NIGHT
ON THE
TOWN

A
NIGHT
ON THE
TOWN

KEVIN LAMPORT

Special thanks to:

Andrew for answering general questions pertaining to police investigative procedures.

Jackie and Carin for answering general questions about the medical profession.

Once again, thank you…

Chad

Colin

Elyza

Kathy Steffan, www.kathysteffan.com

Jason

Sara

…for agreeing to read this book, before it was a book. I'm humbled you'd do that for me.

Thank you, Monty, for reading every single word.

As always, thanks to Shona, who supported me and who, willingly, read this manuscript every time I re-wrote it.

Thank you to the good people at Scribendi https://www.scribendi.com/for their professional editing services and Damonza https://damonza.com/for their cover art and formatting services.

This is for Pauline Bernon

butterfly effect — "Predictability: Does the Flap of a Butterfly's Wings in Brazil set off a Tornado in Texas?" Commonly interpreted to mean: small disturbances in one place in the atmosphere may amplify, leading to drastically different, even catastrophic outcomes elsewhere, as might be suggested by chaos theory.

PROLOGUE

Early 2002

FOUR IN THE afternoon.

The Lucky Thirteen Saloon.

An exotic dancer stared without interest at one of the televisions hanging from the ceiling above the bar. She wore thigh-highs, a black teddy, and transparent shoes with four-inch chrome heels. One leg was crossed over the other, and she bopped her foot in time to the music flowing out of the iPod plugged into her ears.

On the other side of the bar Leo Jarvis and his girlfriend sat side by side, Leo watching Nikki paint her toenails glow-in-the-dark violet. He wore a happy, doting smile on his face that contrasted bizarrely with his steroid fueled bulk and the barbwire tattoo wrapped around one bicep.

And, in the back of the bar, the owner of the Lucky Thirteen sat at his desk with the point of his chin propped on his fist, staring morosely at two wire-bound ledgers.

Gaylord Pryce chewed Pepto-Bismol tablets like they were Skittles (despite the way they turned his tongue black and made his mouth taste like coal), and he longed for the days when he kept a single set of books and the Lucky Thirteen lost money legally, instead of today, when he had two sets and made an illegal profit. Back then (when he operated in the red), there were occasional days of misery and irritability. Now that he was accountable to the nut-job with the ludicrously black hair, miserable and irritable were a way of life.

He bought overpriced supplies—everything from coasters to cleaning products—from companies the nut-job "suggested." Employees who didn't exist drew salaries. Some employees (those who did exist), made several thousand dollars a night washing money in the casinos: buying chips, playing a few hands, and then cashing out.

To ensure the nut-job's ledger remained accurate, the second book, the one Pryce showed the taxman, needed plenty of massaging. It couldn't show too little cash flow. Neither could it show too much. If he misjudged either way and an auditor decided to investigate, Pryce knew he'd end up in jail for the rest of his life.

Managing it all was a crazy juggling act with no attractive options—not the nut-job and his proclivity for violence nor the IRS and their prison cell.

He drummed his fingers on his cheek several times. Smoothed his mustache with his thumb and index finger. Swore. He glanced at the Pepto-Bismol on his desk and then decided against eating two more tablets. When he remembered, he was on a bit of a health kick and trying hard to wean himself off medicinal drugs, Aspirin being the one exception. He needed Aspirin to combat the skull-splitting headaches brought on by the morons who worked for him.

As well as medicinal drugs, he'd quit smoking (except when he drank); he'd quit drinking (except when he smoked); and he'd quit women (except when he smoked or drank or was horny, which was pretty much always, thanks to Dallas the bartender who refused to give it up). In a final effort to reduce his blood pressure and soothe the cankerous ulcer burning a hole in his stomach, Pryce was trying the Atkins Diet on for size, hoping to shrink his belt several inches.

Numerous articles told him all this deprivation—termed a Healthy Lifestyle—would make him happier and more capable of dealing with the stresses of life. It wasn't working. Now, as well as being miserable and irritable, he couldn't concentrate or have any fun.

He looked at the ledgers again and decided he needed something and if it couldn't be Pepto…He tugged open a desk drawer. He pushed a comb and a bottle of Grecian Formula aside, shoved a shiny Glock .26 handgun to the back, threw a roll of space-gray duct tape at the wall in a blinding half-second rage, and finally found a fifth of Absolut standing between a three-hole punch and a stapler. Hyperventilating and trembling slightly in his rush, he twisted the top off the bottle.

A slab of light fell into the Lucky Thirteen.

He paused with the vodka at his lips. With curiosity, he looked past his open office door and saw…a customer?

At this time of day? An hour before opening?

He took a fast pull from the vodka bottle, shuddered when the liquid hit his throat and then retightened the cap. With a grunt, he pushed himself away from his desk. He rose to his feet, smoothed his mustache, and walked out of the office. He almost turned around and walked right back in when he saw Eric Dalrymple standing an arm's length away from the bar.

Dalrymple, aka the nut-job, dangled a pair of Ray-Ban Wayfarers into the neckline of his T-shirt. With his fists on his hips, he held back the sides of a finely tailored sport coat and made a show of scanning the room.

Keeping a tight rein on his expression, Pryce watched the charade from behind the bar. He considered Dalrymple a maniacal clown. Dalrymple insisted people refer to him as Mr. Blonde, an absurd nickname with unknown origins, and considering his unnaturally black hair, a nickname Pryce found impossible to associate with the man. It was also no secret that Dalrymple carried—and happily used—a roll of nickels as knuckle dusters when he was annoyed and a ball peen hammer when he really needed to make a point.

A clown and a maniac at once.

The dancer looked at Pryce, eyebrows raised. He shook his head once and held his hand out, palm down. Dalrymple's only interest in the Lucky Thirteen was business. He never showed any interest in the performers. Pryce didn't know if that had anything to do with the man's sexuality or if some "professional" dictate prevented him from mixing business with pleasure. In truth, he didn't care. The less the nut-job hung around the Lucky Thirteen the better. It was worrisome he'd shown up in the first place. Apprehension fueled Pryce's ulcer like gasoline on glowing coals. He clenched his back teeth against a wave of intense and unrelenting pain.

Dalrymple finished scrutinizing the bar. He shook his head, a mild expression of distaste on his face. "Still don't offer lunch, huh?"

"No." As always when Dalrymple spoke, Pryce was surprised at the timbre of the man's voice. He sounded like a teenage boy. The voice didn't jive with the guy's size, Dalrymple standing six-three or four with shoulders as wide across as an ax handle.

"You open though?"

"No," Pryce repeated.

"But, you can mix a drink?"

Pryce shrugged. "Until Dallas gets in."

"You know how to make a Grey Goose Screwdriver?"

Pryce winced. "You don't ruin Grey Goose with fruit juice. Vermouth or olive juice, sure. But not fruit juice." He filled a highball glass with ice, poured in a fast shot of bar-brand vodka and topped the glass up with orange juice. Finished, he slid the drink across the bar. Dalrymple caught it and held it between his manicured fingertips. Instead of taking a sip he swiveled on his stool and slowly surveyed the Lucky Thirteen a second time. "You need to freshen the place up. It needs a facelift, my man."

Pryce let wistful eyes roam around his bar and saw the same things the nut-job saw. Walls that needed paint. Holes in the acoustic tile ceiling. Dirty wear marks on the floor in all the high traffic areas. He agreed. The Lucky Thirteen did need a facelift.

Dalrymple nodded in Leo's direction. "You think the first thing people want to see is some fuck-wit showing off his tats? A guy like that intimidates people. Chases 'em away before they get in the door. Dress him in a tuxedo. Class up the place," saying it like Leo was a mannequin with no choice in what he wore.

Pryce cut Leo a glance, the man sitting beside Nikki with a hand on her thigh, acting like he wasn't aware of anything going on around him. For the life of him Pryce couldn't figure out what Nikki saw in his bouncer. Leo had a face like a melted rubber boot and as far as he could tell, the personality of a cue ball. He said, "A place like this, guys come in and get drunk. Get horny. Start looking for a fight. What I need in a bouncer is someone who's big and intimidating. Dress a guy in a tux and right away people think he's soft. Think he has good manners. A bouncer with good manners is no good at all."

Dalrymple wobbled his head from side to side, neither agreeing nor disagreeing. "Not a bad point. Still, something to consider." He finally raised the cocktail to his mouth and took a tentative sip. His thick gold bracelet clinked on the glass. He swallowed and then raised his eyebrows. "You put any vodka in this?"

"You watched me make it," Pryce said. "Order a double next time." Instantly he winced. What made him think he could get away with saying things like that? Had all his restraint and common sense vanished along with the carbs in his diet?

Dalrymple's lips thinned. He twitched his head around in a

quick quarter turn. Neck bones clicked and popped. After several long, heavy seconds he said, "Something else you need to do, Pryce, advertise a little. Tell everyone how you have the classiest place in town. Get some walk-in traffic, looky-loos who want to know what the classiest place looks like. You know Sapphires in Vegas? It's the biggest strip club in the world. They call it an adult entertainment complex. People pay five, ten bucks cover just to see what it looks like." He shrugged. "It looks exactly like every other strip club, but you get the idea."

Pryce nodded. He exhaled a quiet breath. The wince must have been enough of an apology. The nut-job hadn't leapt across the bar and crushed the cocktail glass on his forehead. He waited in silence while *Fernando* played quietly on background speakers tuned to a Soft Rock, Less Talk station. He wondered if the nut-job was just making small talk or if this inane conversation had a point. If it did, why couldn't the man simply say what he needed to say? Pryce shuffled his feet and ground his teeth and continued to wait and when he couldn't stand the silence any longer, he blurted out, "Sprucing up the place takes cash."

Dalrymple smiled thinly, no doubt pleased he'd won the silent contest of wills.

Pryce leaned into the bar, knuckles on the counter, keeping his temper in check. He said, "I don't see the banks lining up with reno money. Not when I'm barely breaking even."

"Don't piss in my pocket and tell me it's raining, Pryce. You're doing a little better than barely breaking even." Dalrymple pushed his glass around the top of the bar playing connect the dots with all the cigarette burn marks. "Let's pretend you're as broke as you'd have me believe. If that's the case, and I know you got no reason to lie, you're going to be real happy I dropped by."

Pryce doubted that. He decided he wouldn't ask the obvious question: *Why am I going to be happy?*

The nut-job calmly sipped his drink, and acted like he didn't notice the thickening silence. Pryce acted unconcerned. Below the bar, hidden from the nut-job's gaze, his hands shook. Inside, his guts churned like a pot of stew on the stove. He ground his back teeth into bone meal trying to remain cool. Trying to remain silent.

Without warning his stomach gurgled nosily.

Dalrymple raised his eyebrows.

Face burning with embarrassment, the words spewed from Pryce's mouth. "What do you mean?"

"The people I represent are pleased with our arrangement. They want to get serious."

"No way." Pryce did a palms up, waving off any further involvement with Dalrymple and the people he represented. "No thanks."

"What you need to do, consider everything to this point a dry run."

Pryce said firmly, "Things are fine the way they are." In theory, having more money running through the Lucky Thirteen would be nice. He could give the place the facelift they were discussing. Perhaps he could find a little "grease" in the arrangement as well—at present his only discretionary cash was a tiny percentage of the laundered money he skimmed, as well as the corners he cut, like pouring half a shot instead of a full ounce in a patron's drink. Which in hindsight was a pretty stupid idea when the patron was Eric Dalrymple, but habits were hard to break. He told Dallas to cut the same corners when it got busy and the drunks couldn't tell the difference. He wasn't sure if she followed his instructions.

Anyway...

More money was only good in theory because the more mixed up the Lucky Thirteen Saloon became with Dalrymple and the people he represented, the less ownership and control Pryce maintained over his own bar. He said a second time, "No thanks."

"Did I give you the impression you had a choice?"

Pryce stared at him. Right then he realized he was neck deep in quicksand. No way of getting out. No big branch nearby like on Gilligan's Island that he could use to drag himself free. He sighed heavily. "How much are you talking about?"

Dalrymple threw back his head and emptied his glass. The ice cubes clicked against his teeth. He slurped them into his mouth and then crunched them nosily. He shrugged. "Thirty large a week. That neighborhood. A little more some weeks, other times a little less."

Pryce shook his head several times, still hoping for a way out. "One-twenty a month? I can't clean that much. Not the way I'm operating right now."

Dalrymple nodded. "We've considered that. From now on you're gonna do business differently. How it's going to work, you send one of your employees to New York. Or Philadelphia." He glanced at Leo. "That fuck-wit. He'd be good. Big enough everyone will stay out of his way. I'll give him a briefcase of cash..." He looked at Leo a second time. "No. What I'll do, I'll give him the cash in a gym bag. It will look right. A big guy carrying a gym bag is what people expect to see. We'll meet every two months or so. When you get the money, you blend it into the bar's nightly deposits over several weeks. If your banker asks why your deposits keep growing, brag. Tell him business is picking up. He'll understand if he comes by, sees all the renovations you're doing."

Pryce frowned. What renovations? Then he understood and his shoulders slumped. "I guess that's how you'll be getting your cash out?"

Dalrymple looked around the bar. He nodded like he could see the changes coming. "Renovations are expensive. You'll be scratching checks every other day for building supplies. That sort of thing. Whatever the contractor needs. I'll let you know who that's gonna be and where you'll buy the materials.

"When the overhaul is done, your place will be much nicer. You're going to want security, make sure nothing happens. I know a good company. You're going to fire your garbage contractor. I know a guy who'll do a better job. He's more expensive, of course."

The more Dalrymple talked, the worse Pryce felt. He wondered how many other cash heavy shops the nut-job had targeted. Struggling hair stylists. Fish and chips restaurants. Places that needed just a little extra to take them from red to black, their owners not too concerned about the legalities of it all, and now every one of them in too deep to get out. Owner in name only, just like him.

Dalrymple stood. Rolled his shoulders, settling the sports coat on his large frame. He shoved the empty cocktail glass in Pryce's direction. "I'll be in touch."

Pryce stopped the glass before it toppled off the counter. He stared hate at Dalrymple's back as the man walked out of the Lucky Thirteen. When he disappeared, Pryce stomped across the room to the vending machine. He wanted a snack. Then he wanted some quiet time and some calming music. Perhaps Celine or Air Supply. First though, chips. Or pork rinds! That was a meat product, right? Salty sure, but Atkins didn't say anything about sodium. Not that he remembered.

Standing in front of the vending machine, he swore. It hadn't been re-stocked. All the good stuff—Cheetos, Doritos, Fritos, Ritz-Bits—all of them were gone.

He spun on his heels, looking for someone to blame.

PART 1

9:00 PM to 1:00 AM
September, 2002

CHAPTER 1

JORDON CUTLER PARKED his Ford Escort beside the fuel pumps at a "last chance" Quicky-Mart service station. The fuel was outrageously overpriced, but still cheaper than what Hertz would charge him when he dropped off the car. His bank account was far too anorexic to pay five times the going rate for gasoline. He glanced at the Rolex on his wrist and watched as the seconds rapidly turned into minutes. New Jersey needed to join the twenty-first century and lose the antiquated no-self-serve law. Where was the service station attendant? Time was short. Once the car was fueled, he needed to drop it off, take a shuttle bus to the terminal, obtain a boarding pass and negotiate his way through airport security. If the attendant didn't hustle it, catching his flight would be a near thing.

Jordon's mind was a long way off when the attendant finally rapped a knuckle on the window. The rat-a-tat-tat startled him and he jumped in his seat. He climbed out of the Escort, nerves doing a trapeze act in his stomach, and snapped, "Where you been?" Without waiting for an answer, he headed for the restroom at the side of the building, telling the young attendant over his shoulder to, "Fill it."

With the restroom door locked behind him, ignoring the inevitable graffiti and the stink of ammonia, he leaned on the edge of the counter and took several deep, controlled breaths, doing his best to slow his pulse and steady his nerves. He chastised himself for snarling at the attendant. That wasn't the way to act when a person wanted to remain anonymous. Remaining anonymous… something he'd never given any thought to, prior to tonight. How had he ended up in a situation such as this?

He quickly answered his own question. How was irrelevant. There'd be time for analysis after he put Atlantic City and the atrocity at the Egg Harbor swamps behind him. Right now, he needed to get moving.

He pulled a Ziploc bag out of his pocket. It bulged with a mixture of men and women's jewelry. Working quickly, he balled the woman's necklace into a wad of tissue paper and flushed it down the toilet. He did the same thing with the man's chain. Three rings followed. He felt a momentary spike of regret. He was a paycheck to paycheck guy and Melissa was unemployed. Thousands of dollars' worth of jewelry was disappearing into the sewer. That kind of money would have come in handy and made Mel feel better about the hefty medical bills she'd rung up in the last sixteen months.

Jordon pushed aside his regret and flushed it all. Hopefully, lacking any valuables, the bodies he'd left on the side of the road would appear to be victims of a robbery-gone-wrong. Anything he kept for himself would shatter that illusion and connect him to the crime scene.

Which reminded him of the Rolex. What should he do with it? A Rolex Cosmograph Daytona was worth more than ten thousand dollars. If he were to pawn it, he could buy something pretty for Mel and easily have change in his pocket. But, it was a big watch. Heavy and obtrusive. It was memorable, making him memorable, which, he decided, was answer enough. If the sewer was good enough for the jewelry, it would work for the Rolex as well. He'd drop it down a handy storm drain somewhere between the Quicky-Mart and the airport.

Uncertain if the jewelry would stick in the vapor trap or wash right into the sewer, he flushed the toilet three more times. He guessed he was being overcautious. There was no reason for the police to look for stolen jewelry in this particular restroom. Between flushes, while he waited for the toilet tank to re-fill, he emptied the wallets. He pocketed the cash. All the cards and ID, anything with a name or some kind of identification mark, went into the garbage can wrapped in three or four wads of paper towel. When the water stopped swirling in the toilet bowl and no traces of the balled-up tissue remained, he walked out of the restroom, flipping both empty wallets into the dumpster on his way to the Escort. Everything sort of felt like it was going as well as possible, considering the circumstances.

Halfway to the car, his step faltered.

The gun.

The shiny nickel-plated revolver hidden under his raincoat on the Escort's passenger seat.

The "sort of" good feeling vanished. He'd planned on tossing the .38 into the bushes on the way to the airport. Or, out the window crossing a bridge. Not right away, of course. He wanted to be several miles away from the shooting before ditching it. Far enough that it would take some time and effort for the police to find it, should they cast their net that wide. So, he'd waited. Then, running late, concerned about Mel, thinking about getting home to her before Hurricane Wilfred hit the coastline, he entirely forgot about it.

The young attendant was waiting for him, leaning against the gas pump with his arms crossed and a carefully innocent expression on his face. "Where you been?" he asked.

Jordon looked at him. Said nothing.

After a couple of beats, the attendant asked, "Cash or card?"

"Cash." Jordon pulled forty bucks out of his wallet. "And, you mind picking up the pace? I've got a plane to catch."

"Pump's only got one speed, mister."

Watching the kid shuffle away, Jordon wondered about his ridiculous outfit—the droopy jeans, the gold eyebrow ring, the Mets cap perched crooked on the top of his head, the brim as flat as it was the day it came home from the store. Quicky-Mart must not have cared, but Jordon didn't think the kid's look was the best way to represent the convenience store. He shook his head and told himself to concentrate. The revolver was the problem, not the young man's "uniform."

Leaving the revolver in the rental car wasn't an option. Obviously, he couldn't take it into the airport terminal building. So, what to do? Finding a quiet section of road or a deep body of water before he dropped the car off still seemed like a decent idea, but he didn't have time to search for the right spot. He'd miss his flight for sure and Mel needed him home. Tonight, more than most nights, with the hurricane approaching, she needed him home.

He thought about the problem as he drove to the airport and when he pulled into the Hertz parking lot, he'd decided. After returning the car, while he waited for the shuttle bus to the airport, he'd drop the revolver into the same storm drain as the Rolex. Not an ideal solution but he'd still leave Atlantic City with nothing connecting him to Egg Harbor.

He stowed the revolver in one of the deep pockets of his raincoat, grabbed his roller-bag and laptop off the back seat and strode into the Hertz building. A pair of television monitors hung from the ceiling just inside the entrance, one labeled Arrivals, the other Departures. Thick red lines crisscrossed the Departures screen. Written in bold letters beneath the red lines was the word, Cancelled. With his heart beating faster than a moment before, Jordon scanned the monitor until he found his flight number. A grin tugged at the corner of his mouth. He exhaled a heavy sigh of relief—no red line.

He entered his information into a check-in kiosk the airlines had thoughtfully installed in the rental car office, and then waited, tapping his foot while a pinwheel spun on the screen. And, spun. And, spun.

Half a world away, a butterfly flapped its wings.

A message popped up on the screen. The Atlantic City to Baltimore sector was delayed. Jordon read the words that followed, and a shot of adrenaline stabbed him in the heart and his breath caught in the back of his throat. Atlantic Coastal Airlines had cancelled the second sector of his flight.

He was stuck in Atlantic City for at least another night, his fiancé was home and terrified of being alone, and no more than an hour before, he'd left two gunshot victims lying on the side of the road.

CHAPTER 2

LUTHER MCKINLEY DROVE with one loose wrist draped over the top of the steering wheel. He suppressed a yawn. Afternoon shift was tough. He started work at four PM and if the evening went smoothly, would finish close to midnight. He arrived home a short time later too keyed up to sleep. He wasn't getting to bed before two-thirty AM and for some reason he always woke before seven. Five hours wasn't enough sleep. He was more than ready for a quiet shift. No homicides, beatings, or rapes.

Beside him, in the shotgun seat of the Chevy Caprice, Brenna Hanson said, "You look tired, Mac."

"You know what they say—"

"Who's they?"

Luther grinned and she flashed him an amused half-smile in return. The streetlights shining into the car made her teeth sparkle and burnished her auburn hair with dark copper highlights. "*They* say at fifty a guy's back goes south. Prostate in his sixties, death in his seventies. The forties is all about insomnia."

"In that case, you've got a couple of good years left." A pause. "How are the renovations going?"

Luther grabbed his insulated mug from the holder on the dashboard and swallowed a mouthful of strong, black coffee. They drove past derelict, boarded-up businesses, plywood splashed with graffiti. Teenage gang-bangers wearing baggy jeans, sideways ball caps, and identical Raiders sweatshirts tracked their progress with hard, angry eyes. Occasionally the radio on the dashboard squawked—police officers going on a break or taking calls. He thought about Brenna's question. His little house was beginning to take on a personality. The previous night he'd finished painting his spare room. The oak hardwood flooring came next. Working only a few hours a night, between shift's end and bedtime, the renovation was progressing at a glacial pace. "Slowly. It's looking good though," he answered.

"You stay up too late."

"I know. Marilyn called. That kept me up later than—"

Brenna's cell phone shrilled. The two detectives exchanged quick glances. She flipped her phone open, tucked it between her chin and shoulder and said, "Detective Hanson."

While she handled the call, Luther enjoyed a few quiet moments before the calm of the evening shattered. They'd be working flat out for the next several hours. Probably longer. Probably all night. So much for a quiet shift. He cast a sidelong look at his partner and idly wondered if she ever loosened her French braid or wore blue jeans instead of dark, professional pantsuits. Had he ever seen her with her hair down? He couldn't recall. He thought she'd look nice with her hair down, wearing a pair of faded blue jeans. He didn't care for pantsuits. They made him think of pajamas, but with less style. She couldn't wear jeans to work of course, but a person couldn't wear pajamas to work either—

"Mac?"

He gave his head a quick shake. What was he doing thinking about Brenna in bedtime clothes? "Yeah, yeah," he said. "What's up, Bren?" Raindrops spattered the windshield. He switched the wipers to slow-intermittent. They mixed the rain, dirt, and dead bugs into a sticky paste and smeared it across the windshield in streaky, side-by-side arcs.

"Take a left up here," she told him. "We're going to the Egg Harbor swamps." She glanced at her notebook. "Dispatch got a 911 call. The caller said he and his girlfriend were robbed and shot. That was the extent of the call. Three cruisers are on the scene. The woman is DOA. Paramedics are tending the male."

"That's it?"

"You heard me asking the questions."

Which wasn't exactly true, but Luther went with it. "This happened on the side of the road? Outside, in other words?"

"Yep."

"Perfect."

"I figured that would annoy you."

"No fooling." He blew out a sigh. Instead of the quiet shift he'd hoped for, they'd caught a murder. Not a nice simple indoor murder where all the evidence was confined to a nice predictable space. No. Their killer was inconsiderate and had left his victim on the side of a road. In the middle of the night. With a hurricane twisting up the eastern seaboard. Luther leaned forward over the steering wheel and craned a look skyward. "Let's hope the rain holds off."

"It's not supposed to."

"I know. Who's in charge at the scene?"

"Stonehill? Not a name I recognized."

Twenty minutes later they rounded a corner and the crime scene unfolded in front of them. As they drew closer the drama became more defined. More serious. Red, white, and blue lights flashed, turning the night into an inexplicable, herky-jerky stage play. Three police cruisers were parked on the side of the road. Headlights shone off yellow crime scene tape that drooped between a street sign, a couple of stakes hammered into the gravel shoulder, and several trees along one side of the road. Plastic ribbon encircled a black Porsche and the body lying beside it. Outside the tape's perimeter, paramedics pushed a stretcher into the back of an ambulance. When the stretcher was secure they slammed the doors shut. The siren wailed, and a second later the ambulance sped away.

Luther guided the Caprice into the spot the ambulance vacated. "Was it Billy Stonehill? That sound right?"

"That sounds right."

Luther sighed a second time.

"You know him?"

"He's an insect." He reached for the door handle. "You get the camera, Bren. I'll have a chat with Stonehill. See what's what."

"You wanna know something, Mac?"

He glanced at her, his mind on the irritating and exhausting conversation he was about to have with Stonehill. "What?" he said with a trace of impatience.

"There's more people in China who speak English than in all of North America."

Luther said nothing. He cocked his head to one side, trying to figure out what her statement had to do with anything. "What are you—"

She interrupted him with her crooked, half-smile. "I thought that was interesting. Should we get to it?"

He shook his head once. "Yeah. Let's do it." He climbed out of the car in a slightly better mood than a moment before. Brenna often did that, surprised him with trivia or a joke and lifted his corner of the world into a brighter place.

In front of Luther a cigarette glowed, the tip as bright as a cherry tomato. As he approached, the officer holding the cigarette pushed himself off the fender of one of the patrol cars he was using as a La-Z-Boy. A pair of Oakley sunglasses dangled from his breast pocket. *Nice glasses*, Luther thought, *but too racy. Not conservative enough for a police officer; these young guys overly concerned with image.* He said, "Stonehill, right? William Stonehill?" He paused and then added, "It's a regular midway out here tonight."

Stonehill took the cigarette out of his mouth. "Mac. Yeah. You know it." Then, with a touch of surprise in his voice, he said, "When'd you get back?"

"What?"

"They said you took some time off. On account of your wife."

Luther squinted at him. He didn't say a word for several seconds. When he did speak, his voice was slow and soft. "Who's *they*, Stonehill?"

Stonehill waved a vague hand, sending a swarm of ashes into the night. "You know. Just heard it around."

Every couple of moments the flash on Brenna's camera blinked. Cold gusts of wind blew off the ocean carrying a salty, sandy aroma mixed with the stink of rotten seaweed and dead fish. Fat drops of rain splattered the ground at regular intervals. Several cold drops landed on the back of Luther's neck. His eyes jumped skyward before returning to Stonehill's face. He said, "*Around* better get his facts straight. Marilyn did me a favor when she left. End of story."

Stonehill held two palms up near his shoulders. "Take it easy, Mac."

"You were first on the scene?" Luther asked.

"Yeah, me and Johnston over there."

The uniform Stonehill referred to stood beside the circle of fluttering crime scene tape, clutching an officer-on-the-scene clipboard. He was supposed to write down the names of anyone who entered the cordoned-off area. With the paramedics gone and the crime scene investigators yet to arrive there was a lull, leaving him with nothing to do.

Luther said, "What do we have?"

"I'm thinking carjacking."

"Something to consider, but just the facts for now."

Stonehill replaced the cigarette between his lips. "When we got here, the female victim was lying as you see her now." The cigarette bobbed as he spoke, like someone jigging for walleye. Luther clamped his teeth together and tried to ignore the distracting up and down motion. But after a few short seconds he held up a hand. "Hang on, Stonehill. What are you doing, smoking this close to a crime scene?"

"I'm way outside the tape."

"Put it out."

Stonehill did so, glaring at Luther the entire time. When he finished, he asked, "Can we get to it now? That be okay?" Without waiting for an answer, he motioned with his head, indicating the direction of the departed emergency vehicle. "The mutt in the ambulance was sitting on the ground, propped up against the fender of the Porsche. He was trying to put the pieces of his cell phone back together.

"I told Johnston to hang back while I looked at the two of them. I went to the woman first. She was obviously more critical. I couldn't find a pulse." Stonehill shrugged. "You'll see why when you look at her. Then I looked at the mutt. He was bleeding. He has a bullet wound to his chest, high up on his right side. He was complaining about his head. I made him lie down until the paramedics arrived. They were," he flipped open his notebook, "four minutes behind us.

"Johnston strung the tape. I told him to string it wide. A couple of minutes later the other two cruisers showed up. They helped with the tape. Some pain in the ass civilians stopped by." He chuckled. "You know, the ones who just want to help? I told them to get lost."

Luther nodded. A citizen only stops at a crime scene to get more details for his friends. Never to assist. His next question popped out before he could stop it. "You didn't chase the perp away, I hope."

"Uh, gee Mac. I don't know. Maybe I should have taken their names. Just in case? Is that what a real detective would do?

Someone like you?" As he spoke, Stonehill ripped a page from his notebook and handed it to Luther. His tone hardened, each word like a chip of mortar. "You're not the only guy who knows how it goes."

Luther glanced at the list of names and then folded it once and put it in his pocket. "The victims. Who are they?"

"The mutt goes by the name of Tom Menny. He's from Richmond. Thirty years old. The DOA was local. Menny gave me an address in Brigantine. Her name was Victoria Chesham. She was twenty-eight."

Luther snapped a latex glove over each hand. "Any witnesses step up?"

"Not yet. It's a quiet stretch of road. Two guys are canvassing."

"Where's ID?" Luther asked, surprised the ID Bureau—the crime scene investigators—hadn't yet arrived.

"I called them. They're on the way."

"All right. And, Stonehill? Use some discretion where you light up." Luther turned and walked in the direction of the Porsche and the body on the ground beside it.

Behind him Stonehill muttered, "Bite me, Mac."

Luther's step hitched, but he kept walking, deciding to pretend he hadn't heard. He waited while Johnston dutifully recorded his name on the clipboard. Then he ducked under the ribbon.

A path was marked on the ground with twin rows of tape held in place with rocks at both ends. The path led from outside the cordoned-off area, near where Johnston stood, to the center of the scene where the body lay. It marked the "contaminated" area, the route Stonehill used when he went to administer first aid and later the path on which the paramedics pushed the stretcher. It was the corridor everyone else would take in order to minimize outside influences on the scene. Carefully staying between the lines, Luther joined Brenna beside Victoria Chesham's body.

She glanced up at him from where she crouched. "She was

pretty," Brenna said. "And, put together. Nice manicure. Expensive clothes. Four hundred dollar shoes." She paused. "I doubt the Porsche was hers."

Luther glanced at the sports car, read the vanity plate—UR SLOW—and silently agreed with her. The vehicle reeked of machismo. Either way, they'd find out who owned the car soon enough, assuming Stonehill called in the ridiculous tag. Luther turned his attention to the body. Under the harsh glare of the headlights, he started with surprise. There was something about the victim he recognized. Maybe her dark, chestnut hair. Maybe the shape of her mouth—too big, yet somehow correct for her face?

Her eyes were wide open in an expression of fear. The bullet had entered below one regal cheekbone without making much of a mess. He knew the back of her head would be a different story. Coagulated blood cemented her hair to the gravel.

"Perfect," he said softly.

"You wanna cut that out, Mac? You've been muttering and mumbling all night. I can't hear a thing you're saying."

"Sorry, Bren." He looked at his partner. "I know her."

"Where from?"

"Not sure. It will come to me." He scrubbed a palm down his face. The bristles under his hand rustled. "This isn't starting well."

"Because you might know the vic? Come on."

"Not just that." He glanced in Stonehill's direction. "I've worked with that insect before. We'll never know what he messed up. And, if ID doesn't hurry up, the rain will wash away—" He stopped talking as twin headlights rounded the curve in the road. When the ID Bureau's white Chevy Blazer rolled to a halt, Luther planted a hand on both thighs and pushed himself to his feet. "We should get to the hospital."

They ducked under the tape and side by side walked toward the Caprice, both nodding hello to the ID guys striding in the opposite direction. Once they'd put a little distance between them and ID, Brenna said, "What did Marilyn want?"

"The usual. Checking up on me, is what she said."

"That's nice, isn't it?"

He looked at her, his left eyebrow raised.

"I mean, she trades up, now she's driving a Lexus. Boinking a doctor. But she still has concern for the common man, a guy with a dangerous job and a mortgage." She patted his shoulder. "You don't often see that."

"Why you messing with me, Bren?"

"Nobody knows why you married her in the first place."

He nodded automatically. This was well-worn ground and there was nothing new to say, although Brenna occasionally managed to put a fresh spin on the conversation. *Traded up?* He hadn't heard that before, and he thought he'd heard them all.

His colleagues threw him a party the day his divorce became final. One guy said Luther was lucky Marilyn left him for a doctor. It meant he didn't have to buy someone he hated a house and hand over half his salary. There were silver linings everywhere, if a person cared to look. They gave him a congratulatory greeting card at the party. He stuck it to his fridge with a Budweiser magnet, unsure if it was the sentiment that made him smile, or the idea that Hallmark felt the need to produce a card celebrating divorce.

Brenna continued, "Get out there. A good-looking fella like you, there's lots of ladies who'd go out with you."

"So you've said. I'd still like to know where these women are, think a middle-aged guy with gray hair is attractive." Luther's short hair was salt and pepper. More pepper than salt, but he tended to see the gray.

"Out there." She waved her arm in a random, unclear direction, and then switched gears. "You want me to drive?"

He hooked the keys out of his pocket and slid them across the roof of the Caprice. Then he climbed into the car, still thinking about his ex-wife and her bullshit phone calls, the woman leaving him, but refusing to leave him alone: "Just because it didn't work out, doesn't mean we can't be pleasant, Luther." He wanted her to disappear and quit bothering him. He understood this "wish" was inappropriate for a homicide detective—usually when someone disappeared, he and Brenna got busy. He was left with one remaining choice: tamp down his annoyance and live with Marilyn's phone calls, at least until she became bored of subtly reminding him how she had traded up.

Seemingly oblivious to Luther's introspective silence, Brenna said, "I wonder what this Tom Menny guy is going to say."

Luther shrugged. "Let's get to the hospital and find out."

CHAPTER 3

BERNARD HEWITT STOOD beside a Greyhound bus while the driver used a long, hooked pole to drag suitcases out of the bus's belly. While he waited for his bag, Bernard studied the constantly changing faces in the terminal. He saw the unbridled optimism of the new arrivals, the blue-hairs in their pink tracksuits, enormous purses bulging with a grandchild's inheritance, and he saw those who were in a hurry to leave, the pathetic, broke, and desperate. They put a smile on his face, one and all. America's Favorite Playground could abuse every one of them, but it wouldn't treat him that way. He had a plan. More importantly, luck changed and Bernard figured he was due.

With his suitcase in hand, holding his laptop firmly in the other, Bernard joined the taxi lineup. When he reached the front, he broke cover and strode out from beneath a protective awning into a dark and ominous evening. Low clouds boiled and churned overhead. Sticky gusts of wind carrying humid air and nickel-sized raindrops splattered him. Anxious to get out of the weather, he yanked the taxi door open, looked at the driver, and came to an abrupt halt. He frowned. Indecision froze him in place.

Travelling was like death by one thousand cuts, one headache and indignity after another. Already it had been a long day. Probably the same for the people behind him—

he sensed the lineup pressing forward, everyone impatient to climb into cabs of their own—so the question became, did he really want to pass on this taxi, and possibly several more, just because the driver wasn't an American? Taxis would be busy tonight. Busier than usual with Hurricane Wilfred winding up the eastern seaboard. He could end up waiting a long time for the "right" driver.

After a few more hesitant seconds, he pushed his roller-bag onto the back seat and sat down beside it, laptop on his knees. He shot the driver a sour glare. With barely controlled irritation he said, "Black Horse Pike."

"You need a motel, mang?" the cab driver said in a heavy Spanish accent.

"Yeah."

"Take you to Black Horse, you want. But I got a frien' runs a place on Pacific. He give you a deal, I bet, you pay cash." He dropped the car in gear and pulled out of the parking lot.

"How much? For your friend's place?"

"Eh-teen a night. He give good hourly rates too, you want."

"Motels on Black Horse Pike are fifteen."

"You en' up paying fifteen bucks roun' trip in a taxi, you stay way out there. Not including the room."

Bernard tugged his necktie loose with frustrated jerk. This is what it came to? An eighteen-dollar motel room? He shook his head. How things changed. Two decades ago, when the world was cupped in the palm of his hand, he listened to a proprietor in Puerto Vallarta brag, "I got ceiling fans. An' no bugs!" Bernard forked over the money with a smile, and blew the rest of his budget buying margaritas for appreciative girls on the beach.

"What chew wanna do, mang?"

Bernard looked out the window. They drove past the Presbyterian soup kitchen on one side of the street and the Trump Taj Mahal on the opposite, and then picked up Atlantic Avenue west bound. What he *wanted* to do was check into one of the opulent places along the boardwalk, a place like The Oasis Hotel and Casino where the company used to lodge him. Unfortunately, what little money he had was earmarked for entertainment (peelers) and investment (gambling). Alcohol was a given and therefore not a financial factor. His tenuous constraint in that regard disappeared the day his wife kicked him out of the house. So, staying in a dump, a motel like what the cabby's *frien'* undoubtedly managed, was Bernard's only real option.

That was the problem in America. One outsider digs a tunnel, or back-strokes extra hard and makes it onto US soil, pretty soon a true American can't find decent employment. Suddenly nice hotels are out of reach. All that's left are twenty-dollar-a-night dumps in Atlantic City.

The cabby cast a fast look over his shoulder. "Hey, mang?"

With an effort, Bernard pushed aside his prejudices. He said, "Let's talk to your friend."

"Ho'kay."

"I need to stop, get some beer first."

"7-Eleven, someplace like that?"

"7-Eleven be fine," Bernard answered, inexplicably annoyed with the driver's quiet assistance.

They made a quick stop at the convenience store for a couple of six packs—the taxi's meter running the entire time of course—and before Bernard was completely prepared to accept the dump he was sentenced to, they pulled into the motel parking lot.

The Good Knight Inn.

Bernard looked out the car window at a stuttering neon sign shaped like Sir Lancelot's helmet. Below the helmet, a second sign prompted anyone without a back seat to, "Have Your First Affair Here!" No more than three miles away the tops of the high-end hotels dominated the horizon. Bernard dropped his gaze and yanked a can of Miller Genuine Draft off the plastic retaining ring.

The Good Knight Inn?

"Fuck's sake," he muttered. He cracked open the beer, swallowed deeply and then followed the cab driver into his friend's (or sibling's or relative's) motel. Eventually, after a rapid-fire conversation spoken entirely in Spanish, Bernard paid thirty-six dollars for two nights.

Not bad. Better than Black Horse Pike, anyway.

CHAPTER 4

AFTER STARING FOR a second or two at the red line on the monitor, Jordon Cutler regained his breath and came to the realization that his plans had drastically changed. Melissa would have to fend for herself for one more night. Not ideal, but as long he warned her before she left the house to pick him up, not dire either. Their home was stocked with everything she might need in the event of an emergency—water, dry food, candles. For those rare nights she spent alone, when his business took him out of town, he'd installed extra locks on the doors, stuck emergency phone numbers to the refrigerator, and bought her a personal alarm and a container of pepper spray. She had a Sig Sauer handgun. Chances of something bad happening to her again were slim, but all the extra precautions gave them both peace of mind.

Jordon joined a lineup of people who were either returning or renting a vehicle. They shuffled slowly forward, and he eventually found himself in front of a customer service agent who looked as though she were on the long side of a double shift. Small tendrils of hair dangled out of a short ponytail. She'd melted into her tall chair like hot wax at the base of a candle. He asked, "Do you have any information about the Richmond flight?"

"I don't work for Atlantic Coastal Airlines."

"I realize that. I'm just asking, have you heard anything?

Because the machine," he jerked a thumb in the direction of the kiosk, "says the flight's been cancelled. If that's the case, I'd prefer to keep my car."

The agent sighed her exasperation. "What I heard, everything going south is cancelled. Raleigh Durham. Charlotte. Greensboro. As far as I know, the kiosk information is accurate. I don't work for ACA."

Jordon tapped his fingers on the counter. "You mentioned that." He heard the impatience creeping into his voice, the stress and fatigue. He told himself to take it easy. When the night was over he didn't want to be so much as a foggy memory in this agent's mind.

"You should have called the airline from your hotel. Like the travel agent's itinerary advises."

"About the car—"

"I'm sorry, sir," she said, not sounding sorry at all. "All the vehicles are spoken for. I can't extend the rental. Usually it's not a problem but some other customers were here before you. They had the same idea. There aren't enough vehicles to go around. Not tonight." She smiled weakly and pointedly scrutinized her watch.

He forced a smile of his own. Rapped the ticket jacket vertically on the counter, settling the coupons in the envelope. He nodded. "Thanks anyway," he said. There was nothing left to do but call Melissa, fill her in on the "good" news and then take a cab back into the city.

The pay phones were all busy of course, so he pulled out his cell phone—screw the extra cost, this was the exact situation they were meant for—and thumbed in their home number, hoping Mel hadn't already left for the Richmond airport. The answering machine picked up after four rings. He ground his teeth in frustration. He couldn't have missed her by more than ten or fifteen minutes, probably about the same amount of time he'd stood in line waiting for the rental agent.

He left a detailed message, imagining the machine sitting

on their kitchen counter dutifully recording his voice, and when he finished speaking, he saw the little red light flashing urgently, letting her know he called. Then, lacking any other options, he dialed her cell phone.

A computerized voice answered, "All circuits are busy."

Jordon mouthed a silent curse.

Before she was hurt, when Mel's cell phone was nothing but a fashion accessory, he'd grown used to computerized answers, usually something like, "The cellular customer you are trying to reach is currently unavailable." He hated that voice. He could have easily driven a harpoon through the voice's heart, if it had been something other than a sound bite stored on a wafer of silicone. It was too friendly and completely unhelpful. The message typically meant Mel's phone was at the bottom of her purse, turned off, or dead. That changed after the riot in the nightclub that left her scarred both inside and out. Now she liked—needed—to be in touch. Her phone was always charged and always close at hand.

An, "All circuits are busy," message meant something entirely different. As best as he could tell, "All circuits are busy," typically meant there was a problem with the system, like maybe a hurricane had blown down one of the towers. He didn't know how the system worked, but it was easy to assume a storm of Wilfred's magnitude could do that.

There was nothing he could do but try again later. In the meantime, he needed a place to stay for the night. Longer if the airlines didn't start flying south. This many cancelled flights meant the hotels would fill up faster than Hurricane Wilfred wrecked mobile homes. He hooked a receipt out of the inside of his coat and dialed the hotel he'd checked out of earlier in the day.

"Oasis Hotel and Casino. This is Katie. How may I direct your call?"

"My name is Jordon Cutler. I stayed with you last night. I need to make another reservation."

CHAPTER 5

THE MAZDA'S SINGLE headlight stabbed the night, barely penetrating the black curtain of rain blowing sideways across the freeway. Melissa Bremmer leaned forward in her seat, straining to see through frantically see-sawing windshield wipers. Her grip on the steering wheel was tight and her fingernails carved crescent moons in her palms. She told herself to stop being silly. It was only rain.

Mutant rain to be sure, but still just rain.

Wet.

Cold.

Dark.

Nothing to be afraid of?

She felt like vomiting.

Living outside of the house was bad. Living outside the house in what the media dubbed, "…potentially the worst hurricane since Andrew," was worse. Before leaving the house, she thought she could deal with it. After all, experience made everything easier, even handling fear. But she was tied up in knots and close to hyperventilating. Fear of the weather had layered itself on top of the perpetual fear that lived inside her, the combination like some aggressive, mutating disease. It made her question why Jordon insisted on attending an Atlantic City conference while a hurricane beat up the southeastern seaboard. Why hadn't he cancelled?

Jordon said he couldn't afford not to go. He needed to meet people and shake hands. Network. His business was in its infancy, so there was a kernel of truth to what he said. Mel guessed the more likely answer was Tom Menny's phone call, Tom telling him he was in a jam and since Jordon planned on being in Atlantic City anyway, maybe he could lend a hand?

Mel remembered the call because she asked Jordon not to answer. She wanted to watch *Survivor* without being disturbed. Jordon said, "You know they won't tell you who won until five minutes before it ends."

She'd answered, "Doesn't matter. I want to get in on the ground floor. Pick my favorite before everybody else gets on the bandwagon, you know?"

He raised his eyebrows, but he smiled too. Then he left the room with the cordless phone in his hand so as not to interrupt her program, giving her shoulder an affectionate squeeze as he walked past.

During a commercial, trying hard to keep the exasperation out of her voice, she asked about Tom Menny's newest crisis. Why was he so adamant Jordon meet him?

Jordon shrugged. "He gave me very few details."

The vagueness of Tom's call worried Mel in a way she couldn't define. Something wasn't right with him, not since he broke up with Victoria Chesham. Whatever his problem was, she thought it more significant than a simple breakup. He broke up with girls routinely. This time he'd become moody. He drank too much. Favors went un-thanked. Mel's patience was growing thin. You cut a person some slack, usually more than he deserved when history was as deep as theirs, but at some point, a person had to ask, how long do you let the difficult behavior go? How long does loyalty last? When she broached the subject, Jordon shrugged apologetically—he saw the way Tom was acting—but he said firmly, "In Tom's case, loyalty lasts forever."

There was no way he'd cancel his trip.

A gust of wind buffeted the Mazda. Water, streaming in ruts on the road, grabbed the front tires and jerked the car toward the center median. Mel sucked a startled breath in through her teeth, tightened her grip on the steering wheel and held on with both hands. When the vehicle stabilized, she reached up and massaged tension out of her neck, feeling her hand quiver as she did.

Radio reception faded in and out. The low-quality speakers vibrated and crackled with every high note. A scratchy voice advised her to stay off the roads. The rain would only get worse as Hurricane Wilfred tracked north.

Mel cut a fast glare at the radio. *Really? No kidding?*

Something white and random streaked out of the darkness, jerking her concentration back to the road. She slowed, she had time—she'd left the house extra early because of the weather—and peered deep into the night.

Nothing but rain and darkness.

What then, had caught her attention?

As if in answer, the night filled with plummeting white hailstones. Thousands. Millions. Falling faster and faster. Pounding the roof of the car until the interior rang like church bells. Bouncing off the ground. The gray hue of the road changed to an eerie, washed-out yellow that glowed under the Mazda's single low beam.

Mel swallowed dryly. Her heart beat fast and high in her chest. She hadn't needed a paper bag in a long time. The I90 was no place to start hyperventilating.

Her psychotherapist told her part of the healing process was living life. She said Mel needed to quit hiding under a thick layer of blankets. The world was out there. Go to school. Get a job. Become involved! That's how the woman talked, she was so enthusiastic. Get out there and engage!

Well, this was living life. No question about it. Mel hadn't been this terrified in a long, long time.

A week ago, when Jordon said he needed her to pick him up, a quick trip to the airport didn't seem like a huge issue. Wilfred was nothing but a tropical storm somewhere west of Guadeloupe. Too far away to be a real threat. Mel reluctantly agreed. Of course, she'd pick him up. She didn't mind the idea of the task. Quite the contrary. She was happy to help. The problem was the physical act of leaving the house and driving to the airport.

"It's only rain," she muttered.

Yeah, right.

There's wind too.

And now, hail, the last thing she needed. Hail could wreck a car. Peel paint. Burst windows. She read about a couple who got caught in a mutant hailstorm in North Dakota. Hail stones the size of—

She was freaking herself out.

Lightning smashed the ground. Mel shrieked and leapt in her seat. The flash shone through smoke and steam. Then it was gone, leaving the night darker and more menacing. She thought of a mad scientist in an old movie, the man with spastic gray hair electro-shocking a collection of body parts into a living, breathing monster. Suddenly, the wind, rain, and hail attacking her car seemed to act as a cohesive whole. The monster had no eyes, but the blackness was its face. It lived inside her and Mel knew it would slurp her in and eat her alive. It wasn't the first time the blackness had done it. It thrived on fear and anxiety and left her cowering in a cellar where sunlight couldn't reach.

The stress was almost more than she could ignore.

She whimpered. Tears, hard and brittle, leaked from the corners of her eyes. She brushed them away with the back of her trembling hand. "For heaven's sake," she said and jumped at the sound of her own voice. "Get a grip. It's only bad weather."

No.

Bad weather is a thunderstorm during the dog days of August. This is a hurricane.

Comparing a thunderstorm to a hurricane was like comparing the damage her handgun made on a paper target to the destruction the A-bomb made on Hiroshima. It was the difference between a cold winter's day in Miami and a frigid winter's night in the Arctic. For some reason, Mel imagined a couple of Inuit standing beneath a Miami Beach palm tree wearing their heavy parkas, scuffing the toes of their Sorels through the sand, one of them saying to the other, "What's the big deal?"

The image forced a shrill, hysterical giggle out of her mouth.

She drove by a Hertz sign and a short time later a Best Western sign, the standard airport billboards appearing with more frequency. A sign with an arrow shaped like an airplane materialized out of the night. The nose of the plane pointed to an off ramp.

Almost there.

The tight knot of fear in her belly and the tension across her shoulders slackened. Breathing became easier. Mel shoulder checked, switched lanes and slowed with traffic.

Would his flight be on time?

Delayed?

Had it even left?

She turned the radio off to better concentrate on the people lining the sidewalk in front of the terminal. She and Jordon had a system. He always waited near the last set of exit doors at the far end of the building. Her eyes flicked back and forth, searching. Cars idled in no parking zones, their four-ways blinking indecipherable Morse code. Drivers searched for loved ones through passenger windows, all of them hoping to stay dry and avoid exorbitant parking fees and fervent traffic cops.

She didn't see him.

The band of pressure around her chest re-tightened. Her toes curled in her shoes. The windshield wipers slapped back and forth, the squeak on every up stroke noisy and distracting. Irritating. She accelerated, looped around again and this time slid into an empty spot along the curb behind a tired looking hatchback. Perhaps Jordon was waiting inside out of the rain. He'd spot the Mazda, jog out, rap on the trunk reminding her to open up, and seconds later they'd be on their way home.

She waited, nervously flipping her cell phone end-over-end in her hand.

She still didn't see him. Instead, she watched a man struggle with an overloaded baggage cart that tracked sideways because of a bad wheel.

Was there any point in calling the airline? Was there any point in calling Jordon? Just about anything beat this endless waiting. This not-knowing. She hit speed dial One, Jordon's number. An immediate, "All circuits are busy," message filled her ear. Either everybody on the Eastern seaboard was trying to call at the exact same time and the cellular system was overwhelmed or, more likely, Hurricane Wilfred had knocked out service. She closed the phone and tapped it gently against pursed lips.

The man battling the baggage cart stopped behind the hatchback and began unloading luggage. He wore an exhausted, angry scowl. His expression didn't surprise Mel. Travelling was a miserable experience at the best of times and tonight, conditions were far from ideal.

Among others, Mel mistrusted exhausted, angry people. They were unreasonable and unpredictable. They made her nervous. She looked left and right, ensuring all four doors were locked. Her rational mind told her she was being paranoid, that nothing about the weary traveler's actions was threatening, but she couldn't stop herself from reaching into her handbag and finding her pepper spray. Paranoia never hurt anyone.

She'd never used the spray, but the salesman at Point Blank said good things about it.

"Imagine a blow torch burning your face," he said excitedly. "Imagine having to pry your eyes open with your fingers to see who's searing them with pieces of white-hot steel. That's how much it hurts!"

When Mel pressed him for its limitations, he grudgingly admitted cold weather lessened the effect. He never mentioned hurricanes being a problem, which made the spray a better defensive choice than her SIG, in this particular situation. Even Mel had to admit, seven bullets was probably overkill for a case of paranoia.

The angry man finished filling the hatchback. He slammed the lid down, climbed into the car and the driver drove away, all without giving her a second glance.

There was still no sign of Jordon. Mel frowned. She focused on some distant point and considered her options. There weren't many. She could turn on her own hazard lights like the rest of the losers parked at the curb and dart into the building. Maybe find Jordon at lost baggage claims. With luck, they'd make it back to the Mazda before it was towed.

Or...

She could use the parking garage, go inside and investigate without having to rush. Her stomach twisted painfully.

Mel hated parking garages with a blinding, white-hot hatred.

CHAPTER 6

HOSPITAL PERSONNEL DRESSED in muted green uniforms scurried up and down the corridor. The smell of antibacterial cleansers lay heavy on the air. Luther McKinley knew the innocuous combination of colors and odors scared some people. They associated the blend with sickness and death. He didn't give that idea much consideration. There were other things on his mind, like the seriousness of Tom Menny's gunshot wound, and whether or not he'd have time to interview the man before he went under the knife, or, God forbid, snuffed it on the operating table. He had a homicide to clear and no time for hospital insecurities.

He palmed his badge case, held it vertically in his hand and said, "Evening, Doctor. I'm Detective McKinley. Meet my partner, Detective Hanson. We'd like a word with Tom Menny."

The doctor looked at him blankly. "We've had a lot of customers tonight."

Luther nodded. "A young guy with a gunshot wound to the right side of his chest. A big bump on the back of his head? The ambulance brought him in about twenty minutes ago. He was shot outdoors on the side of the road near the Egg Harbor swamps. His clothes and hair were probably wet."

"Oh yes. I remember. Now is not the best time, Detective. Mr. Menny will be going into surgery shortly."

"How long will that take?"

"Not more than two hours. As long as there are no complications. He'll need some recovery time afterward." The doctor's voice faded away. Wire-framed bifocals slid down the bridge of his nose. He pushed them back up with an index finger. "My best guess? Approximately three, four hours in total before you can speak with him."

"Four hours?" Luther shook his head. "That's too long. We need to have a conversation with him immediately."

The doctor's lips thinned. A flash of irritation crossed his face.

"A short conversation, Doctor. Please."

The doctor cut a glance at his watch, seemed to think about it and then said, "Five minutes. Not a second longer."

"Perfect. Thank you. Thank you very much." Luther handed the doctor his business card. "You'll call me after, right? As soon as he's out?" It wasn't so much a question as an instruction, but he softened his voice and made it sound like a request.

"I'll call." The doctor tucked the card into the breast pocket of his white lab coat. He poked his glasses up the bridge of his nose. "Nurses just rolled Mr. Menny out of the ER. He's parked in the hallway, waiting for an operating room. Remember, five minutes. Follow me."

Luther and Brenna followed the doctor down the corridor until he came to a stop several feet short of a stretcher parked against the right side of the hallway. The doctor motioned to the stretcher and said, "Mr. Menny."

"Thanks," Luther said. He waited. Looked pointedly at the doctor until the man stepped back. With that slim modicum of privacy, Luther faced the stretcher.

Tom Menny was flat on his back, eyes closed. His black hair was limp. There were beads of sweat across his forehead and in his carefully trimmed sideburns. Despite the disarray, Luther recognized an eighty-dollar haircut. Menny's arms lay at his sides, pinning down the sheet that covered him to his waist. Gauzy white bandages were taped to his right side, bright against a darkly tanned, well-muscled chest. He had a defined, young man's stomach, the six-pack Luther didn't have because, as he would have said...*I got thirteen plus years on him*...although he suspected the occasional Boston Cream doughnut had more to do with the softness of his belly than life's mileage.

"Mr. Menny?" Luther waited until the man opened his eyes and focused. "Luther McKinley. Atlantic City Detective. Meet Detective Hanson."

Menny's gaze traveled from their faces to their badges and back.

"We're sorry for your loss," Brenna said.

Luther mumbled something incomprehensible and hoped he sounded sympathetic. He wasn't insensitive to the man's condition, but a healthy dose of cynicism made complete sincerity impossible. Statistically, loved ones were responsible, or involved, in most homicides. Although, in this case, Menny's wound seemed to rule out that scenario.

Menny, his dark eyes on Brenna's face, nodded his thanks. A whisper of a smile touched his lips. He said in a weak, worn-out voice, "If all cops looked like you, maybe I'd change careers."

Brenna nodded. She smiled slightly. Said nothing.

Luther said, "Can you to tell us what happened out there on the side of the road?"

"Now? I'm in surgery in—"

"Yeah," Luther said, affably. "Now is best."

"We know this is difficult." There was genuine compassion in Brenna's voice.

Luther felt a warm rush of affection wash through him, and for a moment his own skepticism embarrassed him. He quickly dismissed the feeling. Brenna was an optimist. He liked and respected her for it. Unfortunately, in most cases his presumption of guilt was the correct emotion, not her belief in a person's inherent goodness. He said, "The sooner we have some information about what happened, the sooner we get the guy who did it. You understand."

"Give us the big picture," Brenna said. "We'll sort the details out later."

Menny shifted on the stretcher. He flinched and his face blanched. After several seconds, he said, "All we wanted to do was go for a drive. Look at the stars. Figure out some dinner plans."

"We? You mean Ms. Chesham and yourself?" Luther asked.

Menny barely looked at him. His attention was fixed on Brenna. He nodded. "Yes. Victoria."

This insect likes the ladies, does he? And, with his build, hair, and appearance, he's probably accustomed to the ladies liking him in return. Luther smiled thinly. Fine. Perfect, in fact. He'd back off and let Brenna ask the questions. If Casanova was hiding anything, her easy manner and friendly tone might distract him. He might say something useful or incriminating and not even realize it. Luther could drop a random question or two into the conversation just to keep him off balance. The tactic pretty much made him the bad cop, something else with which he was fine.

Menny studied the wall for a second or two and when he looked back at Brenna, his eyes were moist. He said in a flat, expressionless tone, "We were out of the car maybe five minutes. Less. Another vehicle pulled in. I couldn't see it very well. The driver left his lights on, shining at us. He got out. His face was all smooth and distorted."

"He was wearing a mask?"

"Not really. A stocking, maybe. He had a gun. He asked for our money and valuables. He was twitchy. I didn't know what he was gonna do. I didn't think I could talk him down, so I dug out my wallet. Took off my ring and chain. Victoria took off all her rings. Her necklace and bracelet." Menny closed his eyes. Shook his head once. When he spoke again there was a catch in his voice. "Then for some reason she says no way she's giving him her watch. It wasn't worth much. A six hundred dollar Gucci. Victoria liked Gucci. It was a gift she said. She wanted to keep it."

He paused.

Both detectives waited in silence, Luther in the background. He wasn't sure if Menny's distress was real or not. He'd seen people in similar situations show no reaction at all, and then come completely unglued a short time later. Or, there was the other kind who immediately dissolved into hysterics. Damp eyes and a catch in a man's voice meant nothing. He'd reserve judgment.

"The guy started yelling," Menny continued, his voice rising, the words tumbling out in a torrent. "'Give me the watch! Give me the watch!' Victoria kept shaking her head. The guy lost patience, I guess. He shot her. I went for him. I wasn't fast enough. He shot me too. I fell straight back when the bullet hit me." One hand gingerly probed the back of his head. He winced and jerked his arm away.

"The doctor says that's how I got the bump on my head. I hit a rock when I landed. The next thing I knew, he was gone. I got my cell phone out of the car and called you guys. But I got dizzy and dropped the phone. I fell on it. Broke it." Menny started to shrug and then immediately stopped. He sucked a breath through clenched teeth. "That's about it, I guess."

"Excellent. This information is a good start," Brenna said.

Luther flipped to a fresh page in his notebook. They had enough information to get the investigation started. Now they needed to sort out the particulars, details that would help them find Victoria Chesham's killer.

As though on cue Brenna said, "Now, a couple of quick personal questions?"

Menny nodded.

"You live in Richmond?"

"Yes."

"Work there too?"

"Yes."

"Who for?"

"A construction company. K and J construction."

Luther cocked his head. This seemed like a good time to rattle Menny's chain. "Good money in construction," he said, sounding skeptical and confused all at once.

"Decent."

"Better than decent. You're driving a seventy-thousand-dollar automobile."

Menny stared at him. "Closer to ninety, actually." He turned his attention back to Brenna. "Is that all? We done?"

"Almost," Brenna said. "Can you narrow the time frame? That will help us reduce the number of possibilities we have to deal with. What time did your evening begin?"

"I told Victoria I'd pick her up at seven. She was late. She was always late. We left about twenty past."

"Where did you pick her up?"

Menny recited an address that Luther cross-referenced in his notebook. It matched the Brigantine address Billy Stonehill gave him earlier.

Brenna asked gently, "What time did you pull over to look at the stars?"

"About nine. Little after, I guess."

"How long before the other car pulled in?"

"I don't know. Five minutes?"

Luther said, "You get a look at the vehicle?"

"Not really. Like I said, the lights were shining in my eyes."

"You see the shooter's face?"

"I just said no, didn't I?"

Luther ignored the outburst. Trying to keep Menny off guard, not give him time to think about his answers, he said, "What was he built like? Tall, short, fat?"

"Taller than average, I guess. Not real heavy. Hundred and eighty pounds, maybe."

"White? Or—?"

"White guy. Staring at the gun, I saw his hands."

Brenna said, "Is there anything about him you'd consider significant? Rings, tattoos, that sort of thing?"

Menny seemed to think about it. "Nothing like that."

"When he shot you, how far away were you?"

"Four, five feet, maybe."

"Okay, about Ms. Chesham. What did she do?"

"She worked as a temp. I don't remember the name of the agency."

"How do you know her?"

"We used to be…We were a couple. We broke up about a year ago."

Luther said, "A couple? How do you mean?"

Menny shot him a hard, unfriendly glare, probably still irritated with Luther's mild cross examination. He said, slowly and deliberately, "We talked about getting married. A couple. That's how I mean."

"That's nice," Brenna murmured, and then louder she said, "You're a long way from Richmond. How'd you happen to get together with Ms. Chesham tonight?"

"In June I went to a ball game in New York. On the way home I stopped in Atlantic City. I saw her walking through a casino. She said next time I was passing through, I should call."

"You remember the exact date?"

"No. The Yankees were playing Kansas." He screwed up his face in disgust. "I remember Kansas won."

"What hotel did you stay in?"

"Taj Mahal."

The doctor suddenly reappeared. "All right detectives. That will be all. Mr. Menny is going for surgery. Now."

Luther looked from the doctor to his watch and then back again. He raised his left eyebrow in a questioning arc. The doctor crossed his arms. He stared back through bifocals balanced dangerously close to the end of his nose. He didn't blink.

Luther quickly decided this was a battle of wills he wouldn't win. He handed Menny his business card. "I guess you won't be in a rush to leave town," he said. "Your girlfriend being dead and all. Where will you be staying?"

"Ex-girlfriend," Menny said, hitting the "ex" hard. "I'll be at the Taj."

"Perfect. We'll be in touch."

Brenna said, "You think of anything significant, write it down. Make sure we know about it." She handed him her business card. As nurses wheeled him away she mouthed, "Call me," with an outstretched thumb and pinky finger near the side of her face.

Luther turned to the doctor. "When will he be released?"

"Shouldn't be any longer than two days." He pushed his glasses to the top of his nose. "The surgery is routine. I don't expect any problems. There's no reason to hold him longer."

"Okay. Thanks." Luther extended a hand. This wouldn't be the last case he worked. He'd have to work with this doctor in the future and bruised egos complicated things.

The doctor shook his hand without hesitation. "I've got to go," he said. He turned and strode down the hallway.

"We'll be back after the surgery," Luther called after him.

Without slowing the doctor raised an arm and gave him a single wave.

Luther rubbed his hand down his cheek and the motion turned into an absent scratch. "That was a short five minutes. That doctor was being overly cautious."

"Maybe so."

"Hospital staff. They don't seem to understand, the time for us to have a conversation with Menny is immediately. I don't care he's going in for surgery. It's a shoulder wound. It's not fatal."

"Mac," Brenna admonished. After several seconds, she said, "You remember I mentioned Chesham was put together?"

Luther nodded.

"All made up. Hair done. Four-hundred-dollar shoes." She shook her head. "No way a lady dressed like that is getting out of a car in weather like we're having tonight."

"It hadn't started raining yet. But, not many stars to look at, that's for sure."

"Since when is a six-hundred-dollar watch not worth much? Far as I know a temp doesn't make enough to blow six hundred on a watch."

Luther hiked his shoulders. It was a good point. "Maybe it was a gift." He paused. "Menny seemed smart to me. He answered you concisely. No nonsense about him. But he didn't tell us anything we didn't already know. Or couldn't find out easily."

"Maybe Chesham's shoes were a gift too, Mac. And, all the jewelry Menny mentioned." Brenna sounded doubtful.

Side by side they pushed through the hospital's twin glass entrance doors, slowing long enough to duck their heads down and shrug up their shoulders. A damp wind whipped the tails of Luther's overcoat around his legs. Marble-sized raindrops splattered the ground like tiny bombs, the shock waves oily, concentric circles on the asphalt.

"He liked you," Luther said. "He got annoyed, but he didn't get confused when I interrupted him. His attention stayed on you. He's cool. Something to keep in mind."

"You know, unless there's more money in temping than I'm aware of, Chesham is spending more than she makes. I want to know where her money came from. Did she win it? Inherit it? Does she have two jobs? Maybe the answers will tell us who wanted her dead."

"Maybe. If it wasn't a random thing." Luther looked across the top of the Caprice. "You notice how he corrected me? Not seventy grand, he says. More like ninety. Where'd he get his money?"

"I noticed," Brenna said. "Back to the scene, then? See if ID turned up anything useful?"

"Might as well." With a scowl, he added, "This weather won't make their job easy."

"Unlock the door, Mac. I'm freezing to death."

"Sorry, Bren." He quickly climbed in the car, reached across and unlocked her door. Living alone as he did, it was easy to forget how quickly most women feel the cold. Or, in his ex-wife's case, how long they stay that way, except with Marilyn it was frigidity, rather than the fuzzy-socks kind of cold.

Brenna slid into the vehicle, and he caught a whiff of apple blossom, the wet weather freshening the scent of her shampoo. She said, "Maybe a witness will have turned up at the scene."

"Maybe he'll confess. We could still get home before midnight."

"Not likely."

"Nope. Not likely." He sighed. They faced a long night. After a quick visit to the crime scene to see if the ID guys found anything obvious, they'd head over to Victoria Chesham's home in Brigantine—maybe she lived with someone who could help them understand the person she used to be. After Brigantine, they'd head back to the office where they'd do a computer search. They'd check out Menny's background, his driver's license and vehicle registration. Did he have a prior criminal history? Did he associate with anyone on the police record?

While they were at it, Luther would call his police colleagues in Richmond, Menny's hometown. He'd ask them to speak face to face with Menny's landlord, friends, and boss. In that way, he'd obtain the intangibles that never show up on a computer screen.

Was he the friendly sort who helped old ladies cross the street, or did he kick dogs and yell at children? Did he have frequent screaming matches with his girlfriend, or did the two of them define happiness?

Next on his to-do list was a second conversation with Menny, after he came out of surgery. Only this time Luther would be armed with the information he turned up in the computer search, as well as anything ID discovered at the crime scene. If there were discrepancies between any of the new information and Menny's story, the man was hiding something. On the other hand, if he was registered as a guest at the Taj Mahal in June, if the Yankees lost a home game to Kansas at the same time, and if every other little thing checked out, they could rule him out as a person of interest.

Luther started the car, pulled out, and aimed for the crime scene. "We got a ton of work to do," he muttered, thinking out loud.

"You ever hear the real story of Little Red Riding Hood?"

"What?" Luther asked, his mind on the investigation, still prioritizing the night's tasks.

"The real story. Everybody knows the fairy tale. But I know the truth. I'll tell you, if you want. Give you something to think about on the drive back to the scene."

Luther glanced at her. She stared straight ahead, her elbow propped on the edge where the door and window met, chin cupped in her palm. Not pushing the idea, just letting him know she had the facts if he was interested. He didn't have any idea what she was talking about, but of course, the way she looked, the way she subtly sold it, he wanted to know.

"Sure, Bren. Tell me the real story. Tell me the truth behind the lie."

CHAPTER 7

TWO HOURS AFTER he checked into the Good Knight Inn, Bernard Hewitt woke up with the stink of stale cigarettes filling his nostrils and the rattle of an anemic air conditioner filling his ears. The nap had done little to dampen the smoldering anger he'd lived with for more years than he cared to remember, but a feeling of cautious optimism had overshadowed it, at least for the moment.

Bernard's plan—perhaps an overly generous description of the course he'd charted—began with entertainment to help him relax and because he couldn't remember the last time he'd enjoyed himself. Once he was in the right frame of mind, he'd start playing the cheap tables. He was ready for them. He'd practiced playing blackjack for hours on his laptop. As his nest egg grew, he'd hit the higher income tables in succession. When he was flush, before his luck went sideways as luck always did, he'd leave town, a defiant middle finger raised to everyone who—

He shook his head. No point in jumping on that train of thought. Not tonight. Tonight was a fresh start…He could have used his remaining cash for a final week in the flea-bag motel to which his wife exiled him. Instead he chose to be proactive. Unlike the host of despondent losers he saw in the bus station, he would create a new beginning and go out big. He grinned. In retrospect, leaving town with his middle finger raised was a perfectly appropriate idea.

He booted up his laptop for a final practice hand, opened a lukewarm beer and started in on a can of Pringles Original (or Classic, or Traditional, or whatever the fuck flavor they came out with first). He played several hands and drank two more beers while watching a half-hour *Seinfeld* rerun, the three fast beers making Kramer's antics funnier than usual.

He called a cab.

While he waited for it to arrive he killed the final two beers in the six pack, consciously slowing his pace because he knew he'd need his wits about him in the casino, when every card on the table became important. He'd need his wits about him in the Lucky Thirteen as well; he didn't want a peeler talking him into more than a couple of twenty-dollar lap dances.

As expected, the poor weather increased the wait times and his taxi hadn't arrived by the time *Seinfeld* ended, so he watched the program that followed—six bantering idiots whose fictional life didn't resemble reality in any way, but without the tongue-in-cheek obviousness of *Seinfeld*. The program had the subtly of a sledgehammer to the forehead. His laughter took on a harder edge. He absently wiggled his wedding band with the pad of his thumb and wondered why losing a job or a girlfriend were worthy of shrugs and jokes. Mercifully, halfway through the program, a car horn bleated three times.

Hand over hand Bernard reeled open the curtains using the rope at the side of the window. A taxi was parked outside his door. The headlights burned into the steadily falling rain like two white lasers. He hurried outside with his shoulders hiked up against the weather, and, just as quickly, dove onto the car's back seat.

He told the driver to take him to the Lucky Thirteen Saloon, then, with his arms stretched across the top of the seat, he studied the ID tag hanging from the sun visor and tried to sound out the man's last name. Two cab rides in a single day, neither driver with enough vowels in his name to be an American? He scowled. Nothing made sense...

Foreigners kept stealing the joe-jobs in America and, in an ironic twist, the high-paying jobs were being shipped to foreign countries. It was harder and harder to earn a decent buck, unless you happened to be a bantering idiot. Executives paid those people one million dollars an episode.

One million fucking dollars.

Meanwhile, he made his mortgage payments doing *real* work. Or, more accurately, before being fired he did real work that barely covered his first mortgage (he refused to think about the second mortgage), and wouldn't earn a million dollars in five lifetimes. His mortification was as bad tonight as it was three weeks ago when the boss dressed him down: "Three straight months at the bottom of the sales list, Bernard? What can I do to help you get those numbers up?" Two weeks after that conversation, Bernard was on the street. According to his lying fucking boss, it had nothing to with do his numbers but rather, semantics. Bernard said, "borrowed," his boss said, "stolen."

Nothing made sense.

The windshield wipers slapped back and forth in noisy rhythm. Rain tattooed the roof of the car. Jangly music played on the radio. Bernard squirmed on his seat, wishing he'd used the bathroom in his motel before getting in the taxi. A single can of Pringles wasn't enough food to soak up a six pack. He closed his eyes, doing his best to regain the inner calm he'd felt after his nap.

The car's front tire dropped axle deep into a pot hole.

Bernard's eyes popped open, the sudden jarring pressure on his bladder making him grunt. The driver met his glower in the rearview mirror. "Sorry about that."

It was the accent. Bernard could no longer bite his tongue. He said, "Where you from?"

"Jacksonville. Florida."

"I mean, what country? Before you came here?"

The driver didn't answer immediately, perhaps guessing the direction the conversation was about to take. "I was born in Iran. My family immigrated here when I was eleven."

"You've lived here, what? Half your life? Why haven't you lost your accent?"

The driver gave an almost imperceptible headshake.

"Couldn't find a job in your own country? Had to come here and take one from an American?"

"I am an American. You think I drive guys like you around for fun? A year from now I'll have a degree in business management. I paid for the entire thing myself. I should have been home studying. Instead, I was hauling people like you around the city."

"People like me?" Bernard, glanced out the window, gathering his thoughts, ready to make an issue out of an innocent comment. He stiffened. "Where you going? We're not on Pacific."

"Traffic is tied up over there. I'll get you to the Lucky Thirteen quicker this way."

"I don't need the scenic tour. I know this city."

"Then you should already know, a ride inside city limits is a flat six bucks. Doesn't matter which way we go."

Further argument was on the tip of Bernard's tongue. Instead he clamped his teeth together. Quicker was better. The pressure on his bladder was becoming painful. He squirmed, searching for the least uncomfortable position on the seat. He wasn't surprised they weren't travelling in a straight line. How was a foreigner supposed to know the best route?

In London, even though they spoke a bastardized sort of English, the drivers were British citizens. They knew the best direction to take. In Mexico, a guy needed to negotiate with the cab drivers. That was to be expected in a third world environment, but at least they were Mexican and spoke Spanish.

Here in America? No! You get a driver with English as a second language, a student who'll eventually work his way up the corporate ladder until he becomes a CEO, who'll then fire your ass for borrowing a measly thousand from petty cash, all because the wife has a garage-sale habit and won't stay away from the ATM—

"That'll be six bucks."

The driver's young, accented voice pulled Bernard back. They were parked in front of the Lucky Thirteen. He had to piss so bad it hurt. His jaw ached from clenching his teeth. His breath came in quick gasps—this kid with his insignificant job stoking Bernard's jealous smoldering anger.

"Six bucks?" Bernard shook his head. "No. I don't think so. That detour didn't save me any time. I think it cost me a minute." He climbed out of the cab, slammed the door and strode away, high stepping over puddles.

The driver yelled at him through his open window. "Hey man. Six bucks!"

The anger flared bright and hot. All Bernard saw was another foreigner with a job and a future filled with potential, neither of which he had. His back stiffened, he swiveled, and then bounded back to the cab, feet slamming into the pavement, water splashing, soaking his trousers from cuffs to the calves.

The driver's eyes widened and his mouth opened into a large O of surprise. He buzzed his window up, into the closed position.

Without knowing what he was going to do, Bernard grabbed the door handle. The kid was a blink faster. He thumbed down the lock button, leaving Bernard shouting useless curses and yanking ineffectively on the handle. When that proved futile, he released it and pounded the side of his fist on the window, making the kid recoil against his seatbelt, despite the protection of the car.

After the third or fourth blow, Bernard's fist bayed in pain and protest, dampening his anger as quickly as it arrived. The driver snatched the microphone off the clip on the dashboard, shooting him an angry glare, no doubt on the line to his dispatcher. Or, possibly, the police.

Panting, Bernard returned the glare for a second or two, and then back-stepped away from the taxi, slowly at first, and then more quickly as the realization of what he'd done filled his head. He scanned the street. He saw nobody, no witnesses. The lousy weather must have driven everybody inside. Either that or his earlier hope was correct and his luck had changed. Finally.

He shook his arm. His fist ached. Rain water dripped off the end of his nose. He speared his fingers through his hair, pushing it off his forehead and then grimaced at the Brylcreem residue that remained on his hand. He headed for the bar. With luck, he'd have a good thirty minutes before the cops walked into the Lucky Thirteen looking for him.

Plenty of time to get the evening started.

CHAPTER 8

PARKING GARAGES.

They were the perfect place for psychos to hide and prowl the shadows. One out of every four rapes took place in a public area or a parking garage. Mel was positive she'd read that statistic somewhere. Or, maybe it was muggings. She couldn't remember. Either way, police officers never hung around parking garages.

Behind her, someone honked. She checked the rearview mirror and saw a vehicle waiting on her bumper. Behind it, a long line of headlights lit the falling rain, turning the night into a mushy smear of yellow light. She huffed out a sigh of resignation. She wouldn't find the information she needed sitting beside the curb in an indecisive fog. She was going to have to park and go inside the terminal building.

She slammed the car into gear and drove to the short-term parking area. Every space, in all four rows, was occupied. She swore softly under her breath and pointed the Mazda's front bumper in the direction of the long-term garage. Driving slowly, she entered the garage, optimistically hoping for a space near the entrance, under a great big spotlight. With a 250-pound security guard standing nearby, arms crossed over his chest, and a hard expression on his face.

One quick glance and Mel smiled. Finally, some good luck!

There were a couple of empty spaces right beside the walkway into the terminal. No spotlight or security guard, but still…

She drew closer.

Her smile faded.

The empty slots were reserved for expectant mothers and the handicapped. She shook her head in exasperation. "Oh, for heaven's sake." The only disabled folk out on a night like this were people such as herself—the ones with mental problems for expecting a plane to land in a hurricane. She slowed to a stop. Maybe there was a sweater or a bulky piece of clothing on the back seat that she could roll into a ball and stuff under her jacket. Waddle into the terminal, instantly pregnant.

One look over her shoulder into the empty back seat and the idea vaporized.

She expanded her search. Eventually she parked in an empty space near a support column labeled with a number letter combination she knew she'd immediately forget.

She closed her eyes, dropped her chin to her chest, and told herself getting out of the car was no biggie. The Black Monster was out there on the freeway and lately it only came out in the dark. She raised her head and pushed hair away from her face. "The Lord hates a coward," she mumbled, and climbed out of the Mazda.

Wind moaned through the parking structure, swirling trash and dust into miniature versions of Hurricane Wilfred. The smell of old exhaust clung to the cement support columns. The air was thick and heavy with moisture, making it difficult to inhale a full breath. She plunged her hand into her pocket and found her handgun's reassuring polymer grip. Clamping her teeth together, she pinpointed the most direct route into the terminal building and strode toward the entrance, eyes glued to a spot on the tarmac twelve feet in front of her.

After several steps, someone behind her shouted, "Hey!"

She quickened her pace.

"Hey, lady!" The voice was closer. A hand landed on her shoulder. "Stop!"

Mel sucked in a startled gasp. She wheeled, the exhalation wedged in her throat. Enveloped in fear, she thumbed the SIG's hammer back. Nobody would hurt her again. Not a second time.

Tires screeched on pavement. A horn blared.

Mel's head twisted around. Out of wide eyes she stared into the front window of the car that nearly ran her over. A flood of hot embarrassment filled her. Hastily she released her grip on the SIG. The pistol settled deep in her pocket.

The driver's stricken face changed to a withering stare.

The hand on Mel's shoulder fell away. Face burning, she looked at the individual who grabbed her. He was older, perhaps fifty-five. There was an unruly tangle of gray and black hair sprouting out of his ears and each nostril. His eyes, behind heavy plastic-rimmed glasses, were concerned. He wore a loose tie, the top button of his shirt un-done. A business man, maybe. Possibly a grandpa. Probably not a predator.

Her stomach rolled over nauseatingly. A quarter of a second longer and she would have blown this Good Samaritan out of his tasseled black loafers. She needed to get a grip.

"Looked like you were on another planet, lady," he said. He added not unkindly, "You need to pay attention. Watch where you're going."

"Thanks," Mel stammered. The embarrassment burned hotter. "I will."

He nodded and hurried past her into the terminal.

Mel took a few moments to regain control and then followed the gentleman into the building. She found a bank of television monitors. Most of the flights were highlighted in brilliant red and marked, Cancelled. She double-checked Jordon's flight number.

Brilliant red.

"Crap," she muttered. A forty-minute drive to the airport. Another forty minutes home. For what? The privilege of standing in a line to ask airline personnel questions she already knew they wouldn't answer. "Crap," she said, louder this time.

Where was he?

CHAPTER 9

A BOISTEROUS CHEER filled the Lucky Thirteen Saloon. The peeler was down to her G-string and thigh-highs, nothing else except improbable plastic shoes with four-inch chrome heels. Which was good. What a guy wanted to see. But the crowd sitting along the front row…

Bernard Hewitt shot them a frown. He shook his head. Kids. Students probably, acting like they owned the place, all of them roosting on stools pressed up tight against the stage for the best possible view. Pounding their draft glasses. Whistling.

He headed straight for the restroom, and while he stood at the urinal, the music started again, something modern he didn't recognize. He wondered if there were any decent rock bands anymore. Bands that made music like the Beatles did, the *White Album* unarguably the single greatest record of all time, or if the noise he so often heard on the radio nowadays represented the best modern music had to offer.

He finished, managing to wash and dry his hands without touching too many surfaces, and then returned to the main room. Slow, heavy bass pushed uncomfortably against his eardrums. On the stage, after several seconds of carefully poised consideration, the peeler tossed her blanket down in front of the students and her writhing floorshow began. The students yelled and cheered.

Cash fluttered onto the stage like confetti. Bernard's frown turned into a scowl. *Get a job*, he thought savagely. *Learn the value of a buck. Maybe then you'll stop throwing daddy's tuition allowance around like there's an endless supply.*

He took a deep breath and, with effort, forced his irritation aside. He told himself to have some fun and enjoy the show, which was the entire point of coming to the Lucky Thirteen in the first place. He wanted to be "up" and riding a high, positive energy and all that new-age gibberish, when he hit the blackjack tables.

He walked deeper into the bar, searching for the table he wanted. It would be in the back, a dark corner with a decent view of the stage. Preferably on a tier like in a movie theatre so as long as the piss-and-vinegar college kids stayed in their seats, he could still see the action across the tops of their heads. Tonight, a dark seat in the back was doubly important. He wanted to see the cops come in the front door long before they saw him. He absently flexed his fingers. It hurt slugging taxicab windows.

He found a place he liked and plopped himself on a chair. Almost immediately a waitress found her way to his table. She propped a tray of empty glasses and overflowing ashtrays on a bony hip and asked what he wanted. Bernard thought for a moment. Something contemplative was appropriate, something he could savor while he sifted through his unusual actions with the cab driver. "Southern Comfort."

The waitress wrinkled her nose. "We don't have Southern Comfort."

Bernard shrugged. He'd cultivated a taste for all alcohol just in case the flavor he wanted was unavailable. "Double JD and Coke, then. Coke on the side."

She nodded and walked away.

While he waited for his high-ball, he studied the Lucky Thirteen through a haze of blue cigarette smoke. Waitresses zigzagged through the crowd with efficiency. Bouncers kept a wary eye on the front row. The bartender, a tall woman with chunky blonde high-lights in stylishly ragged hair, kept up to the drink orders with a minimum of wasted motion. Televisions tuned to ESPN hung from the ceiling, mostly sports of course, but for variety one big-screen showed sports bloopers, which Bernard found more interesting than the games on the other screens.

A voice said, "Lap dance?"

Bernard dropped his eyes from the mayhem on the television. A peeler in a white cotton dress stretched to the point of translucency stood in front of him. The dark silhouette of her panties was clearly visible. Preposterously large and perfectly round breasts strained the spaghetti straps over each shoulder. She flipped thick, black hair away from her face and slowly licked her upper lip. A steel bead glistened in her tongue.

He pointed his finger at his mouth. "Did it hurt when you got that done?"

"Couldn't eat anything but yogurt for three days. Come on." She grabbed his hand and towed him into an area screened off from the rest of the bar with dusty strands of plastic ivy and miniature Christmas lights.

Bernard forked over twenty bucks. He didn't expect, or receive, any change. Clutching his JD and Coke in both hands he watched her gyrate, watched the clothes hit the floor. Three songs later the performance ended. It took a minute for reality to hit. He shifted, adjusting his trousers. When he refocused she stood in front of him, hipshot and fully clothed.

"Another song?"

Bernard said, "You were great, but no." She looked haggard now, like the charade had worn thin. Fine lines crossed her forehead, radiated away from her eyes and surrounded her mouth. Too many nights of bad food, inadequate sleep, and smoke-filled air were aging her in a hurry.

She didn't move away.

Bernard knew she was waiting for a tip. She'd given him a good show, no question about it, but he'd paid for it. If she wanted more money, he was going to have to experience more entertainment. "Care to sit down?"

"Buy me a drink?"

After a brief hesitation, he said without enthusiasm, "I suppose."

"Then, yeah. I'll sit. But you gotta promise you won't ask the two questions."

"What two...oh, I know," Bernard said. "How did you get into the business, and how much do you make. Right?"

"That's them."

"Okay. What's your name?"

"Misty." She winked.

"How'd you get into the biz?"

She smiled weakly.

"Do you make a lot of money?"

"Funny guy," she said, no humor whatsoever. For a moment, he thought she'd get up and leave. That would have been fine, but like a moth to a porch light, the waitress found their table. Misty ordered a Champagne and when it came, it seemed to quell her irritation. To Bernard's skeptical eyes her drink looked suspiciously like ginger ale in a wine glass. He didn't care. His second double Jack looked and tasted exactly the way it should have.

Misty chatted. Bernard nodded and made the right mouth noises. He was as good at pretending to listen as he was at actually listening—both were vital skills for a husband and salesman— and while she talked, he thought about how he'd acted with the cab driver.

He knew different people responded differently to alcohol. Thankfully, he wasn't one of those unbearable types who became maudlin. He fucking hated those people. In his case, he became a little testy. A little angry. He knew this, and he knew he didn't have far to go. The world relentlessly turned the screws…

His wife wasn't the woman he married. The camel jockeys in the desert kept driving the price of gasoline north. The banks made record profits on eighteen percent credit cards and when they were maxed out and a person needed twelve hundred dollars to keep his wreck of a car on the road, they "helpfully" increased your credit limit. Meanwhile, the boss demanded more and gave less. All that shit? Of course he was a little testy. A little angry. At the end of the day, a couple of whiskey sours settled his nerves. If they also happened to spotlight other problems pressing down on his shoulders, well, that was to be expected. It wasn't as though whiskey was lighter fluid on glowing embers…

…Except never before had he turned violent. Charging the cab driver wasn't violent exactly, but it could have turned out that way and for a blind second or two, that's exactly what Bernard wanted. He wondered if his wife had seen a change in him and, in fear for her safety, called the locksmith. He didn't much like her anymore, but the idea she thought he was capable of hurting her made him sad.

Misty said, "Bernard?"

"Yeah?"

"Even though I'm not dancing, you have to pay me for my time. You know that, right?"

Bernard didn't answer. He stared into his glass. The ice had melted, watering the drink down until it looked like iced tea. He cut a sideways glance at Misty. "No," he said heavily. "I didn't know that." He wondered how much this unexpected announcement would end up costing. He asked hopefully, "Maybe you wanna get out of here? Make it worth my while?"

She touched the wedding ring on his finger. "That's not the way I roll."

Bernard wriggled his wedding ring with the tip of his thumb. "She kicked me out a few days ago."

"If you say so. Tell you what, if it's company you're looking for, I know someone. Her name is Nikki. You'll like her. She used to dance here." Misty borrowed a pen from a waitress and wrote a number down on a coaster. "Treat her well. Her boyfriend is huge. And, real protective."

He nodded and distractedly pocketed the coaster—a couple of bouncers and two cops near the front door had drawn his attention. He was probably being paranoid. Cops did spot checks in dive bars like this all the time, but still, it felt like time to leave. He pushed himself away from the table and stood. "How much do I owe you?"

"Like I was dancing. Six dollars a song. Plus, my wine."

Through clenched teeth he said, "How many songs?"

"Four."

Twenty-four bucks. On top of the twenty he'd already given her. Plus, sixteen for two glasses of Champagne. Plus, another twenty-four for the double Jacks. His knuckles whitened around the tumbler in his hand. His vision narrowed, until all he could see was another person in a long line of people, screwing him over. He wanted to throw his glass, watch it smash, watch the shards rip through the air like shrapnel, slicing, cutting, maiming. With a deep breath, he resisted the urge. "I guess that's the end of our conversation."

The huddle at the front door disintegrated. The police officers slowly weaved through the crowd looking at faces and checking identification. Misty rose from her chair. Looking hard and utilitarian, instead of soft and sexy, she planted her fists on her hips and said, "You want to pay me or…?"

"Sixty-four fucking dollars?" Bernard shook his head. "No. I don't think so. I didn't come to a peeler bar for the conversation."

"Hey," Misty's voice rose an octave. She did a little sideways head bob. "You asked me to sit down." She waved at one of the bouncers. The bar-ape immediately lumbered toward them.

Bernard did a fast scan and found a red fire exit sign glowing like a lighthouse. He said, "You want to talk so bad, get a shrink. Maybe figure out why you're doing this job. And, next time, leave your clothes on the floor." He started for the fire exit.

Misty shifted sideways, blocking him.

He raised his arm and brushed her aside. Her eyes widened in surprise and she shrieked and stumbled. Recovering quickly, she flew at him, latching onto his arm with both hands. The bar-ape was only eight or ten steps away. With as much force as Bernard could muster, he shoved Misty a second time. She lost her grip. Arms flapping spastically for balance, she tottered on the points of her high-heeled shoes and toppled into the bar-ape. Chivalrously, he tried catching her but momentum was against them and it carried the two of them over a short round table into an ungainly pile.

Bernard was already halfway across the room, bolting for the fire escape. He pushed the safety bar and the door swung open. An alarm blared. The siren overpowered the music. Every head in the Lucky Thirteen turned and looked in his direction, but he stepped outside and booted the door shut before anyone could get a clear look at him. He sprinted toward the end of the alley and the street lights that glowed like wet jewels in the rain, pushing an abandoned shopping cart aside as he ran, the stink of fresh urine and wet garbage in his nose.

Behind him the alarm shrieked a second time.

Someone yelled, "Hey! Stop."

Bernard's step didn't break. When the alley met the sidewalk, he turned right and joined a small group of pedestrians brave enough to be out in the wind and rain. He tossed a look over his shoulder wondering how much of a head start he had. It wouldn't be enough if cops came for him.

Half a block later, he broke away from the group and headed

for familiar territory—the Oasis Hotel and Casino. Familiarity was comfort, and the largest casino in Atlantic City was a better hiding place than any other Bernard could think of, save the Good Knight Inn, and he wasn't wasting his evening in that dump. Inside the Oasis, he'd be nothing but a nameless blob amongst hundreds of other people in the busy resort.

CHAPTER 10

LUTHER DROVE IN curious silence, waiting to hear what Brenna had to say, what she referred to as the *real* Little Red Riding Hood story. Rainwater splashed the windshield. Whipsawing wipers slapped it away. Thin fingers of mist reached up from dips and hollows next to the road, creating an ethereal atmosphere.

"How it goes," Brenna said, "Little Red Riding Hood is merrily skipping through the woods on her way to Grandma's house. Without warning the Big Bad Wolf jumps out of the forest in front of her! He points a .38 revolver at her. 'Drop the basket and strip, Little Red Riding Hood,' he says. 'I'm going to boink you.'"

Luther raised a surprised left eyebrow. He wasn't shocked but guessed he must have looked that way, because when he glanced at his partner the crooked half-smile she wore widened into the full meal deal.

She continued. "Little Red Riding Hood looks at the gun in the Big Bad Wolf's hand. She thinks for a half a second. Then she pulls a .45 out of her own basket. 'Oh no you're not,' she says. 'You're going to *eat me*, just like the fairy tale says!'"

For a second it was silent in the sedan.

Luther smiled. Then the joke took hold and he laughed. It was a good joke. Not great, but unquestionably good, and the way Brenna told it, the fact she felt comfortable enough to tell it in the first place, seemed to strengthen it in some way. His laughter faded. He bobbed his head a couple of times. "Very good, Bren."

A couple of minutes later they arrived at the Egg Harbor swamps crime scene. Spotlights burned holes into the rainy night. The ID Bureau's Chevy idled on the shoulder of the road. A huge orange tarp was spread out like an awning, creating a temporary ceiling over the scene. Beneath it a crew of four, wearing white coveralls, scoured the ground.

Luther and Brenna sat in the sedan for several moments watching them work. He was reluctant to get out of the car and get wet, and there didn't seem to be much point. The crime scene investigators would be hard pressed to find anything in the deluge, even under the protection of the tarp. However, procedure was procedure. He made a face and sighed. He cracked open the door. Before stepping out he paused. It was time to have some fun at his partner's expense. "Bren?"

"Yeah?"

"I'm supposed to tell my seven-year-old niece that Little Red Riding Hood wants the Big Bad Wolf to eat her? How do I explain that?"

"Shit," Brenna said, shaking her head as she climbed out of the car.

ID had nothing to report. Exactly as Luther expected. Real life and the CSI television program didn't share too many similarities. There were very few instant answers. After ID finished at the scene they'd tow the Porsche to a lab and go through it, searching for any evidence they missed the first time around. They'd spend weeks combing through everything they did find. Nothing happened fast.

Ten minutes after Luther climbed out of the Caprice, he and Brenna were back in the car, on the road to Victoria Chesham's townhouse.

"Hopefully someone will be there," Brenna said.

"No fooling."

"It would be nice to search her place."

"That would be great," Luther agreed.

"Screw her expectation of privacy! If nobody's there, let's just bust in."

Luther laughed. He knew what Brenna was getting at—they didn't have a valid reason to enter Victoria's home. If they went inside without a search warrant and it turned out she had a roommate who was connected to her murder, or who became a suspect, any evidence they found would be inadmissible. But they needed something. With a washed-out crime scene and a boyfriend who looked more like a victim than a perpetrator, they were desperately short on information.

Brenna turned serious. "We need a loose end to pull on, Mac. Right now, we got nothing."

"Jinx," he said. Sometimes it was spooky how closely their thought paths tracked. In that one respect, Brenna reminded him of Marilyn in the early days, when they were new and into each other. They thought along similar lines. Toward the end though, the little irritants had become huge annoyances, and something as silly as a Little Red Riding Hood joke, which at one time Marilyn might have found amusing, was now stupid. She would have given her head a single dismissive shake and walked away without a word.

He said, "Menny might remember something else that points us in the right direction, we wait long enough."

"Maybe so."

He yawned. The clock in the dashboard told him it was near midnight. Any other night he'd be on his way home but with a murder to investigate bedtime was still hours away. Eventually he said, "The thing is, all the pictures I've seen, I never thought Little Red Riding Hood was big enough to handle a .45."

"You spend a lot of time fantasizing about Little Red Riding Hood, do you? That's twisted, Mac. You need a girlfriend."

He smiled.

"And, when you happen to think about Little Red Riding Hood, that's where your thoughts take you? How she couldn't handle a .45?"

He shrugged. "A .45 is a big gun. She's just a little wisp of a thing. Not much more than..." His voiced trailed away. His head rose and he straightened, his weariness fading with a smile.

She turned slightly and looked at him with an air of expectation. "What?"

He slowed the car, did a quick shoulder check and cranked a smooth U-turn. With the Caprice pointed in the opposite direction, he stabbed the accelerator. He'd worked dozens of homicides in his career. For the most part they blended together and the details were soon forgotten. Now and then though, something cropped up and reminded him of a past case.

"Mac, you gonna tell me what's going on?"

"Get ready to be happy. What I remember should be enough to get us a search warrant. I know where I saw Victoria Chesham before!"

He didn't bother adding that even dead, Victoria's involvement changed the case, turned it into something more than a straightforward homicide investigation. It had just become more interesting. And, more complicated.

CHAPTER 11

MELISSA SLAMMED THE front door of the home she and Jordon shared. She slid the deadbolt with a practiced flick of her wrist. The feeling of safety was instant. Almost overwhelming. She slumped against the door while every knotted muscle in her body unwound, her heart rate dropped, and her breathing eased.

For the first time that evening the close to boiling-over-panic was under control. Strangely, or perhaps logically for Mel, her anxiety over Jordon's whereabouts had lessened as well—with the world locked safely on the opposite side of the heavy front door, she was able to think more clearly.

Sure, it was surprising he hadn't called her cell when he realized his flight was cancelled, but there were several reasonable explanations. Maybe his phone's battery was dead. Maybe he tried and got the same, "All circuits are busy," message she got. Reasonable explanations, so no biggie. She was home, safe, and she was certain of one thing—if cell phones were unserviceable he would have used a land-line and left a message on their answering machine. They had a system.

When a business trip went as planned, he checked in once a week. Sunday evening. That was it. Chit-chat could turn senseless and angry in a heartbeat—a telephone was a paranoid device—so he didn't call without a reason except on Sunday. However, if plans derailed, like not being home as scheduled, he phoned, and kept her up-to-date. It was an arrangement they worked out after she came home from the hospital, to avoid forcing a conversation during a time when she didn't feel like talking, when everything he said was wrong and the pauses became long and strained.

There'd be a message on the machine.

Mel shrugged off the door with a fresh sense of excitement. She hurried down the hallway into the kitchen, damp shoes squeaking, leaving wet footprints behind on the tiled floor. She flung her overcoat at a chair. It caught the top rail, hung for a moment, and then the weight of the SIG in the pocket dragged it down. She ignored it. She stared at the answering machine.

All the little lights on the machine blinked rapidly, not just the single red light that indicated a waiting message.

No. Oh crap, no.

Her gaze turned to the digital clock on the microwave. 12:00 PM/AM blinked on and off at her. Same as the clock on the coffee maker. The range read Reset in blue letters. Mel knew the answering machine dumped all its messages after a power interruption, but she pushed the Play button anyway and the machine's digitized voice mocked her.

"You have no new messages."

She backed away from the counter. One step. Another. She pushed an errant lock of hair behind her ear. Goose bumps bloomed on her arms. She hugged herself trying to dismiss the sudden chill as something she'd picked up on the drive home. In the dark, hidden part of her heart she knew better. The fear and anxiety were back. The Black Monster had returned in a rush and it strained against weak chains of time and therapy.

Had he left a message?

Of course, he had. They had a system.

But, the message was gone. Irretrievable. She took several deep, steadying breaths and wondered, *what now?* Her mind was blank. Moving stiffly and uncertainly she picked her coat up from the floor and draped it tidily over the back of the chair. She plugged in the kettle. What now?

After waiting thirty-five minutes at the airport, in a seemingly endless lineup, a US Airways customer service agent told her in his friendliest airline voice, that the flight from Atlantic City to Richmond was cancelled. Mel wanted to answer, *really? No kidding?* Instead she just stared at him. Waited. Gave him what she hoped was a patient and expectant expression.

The oh-so-helpful agent, still as friendly as a Saturday morning TV program, refused to tell her if Jordon was re-routed and halfway home, or if the airline had put him up in a hotel somewhere. In fact, he wouldn't say anything edifying. He did wonder if she was feeling ill. He said she looked very pale.

Mel thought paleness was pretty good, considering it took sixteen months, and several sessions with a Neuro-linguistic Programming Specialist before she could place a single foot out of the house after the stabbing. She hadn't let go of the pepper spray the entire time she was in the airport terminal building.

While she waited for the kettle to boil she wandered into the living room. She fluffed the sofa's cushions. Lined up the magazines on the coffee table until all the edges were straight and parallel. Picked up an old newspaper and wondered aloud, "Why's it always me who carries these things to the recycle bin?"

She was immediately ashamed of herself.

Thoughts like these were supposed to be behind her, from a time when she was an empty husk and the Black Monster did the talking for her, every sentence malevolent and venomous. Her eyes blurred with tears. She wasn't sure if they were for her, for Jordon, or for them both.

In the kitchen, the kettle whistled.

Mel poured boiling water over hot chocolate mix. She walked down the hallway into the bathroom holding the mug near her lips, blowing fragrant whispers of white steam across the rim. She knew she was a creature of habit, neither brave nor daring. She abhorred the unknown. That's why she seldom left the house and when she did she packed her pepper spray, personal alarm, and her SIG 232. She and Jordon eliminated variables by following an established routine.

So, where was he?

Sitting on the edge of the bathtub, mixing wild flower-scented oil into the water with lazy figure eights of her hand, she wondered if he was late and incommunicado because of more than just the weather. Could Tom Menny be involved? After he and Victoria broke up he'd become invisible; a frugal, antisocial hermit, and then the out-of-the-blue phone call, "Can you meet me in Atlantic City?"

Mel's opinion, Tom deserved better than Victoria. He was as deep as a mud puddle. He wore a ten-thousand-dollar Rolex and liked to tell people a Breitling was ostentatious. He was an incurable flirt and typically dated girls whose bra size exceeded their IQ—Melissa reluctantly had to admit Victoria broke the mold on that one—but, despite this showy exterior there was another layer to Tom. This was a man who, after she came home from the hospital, was always close by, helping in every possible manner. Who had been generous with his lottery winnings—

Over the sound of the water rushing into the tub Mel heard something. She stiffened. Tilted her head.

Ringing?

Was it ringing?

Her heart tattooed her chest with hope and excitement. She rapidly twisted off each faucet.

The house was silent.

"Crap," she mumbled, feeling silly and unreasonably disappointed. Since when did water rushing through pipes sound like a ringing phone? She reopened the taps.

When the tub was full she undressed and slipped into water deep enough to touch her chin. Her hair fanned out on the surface like wispy cirrus clouds. She closed her eyes and tried not to think.

But, the thoughts just came.

What if Jordon hadn't phoned? What if he hadn't come home on purpose? What if he'd finally thrown his hands in the air and said, "Enough. I've had it."

It was not an uncommon thought. In the past sixteen months she'd given him, and expected him to accept, a boatload of crap. Bouts of uncontrollable crying. Hysterical mood swings. She wore old, shapeless clothes, her tiny size two getting lost in Jordon's worn-out sweatshirts. Always a ball cap sitting low on her head, covering her pretty blonde hair and the tops of her ears. The psychotherapist said it was a defense mechanism designed to minimize herself, to make herself invisible.

Mel shook her head. No, he phoned. Life was on the upswing. Possibly, at one point, he considered pulling the plug. She had no idea one way or another, but if he entertained those kinds of thoughts in the past, they'd come and gone. He always phoned. He would have done so tonight. Call it woman's intuition, call it whatever you want. Something else was happening. It wasn't just a hurricane playing havoc with their lines of communication.

They had a system!

CHAPTER 12

THE OASIS WAS a nice hotel—deep burgundy carpet, rich wood, granite bathrooms, everything trimmed in brushed steel—but when it came right down to it, his room was nothing more than four walls and a place to sleep. Jordon Cutler wished he were at home in less opulent, more comfortable surroundings.

He flopped his laptop and roll-along onto one of the beds and walked to the window. The revolver in his pocket banged lightly on his hip with each step, giving him rapid, flashbulb images of the bodies he'd left behind on the side of the road. He did his best to ignore them. Instead he let his gaze drop twenty-two floors to the courtyard swimming pool and the spotlights that shot beams of light skyward and traced arcs in the clouds. It was beautiful, and as far as he was concerned, superficial. The city was a gutter; it didn't even have the neon garishness of Las Vegas to hide the desperation. Several years ago, he'd read that casino employees were finding adult diapers in the washrooms. Worse, people who thought their machine might get hot wouldn't get up to use the toilet. Instead they peed in the coin buckets. Modern times, the casinos were moving away from the coin bucket. Now when someone pushed a button (instead of pulling a lever), and three pieces of fruit lined up, the machine dispensed a ticket along with a recording of coins falling with metallic jangles into a tray.

Everything about the place was artificial, including winning at the slots. He couldn't wait to get home.

He yawned widely and rubbed his eyes. The earlier adrenaline had burned off, as had the stress of dealing with the rental car and cancelled flight. Now he was exhausted. He drew back from the window until all he saw was his reflection staring back. The revolver weighed on him, the two-plus pounds doubling and doubling again, heavier with each passing moment. For the first time that evening he allowed the memory of what he'd done rush in. His lean face hardened with angry ridges and plains.

Victoria Chesham was dead. She had an infectious personality that drew people to her like a kid to candy, and a frame that belonged on a magazine cover. It was easy to understand why Tom was infatuated with her. Despite that, Jordon always kept her at arm's length. Pretty girls with good builds were a dime a dozen and he felt Victoria's outgoing friendliness was dependent on her audience. There was something calculating behind her dark eyes, like she was constantly figuring out an angle. Of course, that did not necessitate her untimely death in the rain on the side of a road.

And Tom.

How long had they known each other? Jordon needed more than two hands to add up all the years, and the tribulations, which included Tom's lottery win and the turbulent months that followed, culminating in his breakup with Victoria. Almost overnight he'd gone from enjoying time with all his "new friends" and spending his wealth lavishly, to unsociably taciturn with people he'd known for years and miserly to the point of embarrassing.

Horrible attitude or not, shooting a guy you've known that long isn't something anyone should have to do. Especially after Tom's family took him in as a kid and raised him as one of their own. Jordon wondered how his life would have turned out, had he become part of the "system" after his bastard old man died.

Would he own a nice home and a burgeoning business? Would he have met Melissa?

He hoped she was coping okay on her own. Her night wouldn't be restful, not with this kink in their system, but the message he left on the machine would answer her questions. He considered calling her once more, and then dismissed the idea. No point in phoning just to whine about a cancelled flight, especially this late at night. Not without more information. As much as he wanted to hear her voice and reassure her, calling for the sake of calling didn't work for them. Not since that night in the club...

Later, the cops said the club was over capacity by at least thirty people, a number they couldn't determine with accuracy. Whatever the number, most of the crowd had nowhere to go when the drunks started shoving each other. Within seconds, half the room was swinging fists and, inevitably, bottles and glasses became weapons. Someone with a knife used the mayhem to slash his way out of the club, having fun with it rather than using it defensively.

Jordon figured a bullet was too good for the low-life son-of-a-bitch. He could have easily used the .38 in his pocket and put the slasher down like a rabid dog in the street, someone he'd never met, and then had his best night's sleep in sixteen months.

What happened instead?

Instead of executing a stranger who, by most people's estimation deserved a bullet, he shot a friend he'd known for years. Fucking Tom, putting him in this position, forcing him into doing something he didn't want to do. And, poor Victoria. All her sculpted good looks and manicured perfection gone in an instant. He frowned at the conflicting emotions—anger with a friend and sympathy for a person for whom he didn't care.

Yawning into the back of his hand, he turned away from the window. His entire body felt leaden. The clock on the table between the beds read 23:03. Bed time certainly, but now seemed like a good time to get rid of the revolver. It was a liability, not as urgent as earlier at the airport, but if the butterfly on the other side of the world continued to flap its wings, it was something that painted him with a big, guilty brush. He could not adequately explain it away.

Instead of heading out the door and walking to the end of the boardwalk, he sat down with a noisy exhalation. *Ten minutes. I'll hustle it in ten minutes.* He let his eyes close. His head fell forward and his chin dropped.

CHAPTER 13

BERNARD DASHED ACROSS Pacific Avenue dodging traffic, fighting the urge to run the entire time, knowing running would only draw attention. He hit the boardwalk and turned right, paralleling the beach on his left and the front face of the Tropicana Hotel on his right. The Oasis was a few hundred yards farther along, although it was difficult to tell with any accuracy—the hotel was so huge it appeared much closer than it actually was.

A group of revelers spread five abreast slowed his progress. He skipped sideways, passed them and immediately had to slow again behind two oblivious young lovers holding hands under a single umbrella. A stitch pinched him below the ribs. Every shallow, ragged breath hurt. He cursed the couple under his breath.

It will never last. She'll rip out your heart. She'll chuck the still-beating organ in a dumpster on her way to the pawnshop with the diamond you bought her.

A couple of minutes later, still shooting furtive glances over his shoulder, he walked past the entrance to a nightclub anchoring one corner of the Oasis. A ropy neon sign over the open fire door read: Glow. Inside, a band tuned their instruments and needlessly shouted, "Check, check," into live microphones. One hundred yards farther along, a row of revolving doors spun like ceiling fans, admitting and disgorging a continuous stream of guests from the hotel's main entrance.

Bernard mopped his sweaty forehead dry with his sleeve. He adjusted his sport coat and tightened his tie. Dismissing two uniformed doormen as part of the hotel's architecture, he bounded up the stairs two at a time and at the top, made a show of checking his watch, like all self-important people with full Day-timers do.

The lobby was awash with tourists. Suitcases were scattered like rocks on a beach. Interspersed amongst the tourists were the easily recognizable conference folk. Until a few weeks ago Bernard had walked with purpose through hotels just like them, a briefcase in one hand, a laptop in the other. As crowded as the lobby was, he still didn't feel safe. Glancing swiftly from side to side his eyes grazed past Glow's indoor entrance and landed on a bank of elevators. He smiled. Twenty-six floors from top to bottom, 2000 rooms. He'd be a ghost upstairs.

He slid into the back corner of an elevator that was nicer than the house in which he used to live. Understated luxury was easily affordable with other people's money. A statuesque lady with a diamond solitaire the size of a light bulb on her ring finger joined him. Just before the doors closed, two young guys reeled in as well, all glassy eyes and boozy breath. Bernard wondered if they'd just come from the Lucky Thirteen, perhaps a couple of the college kids whom he'd cursed at earlier?

He let his eyes slip sideways and gave the lady with the enormous solitaire ring a rueful smile and a headshake. *Who could understand the younger generation? If they weren't drunk, they were all on drugs.* She acknowledged his look with a tiny smile of her own and the smallest incline of her head. Laugh lines beside her eyes crinkled. She opened a brown leather purse covered in stylistic LVs and dropped a key chain into it.

The boys pushed the button for floor ten, the lady twenty-two.

Fine. He'd ride up to the twenty-second floor and burn time hiking back down to ground level. Not a great plan—who wanted to trudge down twenty-two levels—but it gave him the breathing space he felt he needed. If the cops bothered to follow up a complaint from a taxi company, or managed to track him out of the bar, they wouldn't look for him hiking down a staircase and they'd be long gone before he reached the lobby. Cops had better things to do with their time.

He pretended to stare at his feet. Instead he peeked sideways at the lady. She looked like a blend of youthful beauty and aging sophistication. Her blouse was obviously expensive, some kind of slippery material. A string of pearls looped around her neck a couple of times and dangled to the center of her chest.

Bernard self-consciously polished the top of his shoes, first one, then the other, on the back of his trousers.

The elevator doors opened and the college kids exited, laughing. Bernard's fellow passenger flashed him a second short smile. After it left her lips it remained on her face in the tiny lines beside her eyes. Her amusement made him curious. Was she remembering a few parties of her own, maybe one night when she and some of the girls in their Switzerland private school ditched their uniforms and snuck over the wall?

She ignored him now, and when the elevator came to a stop and the doors opened, she walked out, turned left and strode away. Bernard automatically went in the opposite direction. He searched for a staircase sign but didn't see one immediately. He did a one-eighty. Down the hallway, the lady dipped a keycard into an electronic lock on a door.

Suddenly, Bernard knew the perfect place to hide. He walked faster. Timing was crucial. She rotated the door handle as he came abreast her. She glanced at him, brow furrowed in a silent question.

"Turned the wrong way," he muttered in what he hoped sounded like an embarrassed tone.

She nodded. She pushed her door open and disappeared into her room.

The door began to swing closed. Bernard stuck his foot between the jamb and the closing door and then straight-armed it open with his fingertips.

She whirled. "What—?"

"Be quiet," he said. "I won't hurt you."

She screamed.

The sound was impossibly shrill. It assaulted his ears. He took two long steps into the room and backhanded her in the mouth, cutting off the scream as abruptly as it began. She staggered backwards, eyes wide with shock. Her feet tangled. She lost her footing and collapsed.

Bernard placed a finger vertically across his pursed lips. "Shh!"

Out of eyes as large as Frisbees, she stared at him. Her breath came in short, panicky spurts. She scooted away from him on her rear, coming to rest with her back pressed into a corner. Her hand went to her mouth. Her fingertips came away bloody.

With both arms stretched out, palms down, he patted the air in a calming gesture. He spoke softly. "Take it easy. I promise I won't hurt you. Just don't scream. Let me help you up." He offered his hand. She ignored it and after a couple of seconds he hiked his shoulders and let his arm fall.

He moved toward the window, between the foot of a king-sized bed on one side of the room and an open suitcase on a credenza against the opposite wall. Spotlights shone up from beside the swimming pool, highlighting the side of the hotel. Lights on the boardwalk stretched left and right, the rain smearing them into a colorful, wet rainbow. "Wow," he murmured. "It's beautiful, isn't it? Sort of romantic, really."

She didn't move. She said nothing.

Without leaving the window he asked, "Why are you still on the floor?"

She stood, sliding her shoulders up the wall, fingers at her mouth.

Bernard exhaled heavily and gave his head a shake. He said, "Quit being theatrical. That little cut is nothing. Don't your kids ever scrape themselves? One of them falls over on his roller blades, comes home with cuts way worse than that."

A drop of blood spattered her blouse. It turned the teal fabric a peculiar kind of purple. It had to be teal, Bernard knew. Ladies like this didn't wear blue or green. They wore teal. And, sometimes aqua or cobalt.

"I don't have children." Her voice was husky with fear.

She enunciated well. He heard a hint of a British accent. "Why not?" He spoke in his friendliest tone, hoping to help her relax. He meant what he said. He wasn't going to hit her a second time. The fact he smacked her the first time still surprised him, although not as much as it would have a few hours ago, before the incident with the cabby and the altercation in the Lucky Thirteen.

"Pardon me?"

"Why not?" he repeated. He poked through her suitcase, looking at the designer labels on the dresses and silk scarves. He dangled another slippery blouse off his finger. "You can obviously afford them. I enjoy the little maniacs myself." He spoke fondly, thinking about his nieces and nephews; Bernard didn't have children of his own, despite trying in the heady, early years of marriage. It saddened him but ultimately it was a good thing. He was on the road a great deal of the time and parenting would have been a challenge for the apathetic, depressed woman his wife had become. "Kids are fun to have around."

The woman strode across the room, snatched her blouse off his finger and threw it into the suitcase. She flopped down the lid. "You've already ruined one blouse."

"I told you not to scream," he said reasonably, saying it like her injuries were her own fault, something easily preventable. "I'll get you a cloth." He walked into the bathroom and slid to a halt on a tiled floor that was slick and smooth enough it might have been ice. "This is a really nice room. Is this granite?"

"Or marble."

He said, "These towels are huge. They're like sails!" He paused, then, "Is that a British accent I'm hearing?"

"Yes."

Her voice sounded different. Muffled. Farther away. He heard a metallic clink. The air pressure in the room changed slightly. He dropped the towel. Swiveled. Flung the bathroom door open. He took two long strides into the short corridor.

The door to the room was halfway open.

Bernard lunged. Wrapping both arms around the lady's waist, he yanked her back.

She screamed, "Help me," but he kicked the door and it slammed shut with a thunderous crash, cutting her off. She thrashed like a marlin on a hook, freeing an arm. She raked a perfect manicure down his face. It burned like twin trails of acid, bringing tears to his eyes. Roaring in agony he let her go and staggered back a step or two, into an end table. A lamp teetered. Fell. Smashed. Hot glass fanned across the carpet.

She sprinted for the door.

Bernard grabbed her again. He planted his feet, rotated one hundred and eighty degrees and flung her at the bed. She bounced off the mattress as though she'd hit a trampoline and came at him, fingernails slashing the air, growling in fury. He ducked and dodged and smacked her with an open palm, the blow snapping her head sideways. She hit the back edge of the bed, lost her footing and landed flat on her back on the mattress. She pushed herself onto her elbows. Her chest rose and fell heavily.

They glared at each other.

Panting, Bernard raised his fingers to the slashes burning his cheek. They came away bloody. He scanned the room. Shook his head. Through tightly clenched teeth he said, "Look at the mess you made." After several deep breaths, he said, "I'm going to lock the door. Then I'm going to get two cloths. One for your mouth and one for my cheek. Move an inch and you're getting more than a slap. Understand?" He raised his eyebrows and nodded.

She nodded along with him.

"We're done fucking around." He backed away, pointing a warning finger at her. "Bitch," he muttered. After latching the main door, he ducked into the bathroom and came out with two hand towels, both larger than his bath towel at the Good Knight Inn.

The phone rang.

They both stared at it.

It rang a second time.

He saw her elbows press into the mattress, her feet dig in. She seemed to elevate, roll of the bed and land in a crouch beside the telephone, all in a single fluid motion. He dropped the towels and leapt toward her. Halfway across the room his feet tangled in the overturned end table. He crashed to the floor.

The phone rang a third time.

She snatched the receiver from the cradle.

He dived, landed on top of her. Her forehead slammed into the floor with a dull whump, and the breath burst from her mouth in a noisy grunt. On his knees, straddling her, he pried the phone from her grip.

"Hello," he gasped.

"Hello. This is Katie, at the front desk. We've had a noise complaint. Is everything all right?"

"Everything is fine," Bernard said. "We had the television on too loud. My apologies." He replaced the receiver in its cradle. The woman beneath him remained motionless, which surprised Bernard. She was a fighter, someone else determined to fuck over his life rather than cooperate. He said, "Are we done?"

She didn't respond.

With a hand on the mattress for balance, Bernard rose to his feet, and flopped himself down in the arm chair. Head tilted, he looked at her out of narrow, suspicious eyes. She didn't move. Was she playing possum? He wouldn't have put it past her but he didn't think so. She was lying so still. Maybe just a little stunned after bumping her head when he landed on her?

Unless—icy hot fear snatched his breath away—unless she bumped her head so hard the impact killed her. Jesus, he only wanted to shut her up. Keep her quiet for an hour or two. She earned the slap, in the same way the peeler earned the shove, but a slap was a long way from dead.

Moving fast, he pushed himself out of the chair and knelt beside her. He rolled her onto her back. Her eyes remained closed. She didn't make a sound. He mumbled panicky curses under his breath. His usual shitty luck was working its usual shitty magic. He lowered his head, putting his ear near her mouth. He heard nothing, but a small, warm puff of breath tickled his ear. He pulled back and patted her cheek several times, until a tiny moan slipped past her lips.

He exhaled an enormous sigh, his relief as dramatic as his fear was only seconds ago.

Before she fully regained consciousness and round two began, Bernard picked her up and placed her on the bed. He propped an extra pillow behind her head and covered her with a spare blanket. A momentary spike of regret stabbed through him. Way back when, he used to cover his wife up like this, tuck the blanket in, tight around her shoulders to keep drafts out, even when the house was warm and there were no drafts.

He took two silk scarves from her suitcase. He wrapped one scarf around her feet and tied them to the bed frame. Using the second scarf, he tied her hands together and fastened them securely to the headboard. He walked into the bathroom and a moment later when he came out, her eyes were fully open. She stared at him.

"For your own good," he explained. "I don't want to hurt you. But you make it so I got no choice." He snapped a burgundy towel monogrammed with a silver O between his hands. "I don't want to gag you either. Keep yelling and screaming though…" He shrugged, snapped the towel one final time and tossed it onto the bed beside her, hoping the mere threat of the gag might keep her mercifully quiet.

Her teary eyes were glued to the towel.

"Just take it easy," Bernard continued. "Before you know it I'll be gone." He wiped his fist across his forehead. It came away oily with sweat. "It's like a blast furnace in here," he said. "Where's the thermostat?"

She said nothing, not that he expected her to, and he found the temperature control without help, a little wheel that stuck out the bottom of a secure plastic housing and rotated from a blue snowflake icon, to Off, and then to a yellow sun icon. The housing was locked, the only access a silver keyhole in the side.

"There's got to be a more precise control than this piece of junk," he said, searching the other walls. When he didn't see anything, he turned his attention back to the little wheel inside the plastic housing. He tried prying the housing off, but it refused to move—heavy-duty security designed to prevent everyone except a few hundred immigrant maids, who had keys to everything and spent their time stealing toilet paper, from tampering with the device. Impatiently, he snatched the remaining lamp off the bedside table and jerked the cord out of the wall socket. He raised the lamp above his head and brought the base crashing down on top of the housing. The plastic shattered. The thermostat sheared off the wall, leaving fine wires dangling out of the drywall.

"I'm sure it will work now."

He gave her a sidelong scowl. "Don't start with me."

She licked the gash on her lip. Snuffled loudly. "Whatever."

"What's your name?"

"Emma," she mumbled.

"Emma. That's a nice name. A good British name."

She turned her head away.

"Yeah, I'm good with accents."

No answer.

"You don't wanna talk? That's okay. I've got some ideas, things we could do that don't involve talking. Seeing as I got some time to kill."

Emma's face paled.

CHAPTER 14

GAYLORD PRYCE WATCHED the weather report on a flat screen TV that hung from the ceiling of his office. With the heavy door shut, the noise from the floor of The Lucky Thirteen didn't intrude too offensively into the room. His chin was cupped in his hand. His fingers drummed a nervous riff on his cheek. On the television, an overly made-up anchor shuffled papers and spoke earnestly into the camera.

"Wilfred reached hurricane status early yesterday morning when sustained winds exceeded seventy-four miles per hour. Only eight hours later she lashed The Virgin Islands with one hundred and thirty-five miles per hour winds, leaving a trail of destruction throughout the Caribbean Islands."

Pryce looked at his watch for probably the five hundredth time that evening. Why hadn't Leo phoned? Neither the cell phone in Pryce's pocket nor his direct landline had peeped all night. He hated, fucking hated, waiting for Leo on those rare evenings when his bouncer went off to Philly on a mission for the nut-job.

"…Meteorologists blame Wilfred's fury on the collision of two systems, a weak system of low pressure centered over the Appalachians and a large high pressure system in the Atlantic, centered near Bermuda…"

With both hands on the edge of his desk, Pryce pushed himself back. He strode to the office door. Every step made the acidic fluid in his stomach slosh and splash nauseatingly. He flung the door open and the bar noise assaulted him, forcing him to retreat a step. He considered slamming the door shut, isolating himself in the relative serenity of his office again but realized hiding wouldn't work—he was slowly going nuts. Waiting in silence was worse than the bedlam in the bar.

The entire scene he looked upon reminded him of one of those programs on the Discovery Channel featuring strange, undersea organisms of the Pacific. Music, heavy on bass, pulsed through the Lucky Thirteen like some mad heartbeat. People, from one side of the room to the other, talked over it. Their voices blended into an unrecognizable foreign language. Lights from the stage burned through low-hanging smoke like tracer rounds.

He fished two Pepto-Bismol out of his pocket. While the pink tablets dissolved into a sweet, chalky paste he continued his appraisal. It looked like business as usual. The bar was about three-quarters full. Things seemed to have settled down after the fracas with the cops and the moron who drank and dashed. Misty was grinding the chrome pole extra hard, likely hoping for additional tips to pay off the guy's sixty-four-dollar tab. College kids slurped down cheap draft by the gallon. Business guys in loose ties drank "expensive" whisky by the beaker. All and all, it appeared the night would even out. Perhaps become moderately profitable by closing.

There was no sign of Leo or Semi-Gloss. Not that he expected to see them. Their first stop would have been his office. They wouldn't have dallied in the bar.

Pryce turned to his bartender. "Dallas," he said. He snapped his fingers and pointed at the floor in front of him. "Right now." She looked good tonight. She looked good every night, Dallas filling out her clothes just right, a big girl who wasn't fat but would never be a model. The pot lights above the bar turned her brown hair copper and made the blonde highlights shine, her hair cut shaggy along the sides and back, framing her face in a three-quarter circle.

She ignored him.

He rapped the bar several times with his knuckles.

Nothing.

And, it wasn't like she couldn't see him. He wasn't invisible—Atkins wasn't working that well, even after several weeks. He stroked his mustache several times with his thumb and finger, and waited. He had to be cautious, keep their interactions strictly boss and employee. A few nights back he told her she needed to smile more. She looked good when she smiled. He told himself the comment didn't mean anything, it was just an observation. But, she'd answered with the flat stare she had, drawing it out long enough he started getting an uneasy feeling in his belly. Then she told him, "I'm normally not into overweight guys with hair growing out their ears like brambles," but yeah, if he agreed to trim that hedge, she'd make an effort to smile more often.

He couldn't look at her for three days after that. So now? Nothing but professionalism. Boss and employee. He crossed beefy arms over his chest, tapped his foot, and waited.

Nothing.

The black pants she wore were slimming. Her white blouse was fastened all the way to the top as usual, the buttons across her chest working harder than the others. He figured she'd do a little better on tips if she undid several and let the pants drop off her hips an inch or two. But she never did and even though he wanted to see more of her, somehow Pryce was glad. She didn't look artificial, like the rest of the women strutting around the place with their overdone everything.

The edge-of-control mayhem in the bar faded as his attention zeroed in on her. He just wanted her to notice him. He was no spring chicken. The daily comb-through with the Grecian hid the gray, except for a few strands right near his temples he purposely kept. A thread or two of gray represented experience. Wisdom. Sophistication. And sure, he carried a few extra pounds around the waist, but he was doing something about it. He'd quit smoking, mostly. He made a decent living. He wasn't some derelict on the street. Not only that, he was her boss. She was supposed to pay attention to him.

He thrust out his head. Coughed.

Nothing.

She didn't even glance in his direction. Just kept popping caps off the Millers and Michelobs. Kept pouring full, one-ounce shots—despite his half-an-ounce-only instructions—into the high-ball glasses.

He didn't try too hard to disguise his growing annoyance. He was careful not to bark either. He didn't want to risk pissing her off and seeing her quit. He liked having her in the bar. Sort of. Aside from never showing him the proper respect, she was the best bartender he'd ever hired. A couple of days back he overheard her raising holy-oh-shit with a distributor for screwing up an order.

He blew out a noisy exasperated sigh. Looked at his watch again. Twenty-five minutes late now. Where was Leo? He couldn't spend all night waiting. Not for Leo or Dallas. He said with forced politeness, "Dallas? You don't mind, I need a moment of your time."

She turned and looked at him wearing a huge, sunny smile. "Sure thing, Sweetie. How can I help?"

"For starters, you can at least pretend I'm your boss. Next, has—"

"I am pretending."

Pryce rocked back on his heels. What did that mean?

Her smile grew. She fluttered her eyelids.

Typical. She was messing with him. That's why he hated her. And, liked her. "Uhm, yeah. Anyway, has anyone called?" He knew nobody had and if they did, in this racket Dallas wouldn't have even heard the bar phone ring, but he couldn't help asking anyway.

"Nobody's called," she answered, saying it in that tone she had, like it was the dumbest question on the planet, like he was a complete moron for even asking it. "You know I'd buzz you on the intercom."

"Where's Leo?" he said with a forced cool in his voice, doing his utmost to ignore the watch on his wrist, Leo pushing twenty-nine minutes late with his phone call, the fourth he was supposed to make that evening.

She shrugged. "He doesn't work for me. I haven't seen him." Casual, saying without actually speaking: *You want me to tend bar? Or, you want me baby-sit absentee employees?*

"What about Semi-Gloss?"

She shook her head.

He smoothed his mustache several times. Every month, give or take a week, Leo drove to some prearranged meeting with Dalrymple. He returned with close to one hundred fifty thousand dollars in a gym bag. Just like the nut-job proposed when he told Pryce the people he represented wanted to get serious.

Each time Leo met the nut-job, Pryce demanded he stay in constant communication. He wanted to know when Leo arrived in Philadelphia, when he got the money, when he left, and what time he'd arrive back in Atlantic City. Most importantly, he wanted to know precisely when Leo expected to walk in the back door, gym bag in hand, full of worn hundred-dollar bills, all tidily wrapped in crisp white paper bands. It didn't take too much imagination to guess what would happen if he lost one hundred and fifty thousand of the nut-job's cash.

Pryce kept imagining the roll of nickels Dalrymple kept in his pocket and the ball peen hammer in his tool box. Worse, every week he saw two of the nut-job's employees, all hard faces and callused knuckles, both of them eye-fucking Pryce the entire time they were at the Lucky Thirteen emptying the dumpster. He was paying five times what he paid a few months ago for garbage disposal.

Leo seemed incapable of concern. "Hey," he'd say with a shrug, "just pick it up and drop it off. No issue, right?" When Leo put it that way Pryce almost agreed. The difference was, Leo wasn't on the hook for the money, so every month Pryce worked himself into a cyclone of worry and swallowed Pepto by the gallon and waited with uncontained impatience for Leo's phone calls.

He said, "Dallas, anyone calls and I'm not around to take it, let me know. Especially if it's Leo or Semi-Gloss."

She snapped him a crisp salute.

Confused once more, he paused before returning to his office. She just never let up. He stared at her, trying to let her know with a look that he wasn't impressed, that he expected some sort of deference. She didn't seem to notice. He continued to stare anyway. The angle of the overhead light had changed. It wasn't shining on her hair anymore. Now it danced on her necklace, a large pendant dangling from her neck on a thin leather cord, the ornament riding high on the nice big rack she refused to show off.

He squinted, trying to figure it out. What was the thing on the end of the leather chord? A miniature sundial, perhaps?

He felt her eyes on him. He looked up in a hurry.

There was an amused smile on her lips. When their eyes met, the smile blossomed. She raised her eyebrows. "Is there anything else?"

A sudden rush of heat burned his neck and ears. "I wasn't, uh...I wasn't looking at..." He shook his head. Pointing at his neckline he drew three or four half circles in the air with his index finger. "Nice necklace," he said. With a twitch of his head he motioned her closer. His voice dropped. "Can you tell? Have I lost weight?"

She appeared surprised. An expression of concentration

crossed her face. She narrowed her eyes, took one step back and studied him from top to bottom. "I don't know. These dim lights, it's hard to tell. You know what? Yeah. Absolutely. You definitely have." She nodded. "I'm almost sure you have. Why do you ask?"

"A few weeks ago, my office chair broke. Chinese garbage. I gave the salesman at Staples a blast of shit. Anyway, I thought I'd try the Atkins Diet. A guy I know says he lost eight pounds in two weeks. Not that I need to, you understand?"

Dallas nodded vaguely. "How long have you been doing Atkins?"

"A few weeks."

"How much have you lost?"

"That's not the point," he said. "Not eight pounds, that's for sure. But I expected my progress to be slow. See, the guy who wrote it says you have to give up all bread. Can you believe that? All bread. Bread products! Crackers, cookies. What not. Pasta too. Pasta!" He shook his head. "I can't do that."

"Isn't that a big part of it? Giving up starchy food?"

"Anyway, I'm following his instructions. Except for the bread part. And, the pasta part." And sometimes, the alcohol part. With one hand on the door he said, "If you see Leo or Semi-Gloss, send them in. And, Dallas? Anybody calls, anybody, I wanna know yesterday," giving her an order without really expecting she'd listen to him. He walked into his office and slammed the door.

Where in the hell was Leo?

CHAPTER 15

THE CHEVY CAPRICE'S tires shushed through the water on the road. The heater fan hummed, keeping the windows clear of fog. After their stop at the crime scene, the temperature in the vehicle was comfortably warm. "This bizarre Red Riding Hood conversation," Luther McKinley said, with a shake of his head. "For some reason, it reminded me of a murder-suicide I worked a couple of years back. Summer of '98. It happened in a suite at the Oasis—"

"Is this going to be a long story, Mac?"

"Yes. Now be quiet. The DOAs were husband and wife. She shot him first then turned the gun on herself. He didn't look his best. Three extra orifices. Comb-over poking up all over the place." Luther waved a hand over his head, his fingers sticking out in all directions as he spoke. He remembered the next day, how he'd shaved his thinning black hair to an even eighth of an inch. The thought of ending up dead and looking as bad as that poor insect in his paisley boxers and black dress socks made him shudder. "Judging from the shocked expression," he continued, "she shot him in the crotch first. Then twice—"

"I bet the guys liked that one."

"Oh yeah. The comments that day were something else. Guy's wife really had him by the balls. That sort of thing. Anyway, the gun she used was huge. A Glock 31. I think that's why your Red Riding Hood story reminded me of tonight's case. You know, one random thought leads to another. Two tiny ladies, two large-caliber weapons."

"Fine. Red Riding Hood reminded you of an old case. Which somehow made you think, 'Yeah! Now I can get a search warrant for Victoria Chesham's townhouse!'" Brenna rolled her hand several times. "I'm not seeing the connection."

"I'll get there sooner, you stop interrupting." Without waiting for a response, he said, "The evidence indicated murder-suicide—"

"But?"

"But the evidence also indicated a third person was in the room. Fingerprints. Lipstick on the wineglasses. Wet towels, except the wife was still dressed in outdoor clothing. The guy had a business card in his wallet. There was a name and a number written on the back of it. Tyffany. I called the number several times—"

"Of course."

"—and always got voice mail."

"Of course."

"I needed to know who she was. Did she witness the shootings? Was she involved? Was she the third person in the room, or only an unrelated phone number in the guy's wallet? I did some of that cop magic we're famous for. Bell Atlantic told me the number was a cell phone registered to..." He glanced across the seat with his left eyebrow raised.

"The phone wasn't registered to Tyffany, is what you're saying. That was an alias, right? And, since tonight is all about Victoria Chesham's death, the only connection I can see is, the phone was registered to her. In '98 Victoria used the name Tyffany as an alias?"

Luther smiled.

"Was she a witness back then, Mac?"

"How it turned out. She was in the suite when the wife came in and ventilated her husband. Later, Victoria told me she thought it was all over, she thought she was dead. Instead, the wife just looked at her, put the gun under her chin and..." He shrugged.

"Shit."

"Yeah, no fooling."

"Anyway, how's that relevant tonight? It's got to be, or you wouldn't be all jazzed about getting a search warrant."

"What's the one thing about Victoria that bothers you the most?"

"Seems like she spends way more than she makes."

Luther nodded. "She was temping back then, too."

"Still with the expensive tastes?"

"Just like now," Luther answered.

"A temp with an alias spending more than she can possibly make, in a suite with a married man." Brenna paused then, with the half-smile on her face said, "Victoria was an escort."

"Very good," Luther said. "We didn't find that out until later. But it did explain why she was avoiding me." Victoria Chesham— Tyffany—had never returned a single call. It wasn't surprising. Witnesses routinely avoid the authorities. He said, "Instinct, I guess, for an escort to avoid a cop."

"And, you're thinking what? The job she had several years ago is going to help us get a search warrant tonight?"

He nodded. "Seems logical. Given her profession, I think we can assume there'd be something in her house that leads to motive. Drugs, maybe. Or, the name of a nervous client. Either would do away with her expectation of privacy."

"What if she was out of the biz?"

"Hopefully it won't matter."

"It's a stretch, Mac." Brenna's voice was filled with doubt. "That was then. This is now. The only thing we know is she spent more than she made."

He clenched his teeth, biting off a quick, irritated response. No point getting annoyed. All Brenna was doing was putting her analytical skills to work. Finding problems and working out solutions before the problems found them. "It's the only idea I've got." His voice sounded testier than he would have liked.

"All I'm saying—"

He held up a hand, stopping her. "I know. You're right. A judge has to take what we know about Victoria's past into account."

"Half the population spends more than they make. That's no crime."

"We get the right judge. Impress upon him that the search warrant is for the good of a homicide investigation. Tell him we believe she was still a working girl."

"Do we believe that?"

"I have a hunch she was."

"Why?"

"I met her. She liked the lifestyle money bought her." He shrugged. "Tonight, at first glance, it didn't appear she changed. Did it?"

"Color me skeptical," Brenna said, and then she leaned over and slugged him on the shoulder. "I'll make the call. What do we have to lose, right?"

CHAPTER 16

BERNARD HEWITT BRUSHED away Emma's fear with a wave and a laugh. "Stop worrying. How many times do I have to say it? I'm not going to hurt you."

She licked her cut lip with the tip of her tongue.

"I apologized for that. And, you have to admit, you earned it. What did I say when I walked in here? I said, 'Be quiet and I won't hurt you.' What was I supposed to do?" He hiked his shoulders, like the entire situation was out of his hands. "Behave, I won't smack you." He gestured at the towel beside her. "Keep quiet, I won't gag you. Simple. In the meantime, since you don't want to talk, I was thinking we could watch TV. Or maybe a movie? Where's the remote?"

She didn't respond.

"Emma! The remote?"

"It was on the table. Before you wrecked my room."

From his perch on the edge of the mattress, Bernard scanned the floor. He spotted one double A battery amongst the broken glass of the shattered lamp. The remote control and the second battery were nowhere to be seen. With an exasperated sigh, he shoved himself off the bed. He propped the side table, minus one leg, beside the armchair. The crippled table tilted crazily into the wall. He flipped up the edge of the bedspread, dropped to his knees and peered beneath the box spring. The remote control lay there, a crushed mangle of black plastic. The second battery had disappeared to the same place one sock goes when the drier stops.

"I hate getting up to change the channel," Bernard said. "You ever see that *Frasier* episode where the old guy lost the remote so he used a broomstick to change the channel from his easy chair? That was a funny one. My wife laughed at that one."

Emma gave a start of surprise. "You're married?"

"Technically, yes," Bernard said. He held up his left hand and wiggled his wedding band. "She kicked me out a few days ago."

It took a moment for Emma to respond. When she did it sounded like she was talking to herself. Bernard wasn't certain what she said, but there was no mistaking the expression on her face: *Too right, I can understand why she kicked you to the curb.*

Anger sent red spots dancing across his vision. What did this British snot with her obvious wealth and classy foreign accent know about him and his marital issues? Nothing! After eighteen years of marriage, half of which he could only describe as miserable, he wasn't about to accept Emma's misdirected judgment. Not when his wife was the catalyst for the situation in which he, and therefore Emma, found themselves.

He'd talked himself into a crimson rage. "Don't make this my fault," he screamed. Spit sprayed. "You're sporting a five-thousand-dollar ring. Ten grand worth of pearls. Don't act like you never fought with your husband."

Chest heaving with exertion, he dropped into the chair. His hands gripped the arms so tightly his knuckles glowed white. He glared at her. Emma's hair was like polished mahogany. She obviously didn't go more than a couple of weeks without seeing a stylist. Her lips would have been perfect cupid's bows, except for the swelling and dried blood at the corner of her mouth. Expertly applied makeup highlighted nice cheekbones. This was what forty, forty-five, should look like, Bernard thought. Not shapeless, oversized sweaters and a two-minute bob that screamed, "I've given up!"

"Sorry for yelling," he said, still slightly out of breath.

"What about hitting me? What about my room?"

"I already apologized for that."

"Let me go then."

He liked her voice, that cultured accent. "I told you, I will. In a while."

"Why not now?"

"Because the cops are looking for me. Not for anything big, but I'd rather stay away from them. Where's the minibar key?"

"Please just go away."

Bernard searched the room and found the key. "I'm going to have a shot or two. Maybe some Pringles. You want anything?"

She muttered, "Screw you."

"Emma. Language! I didn't think you'd say 'Shit' if you had a mouthful." He twisted the top off a miniature, tossed his head back with the tiny bottle clamped between his teeth and let the alcohol flow into his mouth. He shuddered as the fiery Tequila bit the back of his throat and heated his stomach. "I would, you know," he said contemplatively. "Screw myself I mean. If I could. It's been a long time." He lobbed the empty miniature at the trash-can. The force of the bottle knocked the brushed steel garbage pail on its side. "Two points!" he shouted and raised both arms in the air, fists clenched. "What did you decide? TV or movie?"

No answer.

"Emma?"

She didn't react.

"Okay." He shrugged indifferently. "If that's how you wanna be."

He stabbed away at the buttons on the TV until he found the channel guide, and then he poked away some more until he found the program he wanted. "Since you've got no opinion, I vote for *The Night Crew* starring the lovely and talented Jasmine. You ever see her work? She's very good!" Emma continued studiously pretending she couldn't hear him, until the over-the-top moaning on the television reached a point that ignoring was no longer possible.

A lady, wearing nothing but sunglasses, lay on her back with her knees in the air and her heels hooked on the edge of a swimming pool. A man, his lower body in the pool, had his face buried between her legs. She screamed for the Almighty and tossed her head from side to side. Platinum curls whipped her face.

"You know what, Emma? You're getting ripped off. My motel, you don't pay for the adult channels. They're included!" He looked over his shoulder at her. "Can you see? You need me to move?" Bernard slid the chair sideways before she answered.

"This is pornographic." She scrunched up her nose. "I don't want to see."

Bernard said, "What did you expect? You could have decided for us, but no. Instead, you tell me to go screw myself. I just came from the ballet. Of course, this is what I'm gonna put on."

Her eyes narrowed into a question she refused to ask.

Bernard said, "The ballet. A peeler club."

She closed her eyes, shook her head and blew out a puff of air, a sound that was clearly fed up and repulsed.

Bernard ignored her. He crunched a mouthful of Pringles and washed them down with a tiny bottle of Johnny Walker Red. He selected another miniature. Bacardi this time. His vision slowly grew fuzzy around the edges. All the physical activity had cooled the drunken wave he'd been surfing. The miniatures warmed it up in a hurry. He sighed contentedly. He couldn't remember the last time he enjoyed an evening in a nice hotel. And, a dirty weekend? He hadn't wanted a dirty weekend with his wife in years—any husband who said he did was lying—but during all those nights alone in hotels up and down the eastern seaboard, he never once rustled himself a little action on the side. Usually he arrived in town, met with the company's customers and then immediately left. When he spent more time in a city, like at the spring trade show in Vegas, he was too busy for dalliances. Even back then, before his wife's moodiness had transformed into "bitter resentment" and "apathetic depression," the ring on his left hand meant something. And, if he was being honest, by then his booze habit was far more interesting than a one-night romance.

But, here he was in a fancy hotel with a well-stocked minibar, entertainment on the television, and an attractive lady on the bed beside him. Not a stranger either. He and Emma knew each other pretty well. Better than anyone he'd have met in a club. All in all, it was a romantic situation full of possibilities—aside from the room, which was pretty much demolished, and the fear and loathing in Emma's face, which he didn't really understand. He wasn't going to lay a hand on her. What fun would that be?

What he needed was a willing participant.

He straightened. A smile tickled the corners of his mouth.

"Emma, I just had a great idea!" He dipped a hand into his pocket and withdrew the coaster Misty-the-peeler had given him. He waved it in Emma's face. "Where's your purse?"

No answer.

Bernard sighed. Like pulling teeth. Every question was an ordeal. He found her purse, and began rifling through it. "What do we have here?" he asked. He held up a BMW key chain. "Nice car. You a wannabe or do you actually drive one?"

She didn't answer.

"What am I saying? Of course, you do." He found three hundred dollars in cash and stowed it in the same pocket the coaster came out of; then, growing impatient, he upended the purse. An assortment of the worthless paraphernalia a woman refused to leave the house without, fell on the bed. He quickly found her credit cards, the big three.

"You have a preference which card I use? You know, for the loyalty points, something like that?" He didn't expect an answer. Emma didn't disappoint him. He dialed the phone number written on the coaster. While he listened to the phone ring and waited for someone to answer he flicked her Visa card back and forth across the top of his thigh and hummed a tune he'd heard recently, the name of which he couldn't remember.

Someone finally answered. After a short conversation, Bernard disconnected. He smiled. "You ever order an escort before?"

An expression of dawning realization crossed Emma's face. She shook her head slowly at first. As the idea took hold her eyes widened. She shook her head faster.

"Me neither. But Nikki came highly recommended." He made air quotes when he said the escort's name. "She's on her way over. Her agent said, 'all services,' so I assume a threesome is no problem."

The tears started then, silently rolling down Emma's cheeks, leaving red eyes and blotchy streaks in her makeup.

Bernard said, "What's the matter? You got nothing to worry about. The charges show up for a flower shop. Five hundred bucks is a lot of flowers, but that's fine. Rich like you, you probably send that many to a sick friend. You can have sex with Nikki. I'll bang her too. And, you won't have to lie to your husband. I won't touch you, and you won't have slept with another man! It's perfect."

Emma's face was a frozen mask of desperation. He decided a change of subject was a good idea, just for a few minutes while she got used to the whole idea. He asked, "Why don't you have kids?"

"Listen to me, you beastly man," Emma wailed, "I don't want to discuss my life with you. We aren't friends. I don't want to have a threesome with you and some Atlantic City whore. I want you to untie me." She shook her arms and kicked her feet. The scarves held tight.

"Beast?" Bernard's tone turned harsh. "Beast? Quit that

noisy whining. Exact same as my wife. Always crying for no good reason."

"Too bad." She sniffled. "I'm not your wife, am I?"

"No. You're not. And, I'm warning you, I've been down that road before with someone who mattered. I'm not putting up with that kind of behavior again with someone who doesn't. So, do as you're told and stop whimpering."

CHAPTER 17

"THANKS FOR THE lift, baby," Nikki said to her boyfriend. She popped a stick of Cinnamon Extra into her mouth. She dropped the wrapper into a brushed steel ashtray, the sand in it clean, carefully raked, and imprinted with a large artistic O. "I'll be a couple of hours. At the most. I'll call when I'm done. Pick me up?"

"Sure," Leo Jarvis answered. "I'll pick you up."

She scanned the lobby. Aside from a couple of overt sidelong glances she took for granted, nobody paid her much attention. No security personnel were striding in her direction with hotel management on their heels and distasteful scowls on their faces. Like it was some kind of big a deal an escort was in their hotel.

She cinched her belt around her waist ensuring her raincoat wouldn't flap open. There'd be a riot if anyone caught a glimpse of the tiny cheerleader costume she wore beneath it. Husbands' eyes would pop and wives would turn shrill. Nikki looked good and knew it. Security and management would definitely get involved at that point and getting banned from the hotels would be terrible for business.

"Or," Leo said, "you want, I can hang around and wait. Me and Dwayne can have a beer in Glow." He jerked a thumb in the direction of the nightclub.

"Isn't Pryce expecting you?"

"He's waiting for this bag," Leo stabbed a finger at the Adidas gym bag between his feet, "but he can wait a little longer. I'll call him as soon as you're gone. Let him know where I am. Save him from tonight's heart attack."

Nikki stretched up on her tippy-toes. She pushed the gum into the back corner of her mouth and kissed Leo on the lips, careful not to smear her glossy scarlet lipstick. He didn't need to, but whenever he could he saw her safely to the trick and safely home when she was finished. She said, "I'll be fine. Nice place like this, what's going to happen? Thanks for the offer, though." She ran appreciative hands up his arms and squeezed biceps the size of bowling balls. "Where's Sem—" she started, and then quickly stopped. For some reason, Leo didn't appreciate people referring to Dwayne by his nickname. No matter how appropriate the Semi-Gloss moniker was. "Where's Dwayne?"

Leo pointed. "Hitting on one of the receptionists."

Nikki spotted Semi-Gloss over near one of the counters. She shook her head. It was seventy-six degrees outside and pouring rain. Semi-Gloss still wore his leather coat. A pair of sunglasses perched on the top of his head in a tangle of unruly blonde curls. The glasses never seemed to cover his eyes. She made a face. "Poor girl."

"Be nice."

She smiled at him. "You need to get back to work. Pryce will be freaking out, you make him wait any longer."

He nodded. He didn't leave her side.

The elevator settled in front of them with a soft chime. She walked in, her sneakers silent on ankle-deep burgundy carpet. The overt glances would turn into open stares if people saw her sashay by in three-inch heels. They were in her handbag. She'd slip them on upstairs. She did a pirouette for Leo's benefit, and gave him an affectionate little finger wave as the doors clam-shelled closed.

He smiled wide, kind of a dopey smile for such a big, tough guy, Nikki thought warmly. It made her feel good. His skin was bad—adolescent acne scars—but she wasn't so shallow that she cared. He treated her like a jewel. The puckers and scars seemed to disappear when that expression crossed his face, that goofy grin he reserved just for her.

She plunked her handbag between her feet. She leaned into the elevator mirror and checked her eyeliner. It was perfect. Over-applied, thick, and black. No blobs. She grabbed one ponytail, separated it in two and tugged the halves in opposite directions. The little red ribbon cinched up against her head. She did the same with the second ponytail, thinking it was about time for a trip to the stylist. Her hair had grown through what she liked to think of as The Three Stages. Completely blonde to fashionable dark roots to trashy dark roots, which men seemed to like, but if they got much longer she'd just look sloppy.

On the twenty-second floor Nikki exited, turned left and strode confidently down the hall. As she approached 2209, she slowed. This was the worst part. A girl just never knew what kind of weirdo waited for her on the other side of the door. When she was dancing, there were always a couple of big bruisers like Leo hanging around for protection. She wasn't too worried about this job though. She was meeting a couple. Drunk tourists most likely. Probably a husband and wife who wanted to experiment.

After a deep breath, she knocked.

The door opened as far as the safety bar would allow.

Nikki canted her head and looked up into the glassy, intoxicated eyes of the guy staring down at her. His tall, slim frame filled the space between the door and the jam. Inwardly she said: *Thank you.* Fat guys were always sweaty and soft, dead weight on top of her. Their sour stink made her nauseous and stretched her acting abilities to the limit. Comparably, tall and slim was much better.

This guy wore a dress shirt, tie, and slacks. The fabric on the one thigh she could see through the gap was faded a lighter, shinier blue than the rest of the pants but at least he was making an effort. He was older than she expected, middle-aged she guessed, but nowhere close to pension-able. This surprised her slightly. She routinely entertained men whose ages fell between twenty and ninety, and occasionally young drunk couples, but middle-aged couples seldom wanted to party.

He smiled. "Nikki?" A whiff of booze radiated off his breath.

She worked the Cinnamon Extra into a comfortable spot between her gums and cheek. "That's me." The door closed. The safety bar came off with a clank and a second later the door re-opened.

"Come in. I'm Bernard Hewitt." He pronounced every letter, every word clipped. He pushed out his hand.

Nikki recognized the short, precise enunciation. She heard it all the time when she was dancing, from guys who wanted to sleep with an exotic dancer and needed the bottled courage to hit on her. She nodded hello and shook the outstretched hand.

Bernard's smile widened.

She walked into the hallway that led into the main room.

A tickle of apprehension stroked her spine. She pushed the gum around with the tip of her tongue and then started chewing again, very slowly. Something was wrong. Thin wires poked out of a hole in the wall. White plaster dust sprinkled the carpet like icing sugar. A suitcase lay upside down on the floor. Clothes were piled untidily in the corner.

"The maid's day off," Bernard said with a chuckle, like the tired old line explained everything.

Nikki nodded, wondering what really happened. She took another uneasy step, deeper into the room. An end table, missing one leg, leaned drunkenly against the wall. A lamp in several pieces lay beneath it.

When she spotted the woman on the king-sized bed all the flavor in the Cinnamon Extra disappeared.

The woman was fully dressed. A monogrammed hotel towel lay on the bed near her head. A strand of pearls dropped from her neck and pooled on the bedspread like wet enamel on a painter's furniture sheet. Her arms stretched above her head, her toes pointed to the footboard. She was obviously tied in place. Her entire demeanor exuded terror and resignation. She returned Nikki's gaze out of hate-filled eyes.

This was not some kind of kinky husband-wife thing, Nikki realized. The woman on the bed looked like a…

…a prisoner.

At that instant, the woman screamed in a shrill British accent, raw with uncontained fear, "Help! Help me."

Bernard started with visible surprise.

Get out, Nikki thought. *Get out fast!*

She sprang for the door. Reached it in four long steps. The bag dangling from her shoulder pendulumed off her hip. She grasped the doorknob. Turned. Yanked. The door flew open four inches before smashing into the safety bar with a noisy crash. The jolt vibrated up her arm. The knob slipped through her fingers.

The tickle of apprehension turned to dread. Escape was all Nikki could see. She forgot about the pepper spray in the bottom of her bag. As it was, there wouldn't have been time to find it *and* spray Hewitt, *and* get the safety bar off, *and* get out of the room.

"Hey," Hewitt yelled. The words were slurred now he wasn't concentrating on his diction. "The hell is going on? What are you doing?"

Nikki flipped the safety bar back. Her bag dropped off her shoulder and hung in the bend of her arm. She threw the door open. All the way open this time. She jumped for the freedom the hallway offered. And, came to an instant, jarring halt as a bolt of pain blazed from her shoulder to her elbow and rocked her down to her feet.

Hewitt had one of her handbag straps clutched firmly in his fist. "Where you going?" he yelled. "I was told all services."

The lady tied to the bed continued to scream, no words, just a piercingly shrill wail, as uncomfortably loud as a smoke alarm. Between her screaming and Hewitt's shouting, the noise in the room was incredible. Someone had to hear, Nikki thought. Someone would call security or the police. Help would come.

Hewitt slowly reeled her away from the door, deeper into the room.

The door clicked shut.

The woman on the bed stopped screeching, possibly to take a breath, or maybe because she thought the closed door meant all hope was lost.

Nikki thought, *screw that*. Hope was never lost, except perhaps if you were tied to a bed. "Let go of me, you prick," she shouted. She kept her arm bent with the straps of her bag trapped in the crook of her elbow. She knew if she didn't straighten her arm— sacrifice the bag and all her possessions—she'd never get out. Alcohol hadn't affected Hewitt's strength. He would win the tug of war. He *was* winning. But, she could use that to her advantage.

She clenched her teeth and pulled with all her strength, while Hewitt pulled in the opposite direction and grimaced with exertion. They swayed back and forth. The purse straps were rigid with tension. When she couldn't take it longer, when it felt as though the pressure would snap her arm at the elbow joint, Nikki straightened her arm.

The bag flew free.

Hewitt stumbled backward, the weight of his body seemingly too much for his uncoordinated legs to handle. He clutched the bag with one hand. His free arm pin-wheeled the air, reaching for something to keep from falling. "Fuck!" he yelled, and fell on his butt. The breath burst out of his mouth in a noisy blast of pain and surprise.

Nikki flung the door open. It bounced off the stop and swung rapidly shut as she sprinted down the hallway. She glanced over her shoulder. He wasn't following her. Warm relief replaced the terror. Panting, she jabbed the elevator Down button. After three intolerable seconds the elevator numbers began clicking lazily north.

Down the hall, Hewitt poked his head out of the door.

Nikki's heart leapt into her throat. She frantically stabbed the elevator button. A bright violet fingernail broke. She swore.

He stepped into the hall.

Nikki's breath came in rapid little spurts. No handbag. No pepper spray. Emergency stairwell at the wrong end of the hall. Leo always told her, "Look around. There are weapons everywhere." She heard his voice in her head but at that second she was paralyzed.

"Help me! Help!" That British accent once more and Nikki knew without a doubt it was the lady tied to the bed.

Hewitt disappeared back into the room. The door slammed shut silencing the screams.

Nikki shivered, pulled the lapels of her raincoat tightly over her chest and hugged herself. The gum was tough. She chomped it loudly. Frantically. Her foot tapped the thick carpet like a percussionist beats a snare drum. The elevator chimed its arrival. When the doors opened, she charged in without looking.

And, crashed into the individual exiting.

"Sorry," she mumbled.

"You all right, ma'am?" a firm voice asked.

Nikki focused. Navy blue pants. Deep burgundy blazer. A big platinum O and the word, "Security" stitched in silver on the left breast of his coat. A Walkie-Talkie clutched in his right hand.

"Did you hear a disturbance a few moments ago?" he asked.

He looked down the hall. "We've had several noise complaints from this floor."

"I heard screams."

"You all right?" he asked a second time. His attention remained down the hall.

She didn't need these questions. *Who are you? What room are you in?* If the hotel didn't know her before they surely would after this. She kept her eyes on the carpet. "Running late is all."

"Okay," the security guard said. Without looking at her or questioning her further, he walked rapidly away jabbering into his Walkie. Nikki thought she heard him say, "police." She wasn't sure.

CHAPTER 18

JORDON CUTLER'S EYES blinked open. After a second or two of confusion, he remembered he was in Atlantic City, in a room on the twenty-second floor of the Oasis Hotel and Casino. Hurricane Wilfred was shredding the southeastern forty-eight and the airlines refused to fly into her epicenter. He couldn't reach Mel. He'd left bodies on the side of the road near the Egg Harbor swamps. His plans had most definitely come off the rails.

The question was, what awoke him?

He washed both hands down his face. He needed a shave and a shower. His belt and his tie were too tight and his raincoat was bunched under his armpits. He'd fallen asleep without meaning to, without opening a window or turning on the air conditioning. Now he was covered in a thin layer of sweat. His dry mouth tasted awful, like all the contaminants and pollutants in the air were layered on his tongue and coating the back of his throat.

An angry voice drifted through the wall. The sentence was broken but grew clearer as the voice rose. "...are you going? I was told all services."

A woman's enraged voice shouted back, "Let go of me you prick!"

Like the noise of a car crash, the sound of a couple squabbling was universally recognizable—horrible and without any positive qualities, not for the people involved nor for those unfortunate enough to overhear it. Jordon told himself to ignore the argument. It wasn't his business. Now and then couples fought and now and then it splashed over into a public area. It made people sad because when a couple fought like that, the love that brought them together disappeared for a time. It made everyone uncomfortable. It made them wince. The socially accepted thing to do was, try not to hear it and walk away. Create some space. Let the two of them get it out of their system, knowing that in most cases it was nothing but a disagreement they would eventually resolve.

Jordon told himself to ignore it.

He rubbed the back of his hand across his eyes and looked at the clock. His unintentional nap had lasted almost ninety minutes. He had to get up and get out; the revolver was still in his pocket and if he did nothing else that evening, getting rid of it remained a priority.

"Help! Help me," a female voice screamed in a strong British accent.

The voice was loud. It seemed as though the woman was in the room with him. Jordon stiffened and cut a frown at the wall separating him from the room next door. That shrill scream was no longer the sound of two people fighting, it wasn't an angry back and forth. This time it was fear. After sixteen months dealing with Mel's nightmares, he knew what fear sounded like...

...and there was no way he could turn his back.

He grabbed the hotel phone, dialed zero and asked for security.

"Oasis security. How can I help you?"

"I'm in 2207—"

"Is this about 2209?"

Jordon said, "It sounded like a fight earlier. I think it's escalated."

"We've already had several complaints about 2209. A security guard is on the way."

"Oh," Jordon said. "Well, good then." He hung up the phone hesitantly, almost tentatively.

From the hallway, he heard a door slam, and then silence.

He muttered, "Well, good," a second time. He sat motionless for a beat or two, then blew out a frustrated sigh. "Son-of-a-bitch." Security personnel filled him with less confidence than the police. The police tried to find Mel's assailant. Despite all their resources, training, and skill, they were unsuccessful. Security guards had none of those resources or advantages, no matter how commanding or important they liked to act. Trusting a security guard to have more than a stern conversation with the man next door was something Jordon wasn't willing to do. Not after hearing that kind of panicked scream.

"Son-of-a-bitch," he mumbled a second time. He pushed himself to his feet and walked to the door of his room.

CHAPTER 19

ON THE RIDE to the lobby, Nikki adjusted her coat and tightened her ponytails. She removed a Kleenex from her pocket and moistened it with her tongue and then wiped away some smudged eyeliner.

By the time the elevator settled on the first floor the panic was gone. She was equal parts embarrassed, angry, and guilt-ridden. She wanted her handbag back, and the two-hundred-and-thirty dollar shoes she carried in it. She wanted her pepper spray. From now on it was going in her pocket. Burying it under all the other stuff in her purse was inexcusable complacency. And finally, she wanted to help the lady tied to Hewitt's bed. Her terrified, accusing face kept reappearing in Nikki's mind.

She couldn't speak to hotel management on the lady's behalf. They'd have questions for her and they might call the cops, who'd have more questions. That would take time, maybe more time than the British woman had. Nikki thought she knew a better way. She allowed herself a slight smile. Leo lived for situations like this. One detailed phone call and he would come running with a livid, white-hot attitude and the tenacity of an armored tank division.

She stormed out of the elevator looking for the phones—she'd lost her cellular along with her pepper spray and shoes. She saw something far better than a bank of pay phones and her step broke.

Dwayne was still chatting up the receptionist.

Nikki's smiled widened, something that didn't normally happen when she saw him, but she made an exception this time because Semi-Gloss was never far away from Leo. Which meant, Leo hadn't left the hotel.

She scanned the lobby and quickly spotted her man leaning with one foot against a pillar, the Adidas gym bag by his other foot. His arms were folded patiently across his chest while he waited for his friend. He looked bored.

"Leo," she called. He turned, picked up the bag and lumbered in her direction, curiosity on his face turning to concern as he grew closer and read her mood. "What's going on?" he asked. "What happened?"

"That prick upstairs. He's got some lady tied to the bed, like a prisoner." That would annoy Leo but it wasn't enough to get him involved. It wasn't personal. She took a breath. Knowing she was being a tiny bit manipulative, she said, "He stole my bag. Grabbed me. Tried forcing me to stay when I wanted to leave. I barely got out of there."

Leo didn't say anything right away. His jaw hardened. The small pink and white pockmarks covering his cheeks and forehead suddenly glowed crimson. "What room?" His voice sounded like a yard of crushed gravel.

"2209."

"You okay?"

She nodded.

"Really?"

"I'm fine, baby. What are you going to do?"

"Guys like this, they're the reason crime is so bad in this city. They come here, think they can pull this kind of thing and get away with it? Well, he's in for a surprise. Me and him," Leo indicated Dwayne with a sideways head toss, "will go up there and escort this zero into an alley. Beat the living shit out of him. How much you supposed to make? Five hundred?"

"Give or take. He already paid. He put it on his card."

"Don't make no difference. He would have tipped you, so we'll take his cash too. Cops will chalk it up to another dimwit tourist in the wrong part of town."

"See if you can get my handbag back. I had a nice pair of shoes in there."

Semi-Gloss had wandered over while they talked. He clutched one fist in the palm of his opposite hand and cracked his knuckles. He swapped hands and repeated the action. "We'll look into that too," he said, smiling, waiting to be appreciated.

Nikki wrinkled her nose at him. Semi-Gloss looked mean when he smiled. His narrow, too-close-together eyes became untrustworthy slits in his face. He also stunk. His cheap cologne reminded her of a cardboard pine tree hanging from a rearview mirror. Ignoring him she turned back to Leo. "Baby, there's a security guard up there. Got out of the elevator when I got on. I think he called the police. Be careful, okay?"

"I'm not worried. The Zero who grabbed you should be."

CHAPTER 20

BERNARD STOOD WITH his back to the door, fists clenched. He shot Emma a venomous look. "Why'd you scream?" He snatched the towel off the bed and folded it into a long narrow ribbon.

Emma's eyes widened. "You're not putting that thing on me." She rolled her head from side to side.

"What I say? I said, 'Scream and you get the gag.' Now hold still or you're getting a black eye to match the split lip."

She looked at him with an uncertain expression, seemed to decide he was serious and stopped thrashing. Tears welled in her eyes, spilled out, and dribbled onto the pillow. Black streaks of mascara stained her cheeks.

"Smart," Bernard said. He wrapped the towel around her head, covering her mouth. He paused. It was too thick to knot. He cursed softly and then more loudly said, "New plan. Open your mouth. Wide."

"No."

"You don't open up, Emma, I'm going to squeeze your pretty little nose. Hard." He held his finger and thumb six inches away from her face and made pincher motions. "It will hurt. Be uncomfortable. But you'll open up. You won't have any choice." He hiked his shoulders. "I'm trying to make it easy for you."

She slowly opened her mouth.

Bernard stuffed in the towel. Emma's eyes bulged and the sound of her breathing increased as she was forced to inhale and exhale through her nose. "I don't get it," Bernard said in a perplexed voice. "The hooker was here for your benefit as much—"

A firm knock on the door interrupted him. He stiffened. Swiveled. Stared at the door as if a SWAT team were about to burst into the room. What fresh hell was this?

"Hotel security, sir," a friendly voice said. "Could I have a word, please?"

Bernard's apprehension slackened. He puffed out a noisy, relieved breath. He whispered, "Rent-a-cops. Emma, you know what? I hate 'em." Bernard's opinion, they were so inflated with their own importance they didn't realize they had zero responsibility or authority. Throw a problem at them outside of their massive three-page training manual, and confusion clouded their vision like Bar Harbor fog.

But, rent-a-cop or no, Bernard still needed to deal with the man. The security guard had left the excitement of the casino floor and traveled twenty-two levels to investigate the complaints. He wouldn't go away without some kind of answer satisfying his mouse-sized brain.

There was a second knock. "Hotel security. Open the door, please," the voice more insistent this time.

But not yet demanding. Bernard guessed he still had a few seconds. "Be right there," he called back, eyeing Nikki's handbag. He wondered what was in there, considering how reluctant she was to give it up. A weapon maybe? Something he could use? A switchblade didn't seem too far-fetched, considering her profession.

He upended the handbag. The junk that tumbled to the floor was similar to what he dumped out of Emma's purse. High heels. Makeup. Loose change. A spray can rolled across the carpet and came to rest against the baseboard. He grabbed it and looked at the label, and felt a happy smile cross his face.

"Hotel security, sir. Open the door. Immediately."

This time the rent-a-cop sounded as stern and commanding as only a rent-a-cop can. Bernard crouched slightly and peered through the peephole. On the other side of the door, distorted by the magnifying glass, stood a guy in a dark burgundy blazer. The word "Security" was embroidered on the breast pocket, along with a large artistically styled O. He held a Walkie-Talkie in one hand. He raised his other hand and with a great deal of force, hammered the door twice. "Open up, sir."

"Yeah, yeah. I'm coming," Bernard said. He shook his head once, looked at Emma and winked. "You believe this guy?"

With the pepper spray held low along his right leg, he opened the door. He widened his eyes, miming surprise and confusion. "Yes?" His voice came out an octave higher than normal. He recognized the suppressed excitement in it, the rocket fuel blend of adrenaline and alcohol.

Charging the cab driver, shoving the peeler, slapping Emma—these were unscripted reactions, escalating moments in time that were over before he realized they'd begun. This, on the other hand, was a reckoning. The officious rent-a-cop was about to pay for all the times airport security insisted Bernard undo his belt or remove his shoes.

Bernard was going to enjoy watching the rent-a-cop suffer.

CHAPTER 21

JORDON CUTLER LEANED against the door jamb with his arms crossed, holding the door to his room open with his foot. He watched a security guard in a splashy burgundy blazer stride down the hallway, heading in his direction, long assertive steps, brow furrowed with determination. He glanced at Jordon, gave him the briefest of nods, and then came to a halt one door down, in front of 2209. He knocked and said loudly, "Hotel security, sir. Could I have a word, please?"

Jordon thought, *Weak*, although he hadn't nailed down exactly what he'd do…much depended upon how the guard handled the situation. At a bare minimum, the man needed to speak face-to-face with the British woman who screamed in such terror. If he didn't, Jordon would step in…

…*after sixteen months dealing with Mel's nightmares, he knew what fear sounded like, and there was no way he could turn his back.*

The guard knuckled the door twice more, each time more insistently. Whoever was on the other side called back muted excuses. The door remained closed. The guard frowned. He looked in both directions, uncertainty on his face. When his eyes landed on Jordon, he pointed and said, "Sir, return to your room, please."

Jordon kept his face blank, curious to see how the next minute or two played out. He was glad he hadn't tossed the pistol off the end of the boardwalk. The reassuring weight in his pocket counterbalanced the growing volatility of the situation in front of him. For the time being at least, the weapon wasn't a liability. He didn't move.

The guard's frown deepened into a scowl. He flushed. Presumably, he didn't appreciate being ignored by both Jordon and whoever was in 2209. Then the light coming through the peephole went dark and the guard stiffened to attention. He raised his fist and thumped the door twice. In an authoritative voice, he said, "Open up, sir."

The door opened halfway. A tall, skinny guy with slicked-back hair and a face reddened with anger or heat or alcohol, filled the gap. He said, "Yes?"

Even from several feet away, Jordon thought the short question sounded overly innocent. Manufactured.

The guard said, "We've had some noise complaints, sir. Some smashing sounds? Screaming?" He swayed on the balls of his feet, craning his neck, straining to see into the room. "Is everything okay?"

"Everything is fine."

Without warning, a woman's panicked shriek splashed into the hallway. "No. It's not fine. Don't go!"

The sound scraped across Jordon's nerves like an out-of-tune violin in a horror film. The security guard rocked back half a step as though in surprise, and then he reversed direction and lunged into the room. Half a second later he flew out, howling in agony. He fell in an ungainly mess, the burgundy blazer a tangle around his shoulders. His legs jerked spasmodically, his heels drummed the thick hallway carpet.

Jordon's mouth dropped open. He stood frozen in place. What had he just witnessed? He hadn't expected to see the guard enter the room—were they even allowed to do that sort of thing? He really hadn't expected the man to come flying back out like he'd been kicked in the chest by a Clydesdale, coughing and gagging and pawing his face with both hands.

The skinny guy with the slicked-back hair stepped into the hallway. His head swiveled left, then right, and then he pivoted and broke into a sprint, accelerating in Jordon's direction like a Formula One car, his loose neck tie flowing behind him like a droopy-eared dog riding in the back of a pickup, the coat in his hand flapping vigorously. His footsteps were muffled on the carpeting, his eyes aimed at a point over Jordon's shoulder. He closed the gap between them in a hurry, like he didn't have any idea Jordon was standing directly in front of him. Then, as if another part of his lunatic brain had suddenly clicked into gear, his gaze dropped and his eyes widened and he veered left...

...at the same instant Jordon's legs thawed and he doglegged right.

There was neither time nor space for either of them to correct. They collided and went flying, a tangle of limbs flailing the air. Jordon tried to turn sideways, knowing the impact would hurt, hoping to take it on his side, but it was happening too fast and he slammed onto the floor, flat on his back. The wind rushed from his lungs in a loud whoof.

The Lunatic had a fraction of a second longer to prepare. As they collided, he covered his chest with his arms, fists near his cheeks. He landed, blasting Jordon's face with a hot exhalation of his own, forearms smashing Jordon in the chest. An intense pain filled Jordon's chest and then the weight on top of him rolled away. He folded in the middle like a hinge, desperately heaving for air. He blinked water-filled eyes, trying to clear his vision.

The Lunatic stood over the top of him, wiping his hand across his forehead, pushing greasy hair away from his face. Once again, he scanned left and right. For a moment, he squinted down at Jordon. Then, he stooped, straightened, and disappeared.

In the opposite direction, the security guard whimpered and

cursed and staggered to his feet. With one hand scrubbing his eyes, the other arm outstretched as if for balance, he wobbled across the wide hallway and disappeared into 2209.

Jordon's spasming diaphragm slowly calmed and returned to normal. He hadn't had the wind knocked out of him in a long time. Perhaps when he was a kid playing soccer, but he couldn't remember for sure. His old man probably took it out of him a time or two. Again, he couldn't be sure. He chastised himself for poking his nose into someone else's business, but he knew he wouldn't do anything different, if he had it to do again.

He wrapped his arm across his throbbing rib cage. Groaning against the pain, he pushed himself upright until he was sitting with his back against the wall. He looked in both directions. Despite all the racket, the hallway remained empty. Not surprising. In Atlantic City everybody wanted to be downstairs in the middle of the action, not upstairs hiding in their rooms. He swallowed a couple of grateful, pain-filled breaths. It had been a long night. He hoped nothing else went wrong.

Down the hallway, a melodious ding signaled the arrival of the elevator.

CHAPTER 22

BERNARD SCRAMBLED TO his feet. He mopped a hand across his forehead, pushing sweaty hair away from his face. He eyed the hallway in both directions, pinpointed the fire escape a second time, and then dropped a hasty glance at the person he crashed into, the man splayed on the carpet, his raincoat puddled on the floor around him like a no-color pool of mud.

A ragged breath caught in Bernard's throat.

Could it possibly be?

A gun lay on the floor, a brilliant nickel-plated revolver with .38 stamped into the barrel!

He'd never owned a firearm. Not a handgun, rifle, or shotgun. His wife didn't like them, thought they were dangerous. She said, with the complete conviction of the terminally stupid, "... all guns should be banned." He hated that kind of naivety. Guns were dangerous for the irresponsible. In the right hands, though? They were equalizers. A person didn't have to pull the trigger.

Had his luck finally changed?

Without so much as a second thought, he stooped, grabbed the revolver and bolted for the exit. Behind him, the elevator gently chimed its arrival.

Bernard pushed through the heavy metal fire door and hit the stairs running. Took the rubber-edged treads three at a time.

His footsteps clanged on the metal steps. He ignored the vague odor of cigarettes and urine, and briefly wondered what kind of degenerate would piss on a hotel's staircase. With his coat and the revolver in one hand, he used the other hand to swing around the banister at each landing, like a kid playing crack-the-whip. When the door slammed shut above him, filling the stairwell with a hollow, metallic echo, he was already three floors down and dropping like a manhole cover.

By the fifteenth floor he thought his heart would palpitate right out his chest. His Oxford dress shoes weren't designed for running. A blister on his heel shot fiery pain through his foot. Gasping, he slowed and came to a stop. He bent partly at the waist and slurped in huge mouthfuls of air. His throat was dry and raw. His lungs burned. His recovery, however, was unconscious and secondary.

The revolver held his entire attention. He clutched it and swung his arm around the empty staircase, sighting down the short barrel at scuffmarks on the walls. The nickel plating shone brightly in the overhead fluorescents; the catch-light bounced off the walls. It felt powerful. It made Bernard feel the same way. He smiled.

A gun!

Finally, something was going his way. He could have used it in Emma's room. Waved it in her face, seen the fear. The respect. He wouldn't have had to gag her—he still wasn't sure how she managed to spit the towel out—and there was no way she would have screamed like she did. She would have done exactly as he asked, at the precise time he asked it.

And, that was how it was going to be from this point forward.

Too many people on the planet started out aggressive, their misplaced sense of entitlement giving them the idea they could get away with being abrasive. Some pompous talking head psychiatrist might have said he was being overly sensitive, considering his situation—no job, no wife, a shit-ton of debt. Bernard disagreed. The more likely scenario was, people sensed he was in one of life's valleys and took advantage, if not with deeds, then certainly with words.

Well, that ended now. Finding the .38 when he did, after everything that happened this evening, was a sign—you're finally standing up for yourself. Good for you. Here's something to make the journey from the bottom of the valley to the top of the world a little easier. You don't have to pull the trigger.

He placed the revolver on the floor by his feet. He armed the sweat from his forehead and grimaced at the oily stain that ended up on his cuff. He undid his pants and tucked in his shirt, even front to back. Only kids wore their shirts un-tucked. It was a sloppy, unkempt look. Sloppy wouldn't do at all. It didn't match his new and improved outlook. He straightened and tightened his tie. Then he shoved the revolver into the waistband of his pants at the small of his back. It wasn't comfortable, but when he put on his sport coat, the tail hung lower than his waistband, easily concealing the weapon, and that was the important thing.

He started walking, setting a more leisurely pace. The warm rush of excitement still pumped though his body. No more backing down, taking the abuse. Someone didn't like it? Tough. He had a handgun and he planned on using it to change their point of view.

CHAPTER 23

INSIDE THE ELEVATOR rapidly climbing toward the twenty-second floor, Dwayne shuffled and jived and slid his hands between various pockets, seemingly unsure what to do with them. "This is a nice elevator," he said. "All the steel and wood. You ever ride in one that creaked and groaned? Made you wonder if more than one strand of cable was holding it up. You ever get in one that had carpet glued to the walls?"

Leo Jarvis tensed until his biceps strained the fabric of his fitted Henley. In the elevator mirror, he saw an exasperated nerve twitching in his jaw like a greyhound at the beginning of a dog race. Leo knew he was the closest thing to a friend Dwayne had and as far as he was concerned, that counted for something. At the same time, he thought it sad because there were moments when Dwayne's chatter and fidgeting stomped on his last nerve. It took a great deal of effort not to bark at his friend, tell him to shut the hell up. He said through clenched teeth, "What you going on about?" He never called his friend "Semi-Gloss." Not after he learned where the nickname came from, Mr. Pryce telling him with an uninterested shrug, "The boy's not too bright. He's not a dullard either."

"You know. Freight elevators," Dwayne answered. "Or the kind you find in cheap apartment buildings. I liked those. Used to light the carpet on fire with a Harley Davidson Zippo then watch the show! Everyone running out of the building. Bells ringing. Fire trucks." Dwayne laughed. "Good times."

"You a pyromaniac?" Some days more than others, the Semi-Gloss nickname seemed more appropriate.

"A pyromaniac?" Dwayne wrinkled his forehead in what Leo recognized as deep concentration. Eventually he said, "Nah. I don't think so. The carpet never really burnt. It just smoked a lot and set off all the alarms." He paused a beat. A slight smile played on his lips. "Stunk like ass, too."

Leo filtered out Dwayne's drivel and thought about the Zero, how he wanted to drive the guy brain first into a brick wall, the way he messed around with Nikki. Scared her. It's what he deserved. Unfortunately, as much as Leo liked the idea for Nikki's sake, killing the guy wasn't the best choice. The cops would be on a killing like shit in a sty, and Leo definitely didn't want the pigs looking in his direction.

He ground his teeth in frustration.

He'd have to settle for making an example out of the guy. It would need to be dramatic enough to make the newspapers, perhaps the six o'clock news, otherwise the other Zeros in the world wouldn't get the message. A beating fit the bill. Broken bones went without saying.

"How do you want to do this?" Dwayne asked.

Leo made a small, annoyed growl deep in the back of his throat. He hated repeating himself. "Like what I said in the lobby," he answered. "We find this Zero, take him outside, and beat him into a coma. Capisce?"

"Yep."

"You got your piece, just in case?"

Dwayne turned sideways and tugged open his leather coat by a lapel. "Oh yeah."

Leo looked at the molded rubber grip of a Smith and Wesson

magnum under Dwayne's arm, held secure in a shoulder holster. "The .357? Why you packing the heavy artillery?"

"I like this gun. What difference does it make?"

"None, I guess. Anyway, you flash him Mr. Smith. He'll understand he's coming with us. We march him back to the elevator. Simple. In the lobby, you on one side, me on the other, we walk him out the door, around to the car. It's so crowded downstairs, nobody will even notice. We toss his ass in the trunk." Leo nodded at his reflection in the mirror as his plan solidified. "Then we find a nice quiet alley."

"Why don't you just let me cap him?"

Leo smiled slightly. "The pigs, they look hard for someone who does a murder. A beating, they aren't gonna be so worried about."

"Makes sense." Dwayne reached into a pocket. When his fist came out it was wrapped around a set of brass knuckles.

"What are you doing?"

Dwayne squinted at him.

"You bust him with those he'll bleed all over the carpet. Won't be easy walking him out of here, the manager asking how we're going to pay the cleaning bill. Cash or credit? Put 'em away." He smiled a second time and slapped a friendly hand on Dwayne's shoulder. "You'll have plenty of opportunity to use them later."

Dwayne put the knuckle dusters back in his pocket. He said, "Leo?"

"Yeah?"

"You remember a band from the eighties, sang a song called *Pyromaniac*? I like that song. Don't make me a pyromaniac though."

"The song you're thinking of is called *Rock of Ages*."

Dwayne gave him the same questioning squint as earlier.

"It's a common mistake. But you're right. It's a good song,"

Leo said. "Anyway, what I'm saying, I never understood the fascination of watching things burn."

The elevator slowed and then settled with a musical chime. The doors opened. Leo walked out with the Adidas gym bag in one hand, Dwayne a step in tow, Leo wishing there'd been time to drop the bag off at the Lucky Thirteen before bringing Nikki to work, before this all went down with the Zero. He suspected Pryce would be melting down like Chernobyl right now. He glanced right and saw nothing except an empty hallway. He looked left and saw two people at the far end of the corridor. He nodded once and strode in their direction, eyes roaming from side to side, analyzing the scene as he approached.

The security guard Nikki mentioned—had to be him in that awful burgundy and navy uniform—wiped his face with his shirt-sleeve. Weaving and swaying, he stumbled toward an open room, one arm stretched out like he was walking a tightrope. Leo recognized the aerosol can near his feet. Pepper spray. Probably Nikki's. She carried one just like it.

He turned his attention to the only other person in the hallway, some guy sitting on the floor with his back against the wall. A long dark raincoat pooled on the carpet around him, making it look like he was sitting in a puddle of mud. His eyes were clamped shut, his face knotted in pain. The sound of his breath was deep and ragged, like every inhalation hurt. This would be Nikki's client, the guy who got rough, who had someone tied to the bed.

Leo said, "This'll be our Zero."

"Looks like," Dwayne answered.

What happened seemed obvious to Leo.

Nikki runs. Drops her bag on the way out of the room, or maybe the Zero grabbed it out of her hand. How he got it didn't matter. He follows her into the hallway and runs straight into the security guard. They tussle. The guard gets in several hard punches before the Zero doses him with the pepper spray. Now they're both on the floor suckin' wind, the Zero wondering how a security guard got so tough, the guard doing his best to swab the spray out of his eyes.

Pretty obvious.

Standing over the Zero now, his stance wide, Leo said, "Hey, pal. Open your eyes."

Dwayne laughed.

The Zero blinked his eyes open. After a couple of seconds, he pushed himself to his feet, balancing himself with one hand against the wall. Bent slightly at the waist, with his free arm wrapped across his stomach, he raised his gaze. There was a glossy sheen of sweat on his face. His complexion was whitewashed with pain and confusion, like he didn't understand what Leo and Dwayne were doing standing in front of him.

Leo ignored the man's empty expression. In half an hour, in some quiet alley, he'd clear up any remaining questions the man had. He handed the gym bag to Dwayne with a curt, "Hold this," then planted a hand on the Zero's shoulder, steadying him. "You got your breath back? You feeling better now?"

The Zero nodded slowly, his forehead furrowed in puzzlement.

"Glad to hear it." Leo hurled his free fist into the Zero's stomach. The air rushed out of the man's lungs in a heavy, wheezing gust. He deflated. His knees buckled and he collapsed. Leo still had a firm grip on his collar. He dragged him erect and said, "How are ya now?"

Pitiful retching sounds were the only answer.

"Puke on my shoes and it's the last thing you'll ever do," Leo said, his gravelly voice rough and dangerous.

Dwayne laughed a second time but bit it off quickly as though deciding fun wasn't a mean enough emotion. He pulled his coat open, showing off his .357, just like Leo instructed in the elevator. "You're coming with us, bro."

CHAPTER 24

RAIN HAMMERED DOWN. The wipers swiped it off the windshield, and while Brenna worked her cell phone, Luther thought about the last time he'd driven to Victoria Chesham's home in Brigantine, back in '98 when she called herself Tyffany.

He remembered her opening the door four inches—the most the chain would allow—and she stared at him out of eyes as dark as melting Swiss chocolate. She wore a shimmery white blouse tucked into faded blue jeans and understated accessories—a necklace, watch, and belt that all said "money," even to Luther's untrained eye. She smelled delicious, like something that made him think of cherry bark and almonds. He palmed his badge and held it vertically in his hand so she got a good, clear look at it. "Luther McKinley, ma'am. Atlantic City Detective. Are you Ms. Victoria Chesham?"

She dipped her head the tiniest amount. A faint expression of curiosity crossed her face.

"I need to speak with you about a situation at the Oasis Hotel and Casino." Her expression changed to understanding as he spoke. The change was so subtle, if he hadn't been expecting and watching for it, he wouldn't have seen it. "May I come in?"

She gave him an amused smile and her eyes came alive, as

though she was having fun, like a game had just begun. "No," she said, "I don't think so."

He firmly told her she was going downtown, one way or another, and they were going to have a conversation about two deaths in the Oasis.

She answered without a trace of unease, "Are you arresting me? Are you going to put your hand on my head, make sure I don't hurt myself when I get into the backseat of your car?" She widened her eyes and in a breathy, frightened voice he recognized as theatrical she said, "Are you going to cuff me? You can, if you want."

Most people say something like that and he would have answered in his gravest, cop voice, "That won't be necessary, Ma'am." Instead he had to concentrate on holding back a grin. "Let's go, Ms. Chesham."

Suddenly, she was all business. "First I'm going to call my lawyer. Then I'm going to change into something more appropriate. Then we can go. Not before." She slammed the door, left him standing on the step wondering if he should push her doorbell again and ask how long it would take her to change, did he have time to grab a coffee? Would that fit into her schedule?

They spent several hours in an interview room, along with a video camera and her lawyer. Later, when he looked up the attorney's credentials, Luther understood the source of at least some of her confidence. The man was well regarded and very expensive. He forced Luther to tango around her job, but eventually Victoria painted a clear picture of what happened in the hotel, often leaning into him like they were old friends sharing a secret, giving him glimpses of the pink lace beneath her silk blouse, and holding his gaze a fraction of a second longer than necessary. Touching the back of his hand with gentle, polished fingertips. Every time she shifted and crossed her mile-long legs under the table, the whisper of nylon-on-nylon made him dizzy.

By the time he finished the interview, he was a little bit in love with Victoria Chesham. He had to constantly remind himself, she was a witness and quite possibly the trigger that incited the murder-suicide he was investigating.

Years later, the memory still warmed his neck and ears. Allowing a witness to get under his skin in such a manner was unprofessional, although to this day he wasn't sure it was something he could have helped. He snuck a peek in Brenna's direction and saw, with relief, that she seemed unaware of his embarrassment.

The moment of relief disappeared in a hurry.

"What's with you?" she asked.

"Nothing," he said hastily. The flush burned hotter. "Pay attention to your phone call."

"I'm on hold." She stared at him. "You look guilty."

"Nope."

She softly coughed, "bullshit" into her fist. "I don't believe—" Then she was jabbering into her cell phone, free hand stabbing and slicing the air as she made point and counterpoint.

Victoria reminded Luther of an elite athlete or a famous actor, one of those Hollywood types who burn a little hotter than the average person. The common man wants to live inside the actor's orbit, to absorb some of the heat. In return, the actor thrives on the adoration. The relationship never gets deeper than that. It never gets personal or real. It was like a contract. An agreement. You do this for me, I'll do that for you, no different in any great respect from Victoria's occupation. It was her job to impress men, to draw them in with her appearance, style, and personality. She gave them what they wanted and in return, she enjoyed a lifestyle that was quite obviously expensive and lavish. A contract. An agreement. Luther couldn't imagine her breaking it for marriage, suburbia, and pay-check to pay-check trips to Walmart for diapers and dog food.

Brenna shut the cell phone closed on her cheek with finality. "We got the search warrant!" she said, looking pleased.

"Perfect. Good work. Let's go check out her place." After a several second pause he added darkly, "Then we're going back to the hospital. Take another run at Menny."

Brenna looked at him, brow furrowed. "We have to talk to him again when we get more intel. Obviously. But, you sound…" She paused. "You sound like you do when you're convinced a guy's wrong."

"Wrong? No." He shook his head. "But he's holding back. He didn't tell us everything."

"Do they ever?"

"I want to know what he meant, 'We talked about getting married.' That's not the Victoria I met. I don't see her having a boyfriend, never mind getting married."

"Times change, Mac."

He felt the road rise as they approached the bridge that crossed the strait separating Atlantic City from Brigantine. They hit the bridge deck. The Caprice thumped rhythmically over the joints. "Times change. She looked the same to me."

"Other than being dead, you mean."

"Other than that, yeah."

"What aren't you telling me?"

"Victoria had a certain…" he hesitated in concentration. "I don't know, charisma? Menny might have thought he and Victoria were discussing marriage. My guess, she was telling him what he wanted to hear."

"Where do you get that?"

"Just an impression from when I met her in '98."

"Why'd she talk marriage, then? To what end?"

"She was getting something from him." He shrugged. "And, it had to be something big. If she wanted a Gucci watch she could have easily bought her own, the money she was making."

After several seconds of silence, Brenna said, "Menny's story makes sense. Right now, he looks more like a victim than a perp. He was shot. He's in surgery. Remember? I haven't heard anything that makes me think he's lying, that precludes marriage."

"That's because you never saw the way she was; the way she looked and acted. There was something about her." He shifted uncomfortably in his seat. "She was like a Hollywood actor."

"I don't know what that means."

He hesitated once more, longer this time as he struggled to find a way to explain. "Sometimes men lose their minds in front of a pretty lady. Do things or say things they normally wouldn't."

"No fooling?" Brenna using Luther's line, saying it with exaggerated disbelief.

"Watching Martina McBride dance will cross one guy's eyes. The next guy couldn't care a less. Plunk Danica Patrick in front of the second guy though, he's doing her laundry without a second thought." He paused then, and with a grin said, "Although, washing Danica's unmentionables might be kind of fun."

"Yeah, that's definitely what she wants. Some guy who can't say the word 'panties' going through her laundry basket."

Luther laughed.

"Anyway, you decide after two or three conversations she's not the marrying kind? The thing is, Mac, first impressions aren't necessarily your strong suit, are they?"

He assumed she was referring to Marilyn. It was an excellent point and it stung. He said, "Truthfully, Bren? Not really. I mean, I didn't care much for you the first time we rolled, but you've become tolerable."

There may have been a whisper of a smile on her face, but she kept her eyes forward and raised her middle finger in his direction, and he couldn't tell for sure. He thought about how badly he misjudged Marilyn and wondered if Brenna was onto something. How much could he trust his first impressions?

He would have done anything Marilyn wanted for a single smile, even after (maybe especially after), they bought the bungalow and moved in together. But it didn't take long for their plans to unravel. The renovations took too long and cost too much. "I'm done hanging sheets from the ceiling and calling them doors, Luther. I'm done wiping sawdust off my feet every time I get into bed." Then there was the time he spent at work and the cop clique she insisted she could never fit into. "I'm always an outsider at parties and BBQs, Luther."

And, now he was looking at Menny, not necessarily as a suspect but not as straight up victim either, simply because of an impression a witness gave several years before. Perhaps Brenna was right. He said, "I'm curious, is all. If she was working him, how did he handle it when he found out? What did he do? How extreme was his reaction? You want a loose end to pull on? There's one."

"Assuming she was working him. Assuming he found out," Brenna said doubtfully. "A lot of assumptions."

He said nothing. He hadn't expressed his thoughts about Victoria and Menny as a theory or motive. He was simply following a train of thought. It might not go anywhere, but it was worth watching. Given his knowledge of Victoria, the entire scenario wasn't that far-fetched.

Brenna said, "Mac?"

"Yeah?"

"Who's Martina McBride?"

CHAPTER 25

JORDON CUTLER WAITED for the elevator, standing between two people he knew he'd never seen before.

On his left, a guy the size of a telephone booth with a barb-wire tattoo strung around one bicep, a man who either enjoyed superb genetics or a fabulous steroid connection. On his right, the telephone booth's partner, an individual wearing big Hollywood hair, a leather jacket on a rainy, seventy-six-degree evening and a splash of woodsy cologne that stunk like rotting foliage.

Puzzled, Jordon concentrated on the elevator numbers climbing toward the twenty-second floor. Who were these people? What did they want with him? He said, "Guys—"

With sudden urgency, the individual with the big hair leaned back and spoke behind Jordon's head. "Leo? What about her purse? Her shoes?"

"She won't miss 'em. She's got too many shoes as it is. I go shopping with her, she'll drag me into sixteen shoe stores looking at black high heels. Every one of them the exact same thing."

Leo.

The name meant nothing. It didn't come with a glimmer of recognition. It didn't give Jordon a clue to the identity of the men he stood between. "Listen, guys," he tried again. "I don't know who you think I am. I don't know what's going on here."

Without turning his head Leo said, "I don't care who you are. You come here, think you can hassle a working girl? When you picked Nikki, you picked the wrong one." His voice was a low, jagged rumble.

Jordon said, "Who's Nikki?"

"Play stupid all you want. It ain't gonna make a difference." Leo looked at the lights above the elevator doors. "Fuck's sake, where's the elevator?"

The guy with the hair rapidly stabbed the Down button half a dozen times.

"Like that's gonna help, Dwayne."

"I used to go out with a chick who liked shoes," the guy named Dwayne said, as if he hadn't heard Leo at all. "She was the athletic type. Had a nice hard bod." He bobbed his head like an appreciative Pez dispenser.

A muscle began rhythmically twitching in Leo's jaw.

"She had a pair of sneakers for everything. One for aerobics. One for tennis. Another set for whatever else she was doing. She spent a small fortune on Reeboks. Used to tell me they never wore out because she spent good money on good quality. You know what the real reason was?"

Leo's pockmarked face turned a darker shade of red. He gave his head one small, fast twitch. "No."

Jordon followed the conversation with a confusion-fogged mind. Every inhalation hurt, a little bit on the surface from when Leo slugged him, and deeper inside as well, from when the tall, skinny Lunatic guy crashed into him in the hallway. He kept an arm across his mid-section, applying mild pressure to what he felt certain was bruised ribs. He remembered the feeling. One time as a kid his old man clubbed him, Jordon usually lightning fast skipping out of the way, but not that day and the miserable old bastard's cast iron fist connected.

"What about you?" Dwayne asked. "Do you know?"

Jordon wondered, was he seriously being kidnapped by two people he'd never seen before while they discussed an ex-girlfriend's footwear? Was it possible? He said, "Maybe she only wore each pair three times a year?"

Dwayne seemed surprised. "You aren't as dumb as you look."

The elevator arrived and the doors opened. Leo pushed Jordon inside. He and Dwayne followed. After the doors closed Dwayne wrinkled his brow. "The strange thing was, a closet full of shoes, it didn't stop her from buying more." The interior of the elevator was silent for a moment. "Who was the woman had all the shoes? Hey rocket scientist," Dwayne glanced at Leo with a big grin and then turned back to Jordon, "You know who it was, some celebrity, with all those shoes?"

"Imelda Marcos," Jordon said. "She wasn't a celebrity. She was married to a Filipino dictator."

"Sounds right," Dwayne answered, as if the information had momentarily deserted him and all he needed was a quick reminder to bring it all back.

"Okay you two," Leo growled. "Button it."

Dwayne said nothing, nor did he seem the least bit bothered by the noticeable disdain in Leo's voice or the irritated glower on his science-gone-awry face. Possibly he recognized his partner's mood and knew now was a good time to stay quiet. Jordon didn't like any of it—not the big man's tone, his irritation, or his expression. Without saying so, it seemed obvious Leo had more than a pointed conversation in mind when they hit the ground floor. And, even though he now knew their names, Jordon still didn't know who they were or why they were interested in him.

His confusion was quickly turning to apprehension.

CHAPTER 26

VICTORIA CHESHAM'S TOWNHOUSE looked exactly as Luther remembered it, although tonight the floor-to-ceiling windows were dark and black and seemed to stare at Luther like two dead eyes. He rapped on the front door and called out loudly, "Atlantic City Detectives," and without warning a sense of deja-vu rushed over him. He halfway expected Victoria to open the door and brush past him like she did in 1998, after she called her lawyer and changed her outfit. Victoria wearing a skirt and black nylons now, saying, "You're the one who's been leaving all the messages?" and then on her way down the steps, leaving a hint of that delicious perfume in her wake, asking him, "What's your name?"

"I already told you. Detective McKinley," and Victoria had laughed and fluffed her chestnut hair off the back of her neck and said, "You know what I mean. What do they call you? Mac? Something original like that?"

Luther shook his head, chasing away the memory. He rapped on the townhouse door once more, harder this time. There was still no answer, nor did he expect one. The building felt vacant, like somehow the house knew its owner wasn't returning.

"We go?" Brenna asked, already shaking loose the set of keys she'd taken from Victoria's purse.

Luther nodded. "We go." He un-holstered his weapon.

After several attempts, Brenna found the key that unlocked the front door. The deadbolt slid back with a loud clunk. She turned the knob and pushed the door with the tips of her fingers. It swung a quarter of the way open. Off to one side, Luther stretched out a leg and nudged it the rest of the way with his foot. He hated this part, the moment when he had to go from outside to indoors. He always imagined a bad guy jacked up on pills, maybe cradling a sawed-off twelve gauge, waiting in the darkness for someone to silhouette himself in the door. Luther peered around the jam into the foyer, into the long blackness of a hallway that stretched out in front of him like a tunnel. Pistol at arm's length, he edged his way into the townhouse.

The tang of old garbage immediately assaulted his nose. Straddling a jungle of sandals and pumps—no work boots to indicate a male presence—he listened hard for any sound that might mean someone was in the house. All he heard was a refrigerator humming in the darkness and, from behind him, Brenna's breath coming quicker than normal. Without looking, he knew her weapon was in her hand too. To his left in what was obviously the living room, the night spilled in like day-old dishwater, gray and murky from the rain pelting the windows. There was a stereo nestled in a large entertainment center and, beside it, a television. There were books on the shelf.

A body on the couch.

His hand tightened around the pistol's grip. His breath hitched. He took two cautious steps toward the still form before realizing the body was only an untidy bundle of pillows and blankets. He smiled slightly. Someone else who slept on the sofa.

An old newspaper fanned across the floor in front of the couch. Several fashion magazines decorated the coffee table. A plate covered in toast crumbs sat on the pass-through between the living room and kitchen. Beside the plate, a television remote, like

Victoria ate breakfast at the counter while watching the morning news.

He relaxed slightly. The search warrant was unnecessary. She lived alone. Her place looked too much like his own for there to be any doubt. The only difference—her plants were alive and well watered. Still, procedure was procedure. He and Brenna cautiously and conscientiously cleared each room, making sure there'd be no surprises for the ID Bureau when they arrived. Once they confirmed the house was vacant, they holstered their weapons.

In the kitchen, fists on his hips, Luther said, "Start in here, I suppose." They needed some obvious scrap of information that would point them in the direction of Victoria's killer. The ID Bureau would do a much deeper search and dig out the proof that would convict him, or her.

After a perfunctory search, they moved from the kitchen into the living room, and then down the hall to the bathroom and finally the bedroom. Luther had to pull up fast behind Brenna, who'd come to a rapid halt in front of the wide-open closet doors.

She stared at the clothes, rifled through them, and then looked at Luther with her mouth hanging open slightly. "This girl spent money on herself. Nothing but designer labels."

Confident he wouldn't recognize a designer label if it was sewed to his butt, he said, "Is that right?" although he had to admit, Victoria's closet appeared to have more class than his did, with his jeans and shirts from Sears and Target.

"Dior. Chanel. Lots of Gucci. There's thousands of dollars' worth of clothes here." She looked at a tag on one of the dresses. "Bitch was a size two."

Luther didn't hear any malice in her voice and figured she was too grounded to really care about Victoria's dress size. He yawned into the back of his hand, hiding a smile of affection and, for some reason, pride.

Brenna pointed to the clothes and lingerie strewn on the

floor around the laundry basket. "The price didn't bother her. Otherwise she would have treated it better. No way a temp can afford all this." She shook her head. "Sugar daddy, maybe?"

Luther considered that option for a moment, and then dismissed the idea. A sugar daddy wasn't Victoria's style. "Not as I remember her. She was too independent to be kept. Too much of an individual. She was a working girl. Nothing has changed since ninety-eight."

He sat down on the edge of the mattress and opened the top drawer of the bedside table. It was empty aside from a heating pad and a pair of flannel socks. He tugged on the bottom drawer. It didn't budge. With a tingle of anticipation, he said, "When you're done admiring her wardrobe, you mind looking for a key? The bottom drawer is locked."

"Who locks their night table?" Brenna rummaged through the jewelry box on the dresser. "Nothing here." She dipped a hand into her pocket and found Victoria's key chain and then tossed him the entire bundle. "Maybe on that."

He guessed the old-fashioned skeleton key was the one for which he was searching. He tried it and the drawer unlocked with a click. He pulled it open and let a knowing smile cross his face. There was nothing naughty in the drawer. There was something far better.

A black, leather Day-Timer.

"Get ready to be happy, Bren!" He held up the book.

She raised her eyebrows. "This oughta be good." She sat on the mattress beside him, close enough their shoulders and legs touched. "Open it. Come on!"

He grinned at her enthusiasm and cut her a glance. His breath caught unexpectedly in the back of his throat. They were sitting awfully close together, alone on a queen-sized bed. Her hair was tied back in the usual French braid; he still smelled the apple blossom shampoo. There was a tiny diamond stud in her ear lobe. He liked the lines around her mouth and at the corner of her eyes.

She saw his look and showed him a tentative, shy smile, the kind of smile he didn't see from Brenna too often. She looked away fast. A tinge of pink colored her cheeks. The warm pressure of her shoulder and leg against his didn't change. There were about a dozen different things he could have done and judging by the second short look she gave him from beneath her black lashes, any one of them would have been fine with her, but what he did…

…he cleared his throat.

Simultaneously, she said, "Uhm."

The pent-up tension in the room disappeared as fast as it arrived, making them both laugh. Without looking at her, he unzipped the Day-Timer. "Let's see what's in here, shall we?"

"Let's."

The front half of the Day-Timer listed addresses A through Z. The back half held a list of Victoria's day-to-day activities. During the week preceding her death she had several morning appointments. Luther guessed they were her various temp jobs. There was also a scattering of evening engagements. On the day of her death a note read, *Tom Menny. Supper @ 7:00 PM.* Luther nodded. Another indication Menny wasn't lying, even if he wasn't telling them everything.

Brenna pointed at the following page. A line in neat handwriting read, *Jacob @ 10:00 PM. The Plaza.* "A client maybe?" she said.

"Could be," he answered slowly.

"First name only. Might be tricky finding him."

She was right. Then he wondered, could he cross-reference the names? He flipped to the AB tab in the address section.

Nobody named Jacob.

He turned the page to the CD tab.

Brenna immediately stabbed the page with her nail. "Caswell, Jacob."

Luther stared at the name, frowning. Why did it ring a bell?

Unlike most people listed in the Day-Timer, there was no information beside Caswell's name. All the blanks beside most names were filled in—full addresses including zip codes and e-mails. It was all there. But there was nothing except a phone number written beside Caswell's name. With the book balanced on his leg, Luther tapped the page several times with an index finger. He muttered, "Who is this guy?"

Then, he let a smile cross his face.

"What?" Brenna asked.

"Caswell. He's a state judge."

Brenna stared at him. "Oh boy."

"No fooling." Luther considered the implications. If Jacob—the individual who had a ten o'clock with Victoria at The Plaza—and Jacob Caswell the state judge, were one and the same, the murder investigation had just become sensitive and political.

"Let's not jump to conclusions," he said, caution in his tone. "Maybe there's more than one Jacob in this book. Maybe her ten o'clock wasn't a client." He didn't believe it. Jacob wasn't that common a name. And, having a prominent judge as a client squared with what he knew about Victoria. Her clients would all be well off, like the dead guy in the Oasis, a high-priced tax attorney before his wife ventilated him.

He flipped to the front of the book and ran his finger down each page until he came to the next name that stood out for lack of information.

Knight, Clive.

"Whoa," Brenna said, holding up a palm. "Clive Knight? He's the vice president of a bank. I know because I was in re-doing my mortgage the other day and I saw his name on some of the literature."

"Perfect," Luther muttered. He kept looking, thumbing from page to page, working his way to the back of the address section until he came to another name and number combination. "Here's one for you," he said flatly, and read the name.

Brenna sucked in a startled breath. "Senator Radley?"

Luther looked at her, kept his face expressionless.

"You don't think Chesham was fooling around with the Senator?"

"If we're right—a name and number, no address—represents a client, then the good senator isn't getting what she needs at home." They sat in silence for a minute or two, until the doorbell chimed, the ding-dong startling Luther. Several loud knocks followed the bell. He heard the front door open and someone called, "Detective McKinley? Detective Hanson?"

Luther pushed himself to his feet. He looked down the hall to the entrance of the townhouse. A couple of techs from the ID Bureau stood in the open doorway wearing their white coveralls, carrying equipment. "The place is secure, guys," he said. He held up the Day-Timer. "We're leaving. We got everything we need for now."

On the way to the Caprice, Brenna said, "This is huge, Mac. She's got the names of an exec, a judge, and a female politician written down in that book. Those are the names we recognize. We go looking into these people's private lives, into Senator Marion Radley's life, all hell is going to break loose."

Luther sighed. "No fooling." Every person listed in the Day-Timer was a person of interest in her death. Not necessarily a suspect, but certainly a person with whom he and Brenna would have to speak. Most would turn out to be friends and family. It would be easy to lean toward innocent when he talked to them. He had to automatically lean toward guilty when he was dealing with people who had reputations to lose. VIPs abhorred having their name associated with anything sleazy.

"You still want to go hard at Tom Menny?" Brenna looked at him with a cocky, smart-assed smile on her face. "The Day-Timer kind of blows up that theory, huh?"

"You think you're pretty clever, don't you?"

Her smile widened.

Luther said, "It was never a theory, remember? It was just an idea that crossed my mind." He wasn't ready to give up on Menny quite yet. Victoria and the VIPs were conducting business. Extremely risky business for a VIP, but if Caswell, for instance, decided he wanted to end the arrangement, he just never booked her again. He didn't kill her. Business. On the other hand, Menny's involvement with Victoria was personal. The range of emotions and the subsequent reactions were far wider when personal feelings like love and betrayal were involved. As far as Luther was concerned, keeping an open mind and one eye on Menny was still worth his time, no matter how long the suspect list had grown.

He said, "We can't just wake the good senator up, ask her, 'Were you getting it on with a hooker?'" He shook the Day-Timer. "We'll have a conversation with the Captain. See how he wants to handle the situation. Until then, we go back to the station and start running background on Menny."

"After that, back to the hospital?"

Luther nodded.

"You want me to drive?"

"No," he said distractedly, and handed her the car keys. They'd need to tread carefully. One mistake when dealing with a VIP, even if it turned out there was an innocent explanation, meant career hara-kiri.

PART 2

1:00 AM to 5:00 AM
September, 2002

CHAPTER 27

BY THE TIME Bernard reached the first floor his lungs had stopped heaving. They still hurt low down in his chest, like maybe he strained some capillaries, but he no longer thought he'd keel over in cardiac arrest. All those years promising on January first to join a health club, maybe he should have. Maybe after he won some cash, got solvent, he'd buy a gym membership. Pay a king's ransom to run up and down stairs at a club instead of doing it for free in a hotel.

The stupidity of the idea made him smile.

He walked out of the stairwell into a corner of the hotel lobby and stopped abruptly enough the soles of his Oxfords slid on the floor. Bewildered, he scanned the expansive casino in search of an exit to the outside world. The low thunder of countless conversations filled the room. A cacophony of jangling slot machines and rattling roulette wheels assaulted his ears. He took a deep breath, clearing his mind of alcohol-induced confusion. He took a second careful look.

When he spotted a bank of elevators, he thought he knew where he'd find the hotel's exit, assuming the elevators were the same ones in which he rode to the twenty-second floor. Should be as simple as walking past the Boardwalk Buffet on his right, the high roller baccarat area on the left, and a little further along, past the nightclub's interior entrance, directly out the front door. He straightened his tie, adjusted his sport coat, and strode purposefully into the crowd.

Casinos. As much as he loved them, he hated them. They never wanted anyone to leave. Not until they vacuumed every cent out of every pocket. Even then, they still refused to show a person the exit. No arrows, clocks, or windows. It was like an underground garage at a shopping center. A guy doesn't enter the garage in the exact spot he exited; finding the car later on is like finding fly shit in a pepper mill.

Bernard slowed as he neared the nightclub. A sign in a flashing light-bulb frame advertised, "Sunday through Wednesday: NO COVER!" Beneath this, "Thursday: Ladies Night. HALF PRICE Cosmopolitans." A bouncer stood with his back to the casino, his attention directed into the club. He held the entrance door open with his shoulder. A clamor of music flooded past him, the song unrecognizably distorted by the noise of the casino.

Bernard's step broke. He glanced at his watch. 1:40 AM. Still early. Four or five AM was late in Atlantic City. Not 1:40. He peered over the bouncer's shoulder, looking into the club with professional interest. A strange feeling filled him. It took him a moment to recognize it as nostalgia. Cumulatively, he'd spent weeks, maybe months in nightclubs selling the latest and greatest consumer electronics to the DJs and managers. Oftentimes he'd kill a couple of hours in a club the night before a sales meeting so he knew what equipment might transform it into the next "in" place. He'd become a master at figuring out what a club needed.

Bernard licked his lips. A cold beer and a smooth bourbon would keep the drunk alive, in the zone where everything was clear and possible, not to mention how good both would taste after sprinting down twenty-two floors.

Of course, stopping for drinks wasn't the smartest play. Bordering on incomprehensible, really. But, he had some time. He doubted the police would still be looking for him over something as trivial as skipping out on a cab fare or a bar tab, assuming they bothered looking in the first place. In a town like Atlantic City, cops ignored trivial problems. There were too many big problems for them to deal with.

Eventually though, the rent-a-cop upstairs would finish wiping pepper spray out of his eyes. Then he'd free Emma, at which point she'd raise a monumental fuss. When that happened, the cops would most definitely come for him—if a person wanted to get technical about it, he'd kidnapped Emma. It was an ugly word and it had come to him slowly, as he descended the staircase. Kidnapping certainly wasn't his intention when he made the spur of the moment decision to hide in her room, but neither his intention nor his interpretation would matter after Emma finished spinning her version of events.

They would come for him.

He told himself to leave the Oasis. Instead, he took a tentative step toward the club's entrance. Then another. With his second step, all the miniatures he emptied in Emma's room drowned his resistance. Emma, the rent-a-cop, the police—they could all get fucked. The boss who fired him could get fucked. His wife could get fucked too, just not by him in the house he bought and the bank effectively owned. He wanted a drink, perhaps two. He deserved them. He had some time, and if he wanted to wax nostalgic, he was going to do it.

The bouncer didn't look behind as Bernard drew closer. Bernard smiled with malicious happiness. Embarrassing a bouncer was as enjoyable as getting over on a rent-a-cop. He pulled the door the bouncer was leaning on, fully open. The bouncer staggered, his support gone, his nonchalant tough-guy pose ruined as he struggled for balance. Hoping the man would interpret the gesture as apologetic, Bernard gave him a wide smile and friendly nod, but he blended into the crowd quickly, just in case the man decided to become offended.

The dance floor was well lit with a nice light package. Bernard knew of some multi-colored lasers that would light up the fog spewing from the machine in a really cool way. The speakers weren't too bad either although they weren't capable of making the God-awful techno music the DJ was spinning sound good. The stage was empty, the band on a break, presumably. Other than the dance floor itself, Glow was surprisingly dark. He guessed the club's name came from the black lights that made everyone in the place move in jerky starts-stops, and if they wore white clothing, shine like iridescent caricatures.

He elbowed his way into a swarm of people clustered in the center of the room like bees around their queen. When he finally made it to the bar he found himself vying for a bartender's attention alongside a twenty-something in glowing white tights, and a scoop-neck baby-doll T. He glanced at her.

Then took a second, longer look.

The night he'd been living so far—after the ballet and the movie—just about any lady would have grabbed his attention. This one went beyond that. He could have bounced quarters off her ass. Sparkles of silver high on her chest and at the sides of her eyes glittered when the black lights hit them.

Feeling a burst of alcoholic bravery, Bernard said, "How do you get the sparkles to stay on?"

She looked at him silently for a moment before leaning into him. He ducked down so she could shout into his ear. "They're in a cream." She ran fingertips lightly from her neck down across her chest, staring him in the eye the entire time. "Just rub it on, you know?" She pulled back but didn't turn away. "What happened to your cheek?"

Bernard touched the fingernail scratches. He winced. "Cut myself shaving."

She gave him a tiny nod and a small smile. "Right." She kept looking at him, her plucked and shapely eyebrows raised in a silent question.

Did she expect him to elaborate? Was she asking something else? Bernard had no idea what she wanted and the words that were usually on the tip of his tongue wouldn't come. One thing he did know, when a young lady looked like this, when she was waiting for him to say or do something, a guy needed to be confident and speak up, show her something she hasn't seen before, something to hold her interest.

He blurted out, "You want to dance?" and then winced at the stupidity of the question—she obviously heard that all the time.

"Sure." She hiked her shoulders. "Buy me a drink first?"

Her expectant gaze suddenly made sense, something so obvious he couldn't understand how he missed it. He said, "I don't buy strange girls drinks."

"Do I look like an alien? My name is Shari. With an i." She dotted an imaginary vowel hanging in the air. "I'm not strange. I'm normal."

Despite himself, Bernard smiled. "That's not what I meant."

"I know," she said. "Why don't you buy girls drinks? It's a standard business transaction in a place like this. You look like a businessman, you know?" She gave his tie a flip.

To be a good sport Bernard affected a smile and a chuckle. Not much of a bargain, but he couldn't see a graceful way out. He centered the knot and brushed his palm down the tie's length, smoothing it. He hollered at the bartender, "One Miller Genuine Draft. A double shot of Jack." He turned to Sparkle-girl-Shari-with-an-I. "What do you want?"

"Mineral water. Lots of ice."

"Mineral water? That's the biggest consumer head fuck of all time. You realize entire countries wish they had water that flowed out of a faucet? Some genius decides to bottle it and people actually pay for it. Let me get you a real drink."

"Water costs the same as your beer, so what difference does it make?" She spoke directly to the bartender. "Mineral water. Lots of ice."

"No difference," Bernard said begrudgingly. "I guess. How much is a beer in this place?"

"First time, huh? Never would have guessed. Six-ninety-five."

"For a beer?"

Sparkle-girl-Shari nodded.

"That means a mineral water is—"

"Six-ninety-five."

Seven bucks for a glass of water and ice? Not including tip?

The bartender worked fast and the drinks arrived in a hurry. Bernard looked at the glass of water, at the lemon clinging to the rim, and wondered if the slice of shriveled fruit accounted for the price. The anger, already burning hot, flared to life. As far as he was concerned, he'd just been violated for asking how silver sparkles stay in place. He tossed one of the twenties he'd stolen from Emma on the bar, picked up his bourbon and shot it in one smooth motion. The whiskey mixed with the rest of the alcohol he'd consumed that night and ignited like napalm.

He was very aware of what he did next. Curious, in fact, about how it would turn out. "Enjoy your water," he said and deliberately poured it onto the floor between her feet. It splashed up, soaking her suede high heels, splattering her bare ankles. The lemon slice landed on one pointy toe.

Shari's eyes widened in indignant rage. For maybe two seconds she seemed too stunned to react, and then she screamed, "Asshole," and slapped him. Pirouetting on her heels, she stormed away, slicing through the crowd like a ship's bow parts water, heading straight for the bouncer Bernard unbalanced when he walked into the club. The party carried on, the room so loud and dark and foggy that only two or three people in his immediate vicinity saw what happened.

Shari stood in front of the bouncer, her rock-hard body vibrating with anger. She stretched out an arm and stabbed the air in Bernard's direction with an index finger. The bouncer straightened while she spoke. He tapped his bouncer buddy on the shoulder. Mean smiles crossed their dim faces. They started in Bernard's direction.

A chill numbed Bernard's nerves and heightened his senses. Strobes flashed. Smoke made his eyes water. The music was a relentless, painful barrage. He drained his beer, plunked the bottle on the bar and reached beneath the tail of his coat. His hand found the revolver and his fingers curled around the grip. He hesitated. If he pulled the .38 he would become a concern. A threat. Someone who had to be dealt with.

Kidnapping.

In that instant, he realized he was already a concern. When he pushed his way into Emma's room he'd crossed an invisible line, whether he realized it or not. Prior to that moment, he'd been an irritant whose anger and reactionary behavior could be dealt with, if not forgiven…

To his boss who insisted he stole, to the bank manager who refused to renegotiate his line of credit, to the potential employers who wouldn't hire him because he was too old or didn't have a particular skill, even to his wife who decided he couldn't provide her with a house full of children or financial stability, he was an irritant and a failure. None of them had given him a second chance. They refused to listen when all he wanted to do was explain. It wasn't his fault. It was the establishment, large corporations, foreigners…The list was long, but they all brushed him away like he was a mosquito buzzing around their ears.

That all ended in Emma's room. He was already a concern, and if that was true (and he knew it was), it didn't matter what he did next. He washed his free hand down his face. He was tired of being subjugated by people who thought they were better than him. Hadn't he decided (twice already) that he was through letting other people run his life and dictate his actions? He didn't have to pull the trigger.

He whipped the revolver out from beneath his coat. "Don't come any closer!" He swung the .38 straight-arm, back and forth between the two bouncers. "I mean it. Not another step."

For a second or two nobody said anything and then someone yelled, "He's got a gun. He's got a gun!"

Everyone in a small circle surrounding Bernard scattered like cockroaches in a sudden bright light. Outside the circle unaware patrons continued to drink and dance and shout into each other's ears. Girls stood in clusters, pretending they didn't want the glances and attention they attracted, while guys posed and talked too loudly, trying to draw attention of their own. Both bouncers came to a skidding halt, one slightly behind the other. The one in the front held up his hands. "Take it easy, man." He slowly patted the air with open palms.

Bernard thumbed the revolver's hammer back. The rush he felt was like a hit of some powerful, illicit drug. His blood surged. He felt every thump of his heart. *He didn't have to pull the trigger.* With his eyes fixed on the lead bouncer he said, "No closer. Not another step."

The bouncer paced him.

A circuit breaker in Bernard's head snapped. "What I just say?" He squeezed the trigger. Shot the bouncer in the chest. Saw a misty cloud puff away from the man's too tight T-shirt. Watched him stumble into the arms of his colleague.

The DJ must have heard the shot and realized it wasn't base from the subs. The music stopped. Glow was silent for less time than it took for the wounded bouncer to gasp, and then the rest of the partiers became aware of the drama. Panicked screams filled the air and a mass of people fled for the exits.

Bernard jammed the revolver into his waistband and joined the scurrying, frightened throng. Elbows jostled him back and forth. He pulled his shirt out of his pants, letting it hang. The sloppy look hid the revolver adequately. He tugged at the knot, loosening and then removing his tie. He dropped it and it disappeared beneath the mob's feet. He shrugged out of his sports coat, threw it at a garbage can and kept walking. He undid the shirt button at his neck and he ran his fingers through his hair, mussing his careful conservative style.

The way he visualized it, only two people got a studied look at him in Glow's dark and foggy interior. The bouncer, and Sparkle-girl-Shari. As long as he blended in and didn't do anything to attract attention, he figured he'd changed his appearance sufficiently to make it out of the Oasis before someone identified him as the shooter.

The lobby was mayhem. Someone shouted, "Call the police." Small pockets of girls cried. Confusion was written on most faces. Bernard strode past it all, heading for the main doors. A valet stood on the top step, his face wide with curiosity. He bobbed from side to side in an effort to see what was happening. "What's going on in there?" he asked when Bernard got close.

"Some fight in the bar, I heard." Bernard brushed past him, taking the steps two at a time, welcoming the anonymity of night.

CHAPTER 28

HIS RIBS WERE bruised. Not broken. Of that Jordon was certain. He felt the same way now as he did when he was a kid—it hurt to breathe deeply but a cough or a sneeze didn't drop him to his knees in white hot agony like a broken rib would have. When he did cough, a fresh layer of sweat prickled his underarms and seeped into his hairline, and he had to grind his teeth to keep from swearing in pain. His breath came in shallow, noisy rasps that filled the otherwise silent elevator. Leo stood on one side of him, the Adidas gym bag on the floor by his feet. Dwayne stood on the other side.

Leo and Dwayne.

He still had no idea who they were. "Listen, guys. I think—"

"Button it."

"Really, I—"

"I told you once already, shut up. You don't, I'll shut you up. Capisce?" Leo's voice was low and dangerous, his pockmarked face grim.

Dwayne planted his fists on his hips and leaned in, staring without blinking at Jordon, obviously trying to appear as menacing as Leo. "Yeah, capisce?"

Jordon said nothing. He swallowed dryly. His stomach churned with pain and growing apprehension. The last time he was stressed like this and flanked by two jumpy, angry people, he was in a guidance counselor's office, on one of the rare occasions his folks decided to take an interest in him. His father was stone cold sober that day, and embarrassed. He didn't want to hear how his son's exceptional aptitude for computers did not offset truancy and fighting.

Jordon shook his head at the memory. Strange things popped into a person's mind at the strangest times. A lot happened after that meeting, but this was not the time to think about it. He had put himself into a predicament—he just *had* to see how the security guard handled the British woman and the Lunatic—so this was the time to think about extricating himself, not to ruminate about...

Just like that, it dawned on him. He stiffened in awareness. *Leo and Dwayne had mistaken him for the Lunatic.* Why hadn't he put it together five minutes ago when they grabbed him? He should have seen it, except he had other things on his mind and it all happened so quickly. "Hey," he said, his voice stronger than before. "You want the other guy. The tall, skinny guy."

Leo's massive hand clamped down on the back of his neck and in one practiced motion, he straightened his arm and slammed Jordon's face into the elevator wall.

A piercing bolt of pain sped directly to the center of Jordon's brain. A meteor shower of flashing lights filled his eyes. His teeth furrowed the inside of his mouth and he tasted blood. The brushed steel handrail caught him across the tops of his legs like an aluminum baseball bat and his thigh muscles exploded. He staggered, flung out a hand and caught the rail, somehow remaining on his feet.

"I hate repeating myself," Leo said.

Laughter spewed from Dwayne's mouth. "That was great! You see the way his face kind of flattened? Like in a Bugs Bunny cartoon? Imagine that in slow—"

"Dwayne," Leo said, a warning in his tone.

"I'm just saying—"

Leo chopped his hand through the air.

Dwayne's gums stopped flapping with a smack.

Jordon gulped in air. Oily face marks smeared the otherwise spotless elevator mirror. Past the smudges, he saw himself— disheveled black hair, a growing purple bruise on his forehead, drool and blood leaking from his mouth like a string of dangling pink yarn.

His neck and face grew hot with a sudden surge of anger. He swiped the blood away with the heel of his hand. This was ridiculous. They had the wrong guy. Every time he turned around, Leo was using him as a punching bag. And, the worst part? For the time being, there was very little he could do about it. He uncurled his fists, forcing himself to control the anger. He closed his eyes and clenched his teeth, caging his apprehension. A certain amount of anger and fear was good. Anger, when it was managed, gave a guy strength. Fear made him wary. Release both emotions at the same time and the results were unpredictable. Often violent. His old man had inadvertently taught him a couple of life's lessons.

Jordon only needed an opportunity to live up to them.

The elevator slowed. Settled. Jordon's mood improved fractionally. Since talking his way out of the situation was clearly out of the question, maybe this was an opportunity. A group gets on. In the confusion, he twists free and darts out the closing doors.

As if reading his mind Leo grabbed a handful of his belt and tugged him back a few inches, letting him know he had a good firm grip. "If you don't wanna put someone else in the same jackpot you're in, you'll keep your mouth shut."

Jordon nodded once. He wasn't about to put anyone else in danger. But, if a group got on he planned on making a huge scene. In her ongoing psychotherapy sessions Mel had learned that if someone came at her, she needed to scream her head off. As a defensive technique, it would pump her up, make her stronger and startle an attacker, sometimes enough to chase him away. In his present situation, Jordon thought the same technique would help him. He'd yell at the top of his lungs, scare everyone senseless, and while he was at it, he would swing around—maybe jerk the belt out of Leo's grip, maybe not, it didn't matter—and use the momentum to bust Leo as hard as he could on the point of the nose. A time came when a guy needed to quit strategizing and start acting and there was nobody, didn't matter how big he was, whose knees didn't buckle and who didn't tear up after a vicious blow to the nose.

Jordon's legs coiled like springs as he dug his feet into the carpet.

The doors slid open. A single businessman entered.

Jordon blinked in disappointment. The coiled tension backed off slightly.

The suit thumbed the wheel on the side of his Blackberry as though it represented life or death, completely unaware of the sinkhole into which he stepped. He glanced without interest at his fellow passengers. "Lobby," he said in Dwayne's direction, Dwayne standing closest to the buttons.

Dwayne's faced darkened in anger. Presumably he didn't allow anyone to bark at him unless it was Leo, especially arrogant suits with Blackberries. He opened his mouth, but Leo cut him off with another short, chopping gesture and said, "We're going to the lobby too."

The suit raised his eyes, crinkled his nose at the three of them—Jordon guessed it was the stench of Dwayne's something-died-in-the-woods cologne—then he dropped his gaze back to the Blackberry, completely missing the livid glare Dwayne shot in his direction.

Several seconds later the elevator stopped on the ground floor. The doors opened and the suit exited in a hurry. After he disappeared Leo picked up the gym bag and said, "Listen to me. The three of us are walking out of this hotel like we're best friends. Capisce?"

Jordon said, "Capisce," thinking he sounded like an idiot. And, thinking if the slightest opportunity to escape arose he would exploit it to his maximum ability. For now though, he had to follow Leo's orders. He couldn't run. Leo had too firm a grip on his belt. And, yelling would no longer be helpful. He doubted anyone on the casino floor would pay attention to him. If it were Mel stuck between these two thugs—tiny, blonde and cute—and she was shrieking hysterically, people would notice. He, on the other hand, was just an excited guy in a casino.

With Jordon leading the way, Leo and Dwayne flanking him, they walked out of the elevator. They headed down a short corridor and around a corner, into the energetic mayhem of the casino floor. All three came to an abrupt halt.

The lobby was an overflowing amphitheater, people everywhere, all talking excitedly. Near the entrance to the nightclub two police officers, notebooks in hand, spoke with a hotel security guard. Two paramedics were part of the huddle, as well as a couple of individuals in street clothes, one of them a young lady in high heels and white tights, the other a man the size of a skyscraper with what appeared to be a similar amount of intelligence on his face.

Dwayne glanced at Leo, the earlier fun in his eyes gone. "What's going on? Cops all over the place."

"Only two. A crowd this big, dim lights and all the noise, they won't even notice us. Stay cool."

A quick, nasty smile crossed Dwayne's face. "Bar brawl?"

Jordon straightened. He took a deep breath, barely noticing the aching ribs inside his chest. Yelling like a maniac suddenly made sense again. Police officers paid attention to that sort of thing. That was their job. Unlike everybody else in the casino, they weren't supposed to become distracted by their surroundings.

He jerked his arm free of Dwayne's grip and waved frantically. "Hey!" he shouted. "Over here!" No response. Nothing. He barely heard his own voice over the racket and the babbling crowd clustered outside Glow. "Hey," he yelled, harder this time, putting as much into it as his bruised ribs would allow. "Over—"

Leo rabbit punched him in the kidney, not much power in the jab, the goliath too close to really move his arm, but it made Jordon gasp and sag. One of the cops flipped his notebook shut, raised his head and looked straight at him, might have seen him drop too, because his gaze flicked from side to side, and his eyes widened when they landed on Leo. He leaned into his partner and spoke a few words. He pointed.

Dwayne said, "They've seen us, bro"

"Stay cool," Leo repeated.

"Oh, man. One of them is coming over."

Jordon raised his arm and dropped it in a big, sweeping "come here" gesture.

"You're gonna regret that," Leo muttered.

Jordon watched the cop pushing in his direction, less than twenty people between him and freedom. He said, "I doubt it."

"They're waving us over," Dwayne said, the strain making his voice rise.

"Pretend you don't see them." Leo quickened the pace. Pushing with his fist in the small of Jordon's back, using pressure on his arm like a tiller, he changed directions, widening the gap between them and the cop.

"Leo Jarvis," the cop yelled. "Stop right there."

Jordon grinned. He didn't care too much for police officers. He spent too much time as a youngster waiting for them to do something about his drunken old man, and too much time hoping they'd track down Mel's assailant. This particular moment though, he didn't think he'd ever been so happy to hear one yell, "Stop."

A blur of color (perhaps teal), suddenly appeared, speeding across the casino floor toward the cop. A second, larger figure, followed the teal blur, this one dressed in a burgundy sport coat with the word, "Security" embroidered in silver on the breast. Jordon's heart dropped and he mouthed a silent curse—somewhere, on the other side of the globe, a butterfly had flapped its wings.

The woman in teal slid to a stop directly in front of the cop, the security guard beside her. Her obvious rage and the guard's bulk formed a formidable wall. The cop pulled up short with a quick jolt and a surprised expression.

Leo and Dwayne propelled Jordon toward the exit, probably sensing they'd caught a break. Jordon leaned back, digging his feet into the floor, resisting. It was like holding both hands up against an avalanche. He kept his eyes riveted on the cop. Their eyes locked.

The cop's face hardened. With his Walkie-Talkie in his hand, he brushed the woman in teal aside and forged ahead. She staggered. Her face flashed a brilliant, incensed crimson. She swore, the expletive somehow classy in her high-class British accent. Regaining her balance, she leapt in front of the cop, flung out an arm and planted a hand firmly on his chest. She shook a jewel-adorned finger in his face, speaking so fast her words were a jumble.

The gap between the cop and Jordon grew and filled with people.

The cop slammed his Walkie into the holster on his hip. He grabbed the woman's shoulders in both hands and lifted her off to the side.

He acted fast, but not fast enough.

Through it all Leo and Dwayne kept moving, hurrying Jordon out of the hotel, forcing him across the street into an alley. Leo dipped his free hand into a pocket. He pulled out a set of keys and unlocked the trunk of a car. A sudden light flared bright in the dark, wet night. Jordon's feet were swept up from under him and the two thugs rolled him into the vehicle's trunk. He landed on top of a bottle-jack. His ribs seemed to explode, filling him with an all-consuming pain that stole his breath and brought tears to his eyes. The lid slammed down, hitting him on the top of the head. Then there was nothing.

CHAPTER 29

HURRICANE WILFRED MOVED offshore during the night, leaving gusty winds and heavy rain in her trail. Luther McKinley aimed the Caprice toward the Atlantic City Medical Center, the car's headlights barely piercing the lashing rain and oppressive pre-dawn atmosphere. He drove in silence, chewing on the information he and Brenna discovered during the background check they'd performed on Tom Menny. It didn't make any sense. When two detectives question you about a homicide, you tell them everything. You especially don't hide or omit easily verifiable facts.

He raised his voice and spoke over the sound of the windshield wipers and heater fan. "Why do you suppose Menny never mentioned winning the lottery?"

Brenna hiked her shoulders. "Ask him, Mac. He'll tell you he didn't think it was relevant."

"This insect goes out with a girl who loves money. Drives a hundred-thousand-dollar car—"

"Ninety."

"—ninety-thousand-dollar car with a vanity plate that screams, 'Look at me,' and when he gets robbed at gunpoint, allegedly, he doesn't think money is relevant?" With an effort, Luther corralled his irritation. "Listen," he said, "for some reason he seems to like you. I'd like—"

"The guy has good taste, Mac."

Luther cracked a grin despite himself. He said, "He doesn't know you the way I do."

"He's a little creepy. I mean, he was pretty much hitting on me an hour after his girlfriend died."

"Ex-girlfriend. Isn't that what he said? I wasn't sure you noticed him doing that."

"A lady always notices, Mac. Most times we ignore it. Just like a guy is wired to look, we're wired to ignore it." Her voice flattened. She stared straight ahead. "Sometimes when a fellow is a little thick he doesn't realize he's flirting. That can be endearing, if the guy is interesting."

He wondered what she was talking about, wondered if she got that a lot, guys coming at her with lines, but he was too distracted to think about it much. He said, "I want you to ask most of the questions. If he's mad at me he'll likely respond to you."

"Is he gonna be mad at you?"

"I'm going to push him."

"You're in a wretched mood so everyone else has to be?"

"I don't like getting lied to."

"Neither do I, Mac. Particularly lies of omission. 'I didn't mention it because you didn't ask.' That'll be his defense." She gave her head a quick shake, as if trying to dismiss her displeasure. "Anyway, people lie all the time. How's this different?"

Luther didn't answer.

"Am I gonna need to keep an eye on you? Make sure you don't clobber him with a telephone book, he doesn't answer your questions the way you like?"

"Perfect," Luther said. "The good old days." He thought a baseball bat and a thick phone book to disperse the blow and prevent bruising was exactly what the situation warranted. But as much as he liked the idea, entering the room angry and aggressive would only put Menny's back up and make getting answers more difficult. Other than not caring for the man in general, and irritation that most likely had more to do with exhaustion than Menny's lies of omission, Luther had no reason to come at him hard.

He parked in a space labeled "Doctor" close to the hospital's main entrance and then, side by side, he and Brenna hurried indoors. They checked which room Menny was recovering in and then caught an elevator, Brenna saying on the ride up, "Keep in mind he's not a suspect. He's not even a person of interest. We want to clear up some inconsistencies, is all."

"I know," he said.

The blinds in Menny's room were closed, his room dimly lit by a single bedside lamp and the glow of a television suspended from the ceiling. There were no flowers or cards on the bedside table. They'd come soon, from all the people who called this insect a friend and Luther figured they'd come in abundance. A guy who can afford a private room in a crowded hospital attracted friends.

The only bed in the room was tilted up in the middle. The sheets were pulled up to Menny's waist. A washed-too-many-times green hospital gown covered his upper body. Through one gaping sleeve Luther spotted the bandages on his upper chest. Other than that, the man didn't look too worse for wear. In fact, he looked a damn sight better than most people who suffer gunshot wounds and reparative surgery. The thing about an eighty-dollar haircut, Luther guessed, even after getting shot and undergoing surgery, a person still looked good. He irritably washed a hand down his face. Whiskers—a five o'clock shadow or three days' growth, it didn't matter—made him look and feel unkempt. On the other hand, the five o'clock shadow covering Menny's face did nothing to diminish his appearance.

Menny glanced at them both, and then aimed the remote control at the television. The SportsCenter chatter silenced. The television remained on, casting dancing blue shadows on the walls.

Luther wandered past the foot of the bed to the window. He twisted the rod attached to the Venetian blinds until they opened and then spread two slats apart with his fingers. He peered out at the hospital parking lot.

Brenna said, "I'm Detective Hanson, and you remember Detective McKinley?"

He smiled at her. "I remember you both. Especially you."

"Mind if I sit?" She motioned with her hand to a chair beside the head of the bed.

"Be my guest."

Reminding himself to stay calm and focused, Luther said conversationally, "What's a room like this cost? Per night?"

Menny told him.

"That much, huh? Wow." Luther kept his gaze fixed on the parking lot. "The man drives a Porsche. Doesn't think twice about renting a private hospital room. Makes me think I need to get into construction." He turned around and faced the patient. "Isn't that what you said earlier? You were in construction?"

"Yes."

Luther raised his left eyebrow and waited.

"I won the lottery a while back."

Luther nodded. "We know. You didn't think it was important to mention this when we spoke earlier?"

"It's not significant."

"Everything is significant," Luther said. "Very minimum, you let myself and Detective Hanson decide what's significant and what isn't. Not mentioning it bothers me. Makes me wonder what else you're holding back."

"I'm not holding back a thing. You never asked. What did it take? One phone call to find out I had money. Another one to find out she stole a chunk of it? I was real tricky, hiding those two little facts, wasn't I?"

Luther froze. *She stole it?* This was a kernel of information that hadn't made the newspapers. Which meant Menny never reported the theft to the authorities.

Why?

A second disappeared. Then another. Muffled voices and footsteps drifted into the room from the hallway. The heart rate monitor beeped softly. Luther thought furiously, *Victoria stole his lottery winnings?* Had Menny just let slip a fact not widely known, or had he stated a fact so well-known he didn't feel it warranted a comment? Another lie of omission, in effect? Luther guessed time would answer those questions, but either way, the theft added another ingredient for he and Brenna to consider.

Unwilling to show Menny his surprise in case it caused him to withhold something else, he said, "This is more Brenna's department than mine. Trivia, I mean, but here goes. You know the number one reason one individual murders another? An argument. Simple as that. Drugs and alcohol are often part of the mix. Money and love are almost always involved."

Menny stared at the silent, flickering television. He said nothing. The room was quiet except for the near silent tick of the clock hanging on the wall.

Luther continued. "So, we have a victim. We have a significant amount of stolen money. And, we have love. Some bizarre, twisted, sick form of love..." his voice trailed into nothing. He cocked his head and looked straight at Menny with his face arranged into a quizzical expression. "You did know Ms. Chesham was a prostitute, right?"

"Escort," Menny said coldly.

"Tomato, toe-mah-toe." Luther waved a dismissive hand. Brenna frowned at him. He ignored her. "Line up all those facts end to end, and we cops have something called motive. Not telling us your hooker girlfriend—"

"Ex-girlfriend. And, she wasn't a hooker. She was an escort."

"Whatever you say. She ends up dead, and you don't bother telling us she stole a bunch of money? That makes me very curious."

"It happened a long time ago."

"How long?" Brenna said.

"A year. Maybe a little longer."

Luther deflated. A year-old theft was a weak motive. It was too long between sin and sentence. If Victoria had died within a few days of the theft, then definitely. A year later? Not so much. "We'll come back to the money in a few minutes," he said evenly. "Let's clean up some of the details in the story you told us earlier. And, I'd appreciate it if you were one hundred percent forthcoming this time."

Menny's gaze flicked from the television to the clock.

Luther's annoyance flared. "We keeping you from something? Is there a program you're waiting to see? The harpies on The View are more important than Ms. Chesham's death?" He grabbed the remote off the bedside table and killed the television. "Pay attention."

Menny scowled. "We've already been through all that."

"Get used to it. We'll be through it several more times."

Brenna mouthed silently, "Take it easy," in Luther's direction and then patted Menny's arm. "We just want to make sure we didn't miss anything significant. Start at the beginning. Tell us everything about the robbery. From the moment you picked up Victoria to the moment the authorities arrived after your 911 call."

Menny muttered something inaudible and shook his head slightly. Then he re-told the entire story. Listening closely, Luther didn't hear any discrepancies between this version and the one he heard earlier. When he finished talking, Luther said, "Thank you for your cooperation."

Menny gave him a single curt nod.

Luther said, "It was raining."

Menny's face reddened. He glared. "What?"

"You wanted to look at the stars." Luther continued, "It was raining. It's still raining."

"Not when we made plans," he said through clenched teeth. "Not when I parked."

Brenna shot Luther a second, harder frown and while Menny's attention was fixed in the opposite direction, she made a calming motion with one hand. Her expression instantly became sympathetic when he turned and faced her. She said, "That's fine, Mr. Menny. The rain hadn't started. But the stars weren't out. It was overcast. I don't understand why Victoria got out of the car. She was wearing a nice outfit. Expensive shoes. You said the two of you met late. Why stop at all?"

"That's easy." Menny pushed himself upright. He winced, as if he'd forgotten his recent surgery. After several seconds, he said, "She wanted to drive the Porsche. We didn't have reservations. We couldn't decide where to go. We were going back and forth, getting nowhere, so she said, 'Since we have no place to be and it's a quiet stretch of road, maybe I could drive the car?' Something like that."

Brenna nodded. "Tell us about the money."

"It was a small state lottery, about three years ago. I didn't win much. A little better than a million dollars. People come out of everywhere when you win that kind of money. Suddenly I had friends I never had before. And, the women." He blew a noisy gust of air through his lips and shook his head in clear bewilderment, an emotion Luther believed honestly baffled him. "I must have gotten a dozen marriage proposals.

"That's when I met Victoria. She lived in Richmond at the time. She worked in an office building. Some CEO's personal assistant. She was different. She wasn't interested in the money. That's why I liked her." Color tinged his cheeks and his voice dropped and thickened with embarrassment. "At least that's what I thought."

Luther crossed his arms over his chest. He looked out the window, pretending not to see Menny's discomfort. The rain teemed out of a heavy sky. He was glad he parked close to the front door of the hospital.

"Everybody who wins money goes on a spending spree. Everybody. Some people don't stop until it's all gone. Most people end up flat-assed broke within five or ten years. After my spree, I went to a financial consultant. She told me half my money was gone. Turned out the entire time Victoria and I were seeing each other, she was robbing me. She bought the townhouse in Brigantine with my money. A sizeable down payment, anyway."

Luther gave him skeptical eyes. "How'd that happen?"

"She created a credit card in my name. Rang it up on jewelry, other high value shit. She kept some of it, but turned most of it into cash, as best as I can tell. She got my PIN, made a bunch of massive withdrawals." His cheeks tinted pink a second time. "Obviously, I was angry. When I confronted her, she quit her job and disappeared. Turns out she moved to Atlantic City. At the time, I didn't know that." He grabbed a pitcher of water off the bedside table and filled a glass. Every movement was slow and controlled. He was clearly favoring his heavily bandaged shoulder. He swallowed nosily. "That was about a year ago. Then, in June, I was in Atlantic City, like I told you earlier. I saw her walk by. We talked. We promised to stay in touch."

Brenna said, "You weren't still angry about the money?"

"Maybe a little bit." His embarrassed flush deepened. "I guess I was used to it. It was just so great seeing her again."

"And, that was a lucky coincidence?" Luther asked doubtfully.

"Atlantic City isn't that big a town."

"You said the two of you discussed marriage," Luther said.

Menny's face creased in pain. The expression disappeared as quickly as it came. "Back when I thought she didn't care about the money, before I found out she was stealing it, I asked her to marry me."

"What happened?"

"She wanted to think about it." Menny's voice was thin. Quiet. "Then I found about the theft. Then she left."

Already confident what the answer would be, Luther asked, "Were you spending any of your money on her? Gifts, that sort of thing?"

Menny nodded miserably. "I bought her jewelry. Clothes. An Acura. Anything she wanted, really."

Luther nodded once, very slightly. His earlier conjecture was accurate. Acting indifferent to Menny's money was Victoria's hook. She worked him for as long as possible—why buy yourself a Gucci watch or an Acura if someone else will buy it for you—and when he found out she was only pretending to consider his proposal, she disappeared. The only question remaining was Menny's reaction.

Brenna looked astonished. Elbows on her thighs, chin on her fists, she leaned into him. "You bought her a car?"

His voice became almost pleading. "There was something about her."

There was something about her. The exact words Luther used to describe Victoria. "Why didn't you report the theft to the authorities?" Luther asked.

The sheets rustled as Menny shifted into a more comfortable position. "Everybody in Richmond would have heard about it. Or read about it in the paper. It would have looked really pathetic." His voice, barely perceptible, was heavy with humiliation. "Plus, the financial consultant said there was no way to prove she stole it. It would have been my word against hers."

After several seconds of silence Brenna said, "Why did you decide to stay in touch after everything she did to you? After she stole the money?"

"I didn't stay in touch. How many times do I have to say it? Running into her like that was pure chance. But when I saw her again I realized I loved her. That's why I looked her up the second time." He spoke like the answer should have been obvious. "She was beautiful and friendly. Active. Fun and energetic. She didn't put up with any nonsense. Say something to annoy her, she'd let you know, but a person couldn't help but like her. We had fun together. I missed her when she left."

Brenna's expression of astonishment increased. She leaned back in her chair and gave her head a single bemused shake.

In contrast, Luther wasn't the least bit surprised. In fact, his earlier annoyance had evaporated. Tom Menny was responsible for Victoria's death. Luther knew this with a conviction he seldom felt because he understood exactly what Menny was going through.

It wasn't complicated…

One minute you're a couple, the next you're single and wondering where things went wrong. Everything—a song on the radio to the purchase of a home—reminds you of the good times you shared and the potential the future held. Happy memories keep reappearing in different guises—a rerun of a funny television program, a sale at a favorite store, a walk to a coffee shop on a sunny day. But these happy memories are illusions. Standing behind them is the knowledge that she lied and criticized and always said, "No," and was unsympathetic and indifferent. When these negative realizations become powerful enough, the self-loathing kicks in, because, after that laundry list of offences, how can you keep remembering your time together as happy and good? And, if a guy is getting all the good and all the negative confused a year after the fact, how can he move on with his life?

He can't. He has to deal with the powerfully conflicting emotions, otherwise around in circles he goes.

Perhaps he deals with it by taking up a hobby. Or travelling. Maybe he throws himself at his career. Or, maybe he starts a big home renovation project, for instance. Almost anything, other than a murder on the side of the road, no matter how appealing the thought is in the dark corner of his mind where loneliness and recrimination live.

"We're done. For now," Luther said. His voice was level. Unemotional. Out the corner of his eye he saw Brenna's face—tight, her eyes narrow. Recognizable body language. In the same even tone, he said, "We'll be back. Don't go anywhere without letting us know."

"Why? Am I under arrest?"

"Not yet." He dropped the television remote on the mattress near Menny's hand. "We'll be in touch." He walked out of the room.

"You mind re-closing the blind?" Menny called after him.

Luther kept walking. Didn't even look back. He and Brenna didn't say a word to each other as they walked to the elevators. She pushed the down button. Two quarter-sized red spots shone high on her cheeks, brilliant against her pale face.

They waited in silence until she huffed out an irritated breath. "Let's take the stairs." She strode away without checking to see if Luther followed.

He said nothing. He didn't often see her angry. When she was, he found it easiest to give her a little time. Stay quiet. Wait it out. He buttoned his raincoat against the chill in the stairwell. Their footsteps echoed off the metal treads. They didn't talk, not until they were seated side by side in the car, Luther's hand on the ignition key, and he asked, "Are we driving? Or are we talking?" Looking sideways at her with his left eyebrow arched.

Brenna detonated. "What were you thinking? Everything Menny said made sense. He was robbed. Nothing we've seen contradicts that. Nothing. But no. You as good as tell him we'll be back to arrest him. We've got no evidence or proof that he was involved. At best, we've we got a worthless, year-old motive."

Luther said nothing. Best to let her get it out of her system.

"What did he do, Luther? Hold a gun to himself at a physically impossible angle and a physically impossible distance then blow a hole in his shoulder, just to throw us off the scent?" She shook her head. "Shit."

After several long seconds, he nodded. "You've got a point."

"Thank you. I'm glad—"

"He couldn't have shot himself. He might have shot Victoria but he didn't shoot himself. Someone must have helped him."

Brenna swore loudly. She hammered her fist on the dashboard. "Who? Who's this mystery accomplice?"

"I don't know. Someone Menny knew from Richmond, maybe?"

"What about the Day-Timer? Do you know what Occam's Razor is? It says—"

"Everybody knows that old cliché, so keep it to yourself. I'm not in the mood for trivia or jokes."

"—all other things being equal, the simplest solution is the best. Menny said he was robbed. The robbery resulted in Victoria's death. So, the question is not, 'Who helped him stage some elaborate robbery-gone-wrong-homicide?'" She shook her head. "No. Too complicated. The simple question is, 'Was the robbery random or did someone in Victoria's Day-Timer target her?'"

Luther turned the ignition key. The Caprice started. "Listen, Bren. Until we have a conversation with the Captain, our difference of opinion doesn't matter."

"What are you talking about?"

"Right now we have two options." He spoke patiently despite tiredness that made him want to bark at her in return. "First, my opinion. Menny was involved. I'll tell the Captain that he did it because of the money she stole. Even though I'm sure that wasn't the reason."

Brenna threw a frustrated hand in the air. It landed back on her thigh with a slap. "You'll have to explain your rationale to me too. The money is the only thing that makes sense."

He waved her objection away. "Not the only thing," he said. "Now, considering the time between the theft and the homicide, plus lack of any direct evidence pointing to Menny, the Captain won't like option one. That leaves option two. The choice you prefer. Someone in the Day-Timer, maybe one of the VIPs, is responsible for Victoria's death."

He cut her a glance. She sat there, arms crossed, lips clamped together in a thin, angry line. "He's not going to like option two any better, is he? How excited is he going to be about two of his detectives poking around in a bunch of VIP's private lives? Can you imagine the press? Especially if it turns out we're wrong?"

"Shit."

"No fooling," Luther said.

"Where's that leave us?"

"We'll talk to him. He'll weigh the lousy motive and lack of evidence against annoying a bunch of VIPs." Luther smiled. "Then he'll tell us to start interviewing the VIPs in a delicate and discrete fashion. He won't like it. But it's the only logical choice. In the meantime, we'll quietly look into my idea too." He let his smile widen. "Because it's the right one."

CHAPTER 30

JORDON CUTLER WAVED a hand in front of his nose and didn't see so much as a blur. The blackness enveloping him was absolute. The smell of dusty engine oil filled his nostrils. He heard the subdued mumble of voices and a car's idling engine. Rain clattered on the trunk lid above, every metallic drop echoing loudly in the darkness. An all-over ache rippled through him like waves across a beach and his ribs javelined his insides. "Son-of-a-bitch," he muttered. As bad as his situation was in the hotel, it was worse now.

He fully expected to free himself in the hotel lobby. It seemed a sure thing until the butterflies began flapping their wings. Then, after they left the Oasis, he expected Leo and Dwayne to hand him an ass kicking in a nearby alley and he'd discourage them with a few tricks he learned defending himself from his old man. That would be that. Getting tossed in the trunk of a car was something for which he was completely unprepared. Since Leo had not done as Jordon expected at the Oasis, he wondered what the big man had in mind when he parked the car. Imagining a scenario worse than a beating was not difficult. Hopefully Leo wouldn't shoot him through the trunk lid. He saw that happen in a movie once.

He needed a way out.

With a lurch, the car started moving. Music, tinny and

overpowering, pounded out of the speakers mounted in the rear deck above his head. As quickly as it came on, it disappeared. Listening hard, Jordon heard Leo's unmistakable growl, "...ain't listening to that racket while I'm driving."

With probing fingers, Jordon followed the seam where the trunk lid met the body of the car, searching with little hope for a latch that would open the trunk from the inside. Newer vehicles had a latch designed for his exact predicament. Old vehicles, like the Mazda he shared with Mel, didn't have one. Jordon didn't expect this car would either, simply because the size of the trunk meant it was a large vehicle and therefore most likely an older model.

The car slowed and rolled to a stop.

Jordon paused, staring uselessly toward the front of the vehicle, his breath jammed in his throat, a tight band of anxiety squeezed around his chest. After several long seconds, the vehicle accelerated a second time. A red light, he guessed. With a bit of luck, they'd hit several more. He needed the time and a new idea—there was no latch.

He frantically searched for ideas while the stop-start routine continued. He thought pushing his way out of the trunk into the back seat may have been possible but for that he needed time and tools and he had neither. Breaking the trunk lock with the bottle-jack was a long shot. It would take some time, but it was the only thing he could come up with. He maneuvered the jack into position and rotated the top, lengthening it enough for it to fit tightly between the trunk floor and the lock assembly. After four revolutions, he paused. Once again, the car had stopped but this time he no longer heard the running engine. An icicle of adrenaline stabbed him in the heart.

He'd run out of time.

He shot a furious glare at the front of the car. Leo and Dwayne had backed him into an inescapable corner. He'd been there once before, that day in high school after the meeting with the guidance counselor and, against the odds, he was still alive. Just like back then, escape was no longer an option. When the trunk lid popped open, he needed a weapon in hand.

The tire iron was the obvious choice, but where was it? He wasn't lying on top of it, but there had to be one. He searched randomly, palms down patting the floor of the trunk in an erratic pattern, and then forced himself to pause. He scrunched his eyes shut and took a deep breath. Where would it be? Often, they were secured under the spare tire, so as not to rattle around in the trunk on rough roads. He traced the spare's circumference and found it, a hefty steel bar wedged between the floor and the tire.

The car doors opened. A moment later they slammed shut one after another, the force rocking the vehicle slightly. He listened for the characteristic chunk-chunk of someone chambering a round of buckshot, or the metallic crash of someone letting the slide on an automatic pistol slam home but all he heard were footsteps growing louder on either side of the vehicle.

He tugged on the end of the tire iron. It was lodged solidly beneath the spare. With blind fingers, he found a large wing-nut in the center of the rim that secured the spare tire to the floor. He twisted it two turns before it jammed, presumably on threads corroded with years of dirt and grime. He gave the tire iron another yank. A sharp burst of pain reminded him of his bruised ribs. Fresh beads of sweat bloomed on his forehead. The tire iron moved fractionally. Elated, he tugged harder.

Voices now, right outside the trunk, Leo saying, "I open the trunk, I want you looking the other way. Make sure nobody sees this. Capisce?"

"Come on, bro. I wanna go one round with this guy."

Wriggling the tire iron from side to side, Jordon pulled it out from beneath the spare. Keys jangled, and then he heard the metal-on-metal scrape as one slid into the lock inches from his ear.

"Use your knuckle dusters, huh?" Leo's voice was indulgent.

"They're brand new," Dwayne said. "I ordered them from *Soldier of Fortune* magazine. I wanna break them in."

Leo laughed. "You get your chance."

Jordon thought quickly on how this would happen. Leo was his height and a good thirty pounds heavier. That was worrisome but not insurmountable. The last time his old man came after him, he outweighed Jordon by at least thirty pounds. Size wasn't the biggest problem. His injuries were the issue, and the odds weren't even, which meant he'd only get one chance. It would be all about surprise. And, quick feet, something he wasn't sure he had with bruised ribs.

He furiously pushed the negativity away. When a person wants something to happen there's only one thing to do…force it. He squirmed in the trunk, positioning himself so he'd be able to jump out with the least amount of difficulty. Every move jiggled his ribs. He flexed his fingers around the steel bar, tightening his grip.

The trunk lid popped open.

CHAPTER 31

THE SWEET AND sour stink of damp garbage filled Jordon's nose. Rain spattered his upturned face. He blinked. After the obscurity of the locked trunk, even the dim evening light seemed bright. Leo towered over him, one fist on his hip, the other holding up the lid. From down low, staring up like Jordon was, Leo appeared massive. His black T-shirt rippled when he moved. It bunched under his arms and rode high on biceps that stretched the barb wire tattoo taut as prison yard fencing. His arms glistened in the rain.

Jordon flicked his eyes from side to side, searching and then finding Dwayne standing a few feet away with his back to the car. He still wore his leather coat, the collar standing up against the wet weather.

There is no way this is going to work, Jordon thought briefly before his mind screamed back: *See it happen successfully. Then make it happen successfully.* He sat up, the tire iron gripped in his right hand, hidden along his leg.

Leo grinned slightly. It wasn't a jovial expression. "Get out," he said, jerking his thumb over his shoulder. "Fuckin' Zero."

Jordon met Leo's gaze and then quickly looked away, wanting Leo to believe he was scared, hoping to give the man the impression he was harmless. Slowly, deliberately, he kneeled and then stood, taking careful aim at the big man's face. As he did, he inhaled deeply. Adrenaline dulled the pain of his various aches and pains. Then, he pushed his breath out in a raging, demented scream and swung the tire iron.

It swept up from down low, the steel bar accelerating as it crossed the centerline of his body, Jordon twisting as he swung, getting all his upper body behind it. His ribs shrieked in agony not even adrenaline could contain. Fireworks behind his eyes blurred his vision. He ignored it all. Everything he had, all his concentration, rage, and anxiety were behind the tire iron and the primal scream coming from his mouth.

Leo's eyes widened. Reflex made him rock back on his feet.

Too late.

The tire iron slammed into his cheek just below his eye with a sickening crunch. The follow through snapped his head sideways. A crimson fan of blood sprayed, dappling Jordon's arm. Leo's hands flew to his crushed face. He tottered back, wailing.

It was like head butting a power pole. Jordon staggered. Gasped. The impact shook his arms from hands to shoulders. He recovered and re-cocked, ready to bash Leo once more. Instantly he realized it wouldn't be necessary. The first blow had caved in the man's face. He lay supine on the ground, whimpering. Clutching his head. Blood streamed between his fingers. His legs flailed like a baby's in a crib.

Hollering hysterically, Jordon leapt from the trunk. He landed heavily on one of Leo's legs and boiling waves of red pain flushed through his body. His eyes jumped from side to side and found Dwayne five feet away, the man's Hollywood hair waving and rippling, he was reacting so rapidly. His hand disappeared under the lapel of his coat. It reappeared wrapped around an enormous black revolver. His face broke into a happy smile. He thumbed the hammer back.

Jordon lifted the tire iron, knowing he wasn't close enough.

Briefly, he saw Mel, her blonde hair falling down from behind her ears, framing her face. He missed her. At that moment, all he wanted was to be with her.

Something tugged his pant leg. Jordon looked down and saw Leo's hand wrapped around his ankle, the big man sitting up against the side of the Caddy. Leo yanked, pulling him off balance and Jordon staggered. Dwayne, still smiling, squeezed the trigger. The revolver boomed. The deafening sound bounced off the surrounding brick walls like a racquetball. Jordon felt heat blaze through the flesh above his hipbone. With a yelp, he twisted away from the pain, wrenching his leg free of Leo's hand.

Dwayne re-aligned the barrel and Jordon swung the tire iron. It hissed through the air and slammed into Dwayne's wrist with all the force Jordon could muster. The revolver fell from Dwayne's slack fingers and clattered on the pavement at his feet. His wrist dangled, seemingly attached to his arm by skin alone. His scream took a second to come. When it finally burst free, the shrillness stabbed Jordon's ears like needles.

Dwayne howled in agony until he ran out of air and then took a breath and howled some more. He staggered drunkenly into the side of the car and slid down a quarter panel until he was sitting on the ground. His body left a muddy smear in the dust and rain coating the side of the vehicle. He cradled his wrist. His screams faded to sobs.

Adrenaline surging like white water, Jordon took two fast steps and booted him in the ribs. "Who are you guys?"

Dwayne flopped over, flinging out his arm instinctively to prevent himself from falling flat on the ground. When the weight of his upper body landed on his broken wrist, he shrieked once more and passed out.

Jordon kicked the revolver, sending it orbiting deep into the alley amongst the broken glass and cigarette butts. He thought the fight was over, and then the memory of Leo's hand around his ankle startled him back into action. Raising the tire iron, he swiveled, certain he'd see Leo steamrolling toward him, probably pulling out a weapon of his own, but the big man lay motionless on the pavement, hands at his sides. A slick patch in the middle of his chest shone on his T-shirt. He stared skyward out of vacant, lifeless eyes, his pockmarked face now gray and slack.

Fiery pain blazed, making Jordon wince. His hand dropped to his side and he felt warm-wet. When he looked, his fingers were sticky with blood. Confused, he pulled up his shirt and stared dumbfounded at his side. There was a deep, bloody furrow through the fleshy part of his waist. His understanding was immediate—the hot blaze of pain he felt when Dwayne fired his revolver was the bullet burning through him before it struck Leo.

Close.

So very close to never seeing Mel again. To never doing anything again. He remembered a teacher telling him once, in a resigned sort of voice, that it was important to do as well as he could in whatever he chose, but to always remember that other people climb Mount Everest or compete in the Tour de France. Even as a kid Jordon thought it sounded pitiable, as though the teacher had given up and was just marking time. Jordon wanted every minute to count.

He began to quiver. He'd come that close to running out of minutes.

The tire iron fell to the dirty asphalt with a clang. He balled his hands into tight fists, trying to control the shaking, but it seized his body and the speed of the earth's rotation increased. He bent quickly at the waist, resting his fists on his thighs, and slammed his eyes closed while dizziness spun him in circles.

The feeling passed, leaving him exhausted and nauseous. He tentatively opened one eye. The world seemed stable on its axis. He opened the opposite eye and straightened. He swallowed dryly, desperate for something to drink.

Maybe in the Cadillac.

He slid between the car and the dirty black bricks of the building looming above, until he came to the front door. He flung it open, and it smashed into the alley wall with a loud, ringing crash. There was nothing useful on the front seat. He backed up and opened the rear door, taking perverse pleasure in smashing it into the brick wall also.

Leo's Adidas gym bag sat on the floor in the back seat. He looked like a weight-lifting jock with his too tight T-shirt and over-developed muscles. Jordon wondered fleetingly why the man brought his gym bag into the hotel with him instead of leaving it in the car. Not that it mattered. All he wanted was a drink, and there was a good chance he'd find a water bottle in a gym bag. He hoisted it from the floor to the back seat. The weight surprised him. Considering what a person typically put in a gym bag, it was far heavier than it should have been. He unzipped it, pulled the halves open and found exactly what he expected—athletic clothes, a pair of sneakers, and, blessedly, a bottle of Gatorade.

Moaning with relief, he grabbed the sports drink. The bottle slipped from his fingers, hit the ground, and rolled beneath the car. He hurried to the other side of the Caddy, snagging the bottle before it disappeared between the trashcans and dumpsters lining the wall and the refuse that overflowed from them.

The rapid trip around the vehicle induced a second wave of dizziness. When it passed, he broke the seal and guzzled half the tepid Gatorade down before taking a deep, noisy breath. Panting, dragging his fingers along the side of the car for balance, he returned to the gym bag. He needed something he could use as a makeshift bandage for the wound in his side. He rifled through the clothes at the top, rousing the stale odor of old sweat, hoping to find one of the long strips of elastic material gym guys wrap around their knees or wrists.

There was nothing except clothing.

He dug deeper. His searching fingers found paper. Layers of it. Thick and heavy, making him think of a city phone book, or rather, several phone books stacked on top of each other. Curious, he pulled the clothes out of the bag and tossed them on the seat.

That's when he saw the cash, bundles of it, each bundle banded in a crisp ribbon of white paper. His breath caught in the back of his throat. "Whoa," he mouthed quietly, understanding why the Adidas bag was so heavy and why Leo never let it out of his sight. He picked up one bundle and fanned it with the ball of his thumb. It made a soft, buzzing sound.

Well-used bills. Lots of hundreds. Maybe fifty bills in the bundle, which meant he was holding perhaps four, five grand in one hand. The next question came in a rush. How many bundles were there? His eyes jumped from the cash in his hand to the gym bag. The top layer measured three bundles wide by four long. Twelve bundles at conservatively, four thousand per, added up to forty-eight thousand dollars. There were four layers. That meant...

He closed his eyes and did the math. Dizziness and a feverish heat made the problem more complicated than it was, but eventually he calculated, one-hundred and ninety-two-thousand dollars. Give or take. Call it two hundred thousand if he rounded up, or one-fifty if he rounded down, and as strapped as he and Mel were, he habitually planned on less rather than more.

Leo had been casually packing one hundred and fifty thousand dollars around in a gym bag, hidden by a tangle of funky old gym attire. Well, maybe not casually. The guy was big. He probably outweighed a Hyundai. Nobody would consider snatching a gym bag out of his hand, but still.

"Son-of-a-bitch!" This time Jordon's voice wasn't whispered. He thought through the pain, nausea, and dizziness. Legitimate businessmen didn't carry enormous amounts of cash around in Adidas gym bags. Typically, it was guarded by Brinks, not three hundred pounds of muscle and three ounces of brains. So, who had Leo and Dwayne worked for? Who would notice a one-hun-dred-and-fifty-thousand-dollar hole in his bank account?

Jordon nervously glanced in every direction. Was there any way for that person to figure out who he was, if he were to take the cash? He couldn't see how.

All of a sudden, he was anxious to put some distance between himself and the Cadillac. He zipped the gym bag shut and turned his attention back to the clothes. He ripped a thin and faded muscle shirt down a seam, folded it into a bandanna and wrapped it around his waist, covering the bullet wound. Taking a deep breath, he clamped his teeth together and tugged the makeshift bandage tight. His eyes watered and he moaned with pain. He took another deep swallow of the tepid sport drink. It sloshed in his belly like used engine oil. Revolted, he lobbed the empty bottle at the trashcans. His vision tilted crazily. He staggered. The dizziness faded but didn't disappear. Shock, pain, and blood loss. He was in a world of hurt.

His gaze drifted to Leo's body lying on the cracked asphalt and somehow he saw his old man lying there. A chunk of firewood lay beside him, bloody strands of oily gray hair embedded in one end. The miserable bastard's bulbous, alcoholic nose pointed skyward and his dead, uncomprehending eyes asked, "How did my kid do this to me?"

Of course, it wasn't his old man. It was Leo. Jordon wasn't sure how he mistook one for the other. He blinked away his con-fusion. He needed to get home. Mel could help him make sense of this. Together they always found the right answer. All the good days in his life somehow involved her.

Carrying the duffle bag of cash, he walked an erratic path out of the alley. At the street, he paused. In one direction, there was nothing to see but the dark, wet night. In the other, an electric neon glow substituted for the moon. Logically, if a person exits a subway station with no clear idea which way to go at the top of the stairs, he's got a fifty-fifty chance of turning in the correct direction. So why, fifty-one times out of one hundred, does he turn the wrong way? There were variables nobody could understand. Jordon thought in this case he couldn't go wrong if he walked into the light.

With one arm wrapped around his mid-section, he headed for the neon glow. Each time his foot hit the pavement the jolt traveled up his leg, paused to rip the bullet wound open, and then moved north a little further to shake loose his ribs. The gym bag was incredibly heavy. A couple of times he transferred it from one hand to the other. The rain fell harder, plastering his shirt to his body, slicking down his hair until water ran off the ends, down his face and neck. He shivered once. Then a second time.

The neon sign seemed a long way away. It danced. Sometimes there were two. Sometimes three. He'd killed his old man, left him lying in an alley. When the police asked, he'd tell them how the old bastard attacked him after an embarrassing meeting with the guidance counselor, Jordon running too slowly to dodge the chunk of firewood the old man threw at him after they got home.

Nausea overpowered him. He bent at the waist, stumbled to his knees. The Gatorade rushed up his throat. He sprayed the purple fluid all over the rain-slick street. The stomach convulsions were excruciatingly painful. When the retching stopped, he regained his feet, picked up the bag, and concentrated on putting one foot in front of the other. The neon still sent out that warm and welcoming electric glow.

A gust of wind rushed down the street, pushing an empty Big Gulp cup ahead of it. Soaked through, Jordon shivered, making his body shudder. His teeth banged together uncontrollably. When he finally got close, he saw the neon glow was a Miller Genuine Draft sign in the window of an all-night convenience store, the sign shaped like an Indy race car. He'd ask the clerk in the store to call an ambulance. First though, he needed to hide the money. He couldn't pack a gym bag full of cash into a hospital room.

Along the fence at the back of the parking lot, he spotted a dumpster and beside it two cylindrical bulk fuel tanks. He staggered in their direction, found a deep gap behind one of the white tanks, a corner hidden by the dumpster, and he pushed the gym bag in as far as he could reach. Not great. Hopefully good enough. If he came back and the money was gone, well, his fortunes hadn't changed a dime. With luck though, it was adequately hidden and would still be there when he returned.

He lurched toward the store. Peering through a window he saw the clerk talking on the phone, the man staring back at him out of saucer-sized eyes. Jordon hoped he was on the line to the police because he needed to tell them his old man was lying dead in the alley. Then he remembered, it was Leo in the alley. Not his father. His old man had died years before, his head caved in after repeated, panicked blows from a tire iron.

No. That was wrong. It was a chunk of firewood that fractured the old bastard's skull, the same chunk of wood that ended a boy's sprint for freedom when it hit him between the shoulders. The same chunk the boy picked up and used to fend off a violent, abusive drunk.

Jordon reached for the door handle. It was too far away. He wobbled and fell like a sheet of paper, first one way and then the next. For the second time that evening everything went black.

PART 3

5:00 AM – 2:00 PM
September, 2002

CHAPTER 32

MELISSA WOKE FROM a fitful sleep to the sound of wind and rain abusing her house. The digital clock on the bedside table glowed four-fifty. She yawned widely. Jordon would have asked if she was trying to swallow her head. She smiled. As quickly as it came, the expression vanished. This was no time for one of their little jokes. He wasn't lying beside her. He hadn't called. Something was wrong.

She sat up, tugged the blankets toward her chin and planted the bedside telephone on her lap. For a moment, she faltered. Would it work when she lifted the receiver? She wasn't sure she wanted to know. After a second's pause, she told herself to quit being silly. She lifted the receiver. The dial tone hummed in her ear. A happy trill of excitement shimmied up her spine.

Mel figured she had four choices. Jordon's cell phone, on the off chance it had become operational, the hotel in Atlantic City where he stayed while he attended the conference, the airline (which seemed futile after the previous night's experience), and, as a final resort, Tom Menny's cellular, because as far as she knew, Tom was the last person Jordon saw before he headed for the airport.

She started with Jordon's phone and immediately heard the hateful message, "All circuits are busy." She hung up. There was no point in trying Tom's cell phone now. She muttered under her breath, "Cell phones. Can't live with them. Can't throw them in the Atlantic."

Next, she dialed the hotel.

"Oasis Hotel and Casino," the receptionist answered enthusiastically. "This is Katie. How may I direct your call?"

Katie is awfully cheery for this early in the morning, Mel thought, slightly irritated at the woman's chirpiness. Particularly when they were in the midst of a crisis. "Jordon Cutler's room please," Mel said, trying to keep the waspish tone out of her voice.

"One moment." After a series of clicks, a phone rang in a faraway hotel room.

Mel's excitement bounced a second time. She'd found him just that easily! All her fretting for nothing. The hurricane, a dead cell phone, a cancelled flight—none of it made any difference. She'd hear his voice and know he was okay.

The phone rang a second time. Stridently. Urgently.

He must be real tired. He should have picked up immediately. She held her breath.

Three times now. A noise that was impossible to sleep through. She sat a little straighter, felt all her muscles tensing. Her grip on the receiver tightened. The hard plastic pressed snugly against the side of her head, hurting her ear. She twisted the cord around the fingers of her free hand. Desperate to settle the flurry of nerves swarming her stomach, she thought fast, made plans. If he got home…

She shoved that thought into a dark closet of her mind where she didn't have to look at it too closely.

…*when* he got home they would sort out some wedding details. Little things he considered silly. Like the style of her gown. She knew he didn't have a strong preference; what made her happy made him happy. The last time she pointed out a photograph of the perfect dress in a magazine he said, "Even the ugliest hound looks good as a bride. And you, Pumpkin, are a rare orchid. You'll look—"

Fourth ring and Mel knew, absolutely knew, he wasn't going to pick up.

"—amazing in whatever you choose."

She'd savored the compliment. At the same time, she wished he'd offer a stronger opinion. After all, it was his wedding too.

After the fifth unanswered ring the earlier series of clicks repeated itself. A computerized voice instructed her to push One to leave a message or Zero to speak to an operator.

Mel pushed Zero.

"Oasis Hotel and Casino. This is Katie. How may I direct your call?"

Unsure how to start, Mel stammered, "Uhm, you just connected me to Jordon Cutler's room. He didn't answer." The rest of the words spilled out in a worried rush. "Is there a message for me? This is Melissa Bremmer. His wife."

"Just a moment, Ms. Bremmer." After a beat Katie said, "Here we are. Mr. Cutler checked out yesterday afternoon." Her voice faded and then strengthened. "He checked back in at ten-twenty in the evening. There are no messages in the system." She added helpfully, "There were a lot of cancelled flights last night."

"I know about the cancelled flights," Mel said in an impatient rush. "Can you send someone up to knock on his door? I haven't heard from him. I'm really—"

"Ma'am, may I suggest you call back in twenty minutes? Perhaps he's in the shower."

Mel hadn't considered that. After a quick glance at the clock she dismissed the notion. It was barely five AM. He wouldn't be in the shower. The phone should have woken him. Her heart galloped like an afternoon at the Kentucky Derby. "I'd really prefer someone check."

"Does he have a serious illness?" Concern in Katie's voice now. "Is there some reason he'd be unable to answer?"

Confused, Mel immediately said, "Not at all." Half a second later she guessed what was coming and mentally kicked herself. If she'd given Katie a reason to suspect an Oasis guest had a health problem, the efficient receptionist would have sent someone to the room without delay.

"Ms. Bremmer," Katie said, still friendly and courteous, and more assertive all at the same time, "If he didn't answer, and there is no emergency, there is no reason to send security to his room at five in the morning. Checkout is at noon. I suggest you call back at that time."

Melissa told herself to calm down, to get a grip. He hadn't answered the phone. No biggie. There were plenty of possible reasons. Thinking about it, she couldn't name one. Something was wrong. The earlier, vague feeling of misfortune solidified. "I'll do that," she said, her voice high and tight with suppressed tension, her stomach a painful, nervous knot.

"Thanks for calling the Oasis Hotel and Casino."

Mel hung up gently without responding. She whipped the blankets off and climbed out of bed. Searching toes found her slippers. Eschewing the beautiful satin robe Jordon bought her from Victoria's Secret, she plucked his ratty terry robe off the bedpost where she draped it hours earlier. She started down the hallway to the bathroom. Out of nowhere, like a cork coming out of a champagne bottle, an insane thought popped into her head. Her walk broke midstep.

I should go find him myself. Get in the car and go. It's only a six-hour drive. Maybe less.

She heard Jordon's voice in the back of her mind, gentle and rational in its objection. "There's a few more logical courses of action, Pumpkin. Like, maybe talk to the police, you're that worried?"

Mel scowled. Logic. The argument men always fell back on when something they couldn't explain—like instinct or a feeling—loomed in front of them. She wasn't actually going to do it. Driving to Atlantic City was nothing more than a random silly thought.

Back in the bedroom after a quick stop in the bathroom, she dialed Atlantic Coastal Airlines. They must have been catching up. The wait on hold was short. Mel said, "I expected my husband last night on the flight from Atlantic—"

"What was the flight number, ma'am?"

Mel told him. She listened to the faint clickity-clicks of busy fingers tapping computer keys.

"Oh yes. Atlantic City to Richmond. That flight was cancelled."

Really? No kidding? Everyone kept telling her things she already knew. Why wouldn't they give her information she didn't know? Controlling her frustration with an effort, Mel inhaled deeply. She exhaled in a long, controlled gust, blowing a tendril of hair away from her face. When she ran out of air, the hair dropped back in front of her mouth. "I realize the flight was cancelled. What I don't know is what happens next. Does the airline re-book him on a new flight?"

"The airline takes care of rebooking all those passengers who didn't make it to Richmond." He sounded clinical, like he was reading from CliffsNotes, the chapter dealing with distressed wives and missing husbands. "Unfortunately, it is against airline policy to discuss the passenger list."

"I just want to know what flight he will be on." She threaded the phone cord through her hands. "His name is Jordon Cutler." There must have been something in her voice, possibly an audible trace of the fear she felt because when the agent responded she heard sympathy in his tone.

"I understand, Ma'am," he said. "I do. Unfortunately, I'm

forbidden to give that information out. It has to do with security and privacy."

"Thanks," Mel answered weakly. She hung up and crossed her arms, hugging herself. Another seven minutes wasted. What next? Except for the idea of driving to Atlantic City, her mind was blank. She felt her chin quivering and clamped her teeth together to restrain the tears. She realized she was no longer thinking, "random silly thought." Somehow driving had become an "idea." Either way, driving was both insane and silly.

But, if she hadn't heard from him by…What? Eight AM? Maybe by then it wouldn't seem so silly.

Why eight? Why not make it seven?

For that matter, why not six?

She glanced at the bedside clock. Five-sixteen. After some quick mental math, she realized if she left within the hour she'd be knocking on his hotel door before checkout time. She reached underneath the bed and found her suitcase. It couldn't hurt to be ready, packed in case she decided to make the drive.

If that's what the situation warranted.

She folded clothes neatly into her suitcase wondering how many changes she'd need. Four days? Would that be enough? One day to get there, one to get back. Two days to…What? Look for him? Eat crappy buffet food? Walk up and down the boardwalk admiring the beach? Two extra days for something, anyway. Who knew what?

Then she wondered, would the Mazda go that far? Did she really want to test that piece of junk on the highway for five plus hours? She remembered a conversation she and Jordon had a couple of months previous, when they were trying to rationalize not buying a new-to-them vehicle, Jordon saying reasonably and with resignation in his voice, "It should last a little longer. We don't do too much city driving. Most the miles are on the freeway. Highway driving is easier on a car."

So, no biggie. If she elected to go, the Mazda would make it.

A few minutes later she stood under the shower, facing the spray, hoping it would wash some of the tiredness away. Shampoo frothed into thick white suds. It smelled like wild flowers and spring rain. At least that's what the bottle said. Whatever the scent, she thought it was nice and Jordon seemed to enjoy it. He liked smelling her hair when they made love. With that thought, the idea of going to Atlantic City strengthened.

She'd have to leave a good letter explaining why she'd made the trip when he was less than twenty-four hours late. How did a person write that kind of note?

I had a bad feeling. No proof, no evidence, no reason, mind you. Just a feeling. Tightness in my stomach. Breath coming faster than normal. So, I decided to pack a bag, hop in the car and, well, take a drive.

She shook her head. There was absolutely nothing she could put on paper that a man could understand. She wasn't being rational or logical. This felt almost…instinctual?

Drying her hair in front of the bathroom mirror, the top third steamed up so she needed to bend at the knees to see herself, Mel was too preoccupied to notice the jagged red scar that ran from her collar bone down to the center of her chest. And, if someone were with her in the bathroom and had asked about the scar, Mel would have been stunned to realize she'd forgotten it, possibly the first time that had happened in sixteen months. But, at that moment both her conscious and unconscious thoughts were elsewhere. She needed to speak to the police before going anywhere. Was this a nine-one-one situation? It felt like an emergency to her. She doubted the police would see it that way.

That left the non-emergency number. She didn't like that idea. Reporting her husband missing was larger than a phone call to a non-emergency number. They'd put her on hold while they dealt with other calls, some loser complaining about his neighbor's dog, or drunk teens coming home in a noisy car, disturbing the neighborhood. Her missing husband was more important than all of that.

So, finish packing. Talk to the police in person. Then hit the road.

Without warning the blackness inside swelled and the monster attacked. "You're weak. Sixteen months you don't leave the house. Now you're going on a four-day road trip? There's a hurricane raging out there, practically on top of you. Rain like this, the roads are probably closed. You can't do it!"

Mel's busy hands stopped moving. She straightened. Her muscles tightened with edgy fear. The warmth of the house was suddenly oppressive, and it made each shallow breath loud and ragged in the empty bedroom. She stared out of wide eyes at her suitcase and didn't really see it.

What was she thinking? The Black Monster was right. The drive to the airport the previous evening had taken all her effort and concentration. Every fiber in her body had been dedicated to the task. She'd nearly shot someone, for heaven's sake. Less than twelve hours later she was planning on driving to Atlantic City?

Well, yes. And, for some reason the idea was not terrifying. She wasn't curled up in a ball in the corner while the monster gorged itself on her dread. It wasn't growing more substantive as it devoured the scattered bright spots of her confidence, beauty, and love.

Why? What had changed?

The answer came in an instant.

Jordon was missing and her concern for him outweighed the apprehension she felt about leaving the house.

She remembered a birthday gift her parents gave her when she turned six. A fire engine red bicycle. A shiny chrome, thumb-actuated bell was clipped to the handlebars. Her friend Tessa, down the block four houses, was just minutes away! Wobbling from right training wheel to left, Mel pedaled furiously everywhere she went. The wind whipped her hair. Water leaked out the corner of her eyes. The smile never left her face. The world shrank that day.

When her dad announced that she was good enough on the bike to remove the training wheels, Mel cried and pleaded with him to leave them attached. How could she possibly stay upright without them? They were part of the bike, therefore, when she was on the bike, they were part of her. She needed the support. She couldn't do it alone. But, he took them off and once they were gone and she was forced to deal with the new state of affairs, she managed just fine and actually excelled because the bike was so much more with the training wheels gone.

Jordon was like that—her support. Her training wheels. With him gone she needed to step up and become more than she'd been these last sixteen months.

The trembles and shortness of breath disappeared. She tossed a couple of thick paperbacks into her suitcase, a mystery novel off the best seller list and something else Jordon shook his head at and called a bodice ripper. She zipped the case shut with finality, already thinking about her next step.

The cop shop.

She shrugged into her overcoat. She slapped one pocket and felt the SIG's reassuring silhouette. Slapped the other pocket and felt the personal alarm. While she waited for a bagel to thaw in the microwave, she tugged her ponytail through the opening in the back of her ball cap.

The cops would likely smile kindly, pat her on her silly blonde head, and usher her out the front door. Despite that, she planned on starting with them. After she listened to what they had to say she'd take the next step, whatever it turned out to be.

CHAPTER 33

FIVE MINUTES PAST six in the morning. Dark. Rainy. Windy and cold. Streetlights turning puddles into pools of sparkling diamonds. Mel parked in front of a local branch police station, wondering what she was doing walking into a cop shop on a morning like this—any morning for that matter—with pepper spray in her bag, a handgun in one pocket, and a personal alarm in the other.

Crazy. She almost smiled.

She took a deep breath to settle her nerves and climbed out of the car. After a moment's thought she opened the Mazda's passenger door and put the SIG in the glove box, just in case the police station had a metal detector around the entrance door.

The building looked deserted but the front door swung open easily when she pulled the handle. An officer sat leaning back in his chair, feet up on the counter. Laugh lines like spokes radiated away from his eyes. A paperback novel lay open on one leg. His fingers were intertwined across his chest. His shirt was open at the neck, a clip-on tie still dangling from one corner of his collar. Mel thought he was sleeping and, irrationally, she lightened her step so her tapping shoes wouldn't disturb him.

He must have heard something, or felt the blast of cool, wet air that followed her in through the door. He opened one eye and studied her before opening the other. He dropped his feet from the counter to the floor and dragged himself forward, one wheel on his chair squeaking as it rolled.

"Good morning." Mel's voice was faint. "My husband is missing."

He nodded slowly. "What's your name, ma'am?" He had a soft, deep voice. A no maintenance crew cut. Big, kind eyes that looked intense and not even a little bit sleepy.

"Melissa. My husband, well, common-law husband, fiancé really, his name is Jordon. Jordon Cutler."

More nodding. The officer said, "What's your last name, ma'am?"

"Bremmer."

"Okay Ms. Bremmer, when did you last see Mr. Cutler?"

"The afternoon of the twelfth. Four and a half days ago. He left for Atlantic City on a business trip."

"Okay, good. Tell me the rest." He pulled a ballpoint pen from his pocket and twisted the barrel. "When was he supposed to be home?"

"I expected him last night. I was supposed to pick him up. I wrote down the flight number and everything so I wouldn't get confused. But, the flight was cancelled because of the weather. The airline won't tell me when he's re-booked. I called his hotel. There was no answer." Mel knew she sounded silly. Pitiable and frantic. Like she couldn't deal with something as routine as a cancelled flight. The cop didn't comment though. Didn't even raise an eyebrow.

"What airline?"

"US Airways, their little commuter branch. Atlantic Coastal Airlines."

"ACA. I've flown with them. They're reliable. Okay. Your husband is less than twelve hours overdue."

A spike of panic stabbed Mel's heart. He was going to tell her there was nothing he could do. He'd say, "People go missing in Atlantic City every night. Show up in time for the breakfast buffet. Give it time." She didn't want to hear that. She stared at the cop's paperback and did her best to maintain control and not start blubbering like a fragile child. The guy on the cover of the book wore a cowboy hat and carried a rifle in one hand. *The Daybreakers* by Louis L'amour. A person didn't see too many westerns anymore. She'd never read one but remembered her brother reading them all. Max Brand, Luke Short, and, of course, Louis L'amour, just like this cop.

The distraction was enough. Her fear subsided and her chin stopped trembling.

The cop said, "Has this sort of thing—"

"Don't tell me I have to wait forty-eight hours." Her voice was higher than normal, laced with a trace of dread she couldn't entirely control.

"Melissa, right?"

She nodded.

"That forty-eight hours stuff is Hollywood fiction. Suppose someone's two-year-old baby disappeared. You think we'd wait two days to start looking?"

Mel thought about it. Shook her head.

"No. Of course not. Now if, for example," he held up both palms showing her it was a for instance only, "if your fella had a history of this—showing up a day or two late with a powerful hangover and full of regret—we'd probably not be in a rush to go looking for him. Make sense? Maybe then we wait forty-eight hours. Legitimize the movie industry." He smiled. Still warm and friendly. Still with the hard eyes, the ones that said, "I'm taking you seriously."

Mel nodded. She couldn't help smiling herself. Maybe he cared. Naive possibly, but the police had treated her well after the night club stabbing. There was no reason to suspect they wouldn't treat her well a second time.

"So, tell me, has this sort of thing happened before?"

Before he finished the sentence, Mel shook her head.

"Okay then. What was his state of mind when you saw him last?"

She gave him a blank look.

"Did you argue? Had he been drinking?"

"He doesn't drink. His father was…" her voice faded. "Well, Jordon doesn't drink."

The officer asked a few more questions. He wrote down all her answers in his notebook. Eventually he said, "Go home. Stay by the phone. Reach out to friends and family. Any place he might have ended up. Stay in contact with his hotel. We'll enter him into our system and start making inquiries."

Mel felt her chin tremble. She twisted the strap of her bag into tight loops around her hands. When she finally spoke, her voice quavered. "That's it? What do you mean you'll make inquiries? What are you going to do?"

"We'll contact the police in Atlantic City. We'll talk to ACA. I promise, when I ask, they'll answer." He smiled. "We'll check with the hotel. We'll speak to the last person he was in contact with. Find out what time that was. That way we have a starting point. Like a window from when he was last seen to when you were supposed to pick him up. Now go home. We'll be in touch. Try not to worry."

Mel nodded. She thanked the officer for his time. She swiveled and walked out of the police station like she was on a treadmill—no further ahead, and going nowhere fast. Jordon didn't have any family for her to call. As for friends, Tom Menny was it. If Tom were anywhere other than Atlantic City, her first instinct would have been to contact him.

Mel stopped halfway down the rain-slick steps. Tom had said *he was in a jam and since Jordon planned on being in Atlantic City anyway…* It seemed an incredible coincidence that the exact weekend Jordon attended a conference in Atlantic City, Tom found himself in a jam in the same location.

Rain lashed the night at a sharp angle. The wind blew her coat into a frenzy around her calves. Mel raised her shoulders against the weather and thought about the packed suitcase on the Mazda's back seat.

An incredible coincidence.

"Oh yeah. That's what I'm going to do," she mumbled. "Go home and not worry."

CHAPTER 34

JORDON CUTLER WOKE to a soft, regular beep and the instantly recognizable smell of cleaners and antiseptics. He ached from head to toe. His tongue felt like a slab of rotten meat—swollen, dry, and furry. He needed a drink in the worst way. Groaning, he rolled his head to the right. He saw a black monitor with a bouncing green line. Every time his heart beat, the green line peaked and the machine beeped softly. He'd never been hooked up to a machine before—his old man never messed him up that bad—but a kid always had questions, especially when the nurse was young and pretty so Jordon recognized the machine as a cardiac monitor.

There was nothing to drink on the table.

He rolled his head to the left and still didn't see a jug of Evian and ice cubes. Rather, he saw a cop push the door to his room open halfway and study him through the gap. Jordon said, "I need a…" His mouth was so parched he didn't recognize his own voice. He swallowed dryly, cleared his throat and tried once more. "Thirsty. I need a drink."

"The nurse will be back in a minute," the cop said brusquely. "Ask her." He pushed his way into the room and plunked himself onto a hard-plastic chair meant for a patient's visitors. He stretched out, crossed his ankles and arms and pointedly ignored Jordon.

"What are you doing?" Jordon asked.

"Doctors don't like their patients waking up, seeing a police officer in the room. Apparently, it can be scary. Sometimes they have heart attacks and die. Doctors hate that." He hadn't looked at Jordon and he sounded like he wouldn't mind if a patient died of fright. "Now you're awake, I'm gonna wait with you instead of out in the hall."

"Oh." It sort of answered Jordon's question—what are you doing—but not really. He said, "What time is it?"

The cop glanced at his watch. "Eight-forty-three."

Jordon mulled that over for a few seconds. It meant he'd been asleep in the hospital several hours. He absently scratched around the three electrodes taped to his chest. An intravenous line in his forearm tugged uncomfortably. He didn't know what kind of fluid the line was dripping into his veins. He wouldn't have really cared except for the urinary catheter. That was definitely the least fun part of the night.

Worse than getting shot.

Worse than getting beaten.

A nurse had told him the fluids entering his body had to go somewhere. A good indication if his insides were working properly would be the correct amount of fluid exiting his body, via the tube stuck up his…Well, just the memory of her matter-of-fact explanation made Jordon wince.

He wondered why the cop had parked himself like a guard in his room. Which, by extension, made Jordon a prisoner. The cop's entire demeanor seemed unnecessarily hostile. "Why you here?" Jordon asked, which he figured was the question he should have asked earlier.

"Because I drew the short straw and, apparently, my time isn't valuable anywhere else."

"What I mean—"

"Sir," the cop said, "You going to keep talking? If you are, I'm going to read you your rights."

Jordon blinked in surprise. "What are you talking about? I didn't—"

He held up a palm, interrupting Jordon mid-sentence. He reached into his breast pocket and pulled out a laminated recipe card.

"Are you arresting me?" Jordon asked. "What am I charged with?"

The cop looked up from the card, deep irritated furrows like gouges across his forehead. "A person has to be under arrest before he can be charged with a crime. I haven't arrested you. But, I can put you in close vicinity to a gunshot victim. That makes you a suspect. So, I'm going to read you your rights. Before you say something a lawyer could use to drop kick a case out of court." He paused and took a breath and recited, "Sir, you have the right to remain silent. You have…"

It continued. Jordon closed his eyes and settled into the pillow, tuning the cop out. He still didn't have a clear idea of why the man was in his room. He couldn't think of anything that necessitated it, but he wouldn't miss a thing by not listening. Watch one cop show on television and a person knew the spiel by heart.

He remembered confusing Leo and his old man and he remembered the paramedics hustling him onto a stretcher in front of the 7-Eleven. After that, it was mostly a blur—nurses buzzing about, poking and stabbing him. An x-ray. An ultra sound. A doctor sewed the bullet hole closed. At some point hospital staff hooked him up to the cardiac monitor and the annoying beeping started—quiet, but hard to ignore—and someone pushed a tube up his nose, just like every actor on every soap opera experienced when they inevitably make it into a hospital bed. It all felt excessive for one tiny little bullet hole. None of it demanded an armed guard reading him his rights.

Jordon's muscles tensed with growing irritation. Ignoring the pain, he inhaled deeply, and tried to force himself to unwind. He sent a scowl in the cop's direction. The cardiac monitor kept beeping, somehow louder than before, like an alarm clock designed to increase in volume when a person ignored it. He turned his glare on the machine. It ignored him, just as the cop had done. He shifted on the mattress, trying for a more comfortable spot. Barbs of white-hot pain burned up his side. He sucked in a startled breath.

The bruised ribs.

The doctor told him, "Nothing I can do about that," sounding exactly the same as the doctor who'd examined him all those years ago—the time his bastard old man belted him, and then drove him to the hospital in a snowstorm, flipped the car, and blamed his son's injuries on the roll-over. It may have been the same visit the pretty young nurse explained the function of a cardiac monitor.

The incessant beeping bored into his brain like Chinese water torture. Damn, he needed some quiet time. Some comfort. A thin layer of prickly sweat covered his body. The electrode patches on his chest itched. He wanted a drink. He wanted to hear Mel's voice. He wanted the cop to quit talking.

"All right," Jordon said. "I get it. I understand my rights? Okay?" Simultaneously he plucked off the leads taped to his chest. The cardiac monitor switched from rhythmic beeps to a continuous, high-pitched wail. Surprised, Jordon stared at the machine. He expected it to go silent. No heartbeat, no beeps. Louder wasn't part of the plan.

The officer stood quickly, knocking over his chair. He peered at the machine with an alarmed expression. "What did you do? Where's the volume control?"

A nurse rushed into the room, pushing aside the overturned chair. She wore a concerned look. She brushed the officer aside and looked from the cardiac monitor to Jordon, lying on the bed with three leads dangling in his hand. Her concern dropped away. She flicked a switch on the side of the monitor. The alarm went silent. "What's going on?"

"The noise," Jordon said weakly. "The beeping was driving me crazy." Under the strength of the nurse's glare, the heat of embarrassment warmed his face. He shook the leads with the attached electrode patches. "And, these things are itchy."

"Next time you feel like disconnecting something designed to monitor your health, ask." She pointed at a string tied to his bedrail. "Pull it. I'll come."

"Sorry."

She didn't acknowledge his apology. "I don't believe you need the monitor anymore. However, I will consult the doctor. He may decide otherwise." Spine rigid, she stalked out of the room without a backward glance.

"Okay," Jordon said to the closing door.

The police officer cut Jordon a withering glare. He righted his chair and sat down with a noisy grunt and went back to pretending he was alone in the room. It was blessedly quiet, giving Jordon time to finish wondering why he was being treated like a perpetrator instead of a victim.

Nothing between the time he collapsed outside 7-Eleven to the present made him a felon. Prior to his collapse came the kidnapping in the Oasis but, there were a couple of witnesses. The woman in teal saw the thugs dragging him out of the hotel and even better, a cop saw the entire incident, and tried to stop it.

Prior to the kidnapping...

Jordon's heart rate spiked like a solar flare. He inhaled sharply. Thank God he was no longer attached to the cardiac monitor! The rhythmic beeping would have become one long, continuous shriek, like a jet engine in the room. Because, before the kidnapping he was on the side of a road with a revolver in his hand and two bodies lying on the ground near his feet.

Doing his best to appear composed, Jordon flicked a casual glance at the cop. Inside, his stomach boiled in nervous turmoil.

The officer had his cell phone out, was watching him with a curious expression while he said something about, "...the suspect you're interested in talking to is awake..."

Jordon forced himself to calmly meet the cop's look without blinking. His thoughts raced. When the questions began, he'd start out vague. Figure out where the inquiries were going. That was believable, considering the previous night. If the investigation was about the events at the Oasis, he had nothing to hide. Anything else and it was time to call a lawyer.

He read once that there was close to one thousand different career paths a person could take when he joined the law enforcement community. One of the choices was a Truth Verification Specialist. That person could listen for key phrases and read body language well enough to know when he was being lied to, almost instinctively. Jordon hoped the person questioning him wasn't one of those types. Convincing a Truth Verification Specialist that he knew nothing about the shootings on the side of the road was a tall order. And, obviously, he couldn't tell the truth. If he told the truth, he was in the shit at least waist deep.

That damn butterfly.

He muttered several silent curses. For the first time, he was grateful to the Lunatic who had crashed into him in the hallway. Suddenly, he looked like a shining star. He'd walked away with the revolver, the only thing Jordon could think of that undeniably linked him to the Egg Harbor crime scene. Thinking it through had a calming effect. By the time the two detectives walked in, he was ready for them.

The Asian detective was growing thin on top and thick around the middle. He had a cell phone on his belt and on his left wrist, a large Timex Iron-Man, the kind with a fabric strap. His black eyes were sharp and shrewd. Confident. He showed Jordon a badge in a leather folder. "Detective Paul Davis," he said, and stuck out his free hand.

Silently Jordon shook the detective's hand.

Davis stowed his badge. He nodded sideways. "My partner, Detective Duncan Galloway."

Galloway sneezed and wiped his nose on the sleeve of a long, rumpled raincoat. "I'd shake your hand but I guess you don't want my cold." His eyes were red and watery.

"How do you feel, Mr. Cutler?" Davis said.

"I'm thirsty."

Both detectives nodded, looks of understanding on their faces. Davis shot a glance at the police officer. "Officer Samson? Could you have a nurse bring some water for Mr. Cutler? Thanks." He asked in a friendly tone but it was unquestionably an order. Then he turned his eyes back to Jordon. "While we wait for your water, we might as well get started. Can you tell us what happened?"

"You mean how I ended up here?"

"Yeah. How you ended up here."

"I'm not too sure. I walked to a 7-Eleven. I didn't go inside. I kind of keeled over at the front door. I think the clerk called an ambulance because the next thing I knew the paramedics were lifting me onto a stretcher."

"Allow me to rephrase," Davis said, still friendly but somehow more insistent at the same time. "How did you find yourself at an all-night convenience store with a gunshot wound?"

Instantly Jordon felt some of the tension dissipate. They were investigating Leo's death. "Oh. Well, I guess it started with all the yelling and screaming in the hotel room next to me."

He told the detectives the entire story, from the point when the Lunatic bowled him over until he collapsed in front of the 7-Eleven. Occasionally Galloway sniffed or coughed into the back of his hand. They took a quick break when the nurse stomped in with a jug of water. With pursed lips and a stony expression, she poured Jordon a glass. It was a permanent expression, Jordon realized, one that said, "My husband is worthless, I hate my job, my kids are demons." She tapped an annoyed foot, clearly chafed with Jordon and the authorities who outranked her in the room. Jordon thought she and Officer Samson would get along fine. They both seemed to be the type who were only happy when they were angry.

After he drained one glass and then a second, Davis said, "Only a few more questions." Without waiting for Jordon's agreement, he asked, "What hotel were you in?"

"The Oasis."

"What time did you check in?"

"Around ten-thirty, a little earlier."

"Why so late?"

"My flight was cancelled."

They kept going and the detectives dutifully wrote everything down, apparently satisfied with his answers. As they should have been. Everything Jordon said was the truth. None of the questions were tricky or surprising. Thinking about it, he guessed these detectives were coming at their investigation from many different angles, of which he was only one. It explained why they were treating him lightly. All he was doing was confirming what they already knew. They'd probably already investigated Leo's death. They probably found the revolver he kicked into the trash. They probably already knew most of the facts to the story he was telling.

Except for the cash in the Adidas gym bag. They probably didn't know about the cash.

Eventually Davis said, "We're done. We'll talk to the officer you mentioned. The British woman too." He buttoned his raincoat over his belly. "Until that's done, Officer Samson will camp outside your door."

Puzzled, Jordon tilted his head. "Why?"

"One of Atlantic City's residents is dead. Not one of our finest. Still, I would be remiss in my duties if I told the only witness to go home." He emphasized the word "witness," making it sound like a temporary title. He waggled his notebook. "We need to check this information out. We'll be in touch."

Jordon hoped it was a cop's natural skepticism coming through, instead of genuine doubt he heard in the man's voice.

"Why do you care if Samson waits with you?" Galloway asked, his voice hoarse and congested. "You in a hurry to be somewhere?"

Jordon hiked his shoulders. His bruised ribs pushed at his insides, making him wince. The last thing he wanted was to be stuck in Atlantic City while a murder investigation swirled around him. He said, "Anytime you're in a hospital, you're in a hurry to be somewhere else. I want to go home." Home to Mel and the comfort and familiarity they shared. He'd have to track down a phone and call her and somehow try and explain the insanity of the previous night.

"We'll be in touch," Galloway said.

Resigned to a day or two more in Atlantic City, Jordon nodded unhappily.

CHAPTER 35

THE BLACK MONSTER was testing its bindings, telling her she'd have to stop soon, telling her, "You can't stay in the car forever," and asking, "Then what?"

Mel ignored the rising level of anxiety as best she could. When the time came, when she reached the point where she couldn't clench any longer and absolutely had to use a restroom and when the hunger pains gnawing her belly were no longer something she could ignore, that's when she would find a rest stop, climb out of the Mazda's protective cocoon and deal with it.

She killed time tapping the radio's scan button, searching for songs she liked, moving from station to station as one faded to static and the next one became clear. She latched onto a country and western station that lasted quite a while, two wanna-be-funny morning DJs who played off each other and took requests. Why nobody asked for a song without including a lame little autobiography was beyond her. Like this one cry-baby, "I'm a nice guy. I had a lonely night. I'd like to hear *Little Bitty?* By Alan Jackson?"

"Keep whining like that and it won't be the last lonely night you have," Mel said out loud to the radio.

She bobbed her head and tapped her fingers on the steering wheel enjoying the silly song, Alan Jackson having fun with it, not pissing and moaning the way most male country singers carried on. In that moment, Mel discovered she was content. And, strangely proud of herself. She'd driven three, maybe three and a half hours already. She was doing something important, something she wasn't certain she would have been capable of the previous day.

A checkerboard sign appeared on the horizon and quickly grew larger; the sign covered in little square icons indicating food, fuel, and restrooms were only one exit away. Her knees were locked together and her stomach rumbled with hunger. She really couldn't hold out any longer.

Five minutes later, parked beside the fuel pumps at a Sunoco truck stop, she pushed some hair behind an ear, blinked rapidly to clear away nervous tears and asked herself: *What is the fear and anxiety about this time?* She was at a truck stop, for heaven's sake. Road-weary families in crowded minivans stopped at places such as this every hour of every day. There were two police cars parked near the diner's entrance. Judging by all the idling semis in the lot, the restaurant would be packed with macho male truckers. Anyone of them would stand up to protect her because that's what macho male truckers did.

So, what's going to happen?

Nothing.

Go in there. Use the washroom, buy a coffee, maybe one of those apple fritter donuts with all the glazed icing and no real apple—she had an unexplainable craving for one of those—*and then get back on the road. No biggie.*

She swiped the back of her hand across her eyes and climbed out of the car. With one hand deep in her coat pocket clutching the SIG, and the other hand in the opposite pocket wrapped around her pepper spray, she strode across the parking lot, passed beneath the towering Sunoco sign, and walked in the front door.

She paused in the entrance to get her bearings. Her pulse thrummed in her ears turning the dining room chatter into a low background drone. Silverware clanked behind a swing door on one side of the room. The smell of coffee and deep fried food hung in the air. A couple of heads turned in her direction briefly, before returning to their meals or companions on the opposite side of the booth. Oddly, nobody paid any attention to her, almost like she was just another road warrior with as much right to stop here as anyone else.

She found the restrooms sign and crossed the diner in several long steps without meeting anyone's eye. She pushed her way into the Ladies, and then into a stall. The door slammed behind her with a ringing clang. Goosebumps pebbled her arms. She trembled as though cold. Her clothes felt stifling. She planted both hands on the back wall of the stall and leaned her weight into them. Her chin rested on her heaving chest.

Get a grip!

Get a grip, for heaven's sake.

Several minutes later she forced herself to walk out of the restroom, every footstep deliberate. She stopped in front of the counter. "Coffee?" she said tentatively.

"You'll have to speak up, Hon," the lady working behind the counter said. She wore a friendly expression, a dress the color of old mustard, and an apron that bristled with pens. "Linda" was embroidered in red cursive high on the right side of her dress. Her curly brown hair was pulled back and pinned at the sides, wispy strands coming free, fluffing around her ears like it was the end of a long night.

"Coffee. Two sugars," Mel said a second time, forcing some strength in to her voice. "Extra hot."

"That's the only way it comes." Linda blew a little gust of air out the corner of her mouth, making the loose hair hanging in her face dance. "Strong and hot. Just like our men, right? Starbucks we ain't."

Mel smiled weakly, not quite ready for random quips or small talk. She said, "I'd like an apple fritter too." She pointed. "One of those big ones."

"All of it to go?"

Mel nodded. "Yes, please." Her voice still sounded as thin as Jasmine tea. Thankfully it was tremor free. She put a plastic lid on the cardboard coffee cup. A thin thread of steam spiraled out of the pin-hole. It smelled delicious. When Linda slid the gooey fritter into the small brown bag and placed it on the counter beside the coffee cup, Mel's mouth watered. She forgot all about the fear and anxiety. She was doing okay! She was way out of her comfort zone. Literally miles from the familiarity she craved, but here she was, doing what normal people do on a road trip.

And, crap, was she hungry. It was all she could do to keep herself from tearing into the bag and demolishing the donut right then and there. She was doing okay!

She dipped a hand into her wallet.

Shaky fingers betrayed her.

Coins showered the floor in a noisy jangle that sliced through the background noise in the dining room. She crouched and hastily gathered up the change, convinced every eye in the place was staring at her. She kept her head down, letting her hair hide the embarrassment burning her face.

When the money was back in her wallet, she stood.

Too fast.

She bumped a bowl beside the till with her elbow. After-dinner mints went flying, landed, and skittered across the floor like busy little ants. Now people were looking in her direction, curious expressions on their faces. Mel was beyond mortification.

This is how you stay anonymous? This is how you keep the robbers and the rapists and the muggers from noticing you?

"Easy there, Hon," Linda said, and then quieter, "You all right? You seem shook up."

Mel snatched the coffee and the brown bag containing the

fritter off the counter. "I'm doing okay," she mumbled. "I'm doing okay." She strode for the door staring at the floor twelve feet in front of her the entire way.

She ate the fritter on the road and spent the next twenty miles licking sticky glazed sugar off the tips of her fingers. She promised herself a better showing when she hit Atlantic City. Without a better showing, the chances of finding Jordon were very slim indeed.

CHAPTER 36

BERNARD HEWITT WOKE without opening his eyes.

Without moving on the mattress.

Without allowing the moan of pure misery to slip past his lips.

His mouth was dry as sawdust. Every odor in the room hit his hypersensitive nose like an explosion of shit in a fertilizer factory. He lay without twitching so much as a toe and psyched himself up. Because, the moment he moved, the instant he reached for the Dramamine to kill the little acrobat doing calisthenics in his belly, the throbbing behind his eyes would explode into some kind of God-awful nuclear holocaust of agony, and the headache that felt like he parted his hair with an axe would accelerate from zero to sixty, and he needed to be ready for all of it. He'd suffered through some doozy hangovers in his life. This one felt like a four-star leader-of-the-pack.

"Idiot," he mumbled, promising to never, ever mix his drinks again. Before he finished the sentence, he knew he'd break that promise, just like he'd broken it dozens of times before.

He talked to himself a little longer before he risked opening one eye. That turned out okay. It hurt. He needed to squint, but all and all, not too bad. He opened the other eye. Easier than the first. Finally, he pushed himself upright with a groan. The motion was enough to make his stomach capsize, and a wave of nausea pushed up his esophagus. He swallowed it down, ignoring the bitter, burning taste in the back of his throat. Puking was still half an hour away. He never threw up immediately after waking. It was always thirty or forty minutes later.

He staggered into the bathroom, found some extra-strength Tylenol in his overnight bag, and then walked on wobbly legs back into the bedroom. He did a quick scan. No minibar in this crack-house-of-a-hotel of course, so no Gatorade or club soda, which meant the second and third best ways to ease a hangover were out. Then he spotted the gold medal hangover killer—three remaining beers out of the second six pack, sitting on the AC unit. Hair-of-the-dog. He glanced at the ceiling and mouthed a quiet prayer of thanks.

Three Tylenols and two Miller Genuine Drafts later, Bernard decided he might survive after all. There was another thought buried there too, a memory from the night before that tickled his consciousness. So far it hadn't beat its way through the cobwebs, but he knew something happened. Something big. He wiped a shaky hand down his face. Whatever the incident was, it eluded him. He wasn't too worried. He never completely lost his memory when he drank. All the files were there, they just needed to be sorted into alphabetical order. Sometimes, when the hangover was this bad, the sorting took the better part of the morning.

Summoning up the nerve he parted the curtains an inch with a single finger. The day was gray and rainy but still bright enough to slash into the room and stab his eyes like needles. He hurriedly released the curtain. Blinking away the flares of light on his eyeballs, he flopped down on the edge of the mattress, three feet away from the television. He turned it on and ran through the channels until he found the mid-morning news, and then stared at it without really seeing it until, without warning, all the files shuffled into place.

"An evening of care-free fun turned deadly late last night in a popular boardwalk nightclub. One man is dead and many others are asking, 'Why?' after shots rang out in Glow, the popular dance club attached to the Oasis Hotel and Casino. Dead is Alan Gibons, a long-time employee of Glow."

Bernard blew a noisy gust of air through his lips as though he'd been punched in the stomach. The room tilted. The shakes rushed back and his entire body vibrated. He slammed his eyes closed, grabbed a fistful of blanket in each hand and held on, concentrating on controlling the sick panic coursing through him. "Take it easy," he muttered. After several deep breaths, he gained control of his pulse. "They don't know anything, or I'd be in jail already."

The news anchor continued, "Shari Adams was in Glow last night. She spoke to us outside the nightclub. Shari?"

"We were just talking, you know?"

Bernard recognized the new voice. He opened his eyes and looked at the television with curiosity. Sparkle-girl-Shari said, "He bought some drinks. Suddenly, out of the blue, he throws a glass of water on me! For no reason! It happened so fast."

"I didn't throw it on you," Bernard yelled. "Tell them about the part where you slapped me." He made a gun with his finger and thumb and pointed it at the screen. "Bang," he said, and jerked his arm up like he just pulled the trigger.

It was a childish gesture but it made him wonder what he'd done with the real revolver. He scanned the room. When he spotted his sport coat bundled untidily on the floor where he dropped it, he walked over to it and swung a half-assed kick at it. The revolver lay on the floor. He picked it up and sat back down on the edge of the mattress.

"The bouncers saw it happen," Shari continued. "They came at us. Then this nut, he pulls out a gun, you know? I couldn't believe it." Her voice dropped. Her bottom lip quivered, Shari putting in a huge effort, obviously forcing the tears. "I thought I was going to die," she said.

Bernard quickly lost interest as a parade of witnesses searching for their moment of fame came and went. He wondered why the anchor said, "shots," plural. As far as he remembered he only fired once.

He flipped the cylinder out of the revolver's frame. Dull brass surrounded by shiny nickel formed an interesting kaleidoscope pattern in the back of the cylinder. He turned the revolver around and looked at the cylinder from the front, the barrel pointing at his face. Three of the brass cartridges stared back at him like empty black eyes. The other three bullets were dull gray—live rounds. Looking into the business end of a revolver containing three live rounds gave him a sudden, nervous chill. He hurriedly dropped it on the bed.

On the television, the anchor said, "Mrs. Emma Courtney, who declined to comment on camera, described a terrifying evening forcibly confined to her room."

Bernard scowled. Typical female theatrics, these women all putting on a show. Staging a big production out of nothing. Except for the little slap when he entered her room, he treated Emma well and hadn't they agreed, she earned the slap? Why would she describe the night as terrifying?

"At this point the authorities have no proof that Mrs. Courtney's kidnapper is the same man who shot and killed Mr. Gibons in Glow, however they are operating on the assumption that he is. Atlantic City police are searching for this man." The camera zoomed to a pencil sketch hanging over the anchor's left shoulder.

Bernard studied the sketch.

It wasn't a bad representation, he decided, less accurate than the sketches tourists buy when strolling along the boardwalk on a summer day, but still, not bad, considering the artist's only reference was a description given by Emma and Shari, both women overly dramatic and biased. Bernard appreciated that kind of accuracy.

"Authorities describe this man as unstable and unpredictable. They advise anyone who sees him to immediately contact their local police. He is considered armed and dangerous."

A little thrill shot up Bernard's spine. Armed and Dangerous! His new title sounded good. It made him grin. Not because of the power it represented, but because it was only fifty percent accurate. As usual, the media had the facts all messed up. He was armed, certainly. But dangerous?

Not at all.

He fled the nightclub with the rest of the sheep and then he'd walked out of the Oasis as casual as can be, keeping his pace easy and unhurried while his mind screamed at him to run. At the boardwalk, he turned east. Behind him the police sirens grew louder and the flashing red and blue lights lit up the night. He ducked into several bars, ordered doubles straight up and slammed them back before moving on. The alcohol kept his mind steady and his nerves in check, until the immediate risk waned. Then the trembling started. And, the shortness of breath. And, the cold sweats.

He'd killed someone. Murdered him.

Murdered!

His mind wouldn't let it go. The consequences had rushed in next. He wasn't from New Jersey so did that mean he'd be tried in his home state? Would he get the death penalty? Or, life in prison? The questions kept coming, more and more and more, questions faster than answers. He skidded to a halt in his scuffed and worn-out Oxfords and puked over the edge of the boardwalk onto the Jersey shore.

Bernard didn't think "dangerous" guys did that sort of thing.

On the television, the news ended and the weather report began.

Despite the hangover, Bernard was suddenly thinking more clearly. He needed to put some miles between himself and Atlantic City. "They've gotta catch me to put me away," he said. The pencil sketch displayed on television was distinct enough. Every law enforcement officer in the state would be looking for him. Not at the Good Knight Inn. Not right away. But, it would happen. They'd check the big hotels first. They'd watch the airport and bus depot. When they didn't find him in the obvious places, they'd move on to the flea-bag hotels. There were dozens. The owners wouldn't be cooperative. He figured he had some time. Not much, but some.

What he didn't have was transportation.

In the movies fugitives on the run hotwired cars. Nonsense, of course. Who really knew how to do that? Nobody he'd ever met. He could head over to one of the parking garages attached to a big casino and look for an older vehicle without an alarm. Look for a key hidden behind a license plate or stuck in a magnetic box inside a wheel well. That might work. If nobody came by and saw him crawling around the garage. If the garage didn't have surveillance cameras. If security personnel didn't do random drive-bys. There were dozens of "ifs."

So, hotwiring was out, as was stealing a vehicle.

He shook his head slightly. The headache throbbing behind his eyes accelerated. He ignored it and concentrated on the problem for a couple of more minutes. Then he straightened on the edge of the bed. Smiling, he looked from the flickering television screen to the rope-operated curtains. He let the smile grow.

He was going to leave Atlantic City within the next twenty minutes and nobody would look at him twice when he did.

CHAPTER 37

THE CAPTAIN TOOK Victoria Chesham's Day-Timer without enthusiasm. His thick eyebrows were knitted together into a dark frown. He muttered, "Here we go," and then louder he said, "Anything else you want to tell me?" He shook the Day-Timer. "Like this isn't enough?"

Luther and Brenna exchanged a quick glance. She did a palms up and shuffled back half a step, letting him know, he guessed, that it was up to him to tell the story. He could include as much or as little as he felt appropriate. He thought keeping Menny in their collective sights was the important issue; for the time being the specific reason for doing so didn't matter. Not until they had more information. So, he didn't bother mentioning his suspicion that Menny was the killer, embarrassment and humiliation his motivation. Instead, he highlighted the tangible—the theft of Menny's lottery winnings. He finished by saying, "...even with the Day-Timer, I think we ought to keep an eye on him a little longer."

"Of course. Of course," the Captain said, nodding. He held up the Day-Timer. "I need to make some calls. Figure out how to handle this in a discrete fashion. In the meantime, you two go home. Get some rest. I'll put two more detectives on this while you're gone."

Luther said, "I'd prefer to stay."

"What's it been? Over nineteen hours you've been on duty? Several people are working on this. They can handle it for now. Go home. At least until we hear back from Richmond. If something significant comes up, I'll make sure you're notified."

Luther washed both hands down his face. Leaving felt like abandoning the case. But, without a couple of hours of sleep, he knew he wouldn't be able to process any of the background information their colleagues in Richmond discovered. With reluctance, he said, "All right." He and Brenna left the office and when they were safely out of range he said, "I'm too keyed up to sleep. Let's grab a bite."

"You buying breakfast, Mac?"

"Did I say that?"

She shook her head. "Spend all night with a guy, the least he could do is buy me breakfast."

Luther felt his neck and the tips of his ears warm. He hoped he wasn't blushing. "You messing with me, Bren?"

"A little bit."

"Very good." He smiled. "Let's go."

"Where?"

"There's a restaurant near my place. It's tasty." Then for some reason, maybe trying to build it up in her eyes, he added, "They've got a nautical theme going on. Very atmospheric." Nets and anchors and other assorted beach junk hung on the walls alongside bottles of blue and green sea glass. He guessed it was supposed to represent the mystery of the sea. Shipwrecks. Foreign ports. That sort of thing. He thought it was a chain but it didn't feel overtly corporate. And, he wasn't lying. They served a tasty breakfast.

Shoulder to shoulder they stared out the police station's glass entrance doors. Heavily falling rain made the parking lot look alive, as though a carpet of black beetles were scurrying across it. "Perfect," he mumbled. "You ready for this?"

"I guess."

Side by side they sprinted for the Caprice. A short drive later, Brenna guided the car into a vacant spot about as far from the restaurant's front door as a person could park. Luther wondered about families who went out for breakfast. Compared to the other daily meals, breakfast was proportionally more expensive. Figure eleven, twelve dollars before a tip. Cook the same thing at home, you're into it for maybe three bucks, but he still saw entire families in IHOP or Denny's early in the morning. It was a choice that always came as a mild surprise to him.

Inside the restaurant, with coffees on the way, Brenna asked, "What's good?" She looked up from her menu. His was lying unopened, flat on the table. "You've already decided?"

Luther said, "I always order the same thing."

"No point me asking, 'What's good,' then, is there?"

"Not really." Once again, he felt slightly embarrassed and didn't know why.

"Eggs Benny, then." She closed her menu and said, "Okay, Mac. What's up? Why do you like Menny for this?"

The answer was obvious to him. All he needed was a moment to organize his thoughts and formulate his response. He said, "She's a hooker. She's robbing him blind, taking complete advantage of his generous nature. When he finds out, she dumps him without a word and leaves town." He made a face and shook his head. "Most guys? They wouldn't forgive that kind of treatment. They'd never want to see her again. What's Menny do? Instead of running the other way, he spends the evening with her. I can't decide if he's lying about bumping into her in the Taj, the way he's making it out to be a random thing. One thing is for sure, after he saw her he didn't waste any time hustling back for a second date."

"That's love. Or something."

"Obsession?"

"Strong word."

Luther didn't debate her. He thought "obsession" carried the right amount of weight. He continued, "They had a good time, and all that does, it just makes him more confused. He gave her everything she wanted. Why did she have to steal from him? He couldn't understand it. Why would she take advantage of him?

"On top of that, his co-workers are always asking, 'Why you still working? Didn't you win the lottery?' Friends want to borrow money. Family members expect him to pick up the tab. He can't do any of that, or answer any of their questions because he doesn't have half the money they think he does.

"Every aspect of his life has her shadow hovering over it, and he's got no idea when that'll go away. Time goes by. The way he looks, he has no problem attracting the ladies, but he compares every one of them to her. They're never as pretty. Never as much fun. And, he's positive that anyone he gets involved with will take off with the rest of his money. This obsession is starting to mess up any chance he has of a new relationship."

"So, he kills her? Had her killed? I guess that would be more accurate." Brenna sounded skeptical.

Luther nodded.

"You like Menny because of how you think he felt, not because she stole his money?"

"The theft is part of it. But, mostly it was about the way she treated him."

Brenna took a tentative sip of her coffee. She must have deemed it too hot because she pulled back with a grimace and blew air across the top of the mug. "Everything you just said is guesswork. Why are you so sure of his motivation?"

Luther looked out the window at the pouring rain, watched a family hustling to their car. Someone, he guessed the father, had his coat pulled up over his head so his hair stayed dry and instead, the small of his back got soaked. An American flag on an angled pole stuck out from the front of a drugstore, the fabric thrashing back and forth in the wind. He said, "Personal experience."

Without looking at Brenna he continued, "All I'm saying, I understand Menny's highs and lows with Victoria, because I'm going through something similar with Marilyn. Not to the same degree, of course."

"I guess I can understand your thought process."

The waitress arrived with their breakfasts. After she left, Brenna said, "The thing is, as much sense as it makes to you, it's just speculation. Maybe the guys in Richmond will turn some of it into facts. They talk to Menny's landlord for instance; find out he's moping around, a guy who used to go out all the time, now he's home on the weekend. But, it's still speculation. Lots of reasons he stays in on Friday night.

"At best, we might be able to build a case around a one-year-old theft. Right now, we don't even have enough evidence for that. A prosecutor wouldn't look at. And a defense attorney?" She shook her head. "Shit."

Luther had to smile. Brenna was right. A defense attorney would kick the case out of the courtroom like a fourth-quarter field goal. He pushed his plate away. Leaning back in his chair, balancing on the two rear legs with a glass of water in his hand, he asked, "You enjoy your eggs?"

"It was a good meal."

"You ready to go?"

"Yeah."

"Coffee at my place? I'm right around the corner."

"I'll take a rain check, Mac. I'm ready for a nap."

He paid the bill. She left the tip. They stood beneath the restaurant's awning, staring at rain that pelted the ground in sheets so heavy it rebounded when it hit. Luther said sourly, "You think you could have parked any farther away?"

"You could always walk home."

He grinned slightly and then, for the second time that morning, they sprinted through the storm to the Caprice.

CHAPTER 38

THE LUCKY THIRTEEN Saloon didn't look anything like it did the previous night when the dancers pranced around in their glittery costumes and the drunks drooled and yelled and the lights flashed through blue smoke that hung off the ceiling like Beijing smog.

Thank a merciful God in heaven, Pryce thought.

This morning the lights were up and the pulsing music from the night before had been replaced by a soft-rock-less-talk radio station, Celine Dion murmuring something sweet and shallow. Pryce let his concentration drift while she sang and contemplated the interior of his bar with a nostalgic eye, wondering how soon the Lucky Thirteen's spit shine would begin. He studiously avoided looking at his bartender, Dallas, at the other end of the bar cutting limes into eighth-inch slices. He was angry with her and holding onto it like a love-sick teen, which didn't make any sense because he was the boss and it was Dallas who should have been pouting. The previous evening his nerves turned to anger when Leo didn't call. He carried it through the night and into today, and he barked at Dallas, told her she should be doing some of the accounting at the end of her shift when she rang out the till.

She answered enthusiastically enough, almost like she wanted the extra responsibility. "Sure thing, Sweetie. Flat salary, or does an accountant get paid by the hour?"

Of course, he wasn't going to give her more money. He told her it was part of her job and he wouldn't pay her extra for doing something she was supposed to do in the first place. If she wanted a bigger pay check, she knew how to go about it. She worked in a gentleman's club after all. The money wasn't coming out of his pocket.

At which point Dallas' face whitened and when she laughed in his face there was no humor in the sound. She said, "No," and went on to explain, like a teacher to a five-year-old, that she was a bartender not an accountant and, voice rising, if he wanted an accountant he could hire one or pay her appropriately. Then she added, he needed to watch his tone. She suggested maybe the Atkins Diet was making him cranky. Lack of carbs tended to do that. And, if he ever (EVER) suggested she undo a button again, she'd slug him so hard in the mouth he'd be brushing his teeth through his asshole. She actually said that. It was quite a speech. It put Pryce back on his heels.

Celine wrapped up, *My Heart Will Go On* and a sigh slipped past Pryce's lips. Her songs always wound him down. He turned his attention back to the night's receipts and the two wire-bound ledgers on the counter in front of him.

The front door swung open. Weak sunlight poured into the Lucky Thirteen, a welcome change from the rain of earlier in the day. Pryce didn't raise his head. He said loudly, "We're closed."

"We're not customers."

He looked up, eyes narrowed against the light that made the inside of the bar seem dark in comparison. Two men walked toward him with that arrogant chest-out attitude that screamed, "We can do whatever we want."

Cops. Of course.

Pryce checked his watch. It was way too early in the day for cops to be ruining his business, looking for underage college students or drunken troublemakers. And, these two weren't in uniform. Rather, they wore white shirts and loose ties. Cheap, rumpled jackets. Which made them detectives.

Stomach juice squirted onto the cankerous ulcer like hydrochloric acid. He flinched with pain. And, fear. The last few weeks the fear had become as unrelenting as the pain. Mostly he was afraid of Eric Dalrymple. Lately cops had started scaring him too. Every time he saw one, even a cruiser across the intersection, the vehicle turning and driving away from him, he knew—absolutely one hundred percent knew—it was going to circle back and the cops inside would bust his money-laundering carcass.

The detectives arrowed directly toward him, moving with purpose. They wore grim faces that ratcheted up Pryce's fear several notches. Up close, without the outside light shining in his eyes, he recognized both men. Skirt the edges of the law long enough and you're bound to recognize the cops, even if you don't know their names. A pudgy, going-bald Asian was in the lead by a step or two. His partner, taller by a head, sported red eyes and a red nose, all dripping in what looked like a hellish cold or brutal allergies.

Pryce closed the ledgers casually, if there was a casual way to close a couple of notebooks. He stood them up and tapped them on the bar, evening the edges. Casually. Showing the detectives he had nothing to hide. He glanced at Dallas.

She watched the detectives approach with undisguised curiosity, but she didn't stop her work. She'd already straightened the hard stuff on the shelf behind the bar so all the labels faced out. She'd restocked the beer fridges as well as the vending machine. She'd mopped the floor, humming the entire time. He shot her a hard scowl, and then he shook his head. He was all over the place. With Leo missing, along with the nut-job's money, and two serious-as-a-brain-tumor cops standing in front of him, Dallas was the last thing he needed to be thinking about.

The balding, portly Asian said, "Gaylord Pryce?"

Pryce winced and felt his neck flame red. He cut Dallas a second glance. He told everyone his name was Gene. Nobody ever called him Gene. It was always "Pryce," everybody using his last name like it was his first, so when someone called him by his real name—Gaylord—it embarrassed him for some reason. He nodded quickly and said, "That's me."

"I'm Paul Davis. Meet my partner Duncan Galloway." They both flashed their badges.

Pryce said nothing.

Davis said, "We need to have a conversation. Let's go somewhere quiet."

Pryce looked around the bar, making a big show of it, the soft-rock station hardly a distraction. Dallas had finished with the lemons. Cheerful green limes were on the cutting board now, for the occasional guy who figured he'd class up his evening in a gentleman's club sipping on a Daiquiri instead of piss-warm beer from a glass. He shrugged. "This isn't quiet enough for you, we can go into my office?"

The cops waited in silence.

Pryce guessed this was arrogant cop language for, "Let's go into the office." The mood he was in though, he wanted to hear them say the words, so he waited in silence too.

Davis finally nodded once and, with a hint of a smile, said, "The office."

Pryce swiveled, picked up his paperwork and notebooks and said, "Dallas…" He swallowed, his throat suddenly dry. "Dallas, you need anything give me a call. These fellas won't mind. They know I have a business to run." Showing her he wasn't worried about these cops and their arrogant cop attitude.

Without looking at him, she said, "Will do."

Her words were pleasant and accommodating, her voice as frosty as a February breeze off the North Atlantic. He noticed she didn't say "Sweetie" like she usually did. A strange hollow spot found a place in his belly, along with the fear and pain. She wore a red blouse today, distressed silk, maybe. Wide cuffs and collar. A white pearl necklace. And, always with the black slacks, like a uniform with her. No panty lines; something else he noticed. He wondered if that meant she wore a thong. Or, maybe she wasn't wearing panties at all. Did girls go commando? He didn't know. He wanted to rush over and apologize, let her know she looked sensational, let her know he'd been unreasonable earlier.

Behind him someone coughed impatiently. He looked over his shoulder. The cop with the Pacific Rim features stared at him, eyebrows raised expectantly. "Follow me," Pryce said. He took his time walking into the office, walking around his desk, showing them he wasn't nervous and wouldn't rush on their account. He dropped the ledgers into a drawer on top of the Glock and the roll of duct tape and the rest of the stuff cluttering his desk drawer, and he took a second or two to glower at the three-hole punch; the bottom had come off and layered the drawer with confetti. Finally, he sat down in his leather chair. When he was comfortable, with his fingers laced behind his head, he said, "What's up?"

Davis said, "Your bartender, is that all she does? She doesn't work the floor, so to speak?"

"Just a bartender."

A crooked smile crossed Davis' face. "Must sting having the hots for a lady who barely gives you the time of day, huh?"

Pryce shifted in his chair. He turned his head and stared at the framed, *Justification for Higher Education* print, all the expensive sports cars in the garage with their tail lights glowing bright red, kind of like his face, he guessed. When his embarrassment eased, he cleared his throat. "You come to talk about my bartender? That's why you're here?"

"Do you own an eighty-four Cadillac Coupe de Ville?" Davis asked, all business now.

"Yeah," Pryce answered proudly. The car was mint, a classic from the days when Detroit wasn't afraid to build a vehicle with presence. Fucking tree huggers and their Priuses.

"Do you know a Mr. Leo Jarvis?"

"Leo works for me." Pryce felt a tiny flicker of relief. Perhaps the cops were visiting him about something other than money laundering. Maybe Leo bent the Caddy. Except, detectives didn't investigate trivial stuff like car wrecks. All at once, Pryce knew what was coming—something had happened to Leo. He didn't care what. Leo always made out. What concerned him was the nut-job's money. An imminent sense of doom, like water pushing against one side of a leaky dam, filled him. "What's going on?" He barely recognized his own voice for the apprehension filling it.

"Did Mr. Jarvis have reason to be driving your car last night?"

"I loaned it to him. He had some errands to do with his girl-friend. I expected him back in time for his shift. He never showed."

Neither detective's severe expression changed. Davis said, "Mr. Jarvis is dead. He was found in a Pleasantville alley, lying beside your Cadillac. He was shot."

Pryce felt like a heavyweight contender had slugged him in the stomach. The air rushed out of his lungs. He slumped in his chair. With a guy like Leo, "hurt" happened. Fights, what-not. You didn't expect "dead." He was indomitable, a force of nature, too big and solid and reliable to be dead. Soldiers don't expect death when they head off to war, each man thinking he'd be the one who'd survive. It was the same thing with Leo. Dead was impossible.

On the other side of the desk the detectives looked at him, waiting.

Eventually Pryce said, "Are you sure?"

"Yeah. We're sure," Davis said dryly, arrogant cop attitude coming out again, the man saying without words, "We don't make mistakes."

"Yeah, you don't ever make mistakes," Pryce mumbled sarcastically. He stared into the distance feeling only shock. He pulled the plastic bottle of Pepto-Bismol out of his pocket, shook three tablets into his palm and tossed them into his mouth. He crunched them without tasting them. Leo had worked for him for years. He never got excited, never did anything except what he was told. Pryce needed something done, something legal, like, drive this poor drunk high-rolling fool back to his hotel, Leo did it. Or, if it was illegal, like pick up the nut-job's money in Philly, Leo did that too.

Pryce froze.

The nut-job's money!

For a brief moment, in his surprise at the detective's news, he'd forgotten the money. But, it all came back in rush, and all thoughts of Leo disappeared, this man he called a friend nothing but a fading ripple in a pond.

Where was nut-job's money?

Davis leaned forward in his chair, black eyes staring sharply. "Something you'd like to tell us about?"

"What?"

"Looked like something may have crossed your mind."

Pryce shook his head. "What happened?" he asked because that was the next natural question. He was thinking: *Who cares what happened? Where's the money?*

"Where were you between the hours of nine PM and two AM?"

"Here." He waved a hand around the office, gesturing vaguely toward the bar. "Lots of witnesses too." He forced himself to look directly at Davis, trying to make sure the man knew his only concern was Leo's death. He wished he'd ordered Cannelloni for lunch, instead of Chicken Caesar Salad. If lack of carbs had ruined his concentration earlier, as Dallas suggested, then he was swimming upstream now. "Ask Dallas. She'll tell you."

"Were you in the habit of loaning him your vehicle?"

"If he needed it." Pryce could see they were skeptical. He didn't care. Dalrymple told him he was sending contractors. Soon. They'd want to be paid, and he didn't have their money. Suddenly, Pryce was sick to his stomach and it had nothing to do with his diet or his ulcer. He'd lose his bar. That was certain. Dalrymple would take all his savings, all his equity and when he came up short, the nut-job would need to send a message. That's when the ball peen hammer would come out.

Or worse.

Probably worse.

The cops asked a few more questions. Pryce answered automatically. He wasn't paying much attention and maybe they realized they'd have to come back later, after he'd come to grips with the death of his dependable employee and loyal friend because Paul Davis finally said, "We're not done, Pryce. Don't be taking any trips."

Pryce said, "You decide to come back, make it before five PM. You're hard on business." Guilty of something or not, a quarter of the crowd in the Lucky Thirteen made themselves scarce when cops arrived.

Davis and Galloway stood. Davis said, "Before five o'clock, Pryce? Should we put the investigation on hold until it's convenient for you?"

Pryce gave him a flat look.

"By the way, doesn't Dwayne Currie hang out with Leo? Any idea where we'd find him?"

"I don't know where that moron is."

"Were they together last night?"

"How would I know?" Pryce lied. Of course they were together. They were always together, like rum and Coke, those two.

"You see him, let him know we're interested in having a conversation with him."

"Yeah, sure," Pryce answered. *After I talk to him first.* He walked the detectives out the front door. Then he looked at Dallas.

Surprise, surprise. She ignored him. He didn't think it was possible to feel any worse. Remarkably, he did. He walked into his office, and as he closed the door she called after him, "Was that about Leo and Dwayne?"

He said, "Have you heard from them? What do you know?"

"Nothing. I haven't seen either of them. Not last night. Not this morning. So, it just makes sense." Long pause. "Doesn't it, Gaylord?"

Feeling far older than his forty-six years, Pryce pushed the door of his office shut with the tips of his fingers.

Where was the money?

Where was Semi-Gloss?

He wondered, could Dwayne have popped Leo and scampered with the cash? Pryce didn't think so. Semi-Gloss was loyal, not to him but to Leo, Leo the only person Semi called a friend, as far as Pryce knew.

For the first time ever, Pryce wanted to see Semi-Gloss, the moron the only person who might know where the cash was. The only person who might be able to save him from the nut-job.

CHAPTER 39

BERNARD TUGGED THE curtain back with two fingers and studied the Good Knight Inn's parking lot through the narrow gap. Nothing out there yet. But soon. Soon the waiting would end and he'd leave Atlantic City. He only had one idea. One plan. His entire escape hinged on it. The idea was solid—for a person familiar with action and violence. Unfortunately, Bernard considered himself more of a thinker. His nerves were jumping and his breath was coming in anxious little pants he couldn't control. Every move came in erratic stop-starts. He used to be good at waiting. It was a handy skill, a huge part of a salesman's life, but the ability had deserted him, along with his wife, career, and colleagues. He swiped sweaty palms, one after the other, on the bath towel draped over his shoulder.

His edginess made him curious. Did a professional's nerves jump like this before the big hit, or the big shootout, or the big whatever? Did nerves make a professional feel like he was bulletproof while simultaneously making him feel like he had a death wish?

He decided "professional" was an overused word. Outside of a movie or novel, was there such a thing as a professional criminal, an individual who made massive scores using technology the average person didn't know existed, all the while maintaining an icy, sociopathic control?

The answer was, "No." Of course there wasn't. Which meant there were no super cops either. There were only people, some of whom walked to the left of the invisible line and some who walked to the right. Acceptable and unacceptable. Bad and good. Today he was "bad" because he shot and killed a waste-of-oxygen bouncer. Two days ago, he was "good" because he hadn't yet stepped over the line and turned desire into action.

He scanned the room, trying to decide if he'd thought of everything. His suitcase was lined up with the door, several feet inside the room. With the door open, it would be easy to see from the exterior. His fingerprints were all over the room of course, but they didn't concern him. The cops had his description. That made fingerprints irrelevant. He was trying to escape. Not disappear. Disappearing was impossible, at least in the short term.

He heard the sound of a car's engine and peeked between the curtains. A dusty yellow taxi with a black and white checkerboard pattern on its door, pulled into the parking lot. Bernard's breath hitched. He tightened his hands into fists, forcing them to stop trembling. He picked up the revolver and pushed it into the waistband of his pants at the small of his back, once again silently thanking Good Luck for finding it in the Oasis.

The cab driver performed a three-point turn and backed in. A flare of sunlight bounced off the rear window. The tires bumped against the curb and the car came to a halt. The horn tooted and the trunk lid bobbed open.

Bernard waited.

A moment later the driver's door opened. The cabby stood with a contented expression on his face. With his fists planted in the small of his back, he stretched. He let his gaze roam across the parking lot, and then sent a glance up at the drying sky. He smiled.

Bernard waited.

The cabby's face was redder than typical. He wore wire-framed glasses. His salt and pepper hair was cut conservatively, in a style similar to Bernard's. All of which made him appear aged but not old, Bernard decided. Which was good, considering what he had in mind. Unfortunately, the man also looked like an American, which was definitely not good. Getting violent with a foreigner was much easier than with a native. Even worse, the cabby was clearly enjoying the day, and Bernard was going to put an end to that in a hurry. He felt bad about it. Maybe, with any kind of luck, when the guy opened his mouth, a barely understandable Eastern European accent would spill out and wash away his guilt.

Bernard waited.

Still with the unconcerned look, the driver ambled toward Bernard's room.

When he was five or six steps away, Bernard flung the door open. He rubbed his hair with the towel as though he was drying it, hopefully giving the cabby the impression he was running late. And, perhaps the towel would act like a partial disguise, in case the driver had seen him on the morning news while he scarfed down his Cheerios.

"Grab my suitcase, would you?" Bernard said. "I'll be right there."

The cabby nodded cordially. "Sure thing, buddy."

American through and through. Bostonian from the sound of it. Guilt twisted Bernard's stomach. He ignored it. "Thanks. I'm running late. I got a four o'clock flight out of Philly. I'll be right with you."

The amiable look turned into a great big smile, as Bernard knew it would. No taxi cab driver on the planet can resist the long trip. The big fare. Especially in Atlantic City when they typically earned a flat rate all over town.

Bernard pulled back into the room, out of the driver's sight. He dropped the towel. He snaked the revolver out of his pants, thumbed the hammer back and held the weapon out at arm's length. The cabby walked into the room, paused long enough to glance around, like everybody does when they enter a strange room, and looked directly into the barrel twelve inches away from his head.

His red face blanched. His eyes, behind the wire-rimmed glasses, widened in alarm. A moment later the apprehension faded. He cocked his head and stared at Bernard with a hard, analytical look.

Bernard instantly warned himself to be cautious. He wasn't dealing with a simple cab driver. The guy had acted concerned for less than a second. One thing Bernard could do was read body language. It was a salesman's bread and butter. He could see the cabby sorting it out, figuring out how to best extricate himself from the situation. Bernard didn't allow the revolver to wobble. "Move and I shoot."

The cabby remained motionless.

"I'm desperate," Bernard said. "I'm nervous. I don't have a single thing to lose. You understand?"

The driver nodded.

"You got kids?"

The driver nodded a second time.

"You recognize me from the morning news?"

Once more, the driver nodded.

"TV gets things wrong all the time. They omit details. Like the report I saw? The anchor said I was armed and dangerous. But, she didn't say anything about *me*. She didn't say anything about how I keep my promises." He thought about what he'd say next. He shrugged. "Maybe I am dangerous. I don't know. One thing for sure, I'm not dangerous to you or your children. Do exactly what I say and I promise you'll walk away from this. Understand?"

"Yes." The driver stared past the revolver like it wasn't there, stared into Bernard's eyes, acting far more composed than Bernard felt.

Bernard admired him. At the same time a second ripple of unease shivered up his spine. What had he done? Gone and stuffed a revolver in a professional's face, one of those professionals he didn't think existed? Was this guy an ex-soldier, or a cop? Someone who'd grab the revolver out of his hand and beat him senseless with it, if he let his guard down for a fraction of a second? Bernard took two steps backward, determined to maintain the slim advantage he had. "You do anything other than what I say and I'll pull the trigger. You'll be dead. Your kids won't have a father. Me? I'll be in the exact same position I was before you showed up. Understand?"

"Yeah." The man's voice was tight and strained but it didn't waver.

"Lay down on your stomach in front of the television."

The cabby said, "You're making a mistake." He dropped to his knees, and then lay down. His palms were flat on the floor near his shoulders, the tips of his toes dug into the carpet. His entire body vibrated with suppressed tension.

"Won't be the first," Bernard said, looking at his prisoner while sudden fingers of white-hot anger seared through him. "Fact is, I make 'em all the time." He kicked the door and it crashed shut with a bang. He said harshly, "But it's not me making the mistake right now." The cabby may have been a Navy Seal, something like that in a previous life, but Bernard was the one with the weapon, therefore he was the one commanding respect and as usual, not getting it. "I thought you had kids."

"I do."

"Then start acting like a responsible parent. You stretch your arms out as far as they go. Quit thinking about pushing yourself off the floor the moment I get close. Lying there spring loaded."

The driver visibly uncoiled. Bernard knelt near his feet. Down low near the floor, the carpet's smells were more obvious—cigarette smoke, dust, dirt, an artificial wild flower scent designed to hide the other odors. "Everybody wants to push me. You. Emma. I told her, I promised I wouldn't hurt her. All she had to do was be quiet. Same with that idiot bouncer. I told him to stay back."

Working fast, he tied the driver's legs together at the ankles, binding them securely with the rope that pulled the curtains open and closed. "Well, I'm done. The bouncer was the last guy who pushed me."

The cabby grunted in pain when the rope tightened around his feet. "Sorry about that," Bernard said sincerely. When he was done with the driver's feet he tied his hands together behind his back. Then he tied the man's arms and legs together too, so no matter which direction he moved, he was either yanking his arms painfully backward, or his feet unnaturally close to his shoulders.

"Only two reasons you're not dead for pushing me just then, for thinking about jumping me." Bernard shoved himself to his feet with a grunt. He stuck the revolver back in his pants and then smacked his hands together to brush away the grime. "You're an American, and I feel bad about ruining your day. It looked like you were enjoying it."

"I was."

Bernard grabbed a face cloth from the bathroom. "Open wide." When the driver did, Bernard stuffed the cloth into his mouth. Remembering how Emma spit out her gag, he used another small piece of rope to tie the washcloth in place, cinching it tight with a knot at the back of the driver's head.

There was a second muffled grunt.

"You'll be okay," Bernard said. "The cleaners will come by soon." He wasn't being one hundred percent accurate. He'd paid for two nights but only stayed one. With the Do Not Disturb sign hanging on the door, housekeeping wouldn't check the room for another twenty-four hours. At least. The cabby was going to be real uncomfortable by that time. But, he'd be alive and Bernard figured that meant he'd kept his promise.

With his overnight bag in one hand and the Do Not Disturb sign and laptop in the other, he backed out of the room. He dropped the sign over the knob and the room key in a garbage can. With a smile on his face he climbed into the taxi.

A taxi was unobtrusive. Practically invisible. He figured he'd bought himself a good chunk of time. Maybe an extra couple of hours. Maybe more. He tossed his computer and suitcase on the back seat and pulled out of the motel parking lot. The dashboard clock read eleven-thirty-five. Five minutes later he picked up the Atlantic City Expressway heading west.

Hopefully there'd be no roadblocks at the toll stations. If the road was clear he'd be in Philadelphia within ninety minutes. He could dump the cab in a shopping center parking lot, or at the airport, or he could do something pursuers wouldn't expect and press on, get off the interstate and leave the car in some little berg like Claymont or Havertown. Decide where to go from there. The cash he stole from Emma would be enough to pay for a long-distance bus ticket. When he needed more money, he had the revolver. There were options. As long as he avoided the cops until he was well away from Atlantic City, he'd be fine. If nothing unexpected happened...

He scanned the dashboard and frowned. The gas tank was only a quarter full. The frown turned into a muttered curse and he thumped the steering wheel with his fist. He didn't know how far a quarter tank would take him but if he wanted to keep all those options open, he was going to have to stop for gasoline.

CHAPTER 40

BY ELEVEN-FIFTY IN the morning Melissa Bremmer was on the east side of Philadelphia, speeding past various billboards lining the Atlantic City Expressway, signs advertising the loosest slots and the cheapest buffets on the Boardwalk. The mutant rain, which seemed to peak the previous evening when she drove home from the Richmond airport, had backed off as afternoon drew closer. Warm spears of sunlight stabbed holes in the clouds, brightening the day.

Except for her first and only rest stop, and the hour it took to pass through Philly—which Mel figured would have been unpleasant for anyone, recovering agoraphobic or not—the road trip was uneventful. But, now the work was about to start, the reason she came. It was time to find Jordon.

She slowed, signaled and pulled in and parked beside a row of gas pumps at an Expressway Quicky-Mart. She shut off the car. A minute or two later a service station attendant wandered out of the convenience store, a young East Indian wearing droopy jeans, a ring through his eyebrow, and a Mets baseball cap with a flat brim and a gold authenticity sticker.

She hit the window Down button. A third of the glass slid into the door.

The young man asked, "Help you?"

She said through the slim opening, "Twenty on my card." She hoped one day she could fill the tank without wondering if her Visa would carry the weight.

He nodded. "Sure thing," he said, with an easy smile and a care-free tone.

Somehow, he made Mel think life was simple. Enjoy the day and don't worry too much about anything else. She knew better but it was nice to interact with someone who didn't have too many cares or concerns.

While he filled the car, she scanned the parking lot. A telephone booth stood near one corner of the convenience store. A thick phone book dangled on a chrome cord beneath the telephone. She nodded. Good. Not too many places had phone books anymore, but for lack of a better idea, she thought the Yellow Pages was a good place to start her search.

A few minutes later the attendant presented her with a little plastic tray and a credit card receipt. She signed, handed it back and then drove around the store, parking as close to the phone booth as she could manage. She reached for the door handle. Her hand froze in midair. The car was secure. The outside world was not. Anything could happen out there, anything at all.

Of course anything *could* happen, but what *will* happen?

The answer was, nothing. Nothing will happen, just like nothing happened at the truck stop. So what she dropped some change, knocked some candies out of a dish? That sort of thing happened every day. It happened to everybody. Nobody cared.

She stared at the phone booth not entirely convinced.

Maybe, if she got out of the Mazda just long enough to look up the numbers, she could write them down quickly and use her cell phone from the relative safety of the car. She could worry about the long-distance charges another day. They'd add up quickly and she and Jordon didn't have much extra cash, but she liked the idea. It seemed the safest choice.

She unzipped her handbag, looking for a pen and a scrap of paper. The SIG 232 sat near the top of the bag. Would she need it? She'd only be out of the car, sixty seconds—there couldn't be too many hospitals in Atlantic City. She stroked a finger back and forth across the satiny black metal. How could something so beautiful be so lethal? The proprietor at Point Blank told her when she bought the pistol that deciding when to shoot and when not to was the biggest dilemma most people faced. Shoot too fast, without due consideration, and you kill a kindly Good Samaritan, someone in a Richmond parking garage for example, who didn't want to see her become a hood ornament.

"The thing is," the salesman added, his eyes wildly alive behind his round, John Lennon glasses, "Girls tend to err the other way." He knew. He specialized in "Guns for Girls," according to the sign on his front door. "Lots of women buy a weapon for self-defense. Time comes, they don't shoot," he said.

If that was true, Mel thought he needed to advertise a little differently: "Weapons for Women," the title sounding stronger, a little less cute and a little more assertive. Maybe it would put those who were hesitant to squeeze the trigger on the right path immediately.

Twelve feet from the car to the phone booth, with nobody but her in the Quicky-Mart parking lot, and thinking about the fellow in the Richmond airport with the alarming forest of ear and nose hair, Mel decided to leave the SIG in the glove box.

What about the pepper spray?

If she didn't need her pistol, she didn't need the spray. Without really thinking about it, she pocketed it anyway. Leaving the SIG behind was a huge step. Leaving the pepper spray behind was a leap she wasn't ready to take. The personal alarm wasn't even a question. She looped the cord around her wrist, confident that 130 decibels would scare most potential assailants away.

She tucked some stray hair behind her ears and tugged down

the beak of her cap. "The Lord hates a coward," she muttered under her breath. In a single, coordinated rush, like she wasn't certain she could do it if she waited any longer, she opened the Mazda's door and climbed out.

The Yellow Pages had seen better days. The frayed edges of the book were uneven. The front cover was missing, as was the entire hotel listing. Feeling unreasonably guilty, she tore out the single page that named all the local hospitals. Much faster than pen and paper, she reasoned, and the book was ruined long before she arrived in town. After another quick glance across the empty parking lot, the pressure to rush back to the Mazda eased. She scanned the page. There were some specialty hospitals listed—an eye hospital and a children's care hospital—that sort of thing, as well as facilities in Philadelphia. She ignored all those, hoping her search would begin and end in Atlantic City.

When she was securely locked in the Mazda once again, she flipped open her cell phone.

It was dead.

"Crap," she swore loudly. She hadn't plugged it in after coming home from the airport the previous night, one too many distractions on her mind and she'd forgotten all about it. She stared out the window, flipping the useless phone end-over-end in her hand. Traffic zipped by in both directions. In a state with eight million people, she was essentially alone. It was a strangely calming thought. A dusty yellow taxi cab with a black and white checker pattern on the door turned off the Expressway and parked beside the pumps. Mel paid very little attention to it. The taxi was a long way away—on the other side of the parking lot—and taxis were everywhere, so common they were almost invisible. She tapped the useless cell phone against her lips. As much as she didn't like the idea, the easiest, fastest choice seemed to be the phone booth she was parked beside.

She dug around in her handbag and found some quarters.

Then, she talked herself into getting out of the car a second time, this conversation much shorter with experience on her side. She made her first call to the Atlantic City Medical Center. When someone answered, a little flare of excitement tingled in her stomach. She didn't know why. Maybe because it felt like she was making progress. It disappeared when the receptionist told her that nobody named Jordon Cutler was checked into their facility.

She tried a second hospital. Struck out.

Tried a third and struck out again.

On her fourth call, she took an excursion into voice mail hell, had to hang up, re-dial and run through the entire procedure once more.

Over by the gas pumps the service station attendant with the Mets cap passed the driver's change through the taxi's open window. He ambled back into the convenience store, hiking his saggy pants up with one hand and a flick of his hip.

Mel's fifth call was to the Shore Memorial Hospital. When someone answered, she said, "Hello. My name is Melissa Bremmer. I'm looking for my husband. Who do I talk to, to find out if he was admitted as a patient in the last forty-eight hours?"

"That would be me."

"His name is Jordon. Jordon Cutler."

"Please hold." Before Mel could object the voice was replaced with a woodwind rendition of *Penny Lane*. Mel shook her head and pressed her lips together. She leaned on the glass wall of the booth. Her arms were crossed, the phone tucked between her shoulder and cheek. She hummed *Penny Lane* along with the Muzak because once that tune was in a person's head it was impossible to ignore.

The fellow driving the taxi cab climbed out of the car. He was tall. Skinny. His black hair glistened as though heavy with oil. He slammed the door shut with a vicious swing of his arm and stormed toward the Quicky-Mart, giving a sign a solid, ringing smack as he strode past it. The butt of his pants shone as he moved, some kind of cheap, aged polyester, Mel guessed. She kept a wary eye on him, making sure he didn't deviate left or right or alter course in her direction.

"Hello?" The receptionist on the other end of the phone said, "What did you say the name was?"

"Jordon Cutler. My husband. My name is Melissa Bremmer."

"Mr. Cutler was admitted this morning at approximately three AM."

Mel sagged against the booth, unable to contain a whimper of dread. Her breath came quickly and her muscles seized with tension.

The receptionist said, "Ma'am? Ma'am, are you still there?"

Mel struggled to regain her composure. "Yes," she said finally, her voice as thin as early morning mist. "I'm here."

"Is there anything else?"

Mel forced the fear into the bottom of her belly, holding it at bay and allowed the good news to carry her. She'd found him. That was the important thing. Anything else she could deal with in due time. "How is he? Is he hurt? I mean seriously? What happened?"

"Privacy forbids me from saying, ma'am. I can tell you that Mr. Cutler is not in danger and is resting comfortably."

Her relief was palpable. In a firmer voice, she said, "Can you transfer this call to his room?"

"No. I'm sorry. There's no phone in that room."

"Oh." Mel hesitated. "Can you give him a message, then? Please tell him not to go anywhere. His wife will be there within the hour!"

CHAPTER 41

PARKED BESIDE THE pumps, at the mercy of the adolescent half-wit who couldn't get a job anywhere else, Bernard seethed. His stomach churned and his tongue tasted like wet flannel. The MGD hair-of-the-dog was wearing off, leaving him irritable and impatient.

As close to Atlantic City as it was, most people blew right past the Quicky-Mart, anxious to get to the pot of gold at the end of the rainbow. Or, if they were like him, they were done with the city and unwilling to stop until they were in Philly. Except for a shabby green Mazda parked near the corner of the store, its sporty blonde owner making a call from the phone booth, there were no other customers in the parking lot. So, there was no reason, no reason at all, for the young pump jockey to take this long making change. Time was a commodity Bernard no longer had. Waiting this long was nonsense, especially when the till figured out the change automatically. Type "fifty" into the machine and it did the rest. No math skills required.

Movement in the rearview mirror caught his eye and he looked up in time to see the glass door swing open and the pump jockey push through. Unbidden, a small smile of relief touched the corner of Bernard's mouth.

Finally!

The kid sauntered along like he had all the time in the world, his green and orange Quicky-Mart shirt un-tucked, his over-sized jeans hanging low, cuffs dragging on the ground. When he finally reached the taxicab, Bernard barked, "What took so long?" He snatched the change out of the teen's hand. The kid gave him a slight shrug and a bemused sort of look, and then he strolled away without a word, hiking one corner of his pants up with a lazy hand and a flick of his hips.

Bernard shook his head. He was fairly certain the sideways Mets cap wasn't part of the kid's official Quicky-Mart uniform. The thing with young people these days, their parents were always patting them on the head, telling them it wasn't their fault instead of giving them a hard boot in the ass and instilling some responsibility. A guy didn't have to look too far to figure out why every twenty-something on the planet was lazy, sloppy, and stupid. He straightened his leg and stuffed the coins into his pants pocket. Quickly and unconsciously he organized the bills, small stuff to the front, bigger to the back, automatically counting as he did.

He frowned. Recounted.

He gave the kid a fifty-dollar bill. The gasoline, the coins in his pocket and the bills in his hand, added up to forty dollars. The young man had short-changed him ten bucks. Insignificant maybe, but all thoughts of restraint and consequences had disappeared when the circuit breaker in his head snapped. Propelled by urgency, a gut-wrenching hangover, and his earlier promise that he was done letting adolescents, women, peers, bosses, and foreigners screw him over, Bernard pulled the nickel-plated .38 out of the glove box.

He scrambled out of the taxicab. With the revolver stuffed in the waistband of his pants he strode toward the convenience store, giving the sign, "New Jersey State Law Prohibits Self-Serve," a hard smack along the way. He pushed inside. The glass door swished lazily closed behind him. Welcome bells tinkled somewhere above his head. The revolver in his waistband was hard and uncomfortable but it gave him confidence to go with the cold crimson rage surging out of every pore.

The kid sat behind the cash counter reading a *USA Today*. A radio played in the background, someone talking about the weather and hurricane Wilfred's effect on the Carolinas.

Bernard stared at the backside of the newspaper.

The kid ignored him.

Bernard cleared his throat.

The paper dipped. The pump jockey peered at him, the gold ring in one raised eyebrow almost touching the flat brim of his cap.

"You gave me the wrong change."

The kid slowly shook the paper, folded it neatly in half and placed it on the counter. "I apologize." He twisted around on his stool and scanned the register. "Twenty-eight-seventy-nine, huh? You gave me what? Forty?"

Bernard scowled at the sing-song accent. "Fifty." His voice was strained but he was oddly pleased with himself for not leaping over the counter and throttling the young man.

The kid tapped a button on the cash register and the till dinged and the drawer banged open. Bernard saw a neat row of cash, ones through twenties. There was more money in the till than in his pockets. He didn't see a fifty but he knew the bigger bills normally got stuck beneath the twenties.

"You sure you gave me fifty?"

More than anything it was the accent. And, the kid's tone. Sort of superior, saying, "I'm smarter than you," without speaking the words. Saying: *I work here. I'd know if I gave you the wrong change.* "I'm sure." Bernard reached behind him and pulled the nickel-plate out of his waistband. He pointed it at the kid's face. "Empty it. All of it," talking fast now, his breath shallow as the adrenaline hit him.

The kid's eyes widened, all white in his dark face.

"*Hablar* English?" Which made no sense because the kid was East Indian not Spanish and Bernard didn't like either nationality, but the phrasing just popped out. He said, "Come on. Let's go."

The kid reached into the till with fumbling fingers. He found the bills and pulled out the money, his eyes never leaving the revolver.

Bernard's gaze darted around the convenience store. Nobody had wandered out of the restroom. He didn't see anyone else in the store, no other clerks hiding down one of the aisles. Other than his stolen yellow taxicab, there were no other cars parked at the pumps. Everything looked good. "Hurry up. Give it to me."

The kid handed over the cash.

Bernard seized it. He backed toward the door. "How much money you make?"

"What?"

Bernard glanced over his shoulder. Still nobody coming, so he looked back at the wide-eyed kid no more than eighteen years old, stared him right in the eye, and said, "That was a simple question. Foreigners like you, you're the reason I don't have a job."

He pulled the trigger.

The revolver boomed. The re-coil flicked his arm up, the barrel pointing at the ceiling. The young man flew straight off his chair into a shelf of tobacco and cigarettes. His Mets cap toppled off his head, hit his shoulder and dropped to the floor. He slid down the wall, dragging packages with him, leaving a bloody smear on cartons that remained on the shelves. He had an astonished look on his face.

Stuffing the cash in his pocket, Bernard backed out of the store. The welcome bells chimed cheerily. He swiveled and bolted for the taxi, the revolver dangling in his hand. The hangover was gone. He didn't feel like he was going to puke all over his shoes like the previous night when he shot the bouncer. In fact, he felt phenomenal. Shooting the pump jockey was like kicking someone's headlights in after he honked at you in traffic. What a guy had to do. And, putting a bouncer out of his misery made the planet a better place for everyone, never mind it was pure self-preservation, like if a lion was charging him.

He was unstoppable. Invincible. He was smiling like a crazy man. He couldn't help it. There was no way the cops—

He caught a flicker of motion out the corner of his right eye. A brief glance and he saw the phone booth, the receiver hanging straight down swinging on the cord, the sporty blonde he noticed earlier bounding for her Mazda, her ponytail bouncing off her back.

Bernard swore. He'd completely forgotten her. His euphoric feeling instantly dissolved. Panic now. Every mistake and potential problem leapt to the front of his mind.

Like…there was probably a security camera inside the Quicky-Mart, the entire incident on tape. And, what if the kid lived? What about the cab driver he'd hog-tied in the Good Knight Inn? Sparkle-girl-Shari and Emma? The peeler? What was her name? Misty! She'd remember him, no question. What was he thinking, he'd escape problem free? He didn't have a hope. He couldn't run. He couldn't hide. There were exactly two bullets left in the revolver so he couldn't even shoot it out like Butch Cassidy and the Sundance Kid.

Right then Bernard's initial plan—drive to Philadelphia and dump the cab in a parking lot—evolved. Getting as far as Philly and disappearing wasn't going to happen without some negotiating power, some way of ensuring the cops wouldn't put him down like a pig in a slaughterhouse, if and when they caught up with him.

He skidded to a halt. Spinning on his heel, he raced for the blonde, bringing the revolver up as he did. "Don't move," he yelled. She didn't listen. She reefed on the Mazda's door handle. It didn't open. Her hand disappeared into a coat pocket, looking for keys, Bernard assumed.

He was wrong.

An ear-splitting siren went off, the eye-watering sound blaring from her pocket so loudly it filled the parking lot. It startled him. His step broke. He flinched and his hands flew to his ears. The blonde had her car door open now, was reaching across the seat going for the glove box. The siren was so incredibly loud it made thinking difficult. For a second he couldn't decide. Grab her, siren and all, or leave without her?

He needed negotiating power, a bargaining chip. And, he wasn't sure if she'd seen anything significant but there was no way he was leaving a potential witness behind.

He grabbed her ponytail, yanking her backward out of the Mazda. She yelped in surprise. The first few steps he took, dragging her toward the taxicab were easy, maybe because she was shocked and unbalanced.

She got over it in half a second.

Her fists flew. Her delicate features were twisted, her mouth wide open in what Bernard could only guess was a feral scream, but the siren was so loud he couldn't hear her. He moved fast, keeping her at arm's length dragging her with his fist wrapped around her ponytail.

She must have realized digging in her heels kept him out of range. Her struggles ceased. She took two steps toward him and then she was swinging again. One fist slammed into the point of his nose.

His eyes filled with water. He swore loudly. The hangover rushed back and his stomach boiled. The siren's sound hurt like a needle through his eardrum. He had to get rid of the horrendous noise. He jerked the blonde toward him. She staggered. He kept one hand in her ponytail and he wrapped his free arm, revolver in hand, around her, pinning her arms to her sides. Then he let go of her hair, found the siren in her pocket and hurled it away.

She fought like a caged animal, managing to free an arm. Her hand disappeared into the opposite pocket. When it reappeared, Bernard recognized the spray can pointed at his face. Mace! Or pepper spray! Like what he used on the security guard. If he hadn't seen the same thing the previous night in the Oasis, he wouldn't have known what he was looking at until it was too late.

She depressed the trigger at the same second as he swatted her arm to the side. The can went flying and the spray in the air missed his eyes. He cursed his usual atrocious luck, first with the cab driver at the hotel, the man an ex-soldier or whatever, and now this armed-to-the-teeth woman carrying on like a Samurai warrior, everybody he ran into doing their level best to slow him down, make his life difficult.

He let her go. In the split second of bewilderment before she realized she was free, he wound up and slugged her in the stomach. The breath rushed out of her mouth in a noisy hiss. She doubled over coughing, both arms wrapped across her belly. Drooling, she dropped to her knees, body convulsing for air.

Bernard moved fast, giving her no time recover. He scooped her into his arms—she was so tiny it wasn't much of an effort—and plunked her on the passenger seat of the taxicab. He rounded the vehicle in a rush, slid into the driver's seat and seconds later slammed his foot on the gas pedal, the blonde still coughing and spluttering. The tires squealed. The sedan shot out of the Quicky-Mart parking lot onto the Atlantic City Expressway.

His eyes found the rearview mirror. There were no flashing lights behind him. Relieved, he settled into the seat. He was covered in sweat. He slicked his hair back on the top and sides then, with a scowl, wiped the Brylcreem residue on his trousers.

The blonde stared at him out of moist eyes.

He looked at her. "What?"

No answer.

"Put your seatbelt on," he said, talking fast and loud, the adrenaline pumping, his ears ringing from the siren's unbelievable noise. "Don't need you jumping out the moment I stop."

She stared at him. She didn't move. Didn't say a word.

He pointed the nickel-plate at her. "Put it on."

She nodded slightly. She pulled the seatbelt across her chest and clicked it in place. She said softly, her tone distant like she wasn't really in the car with him, "I can't do it, I can't do it, I can't do it. Not again."

"What?" he said, decided it didn't really matter and asked, "You wanna know what's going on, I guess?" He didn't wait for an answer. "We're going to Philly. Or maybe Baltimore, I don't know which. If the cops stop us, you're my insurance. Understand? We get there, I'll go my way. You go yours." He hiked his shoulders, letting her know his plans were fluid and all she had to do was go with them and everything would turn out fine.

She just looked at him.

"Since we're going be spending some time together, my name is Bernard Hewitt. What's yours?"

She said nothing.

"You want, I can call you Pony."

She said nothing but now her expression was confused.

"On account of your ponytail." He thought he was being clever.

She gave him the same slight nod as a few moments before. "Mel."

"Melanie? Melinda? What? It's not Melvin, is it? You don't look like a plumber."

"What's a plumber look like?"

That stumped for a second but he shook it off and said, "All right. Pony it is," heavy emphasis on her new nickname. He drove in silence and thought hard. The thing was, he couldn't just let her go. So, what he'd do, he'd let her think she'd get out of this, even go so far as to allow her out of the car. He'd shoot her then, when she didn't expect it. Keep the blood off the upholstery. Going down for three homicides was no different than going down for two.

He'd hide her body in the trunk. Then back to the original plan—park the car in an airport tow-away zone and leave it there with the four-ways blinking. He'd walk to the opposite end of the terminal building and get on one of the downtown express busses. Casual as can be. It usually didn't take any more than ten minutes in a tow-away zone before the on-call truck hooked up and dragged the offending car away. Without the car, or the witness, the cops wouldn't know where to start searching for him.

He glanced at her. Too bad for Melanie or Melinda or whoever...Pony. She smelled nice, like wild flowers. And, she was cute. Tiny and compact. Petite was how the French would have described her. The French with their pretentious way of making ordinary things sound alluring. *Café Au Lait?* What was so exotic about milky coffee?

Too bad, he thought again. *Wrong place, wrong time.* Very unfortunate for Pony.

CHAPTER 42

THE YOUNG EAST Indian gas station attendant sat on the floor, propped against the lower shelves behind the cash counter. He pushed his Quicky-Mart shirt into the bullet hole with gentle pressure, wincing and grinding his teeth as he did. The unnatural orange polyester slowly turned rusty. He twisted around on the floor until he was on his knees and shuffled to the phone beneath the counter, jaw clenched the entire distance. He wiped his arm across his forehead clearing the sweat from his eyes. Through the store window he watched the guy who shot him drag a diminutive blonde into a dirty yellow taxicab. She fought him every step of the way. He hoped she didn't get herself shot too, the way she was struggling.

He picked up the phone and dialed.

Someone answered after the second ring. "911. What is your emergency?"

The kid's wound was a scarlet curtain of pain. He said, "I've been shot."

CHAPTER 43

BEFORE BUYING HER SIG in Point Blank, Melissa considered a revolver similar to the one Bernard Hewitt was pointing at her. But, the .38 seemed like a "street" gun to her, something punks or hoodlums carried. It was bulky. The SIG's slim profile and ergonomic grips had cachet, like Victoria's Secret lingerie or Steve Madden shoes. With its smooth contours and rounded, snag-free edges, it tucked nicely into her handbag. It fit.

The salesman with John Lennon glasses had hiked his shoulders at that point. "Sometimes that's what it comes to," he said reasonably. "You're slappin' down a lotta cake. In the end, it's gotta be comfortable." His smile was huge. "And, it never hurts having seven rounds instead of only six, does it?"

Mel looked at him, the man standing there in a washed-too-many-times T-shirt sporting the message, *They Can Take My Gun When They Pry it From My Cold Dead Fingers* and she thought, *put it like that, how can I not agree?*

Not that one extra bullet mattered in her present situation.

The revolver on the seat between Hewitt's knees was just as cold, lethal, and impartial as her SIG. He shot the Quicky-Mart clerk with that revolver. The boy was dead as far as Mel knew, and that didn't make any sense, killing somebody who seemed happy making five dollars an hour at a highway gas station. He probably had parents who were proud of him. A girlfriend too, someone who thought he was handsome in his droopy pants and silly flat-brimmed baseball cap. Someone he held hands with and strolled the boardwalk, or took to a concert using the money he made in the Quicky-Mart. Mel's heart hurt for the boy's parents, and for his girlfriend. She knew what it was like to have her life changed in such a vast and fundamental way. The corners of her eyes prickled with tears and she felt her chin tremble.

The speedometer nudged seventy. The tires droned. A small, rhythmic vibration thrummed through the car. She snuck a sideways glance at her captor. His mouth was a thin, rigid line, his jaw set hard in concentration. His eyes shifted between the road and the rearview mirror like the second hand on a stopwatch. Desperation and panic surrounded him like a cloud. She wondered, what else had he done? After the fight in the parking lot he told her, "I'll go my way. You go yours," and then shrugged casually, trying to sell the idea. Looking at him now Mel knew—absolutely knew—that she wasn't just along for the ride. This fresh nightmare might end in Baltimore or Philly but not in the manner he described. He wouldn't allow her to walk away.

The Black Monster came alive and screamed hysterical laughter at her and told her it was all over, there was nothing she could do. The sixteen months she'd lost to convalescence and psychotherapy sessions had been a waste of her time, her friends and family's time, and a waste of Jordon's time. A wave of sadness washed over her. Tears fell soundlessly. She didn't wipe them away.

Then, in a whisper, something else spoke to her, a voice that had been mostly silent these last sixteen months, a voice that a day ago might have remained silent. It asked, "Are you sure there's nothing?"

The speedometer touched eighty.

Jordon would have asked a similar question in his exasperatingly logical voice, "What are you going to do?" Sometimes she hated that voice. Hated the infuriating calmness of it, and the logic that always surrounded it, Jordon always so clinical. More than once she yelled at him, "Quit trying to help." At the same time, she loved that voice because it was the essence of him. Steady and dependable. For a long time, he was the only thing she could cling to, and he always dropped his tools if he was puttering on his boat, or turned off his computer if he was doing business, and held her tightly in both arms, and helped her find a better, warmer place.

In the back of her mind he asked, "What are you going to do?"

Then the whispered voice spoke up a second time, and it was subtler than Jordon and it said, "You've come so far. It seems a shame to give up. Are you certain there's nothing you can do?"

"Am I certain?" she mumbled.

"You say something?"

Bernard's voice was like a hook behind the belly button, jerking her into the present. She shot him a flat stare and didn't bother answering. A trickle of blood had dripped from his nose and dried on his upper lip.

What could she do? There had to be something. Fear, anxiety, and passivity were the old Mel. Hadn't she left the house and parked in a covered parking facility? Hadn't she driven six hours in mutant rain? Hadn't she walked into a highway truck stop, for heaven's sake?

She flexed her fingers and winced at the pain—her hand ached—but it was a good ache and her only regret was not slugging Hewitt twice. She wished she'd put the SIG in her handbag. It was no good in the Mazda's glove box. From this day forward the handgun was going in her pocket, although she acknowledged once again, that the pistol would have been virtually useless in her present situation. She'd use it to defend herself but she couldn't put the muzzle against Hewitt's temple and assassinate him. The way he was driving, close to one hundred miles an hour now, they'd be in a car crash long before they were in a gunfight.

She thought hard. Somehow, she liked the car crash idea. Traffic would stop. Police and ambulances would arrive. If she walked away from the wreck, she'd have escaped a kidnapping crazy who had no compunction about using the revolver on his lap. If she died, well, she was reasonably certain that was how the day was going to turn out if she did nothing.

She hummed as the idea sharpened.

If they didn't hit one of the steel guardrails spaced at regular intervals along the Expressway, she was willing to wager she'd be okay in a crash. The cab was an Impala. Jordon's parents drove a white Impala when they were alive. As far as she knew it was a strong, well-built vehicle. Not like one of those miniature import soup cans. Braced for a crash, with her seatbelt fastened, she liked her odds.

Hewitt said, "*Penny Lane?*" He glanced at her, eyebrows raised questioningly before returning his gaze to the road. "That's what you're humming?"

"Yes," she said.

"Yeah. *Penny Lane.*" In a soft, melodious voice, he sang the first four or five lines before letting the song fade to nothing. Surprised, Mel cut him a fast glance; she hadn't expected his singing voice to be so pleasant, not from someone so violently unhinged.

He said, "There's never been a band like them. Probably never will be again."

"They are way over-rated," she answered.

"What? The Beatles single-handedly dragged Liverpool," he paused, then, "no, Great Britain, out of a terrible depression. The Beatles started rock and roll as we know it."

She laughed once and rolled her eyes. "If they didn't do it, someone else would have. Probably better."

His eyes bulged with incredulity. One hundred plus now, the

tires buzz loud, the vibration uncomfortable. The speed and noise ramped up Mel's apprehension. "Watch the road," she said.

"Don't tell me how to drive," Hewitt yelled. Specks of spit flew off his wet lips. "You're not my wife. She's the only one who gets to nag me about the way I drive." Several seconds later he said more coolly, "You're way too young to know what you're talking about. The Beatles were—are—the best band our generation has ever seen. Ever!"

"A lot of old guys think that."

"You know what? Shut up."

"Why'd you shoot him? They'll come after you, you know?"

Hewitt's eyes jumped to the rearview mirror. "You didn't hear me? I told you to shut up." He worked both lanes, passing on the inside, flashing his high beams to move slower cars out of the way. Vehicles appeared ahead of them and then disappeared behind them in a rapid blur of color and chrome. The black ribbon of highway unfolded before them, the dashed yellow lines turning solid with speed.

She said, "You're annoyed because I don't like the Beatles? Don't take it personally." She inclined her head in the direction of the radio. "I listen to country. Shania. Faith Hill. You mind?"

He seemed to think about it, and then nodded. "Go ahead."

She reached awkwardly across her body to turn the radio on using her right hand. At the same time, she grabbed the bottom edge of her seat with her left hand. In the shadowy part of her mind she wondered if death was more than ten seconds away.

With a quick twist of her wrist, she cranked the volume knob up as far as it would go. A blast of music and static roared out of the speakers.

Hewitt jerked with surprise. His gaze flashed to the radio.

After that, everything happened in a violent, blinding rush.

Mel was already leaning in the correct direction. Taking advantage of his confusion, she yanked the gearshift down, from

Drive to First. The car's engine shrieked in protest. The needle on the tachometer hurtled toward the red arc. The car swerved from side to side, decelerating. Inertia pushed her forward into her seatbelt, which instantly became a steel sash crushing her chest. Hewitt shot forward too, into the steering wheel with a noisy grunt. Gulping audibly for breath, he lifted his foot off the accelerator and stabbed the brake pedal. Fighting the wheel with two clenched fists, he managed to straighten the Impala. With the car somewhat back under his control, Mel saw him relax slightly.

She grabbed the steering wheel and gave it a savage yank to the right.

CHAPTER 44

PRYCE HAD HIS heels on his desk between a carton of take-away Fettuccini Alfredo and a half-eaten chunk of garlic bread. He'd given up all pretenses of dieting. In the corner, the television flickered. He stared at the silent picture without seeing it and played with his Glock .26, popping the magazine out with the thumb-button, a nice solid metallic click, and then slamming it back into the butt of the pistol with his palm.

Click.

Slam.

Click.

Slam.

He knew the expression, "I'm too tired to sleep." He figured he was experiencing something similar. The fear was still present of course, but in the last twenty-four hours he'd added shock and misery to the mix. It all blended together, making him ambivalent to everything around him. Mild nausea had wiped out his appetite so thoroughly that even the pasta and bread tasted like wallpaper paste. He didn't see things improving unless Semi-Gloss walked in the door with the nut-job's money.

His intercom buzzed.

He bumped the button with the heel of his shoe, guessing he was still on Dallas' shit list, the reason she chose to buzz him.

Typically, when the bar was quiet, she knocked and then entered, no pause, no waiting. He didn't know where he was with her. After the detectives left, she seemed okay. Back to her usual efficient, somewhat distant self. Now she chose to buzz him, like she was making an effort to avoid him. "What is it, Dallas?" He kept his tone neutral.

"Semi-Gloss just wandered through the front door." Her voice was an electric, staticky hiss. "I thought you'd like to know."

Excitement stabbed Pryce in the stomach. He rocked forward. His feet slammed onto the floor. He leaned into the intercom, got his lips right up close to the microphone. "Don't let him pass Go, Dallas. Send him right in." There was still hope! Treat Semi-Gloss gently and maybe he remembers something about the money. The nut-job's tool box stays shut and his ball peen hammer remains tucked away where it belonged.

He dropped the Glock back into the desk drawer. Several seconds later the office door swung open, and Dwayne walked in. Pryce had to get used to that—for the next little while at least—thinking of the man as "Dwayne" rather than Semi-Gloss or The Moron.

Dwayne didn't look like the self-impressed golden boy he usually did. His sunglasses were in their usual place, up on top of his head like a headband, but his blonde curls lay flat and unmoussed. His perpetual fake-and-bake tan was faded an unhealthy gray that Pryce associated with pain and sickness. His leather coat was stained and he smelled like he'd spent the night in an alley. An Ace Tensor Bandage was wrapped around his right hand. A cigarette burned between his fingers. Pryce wondered about the bandage. He didn't ask. They'd get to it eventually. He said, "How many times do I have to ask…" His voice trailed away. "You know what? You got any more cigarettes, I'll take one."

Dwayne looked surprised. He nodded and slapped various pockets, the entire search looking awkward with his limited mobility. Eventually he found a crushed package of Marlboros. He tossed them to Pryce.

"And, a light?"

Dwayne reached across the desk and handed Pryce a Harley Davidson Zippo. He straightened, looked at his cigarette, the ash at the end growing long, and then cast a confused glance around the office. Dwayne the Marlboro Man, too cool for school and too stupid to remember Pryce had quit smoking and tossed all the ashtrays.

Pryce shook his head slightly, reminding himself to treat Dwayne gently. He nudged the half-eaten container of Fettuccini across the top of his desk. "Use this."

Dwayne bent forward and stubbed the cigarette out in the middle of the creamy white sauce. "Leo's dead." There was a hitch in his voice.

Alarmed, Pryce thought: *Don't start crying*. He didn't know how to deal with a blubbering female never mind a guy who walks around with a revolver under his arm who suddenly starts weeping. He said, "I heard." He inhaled deeply. The smoke swirled around in his mouth. It tasted fantastic. After holding it as long as he could he exhausted it out his mouth and nose and said, "The cops came by. They told me."

"He's dead. He was my friend." The catch was still there but Dwayne didn't appear sad. He stared at Pryce, his expression accusatory. "I know everybody calls me Semi-Gloss. I don't know why, but they say it. Act like I'm stupid, some kind of idiot doesn't know anything." He took a breath. "Not Leo. He never called me Semi-Gloss."

"Dwayne, where's Dalrymple's money?"

"I can tell you every driver who's won the Daytona Five Hundred going back to Dale Senior in '98. Before then I'd have to look it up because it was before I got interested. I know stuff." His voice rose. "I know stuff! You know who has a lot of shoes?"

Shoes? SHOES? Where's the money? Pryce shook his head. He made an effort, reined in his rising impatience and asked, "Shoes, Dwayne?"

"Imelda Marcos. I'd tell Leo stuff like that. He'd listen. Wouldn't order me around too much. Some people, strippers out there," he waved his arm in the direction of the bar, "I'd be talking, they'd walk away, I'm in the middle of a sentence. Rolling their eyes at me! Like they're better than me. Leo? He always listened."

"The money, Dwayne."

"That's all you care about? Leo's dead, you don't ask me what happened?" He raised his bandaged arm. "I've got a broken arm, you don't ask what happened?"

Pryce didn't say anything. Without warning a wave of sympathy washed over him. His dislike drained away. He saw a boy standing in front of him. Someone who spent his life acting hard because he was scared and sad and out of his element. Someone who just lost his one and only friend and didn't know what to do about it.

He stubbed out his cigarette in the Fettuccini Alfredo, beside the butt that was already poking out of the remaining pasta and sauce. He perched on the corner of the desk. Stroking his moustache with his thumb and index finger, he wondered, what next?

His first instinct was to come unglued and yell at the boy. Rattle him. Scare information out of him. Dwayne was still the last, best, and only chance of finding the money and avoiding the ball peen hammer. But Pryce sensed Dwayne wouldn't respond to that kind of cajoling. Not this time. He was too broken up about Leo. Which meant he had to go slow. Be commiserative. Coax something useful out of him, something more relevant than Dale Senior's Daytona win, whoever he was, and Imelda Marcos' shoes, whoever she was.

Pryce shuddered slightly. He hated deep, soul-to-soul conversations. He did his level best to avoid them. "I do care about Leo," he said evenly. "I care about your arm. But right now, my priority is Dalrymple's money. If we can't give it to him when he asks, we're both dead. You see what I'm saying?"

Dwayne nodded once.

"Do you have it?"

Dwayne stared at his feet.

"Do you know where it is?"

He stared at his feet.

Pryce sighed with disappointment. That would have been too easy. Dwayne walks in, the usual cocky grin on his face, the gym bag full of cash in his hand, or maybe he doesn't have it with him but says it's stashed under the bed in his apartment for safe keeping.

Pryce motioned to the couch. "Sit down. Just shove that stuff out of the way." He waited and once Dwayne settled himself, he said, "I've been looking for you." Which wasn't exactly true, but not a complete fabrication. "Where have you been?"

"Laying low. Mostly walking. I didn't go home."

"Why not?"

"Figured the cops might be looking for me."

Pryce nodded. "They were." He wondered why the Asian cop and his sick partner hadn't staked out the Lucky Thirteen and simply waited for Dwayne to show up, and then he decided limited resources was probably the answer. Plus, the two detectives didn't give him the impression they liked Dwayne as a suspect or considered him a priority. They probably just wanted to speak with people who knew Leo best.

Pryce said, "Do you have any idea what happened to the money?"

Dwayne stared at his feet.

Pryce considered his choices. Possibly Dwayne would remember something relevant if they approached the mystery from the long way around. "What happened last night? How'd Leo get dead?" He waited, feeling his temperature climb while Dwayne, slumped over with his hands clasped between his knees, stared at his feet.

The telephone rang, two short bells instead of the one long trill that was standard, the short bells letting him know it was his private, outside line. Pryce jerked his attention away from Dwayne and looked at the phone like it was a bomb, big and round and black, with a fuse hissing out of the top, waiting to go Ka-Boom!

It rang a second time.

His hand hovered over the receiver. Very few people knew the number. It rang a third time and he picked up and said, "Pryce."

"Gaylord, you know who this is?"

Of course he knew. There was no mistaking the voice, the timbre like an adolescent boy's. It was Eric Dalrymple. Mr. Blonde.

The fear rushed back. Suddenly, his heart beat so fast in his chest it actually hurt. He held the receiver in the hollow between his cheek and shoulder and dug out the bottle of Pepto. He shook two tablets into his palm, and then a second later he shook out two more. A momentary snapshot of his stomach popped into view, gurgling and bubbling like an electric pink lava lamp. He said, "I know who it is."

"How're those new garbage guys working out?"

"They're expensive."

Dalrymple said nothing, which didn't surprise Pryce. Expensive was the entire point. He looked around his office, his sanctuary. He looked at the silent flat screen television, the briefcase, and the duffle bag sitting on the comfortable leather sofa. He imagined Dallas on the other side of the door, efficiently doing her thing. He looked at Semi-Gloss and his dislike returned in a rush. The silence on the phone stretched, just the sound of Dalrymple's breath coming through the receiver. Pryce didn't care. His telephone balls were enormous. He could wait all day on the telephone and when Mr. Blonde handed him a steaming plate of shit, he could hand it right back. The truth was, he no longer cared if he offended the nut-job. The office safe could be emptied in minutes, his desk drawers in seconds. He could be on the road within the hour. Once a person faced the inevitable, decisions became easier. As much as he liked everything about his bar—the flat screen to his tasty-looking bartender and her poor attitude—he liked life better. If Semi-Gloss couldn't tell him where the money was, Pryce figured he only had one choice. He had to run.

Dalrymple finally broke the silence with a short, feminine chuckle. "Very good, Pryce. You out waited me this time. Listen, those building contractors we spoke about? They are on the way."

"When?"

"Tomorrow. Late afternoon. They'll give you a quote. They'll want an up-front deposit. Just so you know, it will be hefty. These guys are good. They don't come cheap. You understand?"

"Is that all?" Pryce spoke more abruptly than he meant. Right away he sensed Dalrymple's displeasure as clearly as if the man were standing in front of him.

"That's all for now, my man." Dalrymple's high-pitched voice was icy. "But I think when my contractor friends visit, I'll come with them. I've warned you about this tough guy attitude. It's fine for your employees. For the bar fuck-wits. But not so much for a colleague. I'll be seeing you soon. We'll chat." He hung up, left Pryce listening to the fast beep of a disconnect, the sound pacing his rapidly beating heart.

He hung up the receiver with exaggerated gentleness.

It was time to run. Or, he needed the missing money. One or the other had to happen before the sun rose the next day. He glared at Semi-Gloss. All he and Leo had to do was carry a bag of cash from point A to point B. Just like all the other times. Nobody was going to screw around with Leo, and if they did Semi-Gloss was supposed to be the bodyguard. For lack of a better word. And, this is where they ended up?

Leo dead.

Cash gone.

Nut-job coming.

Resisting the urge to grab the Glock and blow a couple of fresh holes in the moron's face, Pryce said with forced calm, "You were about to tell me what happened last night."

Semi-Gloss kept his gaze pinned on the floor. He shifted on the sofa. The leather squeaked. "We got back from Philly with the money. Just another bag run, like all the other times." His voice was low. Flat. "Somewhere near the outskirts of the city Nikki calls. She's got a gig at the Oasis. She wants a ride. You know how Leo was with her. He tells her we'll swing by. Pick her up and drop her off. Then we'll come right here. He says it won't take more than ten extra minutes."

Semi-Gloss fished another cigarette out of his pack and then re-did the pocket slapping routine.

Pryce said, "Here," and tossed him the Harley Zippo.

Semi-Gloss raised his damaged arm and tried to catch it. Agony flashed across his face. The Zippo thudded into the sofa cushion beside him.

Pryce waited, watching without sympathy.

After catching his breath Semi-Gloss said, "We parked around the side. Leo's got the gym bag with him. So, we all go in, Nikki gets into the elevator. We hadn't even left the hotel yet, she comes flying back out sayin' some asshole tried stealing her purse." His voice faded away with a headshake. "You know what Leo's like."

"He's still got the gym bag at this point?"

"He never let it go."

Pryce saw where the story was going, because where Nikki was concerned, he knew exactly what Leo was like. "Let me guess," he said. "You headed upstairs? Leo's gonna teach the asshole a lesson?"

"Leo says it's not right, people come to town, treat a working-girl poorly." Semi-gloss kept talking, saying they'd found the guy and walked him downstairs, tossed him in the trunk and then drove to an alley in Pleasantville. They planned on beating the crap out of him, but when they popped the trunk, this guy jumps out and drops Leo with a tire iron.

Pryce was angry and impressed at the same time. Leo was supposed to be able to handle anyone who came at him, especially some asshole tourist. He and Semi-Gloss must have run into some kind of Terminator. "Where's the money when this happened?"

"Gym bag on the back seat."

"Go on."

Semi-Gloss continued and Pryce listened and heard every word he said and a few he didn't say. When he finished, Pryce said, "This guy from the hotel, he—"

"He told us his name was Jordon Cutler."

"Fine. Cutler puts Leo down with the tire iron. You go for your gun. He breaks your arm as you're about to shoot—"

"Not about to. I did shoot him."

"But, you didn't kill him?"

"No."

"Why?"

"Before I could shoot him again, he broke my arm with the tire iron."

"So, then what? You dropped the gun, he picks it up and kills Leo?"

Semi-Gloss refused to meet his eye. He stared at a spot on the wall, high above Pryce's right shoulder and nodded. He was skating around something, Pryce guessed. The question was, did it matter? Did it have anything to do with the money? Pryce didn't think so. He thought it had more to do with the fight. From start to finish Semi-Gloss was unambiguous about the gym bag and its location. His story only became vague when he talked about the fight.

"Okay. Leo's dead. What happened next? Tell me one more time."

"Cutler kicked me and that's all I remember."

"The money was still on the back seat?"

"It was there when he kicked me. When I woke up it was gone."

Pryce thought hard, absently smoothing his mustache. It was safe to assume Cutler had the money. He took it and he's gone and there was pretty much no way of finding him except...

"You shot Cutler?"

"Yeah."

"Hit him?"

"I already said so."

"Bad enough he'd have to see a doctor?"

Semi-Gloss shrugged.

Pryce said, "It's a safe bet. A tourist gets shot, he goes to the hospital. It's not like it happens every day. It's a traumatic experience." He paused. "Dwayne, you have to find Jordon Cutler."

"How?"

"How what?"

"How do I find him?"

"Call the hospitals. When you find him, make him tell you where the money is."

"How?"

"Didn't you just tell me, not ten minutes ago, you know stuff? That was Dalrymple on the phone. He's coming. He'll be here tomorrow to collect that money. What kind of mood you think he'll be in, he finds out you and Leo lost it? Use your head. You got a gun. You're a tough guy. Figure it out. Get back here as soon as possible."

With a sigh, Semi-Gloss stood and walked out the office door.

Pryce called after him, "This time, keep me posted."

Semi-Gloss waved. Kept walking.

Maybe sending the moron on a job as important as this wasn't the best idea. Pryce didn't give him much chance of success. Then again, he didn't figure his own odds would be any better, and he thought his time was better spent booking three separate airline tickets out of town and then checking the train schedule.

He thumbed the intercom switch. "Dallas?"

"Yes?"

"I just got a call. Something has come up. We're not going to open today." He paused long enough to put a worried tone in his voice, which wasn't all that difficult, and gave her a universally accepted and never questioned reason. "A family emergency."

"Anything I can do?"

"I'll know more tomorrow," he said. "Go home; enjoy the rest of the day." He released the intercom button and turned his attention to the duffle bag on the couch and the briefcase sitting beside it. It was time to start packing.

The nut-job was coming.

CHAPTER 45

EYES CLOSED, HOLDING on tightly, Mel waited. At over seventy miles an hour, it was a short wait. The Impala swerved violently. Hewitt over corrected. Skidding severely, the side load on the wheels grabbed the car and rolled it.

Impetus slung Mel sideways. Her shoulder pounded off the door and her head bounced off the window. Pyrotechnics exploded behind her eyes, darkening, and then brightening, everything she saw. The windows burst, showering the inside of the car in a torrent of safety glass. The stench of burning rubber filled the air. Hewitt's mouth was fixed in a wide-open howl she couldn't hear over the screeching jangle of metal, the over-revving engine, and the blaring stereo.

The Impala landed on its right side. It slid with unrestrained forward momentum into a highway guardrail. The hooked end of the guardrail snagged the car's front fender but the back end kept moving, and the vehicle cart-wheeled like a drunken gymnast.

Mel's legs floated, bashing from side to side in the foot-well, bringing fresh tears to her eyes. The roller-bag on the back seat torpedoed forward, ploughing harmlessly into the driver's seat. The laptop missed the seat and smashed Hewitt in the back of the head, driving his face into the dashboard. His face shattered. Blood spurted. He screamed in shrill agony.

The car plunged to the earth. The front end slammed into the asphalt. Unrestrained, Hewitt catapulted through the fractured windshield. Miraculously the car landed on all four wheels.

Mel waited for the next bounce. Nothing happened.

She brushed hair away from her face. The blaring radio was the only sound now, assaulting her ears as relentlessly as the wreck had battered the car. She reached for the volume knob but the seatbelt had tightened to the point where breathing hurt and the radio was out of reach. She twisted sideways to release the buckle and pain sliced from shoulder to hip, making her gasp. When the waves of agony eased she cautiously reached for the buckle a second time, released it and gulped in several deep, glorious breaths.

Where was Hewitt? Was he alive? Would he be coming for her, the shiny nickel-plate .38 in his hand? With her heart beating fast and high in her throat, she leaned forward, frantically straining to spot him through what little remained of the windshield. Where was he? Crap, it would be a terrible irony to survive the crash only to have him shoot her while she was sitting helplessly in the car.

He was nowhere in sight. A thin fog of optimism grew around her. Maybe he was dead. Not too many people could survive a wreck like that—go through the windshield at the speed they were traveling—and walk away.

The radio continued to yell at her. She twisted the volume knob until the sound disappeared entirely and all that remained was the quiet tick of the hot engine and the regular drip of some unknown fluid. One shin throbbed and her right shoulder ached, but when she wriggled, everything seemed to work.

She leaned back, into the seat and something sharp stabbed her between the shoulders. Screaming with pain and fright she lurched forward. Small chunks of safety glass trickled down her shirt.

Still no sign of Hewitt.

For the first time since he snatched her in the Quicky-Mart, Mel thought she might make it to the Shore Memorial Hospital. And, for the first time in several months it occurred to her that she'd finally won a round. Even though she hurt everywhere and the constant black fear and anxiety were still alive inside her, she'd won a round.

She tugged on her door handle. It was jammed solidly shut and she was reluctant to throw her weight into it. What remained of her window was ragged glassy knives. There was no way to climb through it.

The engine had stalled but the ignition key was still in the On position. Not sure it would work, she pushed the window Down button. What little remained of the glass slid into the door, the scraping sound of glass on metal sending shivers scurrying up her spine.

Hesitantly, favoring her aching shoulder, she grabbed the top of the doorjamb and hoisted herself through the opening, whimpering and clenching her teeth against deep waves of agony pulsing in her shoulder. She sat on the edge of the door a moment, feet on the front seat. She brushed hair out of her face with a trembling hand. After a second or two of contortions, she pulled herself the rest of the way out of the mangled taxicab. She planted her feet on the yellowed grass and oily gravel on the shoulder of the highway.

Then she spotted Hewitt's inert form, lying two or three car lengths away.

The trembles hit her and, head hanging, she leaned against the sedan, hugging herself in an effort to control her shaking body. "Get a grip," she mumbled. *There's no reason to be frightened. You won!*

Slowly the strain of climbing out the window abated. She wiped her face with her sleeve, leaving a bloody smear on the fabric. Surprised, she raised her fingers and tentatively probed the side of her head. Thorny slivers of glass in her hair jabbed her fingertips. She jerked her hand away, saw drops of blood brilliant scarlet against the white pallor of her hand.

The shakes faded to occasional tremors. She pushed off the car, grabbed the bottom of her sweatshirt and holding it away from her waist, did a little jig. Cubes of safety glass rained on her feet. She hobbled around to the front of the car, glass crunching like dead beetles beneath her feet. The stench of heat and gasoline rose off the asphalt and mingled in the humid air, wrinkling her nose.

Hewitt's broken body lay like a sack of dirty laundry on the shoulder of the road. His chest didn't rise and fall with breathing. Warily, she prodded him with a toe. He didn't move. With more confidence, Mel bent at the waist and stared into his face. Vacant eyes stared back at her. His lacerated face was frozen in a mask of terror and understanding.

Simultaneously repulsed and indifferent, she pivoted away. Terror and understanding. *What the good-natured clerk in the Quicky-Mart must have felt when you shot him,* Mel thought. *What I felt when you grabbed me. You got what you deserved.*

Vehicles on Mel's side of the Atlantic City Expressway slowed. She imagined their occupants doing their part to ease human suffering—braking briefly, calling the police on their cell phones and then jumping back on the gas. She figured someone a little more caring would stop. Sooner or later.

What then?

She still needed to get to the hospital.

In the distance, she heard sirens, so many they sounded like a symphony. Hopefully they were playing for her.

CHAPTER 46

AFTER BREAKFAST AT the nautical-themed restaurant, Brenna drove Luther home. Before he climbed out of the car, a song he recognized came on the radio. He paused with his hand on the door handle and said, "Good song. You ever hear this before?"

She shook her head.

"For someone who enjoys trivia, this might interest you. The band is called Morphine. The lead singer was Mark Sandman. He had a heart attack on stage, performing in Italy. This song—"

"What's it called?"

"*The Night.* It hadn't been released when he died." Luther considered it the best track on the CD. He continued, "Morphine purists don't like this CD as much as the band's previous efforts. There's acoustic guitar on it. They believe the band should've stuck with their minimalist style. Nothing but string slide bass, sax, and drums."

Brenna listened without interrupting a second time. When the song ended, she said, "Not really my cup of tea."

Luther made a face. "You're young. Unsophisticated. Eventually, with age and wisdom, you'll learn to appreciate great music."

When she showed him her middle finger, he smiled. Another tune he recognized as Morphine's began. He guessed the radio station was doing some kind of special. Morphine wasn't that well known for two songs in a row.

"Luther?

With his eyebrow raised questioningly—she only called him "Luther" when she was angry or serious—he looked at her. She leaned across the seat, placed her palm on his cheek and kissed him. Not a quick peck. She put some effort into it. For one or two seconds, he was too surprised to respond. Then he leaned into her and returned the kiss and for a while time disappeared and he was a teenager again, in the front seat of a car with a woman he was into, and who was into him, and that strange mixture of excitement and newness thrummed through his body like an over-tightened guitar string, and in the back of his mind he wondered how he'd ever become so lucky.

The song on the radio ended.

He tensed very slightly and he felt Brenna do the same, the movement almost imperceptible. They pulled apart. His surprise hadn't worn off. He said, "Wow," and then immediately closed his eyes and shook his head. *Wow?* That's the best response he could come up with? Mid-forties and that's the best response he had? He opened his eyes. She wore the half-assed, crooked smile he liked so much.

"Thanks for breakfast, Mac. Now get out of the car. I'll pick you up at four."

Several hours later she was at his front door, and Luther hated to admit it, but a swarm of nerves buzzed around in his belly. Strange how a short moment in time could potentially change so much.

She said, "Hey, Mac."

"Bren."

He studied her for a second, hoping he wouldn't see embarrassment or regret. She appeared tired, like she napped rather than slept, but her eyes sparkled and when she returned his gaze, her cheeks reddened. The freckles sprinkling her nose disappeared into the flush spreading across her face. She twisted away from him on one foot and giggled. His nerves and worry disappeared in a flash. He could deal with this kind of embarrassment. It meant she was okay with what happened. After thinking about it, she hadn't changed her mind. Cold or standoffish would have been different. This bubbly mood was okay. He found it humorous. Giggly was a side of Brenna Hanson he'd never seen before. He tilted his head and asked, "What's with you?"

"Nothing. Not one thing. Why?" If possible, the blush turned a deeper shade of red.

He wasn't certain what to say next. Finally, he settled for, "All right. Come on in for a sec. Watch out for paint cans. I have to grab something." She followed him into the house. The faint chemical odor of fresh enamel hung in the air. He cut a scowl at the empty cans stacked near the door. *Perfect. Nice way to impress somebody.* He kept forgetting to take them out to the trash, until he walked into his home and tripped on them.

"An easy chair and a television? That's it?" Brenna's voice bounced off the freshly painted walls and the plywood floors awaiting new hardwood. "Where's the rest of your furniture?"

"I sold most of it. It's easier to renovate when you don't have to keep moving stuff from one room to another." He grabbed the Morphine CD off the top of his stereo. "Give this a listen," he said, handing it to her.

She took it without comment, but a wry smile crossed her face.

Now it was Luther who was flushing, the heat rising up his neck and warming his face and ears. Making out in the front seat of a car. Trading music. Not only did he feel like a teen, he was acting like one too. He said gruffly, "We better go, huh?"

"Yep."

In the car, staring straight ahead with both hands on the

steering wheel, Brenna said, "Um, regarding this morning, Mac. I very much enjoyed all aspects of our breakfast meeting."

Luther narrowed his eyes in confusion. Breakfast hadn't been that interesting. Coffee, eggs, toast. Then he decided maybe she was talking about the kiss, but he didn't know. He glanced at her and saw the same tight French braid and pantsuit to which he'd become so accustomed, but now more than ever, he wanted to see her dressed in something other than office clothes. He wanted to see her auburn hair hanging free. He said, "You mean the food, the song, the—"

"That's what I mean."

After a moment, he said, "I was surprised."

"Good surprised?"

"Oh yeah."

"Well, all right then. A lady can't wait forever."

He raised his left eyebrow. "Pardon me?"

"That kiss? That was me pointing the way. How you go down the road is up to you." She squinted out the window for a second or two. The rain had finally stopped. Overhead, dark, low-slung clouds boiled angrily, like they objected to the infrequent slices of warm sunlight knifing through them. She soldiered on. "Let's face it, Mac. You're lugging around some baggage. You unload it one day, give me a call. Invite me back for coffee. I'd very much like to see the rest of your place."

He looked at her blankly.

"You're thick sometimes, aren't you?" Her voice was filled with tenderness that negated any offense he might have felt. She said patiently, "How long have you been renovating?"

He knew exactly when he started but he studied the roof of the car, pretending to do the math in his head while he tried to figure out where she was going with this conversation. He said, "I guess about ten months. Why?"

"Right after Marilyn moved out?"

"That's right," he said slowly. The renovation project had become an exorcism of sorts. It would have been entirely successful except for the bullshit phone calls, Marilyn saying, "I miss our little house, Luther. It's impossible to get competent cleaning staff."

He said, "You're welcome any time, Bren," he said. "I'm almost done." Which wasn't exactly true…

As easy as it was to pinpoint when he started the renovation, predicting when he'd finish was impossible. Time was not something solid he could lay his hands upon; the project would take as long as it took for him to forget Marilyn, and all his associated mistakes and poor decisions. The tangible part of the project—the layout, colors, and materials—that made the bungalow entirely his own were important, but only a by-product of the time he needed to forget that the renovation was supposed to be for both him and Marilyn, not him alone. He had an uneasy feeling Brenna was looking past the fresh paint.

"I can grasp you needing to make some changes after Marilyn left. But, come on! You sold all your furniture and haven't bothered replacing it. Ten months you've been renovating and you're barely finished painting? And now, we get a high-profile murder case and you suspect the guy least likely to have done it? Menny has some kind of love-hate thing going, something you understand, so he must have done it?

"When you get that renovating done—that's what we'll call it, shall we—invite me over. We'll see what my personal circumstance is. Until then, I think we keep our relationship professional. Keep the phone calls and e-mail, that sort of thing, work related."

Emptiness exploded inside him, stealing his breath. He concentrated on keeping his expression neutral. He didn't say a word. He wiped a hand up his forehead and back across the top of his head. She was perceptive, he had to give her that. If he hadn't invited her into his home, she might not have realized how stuck in a rut he was, and maybe she wouldn't be pulling back. Sometimes he was an idiot; he shouldn't have given her the CD. Unbidden, a slight grin tugged at the corners of his mouth. Only a few hours ago, he'd told her exactly that: "Sometimes men act like idiots in front of a pretty lady."

"Luther?" She looked at him, eyes wide and worried, tension radiating off her like heat waves.

He touched her arm. "It's fine," he said. It wasn't, but he wouldn't make her feel more uncomfortable than she already appeared. The hollowness in his stomach faded. He didn't feel as distressed as he had a few moments earlier. She let him know there was still a chance. Down the road at some point. That was good enough. He said, "Do you see the irony in the situation, Bren?"

Her expression was uncertain. "No."

"Well, I do." He was relieved his voice sounded completely natural. He'd read once that effective communication was much less about the spoken word than it was about body language and tone. Whatever, Brenna softened and when she nodded, he knew she believed him.

He said, "We better go see what the Captain wants us to do; hassle a rich kid or panic some VIPs."

PART 4

2:00 PM to 6:00 PM
September, 2002

CHAPTER 47

JORDON TOLD THE hospital staff—as if they didn't know—that he'd been shot in the side. Not the leg. He told them his ribs were bruised. His legs though? They worked just fine. He didn't need a wheelchair. The nurse and the doctor agreed and firmly insisted he ride anyway; the Shore Memorial had its policies. So, he sat down and stopped complaining and for the next couple of minutes enjoyed the ride and thought about how Melissa had shown up in his room with her right arm in a sling, cuts on her face, and a big purple bruise on the side of her head. Mel telling him about the trip from Richmond to Atlantic City and some loser named Bernard Hewitt who went through the windshield in the same car crash that battered her several shades of the color wheel. Telling him how the cops questioned her for what seemed like hours after the crash.

He hardly believed her story. He couldn't decide if he was retroactively angry with her, or terrified on her behalf. One thing of which he was certain; he was hugely proud.

The nurse pushing the chair said, "Here we are, Mr. Cutler. Do you see your wife?"

Jordon refocused and there she was, swinging their faded green Mazda into one of the short-term parking spaces. "That's her." The nurse pushed him toward the doors. They split in the middle, one sliding east, the other west, and a blast of humid air filled the foyer. He stood and walked out of the sterile hospital into the sunny afternoon, a free man once more.

Mel wasn't wearing the ball cap he was used to seeing and her blonde hair flashed in the afternoon sunlight. The car keys dangled in her outstretched hand, Mel saying, "Driving is hard with only one arm," which was probably true, but he smiled anyway. She didn't like to drive at the best of times. If the two of them were in the car, he was the one behind the wheel. The arm-in-a-sling was little more than an excuse. He took the keys and then wrapped both arms around her. She was soft and hard and she fit like the last piece of an enormous jigsaw puzzle. "Pumpkin, you smell good," he murmured into her hair.

"Let's go home."

"We're in America's Favorite Playground. You want to look around first?"

"I picked up your bag and laptop at the Oasis. They had them stored in a little room behind the counter. Let's just leave."

"You got it," he said. When she turned, and headed for the Mazda he gave her a gentle pat on the ass. She looked back at him, chin down near her right shoulder, and she sent him a coy and flirty smile, like something she might have tossed his way sixteen months ago, but better with all the fresh confidence spilling out of her. It was like a million rays of sunshine blowing through his heart.

He opened the door for her and closed it solidly behind her. When he was in the driver's seat he said, "All right. Get some gasoline and we're gone."

"Do it on the highway."

He smiled slightly, thinking about the gym bag he stashed behind the fuel tanks at the 7-Eleven. "I know a better place—"

The left passenger door opened, interrupting him. In a blur of black leather and old cologne, someone lunged into the back seat. The Mazda rocked with the individual's weight.

Mel shrieked in surprise.

Jordon recognized the woodsy smell. *You've got to be kidding me.* He looked over his shoulder and saw...

...Dwayne.

Sitting there in the middle of the seat showing off another hand cannon in his left fist, black not chrome this time, down low in his lap, hidden from the eyes of anyone who happened to stroll past. His face was pale, shining with sweat. His eyes were bloodshot. He was sick or in pain—maybe both—he wasn't just overheating in his leather coat, Jordon guessed. He shook his head. He didn't need this. Worse, Mel didn't need it. He liked her newfound confidence, he just wasn't sure about its sturdiness.

"Eyes forward," Dwayne said.

"Who are you?" Mel asked, surprise in her voice. She looked at Jordon out of wide eyes. "Who's he?"

Dwayne said, "Shut up." He reached across his body, four fingers and a thumb peeking out of the end of a crisp, tightly wound Ace Tensor Bandage and pulled the door shut.

Jordon stared out the windshield. He blew a breath through his teeth, more exasperated than threatened. Leo had worried him far more than Dwayne. Dwayne acted hard, but he took orders, he didn't give them. Unfortunately, here he was in the car with another revolver and a pissed-off expression. Jordon muttered, "I can't believe this."

"You better believe it. Now drive." Dwayne wiped his forehead with the inside of his arm. The sweat glistened on the leather sleeve of his coat. The barrel of his revolver swung wildly all over the car. It found the windshield.

It found the radio.

It found Mel.

Jordon tensed. Fingers of fear clawed at his stomach. How

were they going to get out of this? Dwayne was one thing. Dwayne sick, possibly hallucinating or on medicinal drugs, waving a weapon around, was something else entirely. When the revolver's crazy oscillations steadied, Jordon released a suppressed breath. "Where we going?" he said, sliding the gearshift from Park to Reverse.

"Same place we were last night," Dwayne answered. "Because the way I figure it, you didn't get too far with a bag of cash, being shot and all."

Which, Jordon thought, was reasonably smart for a sidekick named Dwayne.

Mel said, "You know this guy?"

"We've met. We don't get along."

"What does he want?"

"I'm not sure," Jordon said, and then, being cool, trying to keep her calm, he added, "He might be mad about his partner being dead. He might be mad about his arm."

"Both of you shut up." Dwayne stabbed the barrel of the revolver at him. "Drive."

Mel looked at him nervously. She wasn't scared yet—Jordon knew her scared expression—and the earlier feeling of pride washed through him. He marveled at how much she'd changed in the four days since he'd left her. "I was going to tell you on the drive home. This guy," he hooked a thumb over his shoulder, "and his partner grabbed me. They thought I was someone else. There was an altercation—"

"It wasn't an altercation. You busted me up with a tire iron." Dwayne raised his arm so Jordon got a look at the tensor bandage. "You kill my partner? Steal our money? And, somehow you think you're gonna get away with it?"

"Technically you killed Leo."

In the rearview mirror, Dwayne's face went hard. "Your fault. I told Pryce it was you. Turn the heater off. I'm burning up."

Mel said quietly, "You're wearing a leather coat, for heaven's sake."

"You had your gun out. All I did was defend myself."

"Pryce wants—"

"Who's Pryce?" Mel asked.

Jordon shrugged a second time. "No idea."

"My boss." Dwayne waved the revolver in her direction. "Now do as you're told and shut up!" He shook his head. "My preference, I'd shoot you both. But Pryce wants his money. You're taking me to it. It's the only way this works out for you." He glanced at Mel. "Or her."

Jordon said, "I don't know what money you're talking about." Mel's quizzical gaze burned into the side of his head. He ignored it.

Dwayne leaned forward between the seats, said he thought Jordon was full of shit. Said Pryce wanted the money back and he'd do just about anything to get it because it wasn't his. It belonged to someone Pryce didn't want on his ass, a guy called Mr. Blonde, Dwayne saying the name with a trace of fear in his voice, and then telling Jordon that Mr. Blonde was an individual *nobody* wanted on their ass.

"Assuming I knew what money you're talking about, why would I take you to it?"

"I'll shoot you if you don't. I thought I made that clear."

Now more than ever, Jordon was convinced the authorities wouldn't be searching for the money. People with names such as "Mr. Blonde" who carry their money around in gym bags, preferred untraceable cash. That kind of cash—large and untraceable—would come in handy. He could take care of Mel in the way she deserved. He could pay off some medical bills and keep her in visits to the psychotherapist. He could buy a new car before the Mazda disintegrated around them.

There was no way he was giving up the gym bag.

He shook his head. "You won't shoot me. If I did have your money and you shot me, then you'd never know where I put it."

Dwayne said nothing for several seconds. Finally, he said, "You don't tell me, I'll shoot her." He paused. "Who is she?"

Mel said, "Melissa."

"Shut-the-fuck-up."

She straightened in her seat. "Why'd you ask, if you don't want to know?"

"I want to know who you are. I don't care what your name is."

Mel made an exasperated face, propped her chin in her hand and stared out the window.

Jordon pulled the car over and parked. He turned around, faced Dwayne and said, "She's Mel. Just like she told you." His voice was flat and emotionless. "I guess you could try and shoot her. You might get one round off. After that though, I guarantee two things. You still won't know where the money is and," he paused briefly making sure Dwayne was paying attention, "It will be the last thing you ever do."

"I'm the one with the gun, bro. Not you."

"Are you Wyatt Earp?"

"What?"

"Are you Wyatt Earp? Because, unless you're that fast, I'll take that gun out of your hand and beat you into a coma with it before you have time to pull the hammer back a second time. Don't think I could? I was the one stuck in the trunk last night, and I'm still standing."

Miraculous timing, raging adrenalin, and an ungodly amount of luck factored into his escape—Jordon knew it—but the fact was, Dwayne was a mess, his partner was dead, and, against all odds, Jordon was showing very little wear and tear. He doubted he could pull a stunt like that off twice in two days, not before Dwayne started blasting away and, even without aiming, in the confines of the car, someone was bound to get hurt. So, it came down to selling the idea, making Dwayne believe lightning could hit the same place twice.

"Your good arm is broken. You're hanging onto that gun with your left, wobbling all over the place. Looks like you're running a fever. How many of us do you see? I doubt you'd hit either one of us. Not unless you're Wyatt Earp."

Dwayne leaned back in the seat, putting some distance between himself and Jordon. He had a thoughtful look on his ashen, sweat-slick face. "New plan," he said. "We're going to the Lucky Thirteen. Pryce will know what to do. Now drive."

Jordon pulled the gearshift from Park to Drive and eased back into traffic. "Where?"

"Left at the next light."

They picked up Shore Road heading northeast and then hung a right onto the Black Horse Pike and headed back into Atlantic City, Dwayne telling Jordon how he phoned every medical facility in the city from a strip-mall pay phone in Pleasantville until he found the right hospital. Then he sat in the parking lot all afternoon, tapping the scan button on the radio, just waiting for Jordon to show. Every bump in the road made him wince. The bigger bumps made him suck painful breaths in through his teeth.

Mel said, "I'd like to get some gum out of my bag."

After long, careful thought Dwayne said, "What kind is it? Cherry? I like that stuff. You know what? I don't care. I'll take a piece, whatever it is."

She picked up her bag, bent over it and rummaged through it with her good arm. The big cotton sling covered the bag most the time, making it difficult for Jordon to see what she was doing. *Gum? Since when did Mel chew gum?*

After several seconds, she stopped. She turned partway around, said over her shoulder, "I guess I'm out."

"You don't even know what's in your purse?" Disgust was thick in his voice. He shook his head. "Typical."

Nobody spoke for several minutes. The only sound was Dwayne moaning quietly when the car hit a pothole, and his subsequent incoherent mumbling. Finally, he said, "See that alley? We're going down there."

Jordon parked and shut the Mazda off and Dwayne said, "Both of you get out. Blondie, you walk around to the driver's side. Wait there."

"It's Mel."

Dwayne made a face. "Whatever." He met them at the front of the car, said, "March," and waggled the barrel of the revolver at a door halfway down the alley. They walked toward it, Mel first, Jordon behind her a couple of steps, staying ready, looking for an opportunity to wrestle the revolver away, but Dwayne seemed to have caught his second wind because he hung back, stayed alert and the barrel was steady. At the door, he said, "In you go."

Once inside they paused, allowing their eyes to adjust. This early in the day, the Lucky Thirteen was deserted. Without the benefit of music or people, the bar was dim, dingy, and forlorn. Dwayne motioned with the revolver. "Over there," he said. He kept his eyes pinned on them both as they crossed the empty bar and then knocked on a door labeled "Office." Without waiting he twisted the knob and pushed the door open.

An overweight man with a shiny bald head and a polished upper lip like he'd recently shaved off a thick moustache, looked up from a desk. His hand dropped. When it came up, he was holding an automatic pistol.

Mr. Pryce, Jordon guessed.

CHAPTER 48

THE SQUAD ROOM was nearly deserted. The Captain worked in his office, secure behind his door, but visible behind a lightly frosted window. Detective Paul Davis sat at his desk, bent over a stack of paperwork. His thin black hair was combed straight back as though he was trying hard for some kind of style with the few remaining strands.

Luther brushed a hand across his closely shaven scalp and thought his ultra-short crew cut was a better choice than the comb-back the Asian detective preferred. He said, "Hey, Paul."

Davis looked up. "Mac. Brenna."

Luther said, "Did Galloway dump all the paperwork on you?" The desk opposite Davis was empty, the chair pushed back. An open can of Coke sat there, like someone had recently walked away but planned on returning soon.

"He may as well have. At present, Duncan isn't much good. He's got a terrible cold. Or, says he does." Davis twitched his head toward the opposite side of the room. "He's in the john."

Brenna said, "You working anything interesting?"

Davis hiked his shoulders. "Maybe. Do either of you know Leo Jarvis?"

Luther said, "Of course. Steroid freak, right?"

"And, his half-wit sidekick Semi-Gloss," Brenna added. "We know them both."

"That's them," Davis said. "How's this for interesting? Leo got his ass capped last night."

"That's a shame," Luther said sarcastically. "What happened?"

Davis picked up a coffee mug, took a deep swallow, and then grimaced. "Short version: Leo and Semi-Gloss were into something at the Oasis. I haven't figured out what. A tourist from Richmond, some guy in town for a conference, inadvertently crossed their path. As best as I can tell, they hung a beating on him, dragged him out of the hotel and tossed him in the trunk of a car. When they opened the trunk, he managed to get away. During the struggle—the tourist tells me—Semi-Gloss shot Leo."

Brenna said, "Semi-Gloss was the shooter? I'm surprised. He and Leo were tight."

"The way it sounds, Semi-Gloss aimed at the tourist and missed. He shot Leo instead. The tourist's story is credible. So far it checks out."

A door slammed on the other side of the room. The sound of footsteps grew louder as Duncan Galloway slouched toward the three detectives. His eyes were red, his nose glowed. He looked miserable. He nodded hello at Luther and Brenna but didn't say a word in greeting.

Davis glanced at the Timex on his wrist. "What have you been doing, Dunc? We have to get going." He stood, donning his raincoat. As he fastened the buttons he said to Luther, "What about you two? What are you killing yourselves on?"

"Brenna and I are working a homicide, happened out near the Egg Harbor swamps. An escort—"

"What's her name? The escort. Victoria Chesham?"

"That's her."

Davis said, "You two just got in, so I guess you haven't heard. They got the guy. Case closed."

Brenna's eyes widened. She said sharply, "What?"

"Who's they?" Luther said.

The Captain poked his head out of his office at the sound of Brenna's raised voice. "Luther. Brenna. I didn't realize you were in. Let's talk."

Davis said, "Sorry to spring it on you that way." He nodded in the direction of the boss's office. "Cap will tell you more. Late this morning there was a shooting in a convenience store on the Expressway. Ten minutes later a taxi cab heading west rolled itself into a ball. Some guy—"

Duncan Galloway blew his nose loudly, interrupting Davis. He said in a raw scratchy voice, "Sorry about that. The guy's name was Hewitt. The guy who did the escort, I mean. Bernard Hewitt."

Davis continued, unperturbed. "Right. Hewitt. He was driving the cab. He went through the windshield. The gun was in his pocket. Mac, Bren, we've got to run. We've got a few things to take care of." He paused, cut Galloway a nasty smile. "Then, we're going to swing by the Lucky Thirteen again. Annoy Pryce some more. See if Semi-Gloss has resurfaced."

Galloway checked his watch, smiled, and sniffed loudly. "Almost five. I like it."

Luther ignored what was clearly an inside joke between the two detectives. Something else was tickling his brain. Tom Menny was from Richmond. He said, "This tourist you mentioned, do you have his details?"

Davis and Galloway were already halfway across the room. Davis glanced over his shoulder. "Of course. What's he to you?"

"Luther! Brenna!" the Captain called, louder this time.

Luther looked from Davis to the Captain's office and then back to Davis. "I don't know. Maybe nothing." He hiked his shoulders. "Probably nothing. But I'd like to hear his story."

Davis said, "We'll talk later," and headed out of the station.

Luther swiveled and strode to the office, Brenna beside him.

His mind was a tornado. How had the Chesham homicide gone from nearly incomprehensible, with multiple theories and suspects, to solved in a matter of hours? He hadn't been asleep that long! Anger built, tightening his muscles and knotting his stomach. His case, his and Brenna's case, solved? And, he hadn't been involved? Worse, nobody bothered to call and tell him? Who was Bernard Hewitt? Luther was certain that name hadn't come up in any conversations. And, what about all the people named in the Day-Timer? A state judge banging a hooker like a screen door in the wind, and he and Brenna don't get the opportunity to ask questions because some mystery man is suddenly the murderer?

Brenna said quietly, out the side of her mouth. "Take it easy. We need to find out what's going on. Let's see what the Captain has to say."

He glanced at her. Two spots high on each cheek flamed an angry red. She and he were in tune. He took a deep breath, forcing himself to calm down. The Captain's office door was open. Luther knocked anyway.

"Come in. Close the door," the Captain said. He thumbed through a small stack of papers and files on his desk and selected one. "Have a seat. Take a look at this." He handed over a slim folder.

Brenna reached for it.

Luther said, "What is it?"

The Captain dropped his pen on the stack of papers. "Preliminary ballistics report from the Chesham homicide. It confirms Tom Menny's story. He was shot from approximately four feet away. Chesham from approximately six."

"What he told, us," Luther said. "What we expected."

"You remember the weapon was never found?"

"Menny said his assailant drove away with it."

"Okay, stick with me here. It was a damn busy night on the

town. While you were working the Chesham homicide, there was another shooting. The nightclub, Glow."

"Yes, sir," Luther said. "A bouncer was killed. It was all over the news." Anchors, looking suitably concerned, going on about how nightclub security would have to be tightened, maybe some airport type x-ray machines placed at the entrance doors. The song *Dirty Laundry*, penned by the incomparable Don Henley, ran through Luther's mind.

"Correct," the Captain said. "Earlier today a clerk in a Quicky-Mart on the Expressway was shot as well. The entire incident is on the security tape. Not fatally, by the way. The young man will live. The shooter, Bernard Hewitt, kidnapped one of the store's patrons and took off in a stolen taxicab. Several miles down the road he rolled the vehicle. The kidnappee was wearing her seatbelt and survived. A courageous young lady. Hewitt went through the windshield. A .38 was found on his person."

Luther said, "The clerk and the bouncer were both shot with this .38?"

"Correct. Firearms Identification will confirm it, but yes that's what the investigation indicates."

"Let me guess. Menny and Chesham were shot with a .38 as well?"

The Captain nodded. "A .38 slug was extracted from her remains." He leaned back in his chair. He laced his fingers together behind his head. "Hewitt had a busy twenty-four hours. He shot the bouncer. Several witnesses in Glow positively identified him, including a Miss Shari Adams and a Mr. John Staples. Staples was the second bouncer. We've also spoken to the individual from whom Hewitt stole the taxicab. Before all that, he forcibly confined a woman in her hotel room and pepper sprayed an Oasis Hotel security guard."

Luther said slowly, "So, everything Hewitt did has been substantiated, except his involvement in Victoria Chesham's death?"

The Captain didn't answer right away. Eventually he said, "Correct. That won't be confirmed until we hear back from Firearms Identification. However, it's a logical assumption, and until we hear differently, it's the conclusion we're sticking with. The same gun was used in all incidents." The Captain's voice had grown stiffer, more formal, as though he was reading a prepared statement, instead of discussing the case with two of his detectives.

Brenna said, "Who's this Bernard Hewitt guy? Where did he come from? Was he listed in Victoria's little black book?"

"He was not."

Luther knew Hewitt's name wasn't in the book. Brenna knew it too. They'd both thumbed through the Day-Timer several times. He decided to dive right in. He took a deep breath. "Brenna and I," he cut a fast glance at his partner, "have been discussing it. There's something else going on, more than just a bad robbery. We'd like to look into Chesham's death some more."

There was an inquiring look on the Captain's face. "What's on your mind?"

Luther figured his theory would depth-charge the Captain's genial mood in about five seconds. The almost unperceivable tick on the man's left eyelid would start. Luther would get a little more detailed. The twitching eyelid would worsen. Luther would press his theory. The tick would turn to a blur.

"I think it was a setup. I think Menny had Chesham killed. Maybe his accomplice was this Hewitt character. I'm not sure. That's what I'd like to look into."

"What are the grounds for your suspicions?"

"A hunch."

"Based on?" The Captain urged him on with a rolling hand. "Quit screwing around. Talk."

Luther didn't want to get into his immediate dislike of Tom Menny, or the way Victoria drew people to her like a bee to its queen. Nor did he want to discuss how his fractured history with

Marilyn made understanding Menny's motivation easy. It was bad enough detailing that kind of thing to Brenna. He certainly didn't want to discuss it with another man. "Nothing concrete. Just the investigation to this point."

"Didn't Menny's description match this Hewitt guy?"

Luther rocked a hand back and forth. "Menny said the shooter was tall and skinny. He couldn't see the guy's face. It could have been anybody."

The Captain's left eyelid jumped. Just once. "We heard back from our colleagues in Richmond. Nothing, I repeat nothing, indicates Menny wanted to harm Ms. Chesham."

"What about the money she stole?"

"Over a year ago?" He shook his head. "If there were nothing else to go on, that would be a trail worth following—"

"There is nothing else to go on," Luther said, hitting "nothing" loudly.

"Incorrect, detective. We have a boatload of circumstantial evidence. When looked at it in its entirety, it paints Bernard Hewitt with a very wide, very guilty brush. Firearms Identification will confirm it all."

For a second time, Luther heard the oddly stiff and formal tone. He said, "I think we need to look into all that circumstantial evidence. Paul Davis is working a case right now. Some tourist from Richmond got himself beat up last night."

"How's that relevant?"

"Same town Menny came from. Maybe this tourist is part of the setup?"

The Captain rubbed the back of his hand across his fluttering left eyelid. "Doubtful. This is Atlantic City. People come and go every day. It's not surprising two people from Richmond are in town at the same time." An edge of finality crept into his voice. "Victoria Chesham was a hooker who got killed in a robbery. Plain and simple. The shooter has been found."

Time to put the eyelid into overdrive. "Cap, I–"

"This investigation is no longer a priority, detective." The Captain's gaze never left Luther's face. His eyelid was a smudge of angry motion.

"Sir–"

"Detective Hanson? Can you give detective McKinley and I a moment?"

Brenna looked startled. She straightened in her chair. "Sir, I'd prefer—"

"Close the door on your way out."

Brenna stood, quarter-sized spots on her cheeks flaming a deep angry rouge.

Luther stared at the Captain. He didn't hear his partner's rapid footsteps as she walked out of the office.

The Captain leaned forward in his chair. Both palms were flat on his desk. He exhaled nosily. He said succinctly, "Drop it. Understand?"

"I don't get it. Why's this not worth looking into? Nobody's ever heard of Bernard Hewitt. There's a Day-Timer full of more likely suspects but Hewitt is tried and convicted because he happened to have the .38 in his pocket?"

The Captain said nothing.

Luther cocked his head. Like a spoonful of poison, bitter realization filled his mouth. "It's become political."

The Captain steepled his fingers in front of his face like he was praying. He said, "Some of the VIPs were clients. A politician. A judge. There are others. That has been confirmed. These are very rich, very influential people. They don't want their liaisons with a prostitute to become tabloid fodder."

Luther remembered an order he often received as a kid, something he heard from parents, coaches, and teachers: "Stop trying to get the last word in." In hindsight, the authority figures were right more times than not. He should have buttoned his lip and listened. However, there were times when these individuals wanted him to be quiet because they were wrong and didn't want to acknowledge it. One thing hadn't changed in all those passing years—when Luther was right, when he was convinced he was right—he hated to give ground. "People with deep pockets are dictating what we investigate?"

"No!" The Captain slammed an open palm on his desk. He shook his head. His eyelid moved so fast it was a buzz. "The DA's office believes we have the shooter. Nothing, I repeat, nothing suggests otherwise. You've given me supposition. But no evidence. The investigation is over!"

Luther and the Captain locked stares.

The Captain closed his eyes briefly. When he started talking again his voice was calm. "Luther, let's assume for a moment that Hewitt was not the shooter. You're asking me to allow two detectives enough time to chase down a hunch? Based on what? A year-old theft? Some feeling you can't or won't explain?" He shook his head. "Or worse, you want to go off in a different direction and question a state judge and a senator, among others? A female state senator, for Christ's sake? All for a case the DA's office has closed? It's not going to happen, Mac. No way. Tragic as you might find it, Victoria Chesham was a hooker who got killed in a robbery."

The Captain picked up his pen. He twisted the barrel so the tip came out of the end. "I know you've been under some pressure the last few months. Your divorce. Wife moving out. What not. It might explain why you've got an odd feeling about this. But I'm telling you, forget it." He bent to his paperwork, the meeting obviously over in his mind.

Luther waited. The Captain kept writing, as if he wasn't in the room. Finally, Luther said, "I've got vacation time in the bank."

The Captain looked at him. His eyes bored into him, as though he suspected he was being manipulated and was trying to figure out how. Eventually he said, "Excellent idea. Go south.

Drink some beer. Do whatever it is you do on your days off. Don't spend time looking into a dead hooker's past. Am I clear?"

Luther stood.

"Am I clear?" Harder this time.

Luther looked out the office window. He turned his face back and met the Captain's glare head on. "Sure," he said. "Clear as clear."

CHAPTER 49

THE GRECIAN FORMULA was in the garbage can, the duffle bag packed with some personal items Pryce stored in his office. A briefcase on the desk beside the duffle bag was packed too, filled with his discretionary money, ninety-two thousand dollars of grease he'd managed to skim and store in the wall safe hidden behind the *Justification for Higher Education* print. Technically the grease belonged to the nut-job but after losing one hundred and fifty K, stealing another ninety didn't make much difference. Dalrymple, Mr. Blonde, would be just as homicidal.

A manila envelope addressed to the IRS sat on the desk and beside it, a wire-bound ledger—the doctored ledger the tax man was never meant to see. Pryce figured he'd be lucky to live more than a few months, even with the grease. He didn't see why he couldn't make the nut-job's life difficult while he still had time.

He wanted to buy a farewell card for Dallas but greeting cards were a pain in the ass. Finding the correct tone was the difficult part. Something sentimental seemed more appropriate than a humorous card but when a guy moved into that section of the drug store, the cards dripped syrup. Reading them was embarrassing. Giving one away would be worse. He thought he could give her a blank card and fill in the message himself, but that seemed to indicate a lack of thought. In the end, he put five one-hundred dollar bills in an envelope and wrote on the front, "Dallas: thanks for being the best bartender the Lucky Thirteen has ever seen." The message embarrassed him too, but it would have to do. He planned on leaving the envelope on the till for her. By the time she saw it, he'd be long gone. He wouldn't have to face the amused, slightly mocking smile he was sure would cross her face.

His office door flew open, banged on the wall, and started to rebound shut. A diminutive blonde caught it and walked into the room. A step or two behind her was another person Pryce didn't recognize. Several feet behind him, Semi-Gloss holding his .38 awkwardly in his left hand. Absurdly Pryce thought, "So, a guy walks into a bar…" He did not expect to see Dwayne Currie again.

Semi-Gloss said, "Where's Dallas?"

"I told her to go home," Pryce answered absently. His attention was on the two individuals who'd walked in with Dwayne.

Loose hair framed the blonde's face in twin arcing tendrils, giving her a bemused, spacey sort of expression. Her opposite arm, the one she hadn't used to catch the door, was supported across her chest in a fabric sling that was knotted behind her neck. Pryce turned his gaze to the man standing next to her. Before Semi-Gloss had a chance to make introductions, Pryce guessed: Jordon Cutler didn't look like any kind of Terminator. In fact, he didn't look like much at all, Cutler standing maybe five-nine, sporting a face full of cuts and bruises.

Cutler met his gaze with unblinking eyes.

Pryce remembered the actor who defeated the Terminator in the movie. That guy hadn't looked like much either. He said, "You're the guy who punched Leo's ticket." He didn't wait for an answer. "I was expecting someone bigger."

Cutler said nothing.

"I picked him up at Shore Memorial," Semi-Gloss said triumphantly, "just like you said." He grinned like a man who'd accomplished something significant and expected praise. Then his gaze sharpened. He stared intently at Pryce. "Something's different."

Pryce raised his hand to his mouth and was mildly surprised when he felt his smooth upper lip, the moustache gone. In more than one way his escape had already begun.

He looked at Semi-Gloss, wondering why the moron brought two prisoners into the bar. What was he supposed to do with them? He didn't care about the guy who killed Leo; the time for retribution was history. Or, perhaps it was in the future. It definitely wasn't now. All he cared about was the nut-job's money. Two extra people—captives in his office—just complicated matters. He had a train to catch. He raised his eyebrows. "I don't see an Adidas gym bag."

"He didn't have it."

"I told you to make him tell you."

"He wouldn't say. Even when I threatened to shoot him."

Pryce blew out a frustrated gust of air. He looked at the blonde. "Who's she?"

A firm voice answered, "Melissa. You can call me Mel."

Not spacey after all. Pryce ignored her.

Semi-Gloss said, "She was at the hospital. She picked him up."

"You two are what? Married?"

Neither Melissa nor Cutler answered.

Something else that didn't matter. They were a couple, in one fashion or another. He said, "Dwayne, you wanna make this guy talk," he stabbed a finger at Cutler, "you don't threaten him. You threaten her!"

If you really wanted to make it work, you didn't threaten. You acted. Did something dramatic. When you have Eric Dalrymple as a business partner you learn a thing or two. You do a little research and find out how a nut-job like Mr. Blonde handles problems. Like, if you want to get a man talking you break his toes one by one with a hammer—a ball peen for instance—and then you get him thinking about what's coming next. His ankle. His shin. Etcetera.

He'll talk.

With a woman, the principal is the same but since every woman on the planet is vain, whether they admit it or not, you go for their appearance. Cut her. Or burn her with a blowtorch. Either way, give her a scar. Something small. Let her imagine where the next one will be. No threats. Just action.

She'll talk too.

Pryce didn't bother explaining any of that to Semi-Gloss. The truth was, he'd never gone Dark Ages on anyone. He could shoot someone, if it became necessary, but torture them? No. And, since he couldn't do it himself, and it was fairly obvious that as a tough guy, Semi-Gloss made a pretty good poser, it was unreasonable to expect him to scar Melissa or bust Cutler's toes. That was the difference between a real hard ass and a wannabe. If the nut-job had asked Cutler the question, the cash would be sitting on the desk right now.

Semi-Gloss flushed. "I tried threatening her too. It didn't... Well, I couldn't make that work either."

"Damn, Dwayne." Pryce closed his eyes and shook his head. The ulcer burned, scorching his stomach. Once he started eating whatever he felt like, the fire had faded and for the first time in several weeks he'd felt comfortable. Leave it to the moron to bring back the pain, searing hot.

"Listen," Semi-Gloss said in a pleading rush, "I had another idea. You'll like this."

Pryce doubted it, but he opened his eyes and said, "Okay."

"What I thought, you hold onto her. I take him. He wants to see her again he'll show me the money."

Pryce thought about it and then nodded, impressed despite himself. It was a decent idea. An idea that could work. If it happened in a hurry, he wouldn't be on the run by the end of the day.

He'd still own the Lucky Thirteen and Dalrymple would be none the wiser. Best of all, he'd still have a shot at Dallas. He liked the sound of that.

He pointed at Cutler. "You drive. Take Dwayne to the money. Bring it back here. Blondie will be waiting. We can make a nice even trade."

"Mel," the blonde said.

He looked at her. "Like I care. Sit," he pointed to the sofa, "and be quiet."

Semi-Gloss peered hard at Pryce, eyes narrowed in concentration. "What's different?"

Pryce ignored him. He picked up the Glock .26. He popped the magazine, checked it was fully loaded and then slammed it back into the grip of the pistol. He racked the slide, the weapon held high with the barrel pointing at the ceiling. "Get out of here," he told Cutler. Don't come back unless you've got the money." He looked at the clock, nodded once and continued. "Just so you know, time is paramount. I have some place to be. In one hour, I'm leaving, you're back or not. And, when I leave this room, I'm leaving alone."

Cutler turned and faced his wife or girlfriend or whatever. "I won't be long."

Pryce sincerely hoped not. Because, even though he was putting on a show—the way he checked the pistol with such exaggerated Hollywood thoroughness—somewhere in that final little speech he stopped acting and became deadly serious. Before he left the Lucky Thirteen for the final time, one way or another, he'd have to deal with this little slip of a girl. He didn't want to kill her, wasn't sure he could unless he was forced to, but in a fight between Mr. Blonde and Melissa, he'd take on Mel any day.

CHAPTER 50

MEL FIDGETED.

Mr. Pryce's couch might have been comfortable but balanced right on the edge of the cushion like she was, with the band of tension tight across her shoulders and the rest of her muscles rigid with nerves, she couldn't relax and find out for sure.

Where was Jordon?

He'd be back. Of this she was certain. It was in the way he spoke and it was in their history and it was pure logic. Side by side, Jordon was smarter and healthier than Dwayne. Still, she worried. Dwayne was desperate and desperate people were unpredictable.

Opposite the sofa, Mr. Pryce sat at his desk. His face shone an unhealthy crimson. Every breath he took was loud in the near silent office. There were sweat stains the size of pie-plates under each arm. Stale body odor prickled Mel's nose. It wasn't mutant enough to be truly offensive, but it gave her the impression that Pryce hadn't changed shirts since the previous day. Maybe he'd slept in the office. In those clothes. On this very sofa. He avoided looking at her. Every now and then he glanced at the clock. He shook Pepto-Bismol tablets out of a pink bottle and popped them into his mouth.

Music played in the background, a soft murmur out of speakers mounted high in the corners. Mel thought it sounded like—could it possibly be—Air Supply? In a strip bar? Not that she knew for sure, but she didn't think "soft and sweet" created the right kind of atmosphere for a place such as this. She thought raw was more appropriate, like the Red Hot Chili Peppers, for instance. Certainly not Air Supply.

She shuffled her feet and shifted her weight. Were they just going to sit here listening to *All Out of Love* until Jordon and Dwayne came back with the money? What happened after that, after the two of them walked in the door?

Pryce checked the clock. Again.

He did it every minute or two. She realized his nerves were strung as tightly as her own; he probably wasn't lying about his short schedule. Why was he in such a rush? If he missed a plane, all he had to do was dip into the gym bag everyone kept talking about and purchase another ticket. No biggie. What was so important he'd consider walking away from a bag full of cash? Then she remembered the other guy Dwayne mentioned, this Mr. Blonde character, and she felt an unexplainable tingle of fear in her stomach and at the base of her spine. She wriggled, making the leather couch squeak.

Mr. Pryce rocked forward in his chair. He cut his eyes at her and then quickly looked away. "You better hope your boyfriend finds that money. Gets back here," he looked at the clock, "in forty-five minutes."

She said nothing. There was no correct response.

"I wasn't just talking. I'm leaving. If Dalrymple finds out…" His voice trailed away with a few shakes of his head. He rubbed his stomach and winced.

She said, "You'll just leave? You won't wait for your partner?"

Without looking at her he said, "Partner? You mean Semi-Gloss?" He waved the idea away with a lazy flick of his wrist. "That moron gives 'moron' a bad name. He works for me. He's absolutely not my partner. His employment ends," another glance at the clock, "in forty-three minutes."

"Semi-Gloss?"

"Dwayne's nickname." Pryce shrugged. "What we call him."

He didn't elaborate and Mel didn't bother asking. For a while neither said anything. Mel watched the time as closely as Pryce. Now, the deadline was only twenty-seven minutes away. What happened if neither Jordon nor Dwayne—Semi-Gloss— made it back? Had Pryce meant what he said, "…when I leave this room, I'm leaving alone…" Would he actually pick up the pistol? Point it at her? Squeeze the trigger?

Out of nowhere the Black Monster whispered in her ear. "You're out of options. You're not so tough, are you? You're going—" Mel impatiently pushed the static away. She didn't have time for that crap anymore. If the big hand hit the top of the hour and Jordon hadn't walked through the door, she'd make something happen, just like she'd done with Hewitt.

"You're nice and thin. Bordering on skinny," Pryce said. He spoke without meeting her eye. "How do you stay so tiny? The reason I ask, I've been trying to lose weight. Atkins, you understand, but it isn't going well."

"I don't diet, if that's what you're asking."

"What about exercise? Gym, aerobics, that sort of thing?"

She shook her head. "I think it has a lot to do with genetics."

"That makes sense." He leaned back and laced his fingers together behind his head. He muttered, "Eight pounds in two weeks my ass."

Another long silence, and then he said, "Hey, I got a question for you, seeing as you're a lady and all. What would you prefer? Five hundred bucks and a friendly note, or a really fancy goodbye card with a gooey message inside?"

Mel looked at him in silence for a couple of seconds. Who was this guy? Sitting there asking about weight loss and greeting cards, soft rock on the stereo, a loaded handgun on the desk? She said, "I'm not sure. I think I'd need to know more about the circumstances."

"You don't make it easy, do you?" Pryce said. "Women, I mean, not you specifically. Although, I'm sure you're no different. I buy a lady some nice jewelry, she won't wear because it's too expensive. What if she loses it, right? But, if I get the costume kind, well then I'm a cheapskate who won't get her a decent gift." He nodded. "I'm sticking with cash."

Mel said, "I have to ask, is this Air Supply, playing on the radio?"

He answered with a glance toward one of the speakers. "Their greatest hits collection. You wanna know something? They never did a stadium tour. Too bad. I would have loved to have seen that show."

She made a non-committal mouth noise.

Again, the silence stretched, until the phone rang, making them both jump with nervous surprise. Pryce snatched up the receiver before it had a chance to ring a second time. He said, "Pryce." His face turned stony.

Instinctively Mel knew the waiting was over. Her stomach rolled. She put her left hand into the large cotton sling in which the good people at the Shore Memorial Hospital had wrapped her right arm.

Pryce stood. He leaned over his desk with the telephone receiver tight against his face. His knuckles stood out, harshly white against the pulsing purple vein at his temple. It bulged as if it was about to burst, sending blood like molten lava spraying across the room. He said, "Make yourself scarce. We're all done in Atlantic City." He pushed the End button, cursed softly and then threw the phone across the room. It smashed into the *Justification for Higher Education* print, fracturing the glass into a spider web of splinters. The phone disintegrated. Plastic shrapnel flew. "Useless moron!" he yelled.

Moron? Did he mean Semi-Gloss? That kind of made sense. Or, did he call everyone moron? If it was Semi-Gloss on the other end of the phone, where was Jordon? Mel's fingers found the satiny barrel of her SIG, the pistol she vowed she'd never be separated from again, the pistol she'd hidden in her sling when she asked Dwayne if she could get some gum. She wouldn't go with Pryce, if his plan was to take her. Neither would she sit submissively on the couch and let him shoot her.

Pryce hammered both fists down on the desk. Pen and papers jumped. The Glock on top of the black leather briefcase jumped. He kicked his chair. It rolled off the plastic runner onto the carpet. Breathing heavily, he leaned his weight on his knuckles. He took a deep breath. His eyes raked the room, pausing momentarily on Melissa. He nodded the tiniest amount and his lips formed a razor thin line, as though he'd reached a regrettable decision.

Mel wrapped a hand around the polymer grip. Her thumb found the hammer.

Starting at the bottom left, Pryce opened each drawer of his desk, took a fast look inside and then slammed it closed. He moved quickly for a man of his size, and didn't slow until he found a roll of space-gray duct tape.

When he slammed the final drawer closed with a violent crash, Mel thumbed the SIG's hammer back. The oily clicks seemed unnaturally loud and unmistakable in her ears, but Pryce didn't so much as look at her. She slowly withdrew the pistol from her sling. She held it out of sight along the side of her leg, pressing it tightly into the fabric of her pants to keep her hand from shaking.

Pryce held the tape in his left hand. He dropped his right hand and when it came back up, it was wrapped around the shiny Glock .26. For the first time that afternoon, he and Mel locked eyes for longer than two seconds. "Turn around. Face the wall," he said.

"Why?" Her voice wobbled. Her eyes were locked on the pistol in his hand. She guessed she knew the answer before she'd asked the question.

"I'm going to tape your hands, feet, and mouth. I don't need you following me, or calling the cops the minute I walk out the door." He waggled the barrel of his pistol at her. "Come on. Let's go. You drag this out another second, I'll shoot you. I'd rather not, but like I said, I have some place to be."

Mel believed him.

She raised her SIG, wrapping both hands around the butt of the pistol, just like she'd been taught in shooting class. Just like she'd practiced so many times at the range. It hurt her right shoulder, holding the pistol like that, but she wasn't about to shoot one-handed like in the movies. This was real. She needed to hit what she was aiming at. Her mouth was dry as stone dust, her tongue like sandpaper.

Pryce's little slit eyes widened fractionally when he saw the pistol in her hand, the black hole at the end of the barrel zeroed in on his massive belly. His face turned scarlet with rage. "That moron would fuck up a wet dream."

She resisted the urge to pass the SIG from one hand to the other and wipe her palms dry on her thighs. A rivulet of perspiration rolled down her back. Nerves made her arms shake and the gun barrel sketched circles in the air in front of her.

Pryce said scornfully, "You even know how to work that thing? Put it away. Turn around. Let's get this done."

More than anything it was his attitude that irked her, his unspoken certainty that she wouldn't use her pistol. Why would he think that? Did he believe she was a docile lamb and somehow incapable of defending herself? It was annoying. Her breath slowed and her arms steadied.

She said, "I don't want to shoot you either. I really don't. But I will." Her voice was pitched a little higher than normal, but it was even and controlled. She twitched the SIG's barrel at the office door. "Just go. Leave me alone and go. I promise, I won't call the police."

Pryce tilted his head slightly. A look crossed his face, as though he was considering the idea. Then he said, "Can't take the chance—"

The office door burst open.

Mel flicked the briefest glance at it, immediately realized her mistake, and flopped sideways.

Pryce pulled the trigger. The Glock in his hand banged twice.

The bullets buried themselves in the black leather sofa. White stuffing fluffed out.

Mel squeezed off three fast shots. Too fast. Behind Pryce, dark wood paneling ripped open. Splinters flew. A blue haze of gun smoke stung her nostrils. Her eyes watered. The pistol in Pryce's hand came around. She controlled her SIG, kept the barrel down and centered, and squeezed the trigger twice.

A cloud of red vapor misted into the air. Pryce looked at the twin holes in his chest and then back at Mel. There was an incredibly shocked expression on his face. He lifted his Glock, his movements slow and clumsy, as if the pistol was exceedingly heavy. One leg buckled. He tried to catch himself with his desk, but snagged the duffle bag instead. He fell, dragging the duffle bag down on top of himself. He landed with a loud grunt, the impact sending twin geysers of blood spurting out of the holes in his chest.

The gunshots echoed in Mel's ears, sounding like she was still squeezing the trigger. She swung the SIG around, aiming at the figure filling the doorway.

CHAPTER 51

JORDON STOOD IN the doorway, looking from Melissa to Pryce—Mel with her SIG in her hands, the white hospital sling hanging off her neck like a scarf; Pryce on the floor with blood leaking out twin holes in his chest and bubbling out of his mouth, the surprise on his face slowly turning to pain.

Mel said, "Don't get between me and him." Her voice was husky and raw and strained. Her eyes shone feverishly. As she spoke, Pryce lifted his pistol and tried lining up the sights. Halfway through the motion he fell back and his Glock clacked on the floor.

Jordon lurched into the room, favoring his left leg. He reached out and put his hand over both of hers, pushing her arms down so the barrel of her SIG pointed at the floor. She flinched at his touch but didn't resist. "He's dead, Pumpkin." His voice was low.

She didn't respond.

He grabbed her by both shoulders and gently shook her. "Melissa. Come on. We've got to hustle it. The cops won't be far away."

She blinked. She looked past him with a frightened expression, as if the police were already there. Then she caught his eye, his fresh black eye, Jordon, guessed. "Oh crap, what happened?"

She raised her pistol and looked over his shoulder. "Where's Semi-Gloss?"

"Who?"

"Dwayne. Where is he?"

Jordon pushed her arms down. "Remember what I said I'd do if he tried to shoot you?"

"Yeah."

"It wasn't as easy as that but..." He shrugged. "We got to the 7-Eleven. We fought. He was pretty tough for a sick guy. He clocked me here," he pointed at his eye, "and kicked me pretty good on the left knee. Pumpkin, we really have to go."

"Okay." She de-cocked the SIG and stowed it in her sling.

He took her hand and together they walked out of the office, across the bar to the fire escape door. The alarm blared when they pushed through and silenced just as quickly when the heavy steel door slammed shut behind them. They hurried down the length of the alley, around the corner and headed for the Mazda parked a couple of hundred feet down the block. "Stand up straight," Jordon murmured into her ear.

She straightened.

"Shoulders back. Lean into me a little bit." She did and he wrapped his arm across her shoulders and hugged her to him. "Look straight ahead, but don't meet anyone's eyes. Confidence, Pumpkin," he said. "Walk like we own this dump of a town. Nobody will even notice us."

Ten minutes later they were driving west on the Atlantic City Expressway. He snatched glances at her, Melissa staring straight ahead without speaking. He saw a range of emotions cross her face—anger and sadness and guilt and he was happy to see them all. Her face wasn't listless or devoid of life, like it had been so often during the previous sixteen months.

She turned and faced him. She pushed her hair off her face,

trapping it behind her ears. Her chin quivered and her eyes were filled with tears. "I just killed that guy. Mr. Pryce."

"Yes."

The tears fell then, and her body shook.

He put his hand on her thigh and squeezed gently and said nothing, because he didn't have the first clue what to say. She hated it when he tried to fix her problems and he wasn't sure if this was a problem. Maybe it was just stress, and the weekend and the last sixteen months catching up with her.

She said, "He had a mom. Maybe he was married. What if he had kids? But, I didn't have a choice, did I?"

"No."

Her tears slowed and then stopped. She wiped her eyes with the back of her hand. She found a Kleenex in the center console and snuffled into it. "That man who went through the windshield? Hewitt? I took one look at him, thought, *good. Great.* He was married. I saw his ring. His wife is probably worried sick. But, I don't care about him. Mr. Pryce though, he was a gangster but he didn't seem like a bad guy. He was trying to lose weight."

Jordon thought Pryce was a very bad guy. Mel shouldn't have wasted any of her tears on him. He said nothing.

"Semi-Gloss and Pryce? They would have killed us. I know it. We were in their way. But, I didn't have a choice, right?"

"You didn't have a choice," he answered. "You were great. Like James Bond."

She smiled a little bit.

"When you said you wanted some gum," Jordon shook his head and laughed. "I thought for a second you actually said gun."

She said, "Gun. Gum. Practically the same thing." Then she went back to watching the scenery flash past the window.

He looked at her, enjoying the familiar pose—her elbow propped on the window ledge, her chin cupped in her hand. She looked nice without the ball cap. She looked nice when she woke up in the morning, before she combed her hair and put on that slippery red lip-gloss. And, she looked nice before bed when she walked into the room in her ratty slippers and his bathrobe. But, it didn't count for much when Mel wasn't Mel. It had been a long sixteen months. If it had to be a few more, so be it. He'd ride it out. But, he wouldn't waste any sympathy on the people who stole her fresh confidence, if that's how this day turned out.

Without turning away from view she said, "What are you looking at?"

"You."

"You should keep your eyes on the road."

"I know where it is."

"I meant to ask, did you meet Tom after the conference?" She spoke with very little interest, still too inside her head to really notice or care what his answer might be, he guessed. He faltered momentarily before saying flatly, "I met him."

A warm gust of wind carrying the salty taste of the ocean and the pungent odor of the nearby tidal marsh ruffled Jordon's hair. Dead autumn leaves flew by like pieces of soggy parchment. His clothes felt a size too small. A cloying stickiness had gathered under his collar. Humidity or fear? He wasn't sure. He said slowly, "What have you done, Tom?"

Tom Menny stood opposite him wearing black cargo pants, a North Face windbreaker, and thin latex gloves. A plastic garbage bag covered his right arm from wrist to shoulder. "The cops have a test to see if a person has fired a gun recently. It's called a blowback test, I think." He tore the bag off his arm and wadded it into a ball. "They won't be swabbing any evidence off my hands." There was a crazed grin on his face, and Jordon thought the twisted expression didn't reflect the person with whom he'd grown up.

Not even a little bit.

"I met him right after the conference ended," Jordon said, "before I went to the airport for my flight." He didn't say anything else. He didn't want to discuss the events on the side of the road and give her more traumatic things to think about. Of course, there was more to his silence than some noble notion of protecting her.

He didn't want to discuss the previous evening because he felt guilty and tarnished. Guilty because the simple act of showing up and then leaving without reporting the shooting, made him complicit in Tom's actions. Tarnished because no matter how hard he tried to forget what he'd become involved in, he couldn't. It was an oily stain on his favorite T-shirt. The more he tried to scrub it out, the more visible it became.

Mel looked away from the passenger window. She stared at him. "And?"

"And, what?"

"And, what did he want?"

Whatever his justifications were, there was no way he'd allow this dirtiness to touch her and so, Jordon kept his answer evasive. "Tom and Victoria broke up."

She smiled widely. "That's excellent news."

A spattering of large, languid raindrops dropped from the sky, hit the ground and exploded like moths on a windshield. A thin sheen of sweat glistened on Tom's forehead. He armed it away. He tilted his head and looked skyward. "The humidity tonight is something else. Wilfred's advance team, maybe?"

Jordon said, "CNN has been going on about it all day."

"Mel gonna be okay by herself?"

"She'll be fine." The concern in his friend's question was frightening, because Jordon believed it to be genuine. How could six words——one short, fast question——hold that much indisputable concern when…His eyes slid to the side, toward a puddle of ebony blood

pooled beneath the body of the woman lying in deep shade near Tom's Porsche. "That's Victoria, I guess? You killed her?"

"It was easier than I thought it would be," Tom said.

Victoria was self-centered and shallow. She was rude with Mel. She manipulated Tom and until the moment he killed her, Jordon thought his friend was too blindly infatuated to notice. Jordon didn't feel sorry for Pryce, Leo, or Bernard Hewitt. They died as they lived. Victoria Chesham though? A person he disliked intensely? Nothing but compassion. He guessed it was because Victoria had become another victim, just like Mel had become a victim. And why? Because of countless little slights both real and imagined that Tom kept track of until one day he…what?

Snapped?

No.

"Snapped" implied he lost control. Nothing about Victoria's murder was out of control.

Mel asked, "So they broke up. What did he need you for?"

"Their breakup," Jordon stumbled on the word, "was not harmonious. He needed help with some personal things."

Jordon said, "Why am I here? Why did…" his voice was higher than usual. He felt his normally pragmatic control slipping. He cleared his throat. "Why did you call me?" In a blink of the eye the control vanished. "You called me a week ago. A week ago, you freak show," he shouted. He waved a hand at Victoria's body. "You planned this. You're in a jam, absolutely, but you weren't a week ago. This was premeditated. And, you got me involved?"

Tom made the time-out sign several times with his hands. "Lower your voice and listen to me. I have it all worked out." From a pocket inside the windbreaker he pulled out a Ziploc bag. It bulged with a woman's wallet and a variety of feminine jewelry. Tom's own wallet, ring, chain, and Rolex were in the bag. "Get rid of this. Don't pawn it. Throw it in the ocean. Flush it. Whatever. I don't want to ever see it again."

Jordon felt his blood pressure drop slightly. He could do that, not happily, but he could do it. He could take the bag and leave and hopefully this nightmare would end. "That's it?" he asked suspiciously.

"Not quite." The same maniacal grin as earlier touched Tom's mouth. It barely moved his lips and his eyes held no hint of humor. "Take a deep breath. You're not going to like this part." He reached behind him and pulled a nickel-plated .38 revolver out of his waistband. "Shoot me," he said.

Jordon dropped his chin to his chest, closed his eyes, and mumbled, "You've got to be kidding me."

"Right here." Tom jerked a thumb back, touching the right side of his chest, up high near his shoulder. His voice was fast and clipped. "Just once. Then drive away. I've been hitting the gym. I'm strong. In good health. I'll be fine. Once you got a nice head start, I'll call the cops. When they show up I'll have a bullet wound and no clear memory of what my attacker looked like." He glanced skyward a second time. "If it rains any harder the investigators won't even have tire tracks to use as evidence. They don't like working a crime scene in the rain. Rain screws up their evidence. I saw a special on the Discovery Channel. They won't have a single thing that points to me, never mind you. It will look exactly like a robbery went bad." That grin again. "They'll say, 'Sadly, there's one DOA. Fortunately, there isn't two.'"

"No," Jordan said.

"What?"

"I'm not going to shoot you. I'd like to, you getting me into this, but I'm not making myself an accomplice to murder."

Tom looked confused. "What do you mean? Thirty years it's what we've done, looked out for each other."

"No."

Tom muttered, "Bitch. Dead and still screwing up my life."

Louder he said, "You know she was a hooker? All that time we were together, she's on her back getting thousands a night while I pay her bills. I gave her a car." He made a high feminine voice, 'A temp doesn't make much money, Tommy.' She stole my credit card. My ATM PIN."

Jordon felt a stirring of sympathy. These were not things a guy wanted to find out about his girlfriend. He said, "Doesn't mean you kill her."

Tom said, "There's way more to it than that. I'm not going to get into it. Listen, you owe me, and I need a favor."

Mel said, "This was the jam he was in? You couldn't help him with 'personal things' in Richmond?" She shook her head and made a face.

Jordon didn't answer because he recognized the question as rhetorical. The answer of course was, "No." He had to help his friend, and given the circumstances, he had to do it in Atlantic City.

Loyalty was a funny thing. Try and pin it down. When did it start? And, why? Maybe it began the day he and Tom met, all those years ago in grade school. At some point, it came alive. Time nourished it, as did the back and forth of a long friendship, and it grew without awareness, until one of them says, "You owe me, and I need a favor." Suddenly there it is, no longer an abstract concept but rather, a big, black, boiling problem that both of them could place their hand upon.

"I owe you? Are you talking about the cash you loaned me? You want me to pay you back with a favor?" Jordon shook his head. "What you're asking goes way beyond a favor. I'd prefer to write you a check."

"It's not about the cash," Tom said. "I don't care about that. In fact, consider it a gift. I don't want to ever hear about it again. This

is about growing up together. It's about looking out for each other. It's about my family—"

"Don't start with me, Tom. After my father…the investigation, the legal bullshit…it was your family who took me in. Not you. Not you." Jordon yelled the last part. He realized the scales of loyalty would never be perfectly balanced in Tom's mind; the two of them would never be equal. He felt something die inside, or go dark, or disappear over the horizon. In a near whisper he said, "You shouldn't have brought it up."

Both men were silent for several seconds. Tom shuffled his feet. The gravel on the road's shoulder crunched. Eventually he broke the quiet. "Sorry. You're right. I shouldn't have mentioned it. I'm under a little pressure here."

Jordon didn't answer. Pressure hadn't forced Tom's statement. Not by a long shot. He wasn't sure what offended him more, the blatant manipulation, or the fact that Tom tried disguising it as a mistake made under pressure.

"All the drama? Meet me in Atlantic City? I'm in a jam?" Mel held her hands near her shoulders, wriggled them and made ghostly whooing sounds. "He just wanted to cry in his beer, tell you how awful she was? Like we didn't know that?"

"Pretty much. I told him we're getting married in May."

"Oh, yeah? What did he say?"

"He asked if I was nervous."

"Are you?"

"Not today. May is a long way off. He asked if you were making lists."

"…flowers, caterers, music, that sort of thing?"

"She's got lists to remind her to make lists," Jordon said.

Tom nodded. A second or two later, he said, "Make sure you get rid of the gun. And, try not to worry. I've thought it through. I can't see any problems. It's foolproof."

Jordon looked at the revolver dangling on Tom's index finger. He looked at the body on the ground. He looked at the bag of jewelry in his hand. How could Tom make that kind of statement? "Foolproof, huh?"

"Foolproof."

"You ever hear of the butterfly effect, Tom?"

Tom squinted in puzzlement. "What?"

"It's supposed to explain how unpredictable results can occur in conditions sensitive to change. Like, if a butterfly flapped its wings in Brazil it could affect weather patterns in Texas."

Tom made a dismissive gesture. "Get lost with that Buddhist garbage," he said irritably. "You know how big an Andean Condor is? It's the world's biggest flying bird. I saw a special on the National Geographic Channel. It's got a ten-foot wingspan. If a tiny little butterfly can cause a hurricane, than an airborne Condor would cause global Armageddon."

"Buddhist?"

"Whatever."

"It's chaos theory."

"Like I said."

Mel asked, "Did he say anything about the loan? He doesn't want his money back, does he? Because we can't afford that."

"Why don't you look in the gym bag?"

Mel looked at him with raised eyebrows.

"He doesn't want the money back. He said it was a gift. We never have to pay him back. Take a look in the bag."

"Why? Why doesn't he want it back?"

Jordon thought about the best way to answer. A day ago, he might have said, *Because, he's good-natured and he has lots and he won't miss what he gave us.* As far as he knew that would have been a truthful answer. Maybe it still was. Doubtful though. The more likely answer was that in forgiving the loan, Tom was just adding another ingredient to his manipulation. Jordon hoped he was wrong. He guessed he'd never know. "I don't know, Pumpkin. I guess because he's good-natured and he has lots and he won't miss what he gave us."

"Weird." She twisted around in her seat and picked the gym bag up with a grunt. She flopped it on her lap, unzipped it and spread the flaps open. Her jaw dropped and she gave a startled gasp. "Crap! How much is there?"

"A rough guess, one-fifty."

"No wonder Pryce wanted it back."

Jordon said, "I don't know if it's his money. It might be Mr. Blonde's, whoever he is. One thing is for sure, the law won't be looking for it. Nobody carries this much legitimate money around in a gym bag."

"Maybe Mr. Blonde is a gangster. Maybe it's the Mob's money!"

"The Mob's?" He gave her an amused smile.

"Well, something like this happens in a movie, the Mob is always involved, right?"

"Can't argue with that. Anyway, only three people know who we are. Leo and Pryce are both dead. Semi-Gloss is the only one left. He knows my name. He doesn't know yours. He doesn't know where we came from. He doesn't know where we're going. And, the way he spoke about this Mr. Blonde guy, I think Semi-Gloss is going to run far away and hide. We won't see him again."

"It sure would help, if we kept it." She zipped the bag shut, hoisted it off her lap and heaved it onto the back seat. "What made Tom finally see the light? Why'd they break up?"

Jordon felt another stab of guilt, but he told himself letting Mel believe Tom and Victoria had split up was the best choice, for now. Eventually she would ask, "Why hasn't he called?" When sixteen months turned into twenty-two and then thirty, when she was showing off that confidence he'd seen at the hospital, she'd want to know why Tom wasn't dropping by, or sending e-mails. At that point, Jordon figured he could tell her a little more about what really happened. He said, "The final straw? Straws, I guess? Victoria stole half his money. More significant though, she had two jobs. By day she was a temp, by night a hooker."

Mel's eyebrows jumped in surprise. "I knew it. Didn't I say, 'There's something else going on with him?'" There may have been a hint of satisfaction in her tone—her suspicions had been confirmed, her low opinion of Victoria validated. But Jordon didn't believe it was an, "I told you so," statement. He heard too much sadness in her voice for that.

He said, "That's what you said, all right."

"With luck he'll start acting normally, now she's gone," Mel said.

Strangely, as difficult as figuring out when and why loyalty started, it was easy figuring out the exact moment it ended. "After tonight," Jordon said unemotionally, "I don't want to hear from you again. Ever. We're done. Stay away from me and Mel."

Tom looked at him for several long seconds and must have seen something in his face. He said, "If that's the way you wanna be."

"Not ever, Tom. Are we clear on that?" Jordon waited until Tom nodded, and then he took the revolver from his friend's outstretched hand.

"With luck," Jordon repeated. They drove in silence a while longer. Eventually he said gently, "We've got to get rid of your gun, Mel. I don't think anybody is going to be too worried about Pryce. I'd rather not chance it though."

Her eyes brimmed with tears. "I love my SIG."

"I know you do, Pumpkin."

It took her several seconds but finally she nodded. "You're right. I've got to get a grip."

He said, "Take it apart. Wipe every piece clean. Use the cloth from the console."

She knew the weapon far better than he did. With practiced, precise movements she broke it down and meticulously wiped the pieces clean. At the first river they came to, he pulled off the highway. He stood behind her as she tossed the parts into the water. Each of the larger pieces made a faint splash. The current immediately wiped away the ripples, as though the pistol never existed. She looked over her shoulder at him and smiled. "It's pretty isn't it? All the colors. The way the trees droop over the water."

A riot of yellow and orange trees lined each riverbank. Clouds and sky were reflected in the calm waters of the eddies. He wrapped his arms around her and held her close with his palms splayed on her belly. With the point of his chin propped on the top of her head, the scent of her wild flower shampoo was faintly discernible, overshadowed by the thicker stench of gunpowder. He let a teasing left hand roam north, until her right breast was cupped in his palm. "Mother nature is a modern artist," he said.

She giggled. "Cut it out. We're on the side of the road, for heaven's sake. Besides, I don't think I look sexy right now. And," she looked back at him, "I stink."

He lowered his hand. She grabbed it and put it back.

She said, "Maybe I can use some of that cash to buy another SIG?"

"Buy a matching pair if you want."

EPILOGUE

Late 2002

LUTHER MCKINLEY DROVE slowly, keeping his eyes peeled for the address he'd committed to memory. The Silverado's windows were up, the air-conditioning on high. Late September, summer's last kick at the can, and it was hot. His Ray-Ban Aviators kept slipping down his sweaty nose—sunglasses he needed to update, Brenna told him. Buy something a little less eighties, a little more this decade, she said. Wearing them practically screams, "I'm a cop."

Luther told her, "The classics never go out of style." He wasn't sure if he was talking about himself or the glasses. He suspected the expression itself was a cliché, only used by out-of-style old guys such as himself.

He found the right street and the correct house. He parked and climbed out of his truck into a blistering afternoon that immediately made sweat bloom on his forehead and gather around the waistband of his chinos. The gate through the hedge swung open easily on well-oiled hinges. He climbed the front porch steps and, at the top, pushed the doorbell and heard the muffled sound of the chimes.

No one answered.

With no great optimism, he pushed the button again. Just about the time he decided to climb back in the Silverado, get out of this crazy heat and soak up some AC, a circular saw whined. It was an easily recognizable noise after all the work he'd done on his own place.

He followed the sound to the back of the house.

Without the obviousness of a mast, he hadn't seen the boat hidden behind the house. The vessel dominated the backyard. It was cradled in a giant, wooden rib cage. Various parts Luther couldn't identify—he didn't know the head from the jib—were covered in tarps that hung lifeless in the afternoon heat. The scent of sawdust, an exotic wood he didn't recognize, filled the dry air. An orange electrical cord slithered through the grass and then up the side of the boat.

The saw's shrill wail died. Luther heard the tinny sound of a local radio station coming down from the boat's deck. He yelled, "Hey up there."

A man stood. He wasn't big, maybe five-nine, one-eighty. With one hand, he pushed safety goggles off his face into his sweaty hair. He held a plank in the other hand, a rich, red wood Luther guessed was teak or mahogany. He said, "Did the radio just say it was ninety-one degrees?"

The man on the boat glanced briefly at the radio. He said, "Can I help you?" The tone was polite but uninviting, the way a person answered the door to a Jehovah's Witness or a traveling salesman.

Luther said, "I'm looking for Tom Menny."

The response was a long time in coming. When it finally did, the voice had turned cold. "What's that gotta do with me?"

"I'd like to talk to him. But, the man has vanished." Luther shrugged. "You know him. From, what I've seen, you know him well. You grew up together, correct?"

A shadow crossed the man's face. This time the response took even longer. "Tom doesn't live here."

"I figure you could put us in touch. You know where I can find him?"

"No."

Luther looked at his feet and then back at the deck of the boat. He didn't say anything. Maybe if he waited long enough the guy would start talking, hopefully offer a few words of explanation. But, the guy remained mute, and the silence stretched until it became obvious and uncomfortable. Finally, Luther said, "Are you Jordon Cutler?"

"Who's asking?"

Luther gave him with a thin smile. *I'm about to rock your world.* "Detective Luther McKinley," he said. "Atlantic City PD. You are Jordon Cutler, correct?"

A short nod. "Yeah. Was there something else?"

"You want to come down so I'm not yelling up at you?"

"No." Cutler shook his head. After several seconds, he added, "You want, come on up."

"I don't like boats. I get seasick."

Cutler made a show of scanning the neighborhood. "Not much water in this subdivision."

"Maybe its heights I don't like. Take a break. Come on down. We'll have a chat," Luther talking hard, turning it into an order.

Cutler didn't move. He looked into the distance for a beat. When he turned back he said, "You know what? You're a long way from home to be ordering me around on my property. Without a badge. Or a warrant. Or any reason at all, for that matter."

Luther held up an apologetic hand, realizing immediately that he wouldn't be able to bully Cutler. He was the kind who didn't say anything in the interview room except, "I want a lawyer." Ultimately, with time and evidence, guys like this were crackable but Luther had neither of those commodities. Taking a softer tone, he said, "Listen, I just want to have a conversation out of the heat. I'm baking like Thanksgiving potatoes."

Cutler gave him an irritated look and a fast nod. "All right." He dropped the wood. He brushed sawdust off the near-white thighs of his faded jeans, the blue gone a thousand washings ago, being thorough about it, making sure he got it all, so his ripped-in-the-knees Levis looked their best. Luther knew it was just a way of showing he wasn't scared or intimidated and everything was proceeding on his schedule. When he finally climbed down a ladder at the stern Luther saw a message printed on the back of his shirt: *Life isn't short. Death is just* really *long.*

T-shirt philosophy, Luther thought, but often times, true enough.

Cutler faced him, arms crossed over his chest.

"You mind?" Luther motioned at a shady area under the overhang of a large oak. He turned and walked away. After a couple of steps, he looked over his shoulder.

Cutler hadn't moved. He said, "You asked about Tom Menny. I don't know where he is. What else do we have to discuss?"

"Victoria Chesham."

"I thought you guys found her killer."

"You're referring to that Bernard Hewitt guy?" Luther made a face and a dismissive gesture. "Nothing but circumstantial evidence. Seems a dead prostitute ranks low on the priority list. The investigation might be over, but there's a bunch of little details that need looking into."

Officially, Hewitt killed Victoria for reasons unknown. Considering her profession, common opinion was, they'd had a disagreement over a business transaction. Luther thought that was nonsense but several VIPs named in her little black book had applied pressure on the DA's office. The pressure snowballed all the way down to Luther, making his theory that Menny and an accomplice killed Victoria irrelevant. Manpower would not be assigned to a closed case, especially when his theory was based on some wild hunch about Menny's unbalanced psyche. No matter how closely it matched his own.

Cutler said, "The investigation is over? From where I'm standing you're doing a whole lot of looking."

"I've got a theory you should hear." Luther waited half a second. When he spoke again his voice was tough and flat and left nothing to interpretation. "I think your buddy Tom Menny killed her. I think he had an accomplice."

Cutler's eyes widened. "What?"

It was the first unguarded moment Luther had seen from him. He wasn't able to interpret it. Had he hit close to the bulls-eye? Did that account for the surprised expression? Or, was it astonishment at the foolishness of his statement? Luther said, "Menny could have paid a professional. We know he has that kind of money, but that's not the way Ms. Chesham died. A professional hitter would have done them both. That's why I'm leaning toward accomplice." He armed the sweat off his brow. "Damn it's hot. You're in computers, right? Where'd you go to school?"

"University of Minnesota."

"Really?" Luther nodded. "Good school. Got to be smart to go to a school like that. Just like the guy who helped Menny. Smart. Smart enough to work out the details so there wouldn't be much for us to look for." After Luther talked with Paul Davis and discovered the tourist Davis kept referencing was Menny's friend from grade school (and in town the same night Victoria died), he went from sure about his theory to one-hundred-percent, swear-on-a-stack-of-bibles certain. He said, "As I recall you were in Atlantic City that night, correct?"

"You know I was or you wouldn't have brought it up."

Luther smiled, lips pressed together tightly. Cutler wasn't giving him an inch. "You checked out of the hotel. A few hours later you checked back in. Where were you during that time?"

"I've gone through this with the local cops. I told them every-thing I know."

Luther said conversationally, "I doubt that very much."

"I don't care what you doubt. It's all on paper. Read it."

"Oh, I read it. I like a good work of fiction as much as the next guy. What I hate are coincidences. Back to my theory. I used to be married. She—"

"I'm not interested."

"She left me. Her name's Marilyn. She met a doctor with a big house in the Longport area. Everything I did was for her, and she still left. The terrible money I brought home? I rarely spent a penny on myself. I like collecting beer-related paraphernalia. Taps, that sort of thing."

"You didn't hear me?" Cutler had his hands stuffed into his jeans, his cool back under control. He said, "I'm not interested."

"She made me feel guilty if I bought something new for my collection. I always had to pay her off with a gift. I was always paying her off. Making excuses. Apologizing. Sorry for being late. Sorry for being early. Sorry for every little thing." He scratched his scalp. His fingers came away sweaty. He shook his head. "I was miserable when I was with her, but I wish she hadn't left. Pathetic, right?" It was a rhetorical question. He didn't expect an answer.

Cutler didn't disappoint. He only shrugged.

"You see, marriage is comfortable. That's why so many people stay married when they don't want to. It's the certainty they enjoy. It's expected. Divorce is expensive and it takes a long time. It's easier for most people to endure their wretched married life. After a while they think low-grade miserable is normal.

"I know that, so you'd think I'd be happy Marilyn bailed out, right?" He didn't wait for an answer. "But I'm not. I feel like I tried and failed. Like I was good enough to marry but not quite good enough to stay with."

"Late inning relief, but not a complete gamer, huh?"

"Good analogy," Luther said with nod. "I think the worst part is, every time I get close to moving on, she phones. 'We're friends, Luther. Can't we just talk, like friends?' You know what she rolled out the other day? She says, 'I miss our little house, Luther. It's impossible to get competent cleaning staff.' Believe that? She's roaming around 4000 square feet, nothing but Oprah to occupy her time and she can't tidy the place up? Turn the dishwasher on? One of the reasons she left was, 'our little house.'"

"You got a point or no?"

"Yeah. I do. Menny's situation with Victoria? It's pretty much like mine is with Marilyn. He hated her and loved her at the same time. He couldn't get her out of his thoughts. It started messing with his head. Screwing up new relationships. I know what that's like. I've met a really nice lady at work." He held both palms up near his shoulders. "I know. Don't fish off the company dock, but I can't help it. Anyway, I know Menny. I can see inside his head." Luther tapped his temple with an index finger. "My belief? Most men occasionally think life would be easier if they just shoved her off a tall building. At least the incessant talking would end."

"Speak for yourself," Cutler said.

"Hey, no offence. I tend to see the worst in people. It's the job." Luther shrugged. "For all I know women think the same thing every time their husband comes in the house, uses the guest towel to dry his hands after changing the oil in the car. What I'm getting at, if Marilyn disappeared, the love-hate thing would go away. I could start something fresh with this lady at work.

"The difference is, most people only think dark thoughts, occasionally, way down deep where they don't have to look at them too closely. They never follow through. So, I guess, when it's all said and done, this entire Bernard Hewitt thing worked out well for your friend, didn't it?"

Cutler said nothing.

"Hey, this might interest you. The night after you killed Leo Jarvis—"

Cutler interrupted him with a dark glare.

Luther waved it away. "Take it easy. I know you were cleared. What I was going to say, the night after Leo died, a guy named Gaylord Pryce checked out as well. No great loss. Upstanding sort that he was, he owned a fleabag 'gentleman's club.' What's interesting, Pryce was Leo's boss. We can't find a single thing that indicates who killed him. Or why." Luther was hoping for a flicker of emotion. Something that would give him a hint that Cutler, involved in Leo's death, might have also been involved in Pryce's.

Cutler kept his mouth firmly shut.

Luther wasn't surprised. The man was too cool to let anything slip, not even in an off-the-books interview. At best, it was a shot in the dark anyway. He said, "I should hit the road. I have a drive ahead of me. Enjoy the rest of your day." He slid the Aviators out of his pants pocket and slipped them on. He swiveled and walked away.

"Yeah," Cutler said flatly, "take care."

Without looking back Luther threw up a hand and waved over his shoulder. Take care? The way he said it reminded Luther of a line from a Bob Dylan song, something about wishing a person good luck but not meaning it. He made a mental note to look up the reference.

Back in the Silverado, Blue Rodeo's *Diamond Mine* flowed out of the stereo. On the drive south he'd played the song three times back to back to back. Excellent song. A guy didn't get tired of it easily, and it lasted thirteen minutes. A whole bunch of road disappeared in the rearview mirror in the time it took to listen to a thirteen-minute song.

But, Blue Rodeo was wrong now. He pushed CDs around the passenger seat until he found something he thought would better match his mood. Something a little more reflective. He popped in Dire Straits, the *Love Over Gold* CD.

Using his map, he found the roads that took him home. He felt good. Strangely at peace. A person could think dark thoughts all they wanted. It wasn't a crime. It might have been a normal human process. Unwelcome and uncontrollable for most, but normal. Anything more than dark thoughts had a cost attached. Menny may have believed he got away with murder, but Luther knew the truth. And, if Cutler *was* in touch with his old friend, a fly on the kitchen wall would be getting an earful right now— Cutler telling him how the cops knew what happened, saying they didn't have proof but they were digging, they were coming. Watch your back, cover your tracks, don't get caught speeding in that flashy ninety-thousand-dollar Porsche because they were watching. And, they were coming.

It wasn't the traditional punishment Luther would have preferred, not by a long shot, but it was no way to live.

He smiled a thin smile of satisfaction and then flipped open his cell phone and thumbed in a number he hoped he'd be using a whole lot more in the future. When Brenna Hanson answered, he said, "Hey Bren, how's things?"

"Mac. What's up?" Straight-ahead. Cordial and professional.

"You want to grab a coffee tomorrow afternoon?"

The answer was a long time in coming. Luther understood her hesitancy. She'd told him no social calls until he put his past in order, and as far as she knew he was breaking the rule.

"How's the rebuilding coming along?" she said, unease in her tone.

He knew she wasn't asking about the actual renovations. "I got a lot done today," he answered truthfully and easily, more easily now than he would have been able to an hour ago. Maybe there was something to this "closure" thing, putting a period at the end of the sentence so he knew his issues with Marilyn were manageable, if not history. "I just finished up, actually."

"Is that right? Well, you sound good. Hey, you wanna know something? The Feds had an agent working undercover in the Lucky Thirteen. A bartender named Dallas Donovan. In between fending off Pryce and the rest of the horny drunks, she was building a money laundering case against him and some guy out of Chicago named Eric Dalrymple. Get this, the guy's nickname is Mr. Blonde. Like that crazy freak from *Reservoir Dogs?*" She laughed. "The Feds are looking at him for a whole shopping list of felonies."

"Pryce's death put a burr under her saddle, I guess."

"Screwed up her case, that's for sure. Semi-Gloss is gone too. Nobody knows if he's dead or on the run."

Luther shook his head. Where did they come up with these names? Semi-Gloss? Mr. Blonde? Dallas? What was wrong with Ken or Janet, or going safely biblical with Paul and Mary? He said, "He'll turn up. That insect is too stupid to stay gone." He took a deep silent breath, told himself there was no reason to feel like a fifteen-year-old boy and said, "Listen, Bren, how about that coffee?"

The End

As every writer knows, the story you start with is seldom the story with which you finish. I began writing *A Night on the Town* in 2001. The core story is the same today as it was over a decade ago but much has changed, including the world around us, making some of the references sound old-fashioned. Cell phones and voicemail hadn't yet become mainstream. Most people had an answering machine on their kitchen counter that indeed dumped all the messages with an electrical power loss. The iPhone wouldn't debut until 2007. In 2002 people who owned a cell phone had either a "candy bar" or a "flip phone," such as the popular, Motorola Razor. Texting was virtually non-existent.

This novel was never meant to be a police procedural; however, in the early 2000s, I spoke with a friend in the RCMP who gave me general guidelines on investigative technique so that I could sound somewhat authentic. I'm certain the procedures the police use now are far and away more advanced than they were only a few short years ago. Any procedural errors or exaggerations contained within the novel are mine.

For those people who are familiar with the cities of Atlantic City and Richmond, I apologize. I've taken enormous liberties with geography. Egg Harbor exists as a town and as a body of water, but the "Egg Harbor swamps" I reference is an entirely fictional location. Neither the Oasis Hotel and Casino nor the Lucky Thirteen Saloon exist in any place other than the author's imagination. Once again, folks, it's "fiction."

Kevin Lamport is an airline pilot by day and by night he (slowly) writes action-adventure novels. Before joining the airline, he flew small float and ski equipped aircraft in northern Canada, including the arctic territory, Nunavut. He is married. Most days happily. His wife continues to be a source of support and inspiration, after more years than either of them care to count. They live with their pets, (Harley and Malibu), in the always sunny Pacific Northwest. On his days off he enjoys hiking, riding his motorcycle, running for fitness, and travelling, which is tricky because he dislikes airports.

A Night on the Town is his second novel.

Feel free to visit him at www.kevinlamport.com

Follow him on Facebook and Instagram.

www.ingramcontent.com/pod-product-compliance
Lightning Source LLC
Chambersburg PA
CBHW050910250626
47155CB00001B/178